REPORTAGE PRESS

ABOUT THE AUTHOR

Ros Wynne-Jones is a freelance writer and journalist. The *Daily Mirror*'s Senior Feature Writer from 2001–2008, she is a former staff writer on *The Independent, Independent on Sunday* and *Sunday Mirror*, and has written for the *Guardian*. She has worked in conflict zones from Sudan to Kosovo, East Timor to Chad, as well as reporting on UK social issues. Ros studied at the United World College of South East Asia and at Wadham College, Oxford University, before joining the *Daily Mirror* journalism training scheme in 1995. She lives in South London. *Something is Going to Fall Like Rain* is her first novel.

Something is Going to Fall Like Rain

BY ROS WYNNE-JONES

REPORTAGE PRESS

REPORTAGE PRESS

Published by Reportage Press
26 Richmond Way, London W12 8LY United Kingdom
Tel: 0044 (0)7971 461 935
e-mail: info@reportagepress.com
www.reportagepress.com

British Library Cataloguing in Publication Data.

A catalogue record for this book is available from the British Library.

ISBN-13: 978–1–906702–04–5 paperback

Cover design by Sheridan Wall.

Layout by Florence Production Ltd

Printed and bound in Great Britain by Cromwell Press Group.

DISCLAIMER
Although set in a real life warzone against a backdrop of true events, this book is a work
of fiction and any resemblance to persons living or dead is entirely coincidental.

Endorsements

"An authentic, well-written and deeply-felt portrait of the tragedy that is South Sudan." – John Le Carré

"A moving, beautifully written book that captures Africa in all its humanity and heartbreak. Written with controlled rage and a clear-eyed love for a people and a country, the author makes us taste the red dust of South Sudan, and feel the horror of the East African dying rooms, and the weight of a world where tears are too small. A book of meat and emotion, blood and fire – it is a story of our time. And a masterpiece." – Tony Parsons

"As the tragedy of Darfur continues Ros Wynne-Jones reminds us of the time when the Government of Sudan rehearsed genocide in the South of Sudan. This is a dramatic story of the courage and endurance of the women and men of Sudan and of the aid workers who are so dedicated to making a difference there. Sudan has now found a literary champion who has a long commitment to following the longest ever civil war and its man-made famine. Her writing is evocative, moving and gripping and if only one person sits up and listens to what is going on inside Sudan's borders then the telling of this story will have been worthwhile." – Glenys Kinnock

"Ros Wynne Jones' first novel takes the harshest of grounds and subjects and turns it into fertile, febrile, feverish territory. This is tough and tender writing, as welcome as water splashed onto parched skin. Through the understated passion and politics of her writing she grows hope and life and love in the most barren of places. Remarkable." – Suzanne Moore, *Mail on Sunday*

The sky is darkening like a stain
Something is going to fall like rain
And it won't be flowers

WH Auden, 'The Two', 1932
Collected Poems by W.H. Auden
(Faber and Faber Ltd)

I was reminded of a conversation I'd had a few years earlier with a friend of my mother's, an Englishman who had worked for an international aid organization throughout Africa and Asia. He had told me that of all the different peoples he had met in his travels, the Dinka of Sudan were the strangest.

"Usually, after a month or two, you make contact," he had said. "Even where you don't speak the language, there's a smile or a joke, you know – some semblance of recognition. But at the end of a year with the Dinka, they remained utterly alien to me. They laughed at the things that drove me to despair. What I thought was funny seemed to leave them stone cold."

I had spared him the information that the Dinka were Nilotes, distant cousins of mine. I had tried to imagine this pale Englishman in a parched desert somewhere, his back turned away from a circle of naked tribesmen, his eyes searching an empty sky, bitter in his solitude.

Barack Obama, *Dreams From My Father*
(Canongate Books, 2008)

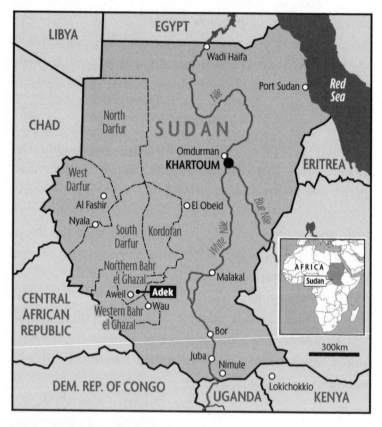

Map by Lawrence Goldsmith

For my family

Prologue

Massacre is just a word, and has no power to hurt. 'Slaughter' is without teeth or sharpness, no machete edge on which a finger might be cut. There are no words for what happened in Adek village during the hunger-gap of 1998 when the rains had been gone so long that the smaller children had only heard of water falling from the sky, and the forty-year war had overlaid a people's memory of peace with the thick sediment of loss. What happened that dry season was the desiccated flutter of a dying bat's paper wings in an arid, airless African desert. It had no evident knock-on effect anywhere else in the world, no apparent after-tremor. Afterwards, nobody sat down to learn the lessons of tomorrow. No flags were lowered. No minutes of silence stopped the commercial centres of the world. No memorial was hewn from white stone or garlanded with paper flowers. Nobody made a film about the deceased's last moments and the final whisperings with which they went to Lual Aghony, the Promised Land. Their fierce love for their families and their friends, their vain yearning for peace and freedom and their unsatisfied and impractical desire to go on living, went unrecorded. No heroes were honoured. How can there be heroes when nobody knows the names of the dead? How can the world weep, when its eyes are closed?

Yet something in the world changed that day. Everything that is bleak and dark and empty became bleaker, darker and emptier, and everything that is good and light flickered with a sudden bright pulse of electricity as if the world's moral circuitry were overloaded and blinking. Depending on where you were on May 12 1999, you might have felt its pulse. Maybe you were walking to work in the Manhattan sunshine, and you felt a sharp coldness needle your exposed cheek. Maybe you were travelling on the Underground beneath London when the train stopped in the tunnel shivering like an animal and you felt the lights shudder. Perhaps you saw the yellow Caribbean sun hang its head in shame at its own childish optimism, or a field of cows lie down on a Greek hillside without any sign of rain. Maybe you were sitting with your sweetheart under a mango tree in Gokar in the west of Darfur and you noticed the fragility of the leaves against the impossible blue of the sky. You couldn't have known that what happened that day several hundred miles to the south would soon become your own daily reality. That the Government of Sudan was rehearsing a genocide that would mean within six years there would be no mango trees left in Darfur.

Everything has an effect. Everything means something. The Dinka tribespeople lying dead in the marketplace understood that, deep in the sinew of their stilled hearts. But you, you only saw the hairs standing up on your arms and mistook their sign for a wintry chill in the summer air. You missed the moment. You were not listening for the drumroll in the sky.

Chapter One

I am lucky to live this near to the river. You can't see it from here, but you can smell the dirty damp of the Thames coming up through the earth, and up above the occasional seagull wheels by, miles off course, drawn by the glittering curve of the water. You are aware always of the river's presence, just fifty yards away, winding towards Waterloo Bridge and the upended Wheel and the concrete hulk of the South Bank. Even when I am sleeping the winding space is still there, prising London apart, dividing the capital into two distinct halves. Without the water we would be hemmed in to our tiny plot, surrounded on all sides by a splintered forest of shiny office skyscrapers and luxury apartment blocks of glittering glass and strengthened steel. The longer I am back in England, the more I find I am obsessed by water. Without the river, it would be hard to breathe.

Our housing association flats were put up in the 1930s for unmarried mothers and other outcasts from between the wars, when living within sniffing distance of the Thames was undesirable. Eight decades later, babies born in wedlock are still a rarity on this estate, but today we are a miscellaneous collection of students, shiftworkers, unemployed and other non-participants in nine-to-five life, each of us refugees of one kind and another – an old-fashioned, untidy narrow boat adrift in a sea of blank buildings. Our tiny, cluttered balconies spoil the flat glass aesthetic, tumbling with potted plants and bicycles and washing and broken things waiting for mending.

My Japanese neighbour is a bonsai gardener with an entire forest of trees in a two foot square space. The walkways are kept spotless by the lady downstairs. Next door but one, a grey-faced white boy with a wardrobe entirely devised by Adidas – socks, shirts, shoes and baseball caps – knocks out shrink-wrapped cannabis to a steady stream of teenagers in matching, monobrand sportswear. In our block, named appropriately enough for Desmond Tutu, we have families of Ghanaians,

Angolans and Somalis, a young Bangladeshi couple, a Chilean girl and an elderly Irishman. Michael was shocked once to hear there were so many Africans living in London. He felt sorry for them, he said, having to live somewhere cold and cramped, without room to keep cattle. But people here were kind to me when I first arrived, garlanded with my own macabre brand of celebrity, the press knocking on the neighbours' doors and standing in the bitumen car park down below craning upwards with their cameras. The Ghanaian family were the ones who showed me how to get up to the roof through the firedoor, where if you stand on tiptoe you can see out across the capital's broad, round horizon and get a sense of sky and light and curving city, unparalleled in any of the nearby office blocks. That space and skyline have helped me keep on going these ten years. People pay good money for the same view from the sterile capsules of the London Eye.

Today, despite the weather, I am sitting on a tiny plastic stool on my miniature balcony five floors up above London, nursing a winter flu, looking out towards where I know the water is, seeing the river in my mind's eye. I could afford to move from here now I am a fully qualified doctor, a consultant in geriatrics. I stay for the brief walk to work and the closeness of the river, but also, I think, for the transitory feel of the building and its people. Being here, I'm only really visiting, taking time out from some much bigger life plan. My half empty flat adds to the illusion and my few possessions are not out of place. When so many families here are dislocated, uprooted, far from the lands they know, no-one notices my lack of visitors. I keep myself to myself, and enjoy an arm's length friendship with my neighbours. In any case, if I moved downriver to a shiny, high-up box with glass windows and an actual view of the Thames, I would miss the way I imagine the river from its sounds and its smells. And I would miss the joyful merengue music from the Angolan family downstairs.

Geriatrics suits me in a similar way, even though as a trainee doctor my ambition was to work with children. After what happened, paediatrics turned out to be too visceral, too painfully exposing. The ward I work on is quieter and I enjoy the patients. The ambitious doctors leave geriatrics out. There is death, of course, all around – sometimes daily – but there is a sense of life lived too. Most of the patients are resigned, even ready, passing from day to night, often without pain; missing the shocked stare of a dying child that says 'this is not my time'. We eye each other with cautious recognition: I from my closed off, locked up world, they from their end point, already in transition. With so little of a life outside of work, some nights I sit and hold the papery hands of the patients without visitors, a midwife to the dying, whispering them on their way. They comfort me, I think, more than I do them.

My fever is down a bit today, 38°C, or thereabouts, but my joints still feel thick and heavy and the single long headache I have had for four days whines relentlessly on. I struggle with the isolation of illness and they will be short at work, but with vulnerable elderly patients it would be unhelpful to come in with flu. So I'm sitting here, the impatient patient, wrapped in one of my mother's old blankets, orange-patterned and scratchy from before the days when softness was prized equally to warmth. It irritates my skin, but it smells of my mother, even after all these years.

Sitting there with the cold wind scratching my face alive, enjoying the play of air on my hot cheeks, I can ignore the fact that the phone is still ringing and that the answer machine has not kicked in. It is a sign that the mailbox is blocked up with messages, but I am not going to listen to them or answer the phone. She can ring all she likes. It has taken me a decade to forget what happened, to forget Grace and Billy and Sean and Bol and the Commander and everything that happened to us then. I wrap the blanket tighter around myself and pull the hood of my sweater up around my ears to muffle the sound of the ringing telephone throbbing in time with the rhythmic pain in my head. I squeeze my eyelids shut against the flooding images.

Yet, when I open my eyes, Southern Sudan is there, spread out like a panoramic photograph in front of me: a vast landscape of red desert and blue sky, split equally in two by the long goodbye of the horizon. I am surprised as always, by its hard beauty, by the perfection of rock against empty sky. The picture begins to move, almost imperceptibly at first, with the silhouettes of men moving their tiny specks of cattle against the reddening of the dying sun. I shake my head to dispel the moving image, and go inside to put the television on, needing someone else's reality to confront my own. I am suddenly deathly tired as well as angry.

Damn Grace. What does she want, an anniversary get-together? Surely even she must know that formal remembrance is unnecessary when memory has the power to repeat an event over and over, playing like a shaky film in the background of every waking moment. Even Grace can't have escaped that.

Chapter Two

In late October 1997, on an early-middle day of the week, I was flying in a tiny plane above Africa marvelling at the curvature of the earth. There were still three of us then: Me, Billy Finn, a thirty-five year old former ranch-hand from Tennessee, and Sean Connelly, thirty-eight, born on the Bogside in Derry. Both Billy and Sean were experienced aidworkers, with almost three decades' practice in the field between them. I was the inexperienced third of our party: just turned twenty-three, a medical student still a year away from taking my finals. My mother had died a few weeks previously after a long and cruel contest against unfairly advantaged cancers. Her death had taken place two days after Princess Diana's fatal car crash and three days before Mother Teresa's death from cancer in Calcutta. My own grief was washed away by the wet, saccharine flood of unprecedented national mourning, and I felt lost, lonely and adrift.

In London, after twenty years as a straight-A student, I had found myself drifting away from my studies towards long nights in the subsidised college bar, and longer days in the narrow straitjacket of my single student bed. Watching the shadows lengthen across the white walls of my tiny room, I immersed myself uninterrupted in a childhood trick, day-dreaming of the wide African plains my mother had told me so many stories of when I was a child. So when I saw the Africaid advertisement offering "Sabbatical Opportunity for Student Doctor in East Africa" on the scuffed noticeboard at the nurses' station at the hospital, it seemed as if it had been placed there for me in particular, and I slipped the pins out carefully so as not to tear the thin newsprint.

Concerned by my ever-decreasing third year grades, Professor Yurie signed my sabbatical papers wordlessly.

"Twelve weeks, Maria," she said, after a long pause, handing me the papers back with a pale blue leaflet bearing the word 'Bereavement' in a friendly font, like handwriting, tucked discreetly into the bundle. I folded it neatly into four and placed it carefully inside the back pocket of my jeans. "You can pick up your fourth year again in January."

My only remaining relative – my twenty-one year old brother Matt – had just got a job in an almost famous Soho kitchen and disappeared into a cloud of work and steam and late nights. He gave me his blessing to go and leave him alone in London, and seemed relieved when he said goodbye. In my grieving imagination, my dead mother took longer to convince, standing on the only patch of clean and tidy carpet in my student bedsit as if too repulsed to set foot in the untidy room itself.

"And get a year behind?" her voice echoed until I turned up the radio.

I didn't know how to listen to dead people then.

*   *   *

Four weeks later, and I was flying across the wide African skies with a small Food Security assessment team, exhilarated and astonished at my own luck. I looked out of the window and watched the sprawling UN airbase at Lokichokio dwindle into nothingness until all that was below was blank, bare scrubland. Shouting above the roar of the plane, Sean, the team leader, explained again how my six weeks would unfold. A day and night on the ground in this first village to conduct an assessment of the food needs of the people there, then back to the safety of 'Loki', a tented and hutted city of humanitarian workers perched on the very edge of Kenya. It was too dangerous to stay in the warzone itself, so we would pass in and out on light aircraft, staying no longer than a day or so at a time in Southern Sudan. In between trips we would write reports at Africaid's small, occasionally air-conditioned outbuilding in Loki, and there would be breaks for 'R&R' when I might even get to pick up a cheap safari deeper into Kenya.

Loki had seemed both exciting and frightening to me when we had arrived from Nairobi in a narrow ex-Cold War plane that still smelled of the Soviet Union. The airbase bars and mess areas were full of lost souls. Dirty looking Russian pilots making a killing by flying into the warzone, earnest young Valley Girls marching around self-importantly with clipboards and walkie-talkies. Well-built American men with their shirts off, playing volleyball in the dust, and daughters of African ministers writing emails to their sweethearts in Mombasa between earnest papers on drought and food security. Heightened by the perilous closeness of death and war and famine, there was a feral scent that floated on the hot night air and on the winds blowing across the dust bowl of the makeshift airstrip. At the Loki beach-bar stranded 1,000 miles inland, the Tusker beer tasted stale and flat, and the gin was served warm in dusty glasses, but it brought its own rewards in dampening down the harsh realities all around. It was as strangely thrilling and as frighteningly adult as the warzone itself, a reminder of how far I already was from home.

During those first couple of days it was the faces of the ragged children looking through the barbed wire that fenced off the airbase from the flat red desert beyond that gave me most cause for disquiet. The children's bellies strained at the cloth of their filthy, tattered T-shirts, and I tried to imagine what it must be like to see so many tonnes of food fly out daily from your own country, while your own belly grew hard and distended with all the signs of malnutrition I had studied in lectures thousands of miles away in London. But, after a day or two of pushing Heathrow-bought boiled sweets and curiously sour green Kenyan oranges through the perimeter, I tried to harden my heart and tell myself that I was already doing my bit for Africa, and after the first few days I stopped seeing the children's faces at the barbed wire.

On the Tuesday or the Wednesday – I soon learned days are for civilians, and do not encroach on UN life – we reached the airstrip at dawn and climbed the shaky aluminium steps up into a tiny, mosquito-sized plane. I was hungover from the night before, staying up late with the gin-ravaged pilots, but also filled with an anxious excitement at the possibilities ahead. Our tiny aircraft took off suddenly at a fierce angle, and on all sides the mountains rose up around us so that I realised Loki was located at the centre of a giant dust bowl. As we flew between the steep hills, I saw the carcasses of a dozen aircraft where they had been dashed into the rocks. Yet, even then, I did not feel the pull of my own mortality. Flying up there in the cloudless sky I had never felt more alive.

It was freezing at altitude, so cold it was impossible to imagine the heat-haze raging below. For three hours nothing disturbed the horizon, only the thatched roofs of remote homesteads strewn like sunhats scattered across an empty beach. My heart rose and fell with the lifting and falling of the plane as we bobbed like seagulls on an air current. The Kenyan pilot was reading a battered Wilbur Smith novel and looked up only every now and then to study his course.

"The Sudan People's Liberation Army is reporting a famine in Northern Bahr el Ghazal," Sean explained for my benefit. "But we can't take their word for it. Famine is political in Sudan: a weapon of war used by the Northern Government, and by the SPLA to lobby for Western support in the South."

How many starving people make a famine, I wondered, but behind me Billy grunted.

"Commander Wol never lied to us before," he shouted, looking up from the scuffed six-string guitar patched up with masking tape that he had been strumming soundlessly and wordlessly for most of the journey.

Billy was handsome in an unkempt way, all stubble and scars and angular bone structure. A mass of physical contradictions like a blunt knife, his forearms were stained brown by the sun like two long Montecristo cigars but his fingers were girlish, while his teeth were crooked behind a neat mouth. He looked ten years older than his age and his face was lived in enough to suggest reincarnation, but under his lined forehead his eyes were a clear swimming pool blue.

Sean, in contrast, was poorly built for Africa. Red-haired, translucent-skinned and freckled, his face was permanently crumpled by earnestness and hidden by a thick, salt-and-pepper beard and scratched metal glasses that slid often down his nose. He spent the three hours of the flight sheafing through piles of papers, marking them in red, blue or green pen, reading to me the details of the assessment – but I could hardly hear him over the roar of the plane and my excitement was too profound for me to concentrate. I knew already what was required of me: the weighing and measuring of children to assess the degree of famine in the area. I also had basic medical supplies with me from the store at Loki in case there were urgent cases to treat. "Patch up and piss off," Sean called it. "It's about the report, not the intervention."

Three hours in, and the pilot closed and bookmarked his novel with an air of reluctance, pulling out a faded Ordnance Survey map from a plastic carrier bag on the empty co-pilot's seat. Billy struck a resounding chord on his guitar as if finishing a stage performance, and got up to urinate in the metal bucket at the back of the plane, whistling as the steam rose from the arc of his urine. Sean began rubbing his freckled arms and legs with sunscreen.

"Ten minutes," he said. "Adek is the village coming into view."

I looked down at the cluster of circular huts, which spread out across the emptiness of the barren scrubland like a small island, wondering how he could tell them apart from any of the others we had passed. Then I remembered he and Billy had worked in Adek the previous year, before the Government in Khartoum had suspended all aid flights into Bahr el Ghazal, increasing the likelihood of famine among the rebel tribespeople of the South. I wondered about the proud people I had read about, who were armed only with spears and rusted guns against the industrialised might of the Islamic state of Sudan. It seemed an easy enough war to understand: North versus South, Muslim versus Christian, rich Arab against poor African. But then I had never been to a warzone before.

As the plane began to lower itself, I heard Billy swear behind me and turned to see him rubbing his breath from the steamed-up glass of the dust-spattered window as he squinted to see the village coming into view. Down below, the ground was crawling with moving bodies, a dust-drowned torrent of precise human choreography that made the earth itself seem curiously alive. People were running from all directions, dragging themselves through the dirt, pulling themselves forward on sticks towards a rough line carved into the scrubland where I realised the plane was going to land. The effect was one of coloured ants, blue and brown and red, being drawn towards a spilled bowl of sugar, and I realised suddenly that our poorly stocked plane was the lure.

"Shit," Billy said, wedging his wooden guitar between two boxes for landing.

The pilot was hollering at Sean, and as the plane flew straight at the strip, he flung the controls suddenly upwards, jerking the aircraft straight back up at the sky. My heart was in my stomach and my stomach was in my mouth and I thought I might bring up the greasy breakfast I had eaten in the Loki mess hall that morning, but the plane swung round again and I realised the pilot had dummied the landing to clear the people from the strip. Second time round we landed abruptly, bouncing three times before the engine shut off and we sat sweltering in the sudden heat watching a bead of sweat trace the neat perpendicular of the pilot's hairline and drop as if in slow motion onto the collar of his pressed white nylon shirt.

In that moment, as the droplet of sweat exploded against his collar, a confusion of shouts and gunshots and a tumult of human voices became audible outside. We were surrounded by faces and arms and legs pushing at the windows, and the dim glass was filled with staring eyes and pressed cheeks and squashed noses temporarily disfigured by the proximity of the glass and the pressure of the vast crowd behind. I heard myself counting under my breath, steadying my hands where they gripped the reassuring heaviness of my medical kit. For a moment, in my shorts' pocket, I held my mother's engagement ring between my fingers. It fell to Sean to break the internal silence of our besieged aircraft.

"The Commander was right," he said. "Look at the state of these people."

I followed his pointing finger to the front windows where a group of naked children were peering in, one balanced on top of the other, ribs protruding from above swollen stomachs, arms and legs thin as shoelaces; immobile, staring eyes moving in faces covered with thick dust.

"How much food do we have?" I asked, and was surprised to hear that my voice was not shaking.

"Not enough," Billy said, hunching his tall shoulders to move through the narrow body of the plane.

He opened the heavy door slowly so as not to harm the crushed bodies, and said something in the Dinka language that made people move politely back, their gaunt faces like a rebuke. As we climbed out down the rickety steps, stretching our cramped limbs, the heat hit like a sheet of hot metal, slicing away our breath.

I was immediately struck by the height of the people surrounding us, most of them two metres tall at least. The length of their limbs and the span of their hands and feet only served to emphasise their terrible thinness. Naked or dressed in filthy rags, their skin was a startling powdery black, like charcoal or obsidian coated in dust. Even in such an extreme state of emaciation and dry dirt, it was clear they were a strikingly beautiful people, high-cheekboned and proud-standing, their bone structure like that of no Africans I had met in London or Lokichokio.

For a moment, we all stood blinking in silence on the airstrip, overwhelmed after the cold of altitude by the terrible force of the dry heat, and then an emaciated woman grabbed me hard at the elbow, screaming into my shoulder and pulling at my hand. Propelled by her movement and disorientated by the wall of heat and acrid collective smell of the violently sweating crowd, I followed her, and a knot of people came with us, whispering urgently, tall as trees. I don't remember how I felt – too fat, too well-dressed, too short and insubstantial? At five foot nine, I could no longer see around me, hemmed in by flesh and suffocated by the heat, and lost to the aircraft I simply let myself move forward.

We advanced to the short midday shade of a stunted, blackened tree, where I saw there was a tiny scrap of a child laid out on a piece of brightly-coloured cloth. His breathing came thickly and too fast, and the skin of his face was so taut that it held his mouth rigid and open. I did not dare to lift him, only to gently stroke the papery skin of his burning forehead, and I had the feeling it was like touching a child already dead. My hand shook and I realised my mistake with a start. Escaping the death of a loved one, I had come to Africa's dying rooms.

"So you see how we are living in Adek village," said a voice behind me in clear English, and the people shrank back to reveal a tall, powerfully-built man in a long mid-blue robe. For a moment, his tall silhouette blocked the sun from the spectacle of the shrunken child so that the sticky spiderwebs of her infected eyelashes blinked briefly open.

The man introduced himself formally in clipped English with a sing-song accent, straightening his royal blue robe with his hands as he spoke.

"I am Chief Deng, leader of the Dinka of Adek village."

Under the tree the tall man continued talking but his words were lost to the roar in my ears as I stood under a blasted tree in a barren desert amongst dying people.

Struggling nervously with the clasps of my knapsack, I took out a small dropper and filled it from the flask of sugared tea I had taken from the mess hall that morning. I felt Professor Yurie tutting at my back, but I put the dropper to the child's taut mouth and, gaining gentle leverage, squeezed a drop of moisture onto his hard tongue.

As I did so, I heard Billy's voice approaching, talking to Sean or the pilot behind him.

"Don't wander off like that," he snapped when he saw me there, but his voice trailed off as he noticed the child and he dropped to his knees, cradling the boy's tiny, paper-light head in his long fingers.

"There's Unimix in the plane," he said. "One part mix to three parts water. Use the water in the drums at the back."

I handed him the dropper.

"What's in that?" he said.

I stared down at the red dust on my bare leg and it looked like blood.
"Tea."

I had never felt less like a doctor.

"It's got sugar in."

"Good," Billy said.

*   *   *

12

The rest of that first day passed in a blur of work and a relentless burn of sun, from which there was neither shelter nor shade. Measuring the children seemed a pointless formality given the state of the village, and we simply moved from family to family with droppers and bowls of water blended with Unimix, a special United Nations formula for malnourished children, filled with sugars, salts and proteins. Billy and Sean worked together in eerily silent tandem, and I tried not to ask too many stupid questions. I don't remember hearing the plane leave, only looking up to see a small dot on the horizon flying straight at the dying sun.

"He'll come back for us tomorrow," Sean said, placing a reassuring hand on my back, where I knelt mixing more of the Unimix porridge.

*   *   *

That night, I lay down fully clothed on a wooden platform bed as hard as a stone floor, under a tukul hut made of mud and straw and inside an encampment protected by a thin wooden fence, and I felt the strangest sensation that all of my life had been leading up to this drawn-out point of arrival, the first thing I had ever done that truly mattered. Exhaustion cut through my muscles and into my bones, but my mind was alive with colours and ideas and possibilities, all dancing in the grey starlight that leaked through gaps in the thatching like thin smoke. I wasn't yet afraid of the powerlessness of sleep or its lack of protection against the night and I barely understood the dangers by which I was surrounded, and perhaps it is this narrow window of naivety that makes the memory so powerful. But I remember that at some sudden impulse I rose slowly and lowered my feet into my boots, shaking my stiffened shoulders into movement and pushing my way through the white buzzing cloud of insects dancing in the light of my torch, dragging at the heavy wooden door and scraping it aside. I remember the moment the way a lover does, irresistibly drawn to mysterious Sudan, already intoxicated by Africa. I can still feel the light breeze plucking at the hair of my arms, and the sweat pooling at the band of my shorts, and my bare feet against the leather of my new boots, and I can still see above me as I stood outside in the black night the light-studded brilliance of the bare night sky.

A billion pinprick stars blazed brightly overhead so that I felt small enough to slip between the stones of the red earth beneath my feet. The smell of wood smoke was at the back of my throat and the distant drumming coming from the village thundered along my spine and into my skull as I listened to the whispering sound of the distant in and out-breaths of a continent. It might have been the ragged pain of an exiled land mass calling out to continents far beyond, but perhaps it was only the pain of my own recent bereavement I heard, held captive in the silence, radiating from the hot earth and into my ears and mouth.

This is how I remember it, but perhaps it took longer than that. It may be that that first night has come to be all of the hundreds of nights I would come to spend in Southern Sudan. But it seems to me I was already awake to Africa and its curious breathing.

Tonight, so many years later, lying here feverishly in the emptying shadows of evening, in the bedroom of my little flat by the Thames, I feel that wind again: a hot sweet air like a deep sigh, laden with sand and regret, a dry heartbeat flickering at my temples. And I shudder, because I can hear that in the hallway the phone is ringing again, calling me to remember that which I would rather forget.

Chapter Three

That first night something happened in Adek that was to change the course of all our futures. Some time in the dull pause between night and day, as the sky was already lightening and I was still wrestling with sleep, bombs began to fall from the sky.

I stirred suddenly from a dream in which my mother was struggling to sit up in a vast white-canopied hospital bed, to the screaming sound of the falling barrage: a crashing, droning, mechanical thunder that drilled right through the wooden platform I slept on and made every sinew in my body vibrate. In those first brutal seconds of immediate wakefulness, it seemed as if the noise might be only the physical, aural manifestation of the fears in my heart, but then I felt the first juddering tremors as the high-impact bombs began hitting dry earth.

I felt myself struggling for breath, and a liquid coldness spread upwards through my limbs from my lungs towards my sweating hands and feet, and I understood for the first time in my life the paralysis of fear. My tongue was too large and thick in my mouth and my heart was pumping as if it might flee the barred prison of my ribcage. I lay in an agony of indecision, not knowing whether to throw myself under the bed or run from the hut into open space. After a few moments of frozen time, the door to my tukul bumped rudely open and I half sprang from the bed, arms and legs twisted up in the sheet like a mummy. A tall figure appeared through the grey shadows and pulled me from the bedclothes, tearing at my brand-new Youth Hostel Association mosquito net and lifting me through the doorway, so that my arm scratched on a wooden nail and my hair was in my face and my bare feet were swinging wildly.

"I must apologise," said the voice somewhere above my hair, and it was a low African voice, not English. "I am most terribly sorry."

The man put me down in the middle of a stampede of fleeing silhouettes.

"Follow them quickly to the shelter," he said, and vanished into the crowd.

15

As I stood there amongst the running people, I was aware that the blue-black sky was closing in on us, a grey-silver shape lowering itself between the thin shadows of bending trees, and I began to run. I ran with the others towards the edge of the camp, every minute sensing the threatening shape above us would land and crush the sky against the earth. After a few moments I reached the entrance to a bunker, covered with branches, leaves and earth, and hesitated, watching the people climbing in.

"Quickly. There you go . . ."

I heard a voice behind me, and saw Billy lowering children into the bunker. I recognised the shape of his guitar slung across his back, and it touched me to think he was saving it from the bombs.

"There you are," Billy said.

He saw me hesitate to climb into the bunker, and for the second time in ten minutes, I felt myself propelled. He pushed me down inside the shelter with impolite force so that I was gasping for air inside the darkened burrow, arms and legs struggling against the unfamiliar flesh of shadowy bodies, my hand catching at someone's mouth, my bare feet against a person's hard shoulder.

My fingers scrabbled with a matchbook in my pocket, and with shaking hands I lifted a flaming match. As I did so, Billy climbed into the bunker and then Sean. The remainder of the space was filled by 100 or so people crammed into every corner, several tied up and terrified goats and the furious noise of captured chickens. Overhead I made out the shadow of an enormous dust-covered spidersweb hung with threads that seemed as thick as rope. Then darkness, as the match expired, so that in its last light I saw it was from the student union bar in London, and felt myself a long way from home and the things I knew.

The space fell silent after that, so that I could hear my own ragged breathing and I worried that the thudding of my heartbeat would call in the plane to our exact position under the earth. Struggling against the weight of the people pressing against me, I closed my eyes and tried to focus on the soothing scent of slightly damp, deep soil. I didn't yet know even the names of any of the dozens of people in the bunker – only Sean, Billy and Chief Deng – but we were all squashed together: anonymously terrified people breathing in each other's outbreaths, lying in the acrid, unfamiliar scent of each other's fear.

Sean was the one who lit the candle, but it was Bol who broke the silence. Little Bol the boy-poet with the earnest face and deep voice. Bol, who I did not yet know, and who was sitting next to me crushed in the bunker, holding his tiny sister Atong against his thin body. In the candlelight the outlines of their faces blurred into the surrounding blackness, but their eyes shone brightly.

"My name is Bol," the boy said, slowly, with the concentration of someone who knows only one phrase in English. He smiled shyly and I shook his awkward hand above the head of the fragile and too silent child on his narrow lap.

"My name is Maria," I whispered, and my voice rang in my ears.

As I spoke, the ground vibrated with the impact of the next wave of bombing and dust rained down from the ceiling of the shelter, snuffing out the candle, and with it the last whispers of our collective courage.

The screams of the village were in my ears, its sweat in my eyes, its fear scratching at the pit of my stomach. My straining ears picked up every heartbeat, every murmur, every high-pitched whine in the sky, my senses superhuman with adrenalin.

The bombs dropped and stopped, stopped and dropped, like in a game – like someone throwing stones into a river. Images came in swift succession, a series of thought fragments: my mother in the endgame of her illness, the impossibility of what she had asked me to do clouding the last days that we had together. Sitting below the surface of the earth under a screaming sky, I knew that she would have given anything in the world to have been killed by something as kind as a falling bomb.

I felt a wave of nausea and tried to empty my mind, beginning unconsciously to do what I had always done in times of grief or trouble or boredom and to think of Africa – of its soothing savannah, where grasses moved hypnotically across an endless horizon, grazed by straggling antelope and circling prides of lions, hunched low against the waving tips of yellowed foliage. But even as I entered the daydream I was aware it could not hold, not with the real Africa crashing and wailing outside, its bare fields burned, its wildlife dead and its hard soil barren of everything but stones. In that lonely moment I realised the Africa I had imagined for twenty years, my mother's dreamed-of Africa, did not exist, or at least not here in the harsh and sterile crater of Southern Sudan.

We all lay there in silence for a long time, many minutes after the wailing and banging and thundering faded into a deafening silence. Then collective relief flooded through the shelter like warmth from the sun.

"The bastards have gone back to Khartoum," Sean said, re-lighting the candle once more with steady hands.

We climbed out one by one, exhilarated by survival, dusting down each other's clothing, laughing at nothing, close to tears of relief.

I lost sight of Sean and Billy in the melée, and found myself standing bewildered in the already warm light of a pale early dawn. Disorientated, I could not think which was the way back to our tukuls, and instead found myself following the boy, Bol, and his sister, who each carried a sleeping child in their arms.

The children stopped as they reached the twisted trunk of the tall blasted tree beneath which I had treated the dying boy only hours earlier. Its mighty branches were shattered into a split fork where a bomb had landed exactly in the middle of its spreading shade. Circling its ancient root system, a nest of craters left by the air attack overlapped each other in a near-perfect Venn diagram. That was the moment I realised we had all been as close to death as the boy with the shoelace arms and legs, the intended victims of deliberately calculated murder. Suddenly I began to wonder about the man who had dragged me from my tukul, and whether he too had escaped the falling bombs.

It was close to dawn now, and the sky was warming slowly, pale yellow against the dirty brown of the disturbed earth. A bat lay stunned on the ground by the twisted tree, breathing too quickly. I was still burning with adrenalin as if I had run a dozen miles, and my thoughts were disordered and out of synch. I don't think that I wept. Tears would have been too small for the foreboding I felt.

I stood there looking at a blue biro standing upright in the earth like a fallen missile, realising I had bought it a week ago at Heathrow airport, and smiling to myself as I watched the girl, Bol's sister, pick it up and fix it neatly into the weave of her tangled hair. Then I watched the children walk back in the direction they had come, the blue lid of the pen bright against the dusty black of Atong's short, knotted curls. Finding my way from the shattered tree, I remembered I was the only doctor for a thousand miles and that there would be people to treat and bodies to bury. It was a dividing line between my life as a passenger and my future as a person, and I stepped over it knowingly, a line in the dust like the prints left in the hard soil by the bombardment.

Chapter Four

An hour or so later, as the sun began its scalding ascent, Sean stood in front of the campfire staring fiercely at the fire, while Billy and I ate a silent breakfast of tinned sausages and smoky-tasting baked beans.

"The airstrip is destroyed," Sean said, quietly, the still air swallowing his words. His arms hung at his sides, and his face beneath the red beard looked curiously pale and defiant all at once.

Billy lifted a blackened kettle of water onto the fire, steadying the long, nursery-rhyme spout so that it splashed cold water across his dirty right hand.

"And the vehicle?" he asked.

"Commander Wol had it safe under camouflage at the barracks," Sean said.

In my mouth, the beans turned to burned wood. I drank from my canteen of warm Loki water, ignoring its overpowering taste of chlorine.

"Is there another one?" I asked, swallowing the food down. "An airstrip, I mean."

Billy made a curious, dry, half laughing sound in his throat, and resettled his leather cowboy hat onto his head. Underneath, his hair had the texture of dirty brown suede.

"The nearest is Rumbek," Sean said, in his Derry drawl. "It's five days in the Land Rover, and it's under siege from all sides by Government forces."

My leaden brain clicked and whirred and scratched as it attempted to process this information, struggling with the heavy exhaustion of the night before. I had been sitting by the fire since dawn and I was numb with tiredness.

"So, what do we do?" I asked.

"We need to fix the radio," Billy said, spooning coffee from a plastic container. "The communications hut has taken a battering, but the transmitter itself may be intact."

The men continued talking, but I hardly listened, made strangely confident by their apparent calmness, the way I always felt while watching the surgeons at the hospital in London deal with a bewilderingly complex operation and knowing my own role was only to follow instructions and watch and learn.

I ate my breakfast, drank my water, and gratefully accepted the metallic mug of strong, black coffee proffered by Billy. He lit two cigarettes from a burning log on the fire and passed one over to me. My left leg itched violently, and I saw it was covered in a roadmap of bloodied bites, conurbations of cities and smaller satellite towns appearing where the mosquitoes had drawn blood.

"Are there injured people from last night?" I asked Sean.

"Five dead. A whole family who stayed in their tukul," Sean said, rubbing his own freckled arms unconsciously so that wiry golden-red hairs stood up against his pale skin. "The villagers will bury them."

"Any injured?"

"No," Sean said. "Just cuts and scratches. The local medicine men will treat them."

I hesitated.

"Did they attack the airstrip because of us?" I asked.

"Probably," Billy interrupted.

"We don't know," Sean said. "It's possible. They also randomly bombard villages in this area, sometimes weekly, sometimes monthly. But it may be they were aware we were flying in, and wanted to discourage interference in the developing food crisis. Don't forget this is a man-made famine we're dealing with."

Before I could ask him what he meant, a tall man slipped from the shadows and into the light, and I pushed away thoughts of the dead family crouched together in their tukul. Five people who yesterday had hopes and dreams, and today were stopped like smashed machinery in a place where the line between life and death seemed increasingly transparent. By comparison, the man standing tall in front of me seemed vibrantly alive.

"Good morning," the man said, in moderately accented English.

His face was long and sharply oval in the shape of the Dinka Sudanese and a deep, dark almost bluish black that was empty of the tribal markings I had noticed on other men of his age. Instead of the long, blue gown worn by the elders, the man wore threadbare but neatly mended Western clothes: mid-blue jeans, clean white trainers and a pale green, much-washed T-shirt bearing the Africaid slogan. Even in Western clothes, however, he would have stuck out on a British or American street as solidly African. Tall and sturdy-looking, with an air of quiet authority, his startling light brown eyes carried a heavy sadness. As he squinted into the sun, the skin creased sharply along the bones of his cheeks.

"This is Michael," Sean said. "Our logistician. He's been running the camp for the last few months while flights have been denied from Loki by the Government."

He clapped Michael on the shoulder and the two men hugged warmly.

"We're extremely lucky to have him," Sean said. "He's from Adek but educated at the Kakuma Refugee Camp in Kenya. There's no better logistician in Southern Sudan."

Michael half turned towards me as if embarrassed by this introduction, and I saw he was younger than I had first thought, although I struggled to place him between mid-twenties and mid-thirties. He wore a white necklace at his throat that glittered in the sun.

"I am sorry for your welcome to Southern Sudan," he said, addressing himself to me, and I realised he was the figure who had come crashing into my tukul the previous night when the bombings had started. "It is ungracious of the Khartoum Government."

I shook his large hand awkwardly, embarrassed of how frightened I had been the night before, and of having been lifted from my tukul like a silly child. With his refusal to properly meet my eyes and his arms locked tightly across his chest, I found Michael both intriguing and intimidating.

"I am extremely grateful . . ." I began, staring at his clean white trainers.

Michael said: "It was a precaution. The encampment itself did not take a direct hit."

He took a coffee from Billy.

"In any case, it is you I came to thank," he continued. "The family of Wut, the boy you helped at the airstrip yesterday, asked me to pass on their gratitude for your kindness."

"Is he any better?" I asked, with a stab of hope.

Michael shook his head slightly.

"I am sorry that he did not survive the night," he said.

I thought of the tiny baby with his tightly drawn mouth pulled up into a dry triangle and his unfocused, bluish eyes, and I tried to reply, rejecting every phrase my mind formed as too thin, too clichéd or too inappropriate. Instead, I stood there watching Sean's bare feet grip and ungrip his green flipflops.

"He was a relative of mine," Michael said, after a while. "A nephew. We are all very sad."

The child's pain was over, I thought, passed on to his parents and his family like a scalding kettle.

For a while, we all stood there drinking our milkless coffee, listening to the strange silence brought by famine – a lack of birds and traffic and words. In the far off distance I could hear light voices, a whispering of the wind in the dead trees, the shout of a child.

Sean threw the dregs of his coffee from his mug into the parched soil, where they darkened like a stain.

"Since we're going to be here longer than we thought, we can organise a proper feeding," he said. "We can use the banyan tree as the distribution point. Let's get some men to shift a quarter of the sacks of food over there this morning. Children to be fed first. The women can bring their babies to the front of the queue."

Michael nodded.

"I will tell the village," he said. "Give me an hour to arrange it."

"And we'll need water if we're going to be here a while. How far is the nearest borehole?"

"Three kilometres. An hour by vehicle."

"I'll go this afternoon," Billy said.

Michael hesitated.

"What will you do about the airstrip?"

A shadow passed across Sean's face.

"We'll speak to the Commander."

He clapped his hands together.

"Let's make the best of it while we're here."

*　*　*

While Michael and Sean organised the feeding, I helped Billy pick through the jagged debris of the shattered radio hut, busying myself against a feeling of growing anxiety. The shack's narrow wooden structure was splintered around a crater the size of a garden shed. Bits of twisted metal lay in shards, and they seemed still warm to me, but perhaps it was only the reflected heat of the already burning sun. My watch said 9.25am, but it already felt like noon.

Billy worked wordlessly with his shirt off, and his hat slung on its leather string across his tobacco brown back, pulling the debris apart piece by piece and occasionally picking up mysterious pieces of machinery and putting them into a neat pile on a groundsheet he had dragged from his tukul. As he worked, I noticed a long scar across the hard ridge of his torso, tracing the edge of his ribcage the way a railway line hugs an escarpment.

"Here she is," Billy muttered, easing a small black box the size of a cassette player from under a giant section of wood that took two of us to lift.

As I continued to pile up the shattered wood, trying to ignore the splinters that snagged at my skin, he sat cross-legged on the groundsheet, tinkering with the box and shaking it, putting his ear to the dull casing and whistling to himself. His long fingers were strong and agile with short, manicured nails on the left hand, and longer nails on the right, presumably for playing the scuffed wooden guitar he had brought with him on the plane. From time to time, my tired mind wandered to the boy at the airstrip, but it could not seem to process the news of his death, flickering over the fact of it like a far off storm.

We had worked in silence for an hour or so, when Billy set the box down to wipe the sweat from his face with his faded brown T-shirt.

"So Maria," he said, pausing to drink heavily from a battered khaki water bottle, "what you running away from?"

"Nothing, I hope," I said, squeezing a splinter between thumb and fingernail and deciding it would need a safety pin.

Billy looked at me tiredly for a moment, and then returned to tinkering with the box, using a blade from the Leatherman knife permanently clipped to his belt-hook.

"I've dreamed of Africa since I was little," I said. "I wanted to see if the reality matched up, I suppose."

Billy made a sound like a laugh, but his face was pressed to the small black box and I couldn't tell whether he was communicating with his handiwork or with me.

"Why Africa?" he said, without looking up.

"I don't know," I said. "The opportunity seemed too good to miss."

That sound again, an empty pistol-crack of laughter.

"Well, there's always a reason."

Silence hung briefly between us, broken only by the chipping and clacking of Billy's knife.

"What are you running away from?" I asked him.

Billy ignored the question and pulled out a battered leather tobacco pouch from the back pocket of his jeans, rolling a thin cigarette, then licking the paper and smoothing it down with a neatly-trimmed fingernail.

"Smoke?" he said.

I nodded, and caught the cigarette as it landed in my lap.

"I've seen 'em all you see," Billy said, starting to roll a second cigarette. "I seen the Mid West girls in the Peace Corps wanting to give something back cos Daddy's so filthy rich. I seen the Irish nurses coming to find theirselves a husband. I seen the Norwegians coming to Africa just to see the sun coming up and down at the same regular time every damn day. And the Brits, that Live Aid Army, saw Madonna jumping up and down like a hooker on television and decided theirselves to be aidworkers."

"Is this the welcome speech you give everyone?" I asked.

Billy rolled the cigarette into a perfect cylinder.

"I just like to know which category new people fall into . . ." He licked the edge of the cigarette paper. "You're young. I'm guessing Category D – unhappy childhood. Or Something Bad Just Happened to You. That's Category E."

"You still haven't said which category you fall into," I said.

Billy laughed.

"That's for me to know and you to find out."

"Anything else I need to find out?"

Billy was starting to get on my nerves.

"Lesson One: We're all playing God here, Maria. That's the first thing to understand."

He gestured at the makeshift encampment with the tobacco pouch.

"I mean . . . why this village out of every village in Bahr el Ghazal? Why Bahr el Ghazal out of Southern Sudan? Why Southern Sudan out of all of Africa? Why this child, not that child?"

He patted his pockets for a lighter.

"I saw your face this morning when Michael said that boy had died."

I looked away from his face, its shadows lit eerily by the flare of his lighter.

"Just remember it's a numbers game out here," Billy said. "Save who you can, walk away from the rest. Don't get involved. Take it from me, okay? Whoever's life you save here, there's 1,000 dying in the next ten villages."

I got awkwardly to my feet, up to my shins in shattered shed and unable to move either forward or backwards, momentarily marooned in a splintered desert of broken wood.

"I appreciate the pep talk," I said. "But I really didn't come here to play God."

"No, you're here to play some fucked up Florence Nightingale," Billy said, smiling at last, as if this was the point he had been driving at all along. "It's written all over your sweet face."

I dusted down my knees and picked up my daypack.

"I'm going to help with the feeding," I said.

Billy blew out a thick plume of smoke that exited his nose and mouth simultaneously in an amorphous white cloud.

"Running is running is running," he said.

* * *

The feeding began at 11.00am, when the sun was already a giant red ball in the sky, and the heat came down hard in oppressive sheets as if from an invisible oven. The women of the village, many carrying tiny children tied to their backs, stood in a long line that seemed to stretch to the horizon, their lively, brightly-coloured sarongs contrasting with the tiny movements they made to conserve energy. Most were of an arresting height, six feet in average, given the illusion of being even taller by the slight width of their narrow frames. Their faces were as taut as drumskin stretched over bone, marked by striking scars that divided the area between hair and eyebrows in a series of deliberate parallel lines. Above the faded material of their skirts and below their protruding collarbones, their breasts hung without shape, and some of the children they carried were so thin and disfigured by hunger I found it hard to look at them until my eyes and brain began to adjust to the reality of famine. Along the queue, I recognised Bol and his sister from the night before, and I wondered if they were orphaned, or if their mother was unwell. For the briefest moment, in the surreal semi-silence, the whole scene had the feeling of a photograph, a still black and white image lit harshly from above, framed and placed behind glass. I felt as if I were watching television while being inside the experience at the same time; trapped in a looking glass reality that reflected nothing I knew or understood.

Under the shade of the banyan tree, men stood behind the sacks with crude measuring bowls, supervised by the tall figure of Michael and the imposing silhouette of Chief Deng, whose voice rumbled like a deep, subterranean tremor from under his clipped black beard when he spoke. Each woman received a ration of sorghum, a type of grain used to make porridge, a bowl of beans and a slug of cooking oil, depending on the size of her family. Michael had a pad of paper on which he wrote each woman's name, the ration she had received and the number of her children in careful handwriting, handing a copy to the women themselves that would act as a temporary ration card. It was a meticulous operation despite its hurried organisation, far more orderly than a British supermarket queue. The feeding took place in almost complete silence, with only the murmuring of the women and the sound of grain falling into bowls of hard gourd.

I had no defined role in the process of the feeding itself, so I walked along the queue examining the weakest children, patching up occasional cuts from the midnight attack, and making a note of those families worst affected by malnutrition. The part of my mind that had paid attention to Professor Yurie's lectures on tropical medicine began to pick out details and symptoms, a remembered code of signifiers strung together like shrunken, misshapen beads. I saw severe malnutrition in the reddish hair of the children and registered a hundred infections in the eyes that turned to stare at me as I passed. I examined goitres that spoke of a lack of minerals and of thyroid problems, and listened to dozens of tuberculoid coughs. I examined infected bullet wounds, badly-healed machete scars, and the lesions of HIV/Aids. Had the London School of Hygiene and Tropical Medicine existed solely for this single, African village, it would have been overrun. And there I stood, with a modest box of medicines, some patchy medical experience and a dwindling supply of optimism.

The morning's conversation with Billy weighed on me, but I dismissed it irritably. He was the one on the run, I thought. Growing up on the lower middle class edge of a tough south-east London council estate, I had met a hundred Billys: cocksure in their swagger, tight clothes hugging their pecs and biceps, terrified inside of themselves. Billy Finn was just the cowboy version and I was more than capable of dealing with him if necessary.

The feeding went on all morning and into the blistering heat of the afternoon, a long queue of skeletal shapes shrouded in bright material that kept the sun from the women's faces and hid the babies from view. I began to work, and found in medicine's familiar routines a kind of quiet: dressing wounds, administering antibiotics, listening to rattling chests protected from the outside world by only the thinnest parchment instead of the insulating thickness of layers of flesh and skin. At least a quarter of the queue was malarial, and some of the TB cases needed treatment more urgent and involved than I could possibly provide. Meanwhile, I noticed greater evidence of HIV/Aids than I had expected, thinking that the village's proximity to the civil war's frontlines might have sealed off the area from infection like the Derbyshire plague villages of the Middle Ages.

I had been working for three hours or so, my tongue thick and swollen in my mouth and my face burning red despite the suncream I had slathered on that morning, when I noticed a tiny dustcloud appear behind the food-servers, growing larger and cloudier until it became the figure of a small boy dragging himself purposefully towards me through the dirt. I began to move towards him, thinking he must be hurt, but as he reached the serving area, a man turned around and shouted angrily, pushing him roughly away. By the time I reached the head of the queue, the boy had dragged himself to the front and crouching down to his level, I saw his face was bright with mischief and completely without fear.

"My name is Polio John," the boy said.

"My name is Maria," I said.

The boy shrugged.

"I know."

"Really?"

"Yes, Michael told me."

He wriggled awkwardly as I tried to examine his legs, touching the toughened skin on his knees thick with scarring from years of dragging himself across the hard earth. He spoke far more fluently than Bol had the night before, his small hand clamping hard onto my leg as he pulled himself into a sitting position. Then he pulled in his narrow chest and cleared his throat.

"I'm having Polio," the boy said importantly, in case that might not be evident from his name and the legs twisted beneath him.

I wasn't sure how to reply to this, but the boy interrupted me.

"Do you have cigarettes?"

"How old are you?" I asked, taken aback.

"I am ten years old," John said.

"Well, no, in that case," I said. "You're too young to smoke."

"How do you know?"

"I'm a doctor," I said. "Well, nearly a doctor anyway."

"How old you are?

"I'm twenty-three," I said, and John made a face as if I were unimaginably old.

"When did you contract polio?" I asked him.

"Since I am small," John said. "My parents are carrying me a long way to missionaries. We are walking for more than a whole week, and we stay many months, but the nuns say I have bad spirits called Polio."

"Polio's not bad spirits," I said. "It's an illness you can catch through dirty water. Anyone can get it. Even a nun."

John received this information dubiously.

"Is that where you learned English?" I asked. "From the missionaries?"

He nodded.

"The nuns teach me," he said. "They are nice ladies."

He allowed me to put a dressing on one of the worst sores on his legs, flinching as I dabbed at it with antiseptic.

"If you are doctor you are needing hospital," he said.

"That would be great," I said. "I work in a hospital in London. But I guess we'll have to make do with here, under the tree."

"There is Adek hospital. From the time before," John said.

I was immediately curious.

"What time before?" I asked.

"Time before when doctors came. White people. Long ago when I am still walking on my legs. Everyone killed by militias. White people ran away."

The thought of this mysterious time before sent a shiver through me and I was suddenly both curious to see the hospital and instinctively afraid of its history.

Just then, two incongruous white and freckled legs advanced into view from our vantage point on the floor. I looked up to see Sean standing above us with a small package in his hand.

"I see you've met John," he said.

John made a face.

"I hope he's not telling you any of his tall stories."

I pulled myself to my feet.

"He was telling me about the hospital – the one the white people built before. Is that a tall story?"

"Ah, no, that's true enough," Sean said. "It's still there but it's derelict. Médecins Sans Frontières Belgium built it a few years ago, but it's a shell now, full of weeds. We've never had the presence on the ground since to justify rebuilding it."

"Do you mind if I take a look?" I asked. "There might be something useful there. John can show me."

"Sure," Sean said. "We've finished feeding now anyway. The heat is too much and people need to be getting home to the outlying villages. We don't encourage people to move around in the late afternoon because of the militias, but you should have plenty of time to get there and back."

He hesitated.

"I would offer you a radio, but with the transmitter destroyed in the bombing, they're useless," he said. "Just come back if anything feels wrong, okay? Instinct is the best guide out in the bush."

He lifted John up onto my shoulders.

"Billy says he'll make him a wheelchair, but otherwise, John mostly travels by piggyback." Sean placed his hand on my arm. "Keep an eye on your feet. Lots of the area round here is mined. I'll send one of the SPLA boys down after you when they've finished up here. And watch out for snakes. It's very overgrown down there."

He handed me the parcel he was holding.

"Lunch," he said.

"Good," said John, in my ear.

It was a long walk to the old hospital with John on my back and we stopped under the shade of a tree to open the picnic parcel. There were two triangles of sweaty cheese and tomato sandwich made from strange, sugary white Loki bread, and a near-black, battered banana. John and I ate half the sandwich each and washed it down with a small carton of sickly yellow viscous liquid labelling itself as 'orange juice'.

"Nice," John said, wolfing down his half of the banana in a single bite.

Relieved to have finally made a friend, I found myself still wondering about Bol, the boy from the shelter, and I asked John if he knew him.

"Young Bol?" he asked. "The wedding poet?"

"What's a wedding poet?" I asked, curious.

"When a boy wants to marry he must have poem," Polio John said. "Then they will ask Poet Bol for a verse."

"And has he written any for you?" I asked, teasingly.

"Many poems," John said. "But not many girls are marrying a cripple."

I was stung by his direct response to my flippant question, and felt a need to cover the silence.

"I expect you're a bit young for girls anyway, John," I said.

The sun was high in the sky and hammering down on the top of my head in the rhythm of a headache, pressing down like a heavy sheet of metal, and I took a sachet of oral rehydration salts and poured the white powder into my water bottle, swallowing long drafts with a pair of shiny Nurofen. My body was in a feverish revolt, I realised, struggling against sun and sleeplessness. We sat for a while in the shade, and then set off again, better for the small amount of food.

"One day soon, Poet Bol will be a great soldier like his father," John volunteered as I lifted him onto my back once more.

"Not for a few years yet, I hope," I said, adjusting his weight so that his thin legs hung around my waist, supported by my arms. I changed my grip to avoid hurting the blisters and sores on his knees and thighs.

"This year," John said. "After initiation. He will avenge his father's death."

John kicked me then, a light squeeze of the ribs, like a rider encouraging a horse.

"Let's go!"

"What happened to his father?"

I was already feeling John's light weight in the heat.

"He is killed in the militia attack. The one from before."

John spoke in a low voice right into my left ear.

"He was very brave. Not in the army – traditional warrior with spear. But the Arabs had horses and guns and fire and killed hundreds of people and burned everything. Bol's father the warrior he was killed fighting the horsemen."

* * *

We reached the charred remains of the old hospital at around 4.30pm: a ruined building that bore living testimony to the story John had told of the burning village. Having only seen mud and stick tukuls in the village so far, I was surprised to find the hospital was a crumbling, stone building, pock-marked with great peeling holes as if eaten from inside by giant insects, and toothless where the wooden roof, window frames and door had burned away. Inside, amongst the shattered glass of broken bottles and empty phials of morphine, the building had a waiting air of dereliction as if expecting its occupants to return. Thick weeds grew up through cracks in the dry earth and a curiously glossy and symmetrical shrub grew at its centre, reaching upwards towards the open roof. Worried that John would cut himself on the broken glass or disturb a buried mine, I hoisted him up onto an upturned, blackened fridge that had survived the fire, pulled on a pair of plastic gloves from my medical kit and began picking through the debris. The place had been ransacked, and in between the weeds I found scores of empty blister packets of drugs, and the charred cardboard remains of their boxes: amoxicillin, ciprofloxen, codeine, fluconozole. There were empty packets of TB medications and even anti-retrovirals to treat HIV, and some advanced malarial drugs, and I scanned every one for a single tablet, knowing my own medical supplies would soon be exhausted and that there was little chance a plane was coming any day soon.

Médecins Sans Frontières had run an established field hospital here, I realised, and I sifted through the wreckage with hands that prickled with the sense of a living past. In my mind's eye, I could see the hospital as it was, the nurses and doctors moving between rows of camp beds, the giant fridges running on solar power. I could hear the calls of the patients, and smell the iodine, the disinfectant. I imagined rebuilding it, as if its reconstruction could somehow mend some of the hurt and damage done to the village, the way that Billy's patient tending of the shattered radio had felt as if it were at least a tiny sticking plaster on the horror of the night before. Perhaps a part of me even thought rebuilding the hospital would somehow bring real doctors and nurses to Adek to help me, a shameful imposter who knew nothing but textbook, parrot-learned medicine and had paid far too little attention to anything that might actually save a person's life.

I explored the building thoroughly, section by section, making a heap of burned and ruined medicines by the doorway, so that the place took on the air of a junkie's squat. I pulled up the weeds where I could so that the air began to smell fetid and overripe, as if the vegetation had begun rotting as soon as it became detached from its roots. A part of me knew I ought to be getting back to the feeding, but I was tired and the shade and the rhythm of the work were enticing to my overheated brain.

John chattered away as I worked, and fired questions at me in his interrogative way as I sweated and strained, pausing to study the answers with his head on one side, and shaking his whole body if he found them unsatisfactory.

"Where are you from?"

"England."

"Is England a village?"

"A country. I come from a big village in England, a city called London."

"Is there food in London?"

"Yes . . ."

"No-one is hungry?"

"No."

I heaved a large chunk of stone to one side, and stood breathless, leaning momentarily against the cobweb-encrusted wall until I felt something dark scuttle across behind me. I thought of Sean's warning about snakes and spiders, and shuddered involuntarily.

"Is there war?"

I thought of Kosovo, but the way England would experience it seemed a vast way away from the forty years of civil war that had shattered Sudan into brittle fragments.

"Well, we are becoming involved in a war. But it's not in England," I replied.

"England is attacking another country?"

"It may do. That country is attacking its own people in a civil war."

"Like Sudan."

"I think like Sudan. I don't understand it enough."

"So will England attack Sudan?"

"I don't think so."

"Why?"

"The other war is nearer. People can see it."

"Are you married?"

"No."

"How many children do you have?"

"I don't have any."

John's eyes widened at this.

"Why did you come here?"

"That's what I'm wondering John," I said, out of breath, and examining a splinter in my left thumb that had drawn blood across the white spiderweb of my thumbprint.

"Polio John," John said.

"Okay, Polio John," I said. "Now, look over here in this corner. It looks different to me. What do you think?"

At the far end of the half-dark, unroofed hut, which was overhung by sickly vines, I had seen that the earth was flatter and harder, as if it had been stamped down, and I pulled out a penknife from my pocket, moving entirely by instinct now, my mind dislocated from the present by exhaustion and sleep deprivation. I half heard John jump down and join me on hands and knees, and together we began scrabbling at the earth, until it seemed clear there was something buried beneath.

I took a deep breath then, knowing Adek's bitter history, how it had been attacked and burned multiple times by the Arab militias, and then rebuilt again in defiance on the charred embers of its own buildings. Steeling myself for a grisly discovery, only impatience and curiosity kept me digging on without going to fetch the others, and with John's ten-year-old help, we uncovered the lid of a giant metal box, preserved from rust by the dryness of the red-orange soil. We both sat back on our haunches for a minute, and I looked at my hands where they rested on my knees and saw my gloves had come off somewhere in the digging and that my fingernails were bloodied and ragged like a warning. I paused for a moment, knowing I should not open the chest alone.

Then I stuck my penknife into the narrow crack between the buried container and its lid, and began prising it open, slowly, working my way methodically around its edge. After the heavy lid had come up a millimetre or so, I took the broken handle of the old metal fridge, and pushed it under the rim, levering with all my strength, and John pushed his weight onto me so that together we pressed the handle downwards. We did the same at two other points, and suddenly the lid came flying up, knocking my forehead so that I fell backwards into a pile of rubble. I got up, dazed and in pain, to see that John was lying at the edge of the hole we had uncovered, his eyes dancing with jubilant mischief.

"Riches!" he shouted.

Inside the dark space were myriad treasures bequeathed by unknown predecessors. Boxes of neatly-stacked drugs shone in their packaging, bottles of iodine glowed an unnatural, iridescent orange in the sunlight. There were droppers, and syringes, and sterile dressings, and blood transfusion kits. The box went deep, and I had to lean in with John hanging next to me, to reach a bottom that was lined with several wooden boxes of snake antivenom, and some mysterious packages of dried herbs.

Perched awkwardly, I sensed rather than saw a slight movement to my left in an area of rubble in the corner of the derelict building, and pulled myself up in time to see a shadow flit across the back wall. I wondered if it was the SPLA man Sean had said he was sending, but the man standing there framed by the burned out doorway like a portrait – a tall man, slender and painted white all over, holding a long spear decorated with painted feathers – was not a soldier. His eyes, black hollows against the unnaturally white shape of his face, seemed to lock with mine briefly, and next to my skin I thought I felt John shiver. And then the figure was gone, and I was left wondering whether it was heat exhaustion or the dizziness of my excitement that had conjured him there, or whether it was the opening of the box.

*　*　*

Polio John and I covered the mile or so back to camp in a blur of excitement, and his thin body felt light up on my back against the exhilarating force of the adrenalin pumping through my bloodstream. John chattered on excitedly, but I hardly heard a word he said, thinking only of my discovery and of the new possibility of treating so many people in the village. For the past three-and-a-half years of medical school, I had stood in the teaching hospital under the strip-lights observing the nurses administering shots and swabs and drips and pre-meds and watching the doctors work, physically disconnected from what I was learning. Now, jogging across an African warzone with a ten year old boy with polio on my back, I felt suddenly alive to the possibilities of medicine. The sun had begun its rapid descent across the sky by the time we had left the hospital and if it hadn't been for John calling out the route left and right, round family tukuls and between clumps of stunted trees, I would never have found my way back to the camp.

By the time we arrived it was pitch dark. Billy was sitting silhouetted by the campfire picking out some quavering melody on his guitar, and stood up abruptly when he saw us approach.

"Where in hell have you been?" he said quietly.

I lowered John to the floor and Billy placed his guitar carefully on the tree branch, as if we were each laying down our weapons.

I felt defiant and embarrassed all at once.

"At the old hospital," I said, evenly. "Sean said I could go."

"Well, Sean had no goddamn business saying you could go. He must have had heatstroke."

Billy's accent was loosening and spreading, although he still spoke softly.

"I found medicines . . . Medicines that could save a lot of people's lives."

"I don't care what you found. It's after curfew and Sean and Michael are still out looking for you," Billy said. "So now they're in danger too."

"John was with me," I said, but John had already vanished into the shadows.

"And you thought a polio boy protection enough?"

"He got us back to camp."

"Let's get something straight, Maria," Billy said, and his mouth was a short razorblade of anger. "This is a warzone, not some African safari camp for you to go wandering off to wherever takes your fancy. Some of the land round here is still mined, there is unexploded ordnance all over the place. The militias can come without warning and they will kill you, Maria, and probably rape you first. There are a dozen spiders out there that will kill you with a single bite, not to mention the scorpions, the green and black mambas and some pretty lively spitting cobras . . . This ain't some little piece of English countryside, you know? This is hostile fucking territory."

He might have continued, but I interrupted him.

"Well, perhaps if all this had been outlined truthfully to me before I came, I wouldn't be here," I said, angrily. "I don't remember green mambas and unexploded bombs being on the job advert next to "unmissable opportunity"."

I rushed on before Billy could interrupt.

"And I'm also not responsible for us being stranded here in the middle of bloody nowhere with no chance of getting home. So if anyone is irresponsible, I would think that were you."

Billy stared at me for a moment in apparent disbelief.

"Answer me one thing," he said. "What do you think is actually going on here?"

"A famine."

"Wrong. It's a genocide. And a genocide surely is not the time to be running around after dark. You got forty-eight hours to prove you ain't a liability to this mission."

"Or let me guess . . ." I said. "You're going to send me home via that bombed out airstrip?"

Afraid I would cry or lose my temper completely, I turned on my heel and pushed open the door of my already dark tukul. I climbed inside the mosquito net fully clothed and lay down, feeling my exhausted spine unfolding its vertebrae one by one against the hard wooden bed, pulling a sheet over myself so that the clumsy shadows of my dusty hiking boots stuck out at the end like a joke, as if they belonged to some other grown-up person. Feeling oppressed by the thick blackness and the heavy, oppressive heat of the airless cabin, I pulled my torch out from under the pillowcase I had stuffed with clothes, and clicked it on. Above me, countless insects violently attacked the lit shape of the mosquito net so that it became a restless, amorphous shroud moving and buzzing in time with the throbbing of my head where I had banged it on the metal lid of the buried medicine chest. Something scuttled and scraped beneath the platform of the bed, and I imagined a rat, then a scorpion, then a green snake in the shape of what I thought a mamba might look like. The thatch was alive with insects, a tiny ecosystem in which I was an unwelcome intruder, and I tucked the net in tighter around myself, wondering if the Government bomber was already taking off from a dusty airbase somewhere in the North of the country to annihilate the village while I slept. I was hungry, desperately thirsty and had no way to go home.

"What are you doing, Maria?" I whispered to the familiar worn floral-pattern of my old pillowcase, determined not to give Billy the satisfaction of my tears. "What the hell are you doing?"

Outside, I heard Sean's voice whispering urgently at the doorway.

"Maria? You awake?"

I snapped the torch off quickly, feeling the absolute, blanket-heavy blackness pressing down on me like a great weight, trying to imagine myself at home in my mother's tiny, dark, falling down house, lying between cool, clean sheets with a glass of water by my bedside I probably wouldn't even drink. But my mother's house had been sold at auction the previous week, and instead I lay there listening to Billy's mournful guitar and hating him for his patronising macho superiority and his phoney cowboy drawl.

I lay there wide awake in the boiling heat long after the music faded and the others had gone to bed, listening to the roar of the cicadas and crickets outside, wondering where on earth they could be living in this dead place, where every blade of grass had been eaten, used for matting or killed by drought, a bare and empty dustbowl without birds or cats or howling dogs, where only giant insects thrived on a diet of death and dust. I lay there grieving for my old Africa, the dreamed Africa of my childhood, a place that existed only as a flickering pattern of colours and sounds in the synapses of my brain, a place of swaying Saharan grasses and flat trees and lush jungle vegetation alive with lions and buffalo and giraffes – a place as familiar to me as childhood pyjamas and storybooks, as my mother's voice or the lines on the palms of my own hands. I had known this continent remotely all my life. As a child, I had watched its great hulking landmass from the shores of my grandmother's town of Tarifa at the very bottom tip of Spain and held its sand in my fingers when it blew ashore. I had known it in my mother's endless stories and in her dreams of travel. But of course I had not known it, not really, at all.

Then exhaustion pulled me into itself and the scratching and the scuttling and screaming of the insects to one another blurred into a single static noise of unknown fears, and with the torch still gripped tightly in my left hand and my penknife in my right, I fell asleep thinking of the man with the spear and of the hollow sockets of his black eyes.

Chapter Five

I awoke early the next morning in the already stifling warmth of my tukul feeling curiously rested, and was surprised to find I had slept for almost eight hours. My limbs were heavy with a feverish ache, as if I had run a marathon the previous day, and my hands were sore and filthy with the effort of digging the box from the ground, but the sense of elation I had felt at the derelict hospital persisted in choppy waves of cautious optimism. During the night I had dreamed of the bleached silhouette of the man in the doorway, but in sleep he had seemed quietly benign, and in the cool early morning light already pooling on the mud floor of the tukul he seemed to be only the product of too much heat and lack of sleep – a warning to look after myself better in hostile territory, as Billy had put it.

My clothes were wet with sweat where I had slept in them, and I towelled my damp skin as I changed, hanging my sleeping sheet up to dry on a wooden nail on the back of the tukul door. After draining my flask of water, I pulled out a packet of baby wipes and carefully washed my filthy hands, face and neck, removing the streaks of dust from my arms and legs, and dressing in clean, dry clothes. I clipped my fingernails where they had torn and removed two large splinters from my thumb, bathing the cuts in antiseptic and then applying plasters. I dabbed some antiseptic on the raised lump below my hairline where I had banged my head, but with only a fragment of poorly lit mirror and in the dark of the tukul I couldn't see whether it was cut or only bruised.

There was nothing I could do with my filthy hair, so I tied it back, and then set about tidying my tukul, dividing my clothes into clean, cleanish, dirty and filthy, and using a red dust-stained pair of khaki shorts to flick the worst of the cobwebs that overhung my sleeping platform. Two spiders shot across the floor in awkward succession, a pair of poor ice-skaters or unfortunates fired from an arachnid circus cannon, and I realised I had just made them homeless. The first had long, thin, hairy legs, skittish movements and a tiny brown body; the other was fat and black with short stubby legs and an air of self-conscious intellectualism. In my head, I named them Laurel and Hardy to avoid having to think of them as actual insects. Laurel, the eternal follower, scuttled off after fat Hardy under the bed.

Tying my mosquito net up into itself so the bed platform could air, I repacked my pillowcase with the clothes that had spilled out of it during the night, and hung a piece of string across the hut so that my sweat-dampened clothes could dry a little. Then, checking my boots for scorpions or spiders by banging them on the ground, I pulled them on over clean socks and I felt ready to face the day. As a final touch, I pulled a faded photograph of my mother from the front pocket of my rucksack and pinned her to the wall next to where I had wedged the tiny fragment of hand mirror into the mud wall.

"See where you are?" I said to the photograph.

My mother had been born at the southern most tip of Spain in a town that looks out across Africa, and had dreamed all her life of crossing the water to the landmass beyond. As a young student nurse she had yearned to sail across to Morocco, Algeria, Tunisia and down to Egypt, Ethiopia, Sudan and Chad. Just once, she had made the crossing from Tarifa, stowing away on the morning boat to Tangiers. She spent the day in the souks and marketplaces, speaking French with the women at the dockside cleaning fish and mending nets. She came home on the evening boat longing already to return. Instead, that same summer of her nineteenth birthday, she met my father the Englishman and travelled to London to be with him. Within two years he had left her with an eighteen month old daughter and five months pregnant in a two-roomed 1970s council flat in an un-noteworthy urban suburb of the city. By the time I was five, my mother's sense of shame was so great that we no longer went to Tarifa for holidays. The tiny window into the African continent she had experienced might have closed had she not kept it propped open, supplementing memory with documentaries and wildlife programmes, and dog-eared copies of *National Geographic* borrowed from the doctor's waiting room.

Now, experiencing the adventure she had dreamed of all her life, I knew it was time to pull myself together. I could smell wood burning and I was hungry. It was 7.00am and already heat was rising from the ground below the tukul as I pushed open the door. Rounding the barren mango tree at the centre of the camp, I prepared myself to face Billy, but instead there was a small girl boiling water by the fire who stood up with a start as I approached. She wore a neat brown sarong dotted with faded green flowers, and her thin, black upper torso was naked. Not quite flat-chested, she wasn't yet old enough for breasts, and I thought she must be about eleven years old.

"Hello," I said.

The girl sat down without speaking.

I knelt at the fire with my mug, looking for teabags in the cardboard carton of our provisions from Loki.

"My name is Maria."

"Adel Deng," the girl whispered without looking up, so that it wasn't exactly clear she had spoken at all.

"Chief Deng's daughter?" I asked, suddenly noticing the similarity, the oval, high cheek-boned face and the almond-shaped eyes.

The girl nodded, adjusting her sarong so that it fell neatly across her knees. I noticed her eyes were unusually light, a mid-brown that was almost mauve.

"My mother is sick," she said, and I realised that was why she was here, tending the white people's hearth.

"Perhaps I can help her?" I said, thinking of the box of drugs in my tukul. But the girl shook her head.

"The Spear Master is there," she said, with a fluttering hope in those teardrop eyes that I recognised from many months at my own mother's bedside, waiting for the verdicts of doctors.

"Perhaps I could talk to him," I offered, but Adel shook her head emphatically, and stood up to signal the conversation over. In the silence, I sat drinking my black tea at the fireplace and watching the early-morning shadows of clouds crossing the dusty floor of the encampment, listening to the distant sounds of the village coming to life.

"Would you like some milk from the goat?" Adel asked after a while.

The milk tasted like a thick, bitter cheese, with a faint odour of goat dung, and it was all I could do to swallow it, but it was liquid and laden with vitamins so I drank as much as I could before setting my tin mug down again on the earth. As I did so, I saw Adel's almond eyes watching the mug with regret and realised she had probably not had any breakfast.

"Are you having some milk?" I asked, but the girl shook her head.

I poured some in a mug for her anyway, and offered it to her. She took the cup in both hands and finished it in a terrible swallow as if her stomach were on fire. I went and fetched her a banana from the box, which she ate rapidly in a dignified silence.

"You're hungry," I said.

The girl looked back at me through mauve eyes.

"Yes."

I made a cheese and tomato sandwich and gave half to Adel, and we were sitting eating happily in silence when the girl suddenly scrambled to her feet.

Two men with Kalashnikovs were lazily approaching the camp, as if on a Sunday stroll. The taller had a tight-curled grey beard and a scar across his face, and was wearing a cerise-coloured woman's dressing gown over a pair of army fatigues and shined army boots. The second man, slightly smaller although still above six feet tall and neatly dressed in a uniform of not-quite matching camouflage, advanced a step behind him and was carrying a wooden chair. Somehow, the presence of the chair and the bathrobe seemed to cancel out the Kalashnikovs, so that I felt the men weren't quite enemies nor exactly friends.

Adel greeted them in the Dinka language, handing each a cup of water ladled from a bucket.

"Commander Wol," Adel said, bowing a little towards the taller man, and I felt myself unconsciously mimic her gesture. The Commander was over seven feet tall, but with a girlish waist and long lean limbs. The angular set of his face was striking, the line of the high cheekbone on his left side given a curious expression by the five-inch scar that bisected his eyebrow and puckered the skin of his wide top lip.

"Good morning," I said, feeling tiny in the presence of a seven-foot rebel army commander, and wholly perplexed by the dressing gown.

The Commander nodded at his companion, who placed the chair down in front of him and removed a speck of dust from its seat. Commander Wol sat down heavily, arranging the bathrobe carefully across his legs, and laying his rifle across his knee like a walking stick. He downed the water in a single swallow and returned the cup to Adel's outstretched hand.

"Where are Finn and Donnelly?" the Commander asked in heavily accented English, looking around him unevenly. His words slurred slightly, and although it was barely 7.00am, it was clear he was more than a little drunk.

"They're asleep, sir," I said, hating the servility of my tone.

"Then, wake them up," the Commander snapped.

"Perhaps I can offer you some tea," I said, politely.

Just then, Billy appeared at the door of his tukul in a pair of long surf shorts, a blue toothbrush sticking out of his mouth and a ragged yellow towel around his bare shoulders.

He saw the Commander sitting there and offered him a half-salute that seemed to me to be mocking, although the soldier took it as sincere.

"Give me a moment, Commander," he said.

We all sat in silence waiting for him to complete his al fresco ablutions, and Adel gave the old soldier a mug of steaming brown Nescafé, into which he poured a generous slug of amber liquid from an antique hip flask. I found myself staring at the scar across his cheek, and at his left hand which appeared to be nerve damaged, twitching unconsciously and unable to grip the rifle where it lay in his lap. I had never seen a real gun before except on television, and it seemed a shocking, menacing thing, despite its evidently ancient exterior.

"I've heard a lot about you, Commander Wol," I said to break the silence.

The Commander grunted into his mug, and then spat the last of his coffee onto the parched ground by his chair, ejecting the liquid through the sizeable gap between his two front teeth. The dry soil drank the moisture greedily.

We sat in silence again until Billy reappeared, shaking hands with the Commander and then slapping the back of his companion, a younger man he greeted as Lieutenant Dit. There appeared to be a genuine friendship between the young Lieutenant and Billy, and a relationship of mutually wary respect between both men and Commander Wol. I was also fascinated to see that Billy seemed to accept the dressing gown as a part of the Commander's normal military attire.

Apparently ignoring my presence altogether, Billy took a black coffee from Adel's outstretched hand.

"What news, Commander?"

As he spoke, he sat down on one of the upturned logs by the fire, pulling it forward so that he faced the soldier and his man.

"No news," the Commander said, stonily.

"I'm sure you didn't walk two miles to tell me no news, Commander."

Billy spoke lightly and evenly, almost smiling.

"We have a unit due back today," the Commander said. "Then we will know news. You are the one who has just come from Kenya. And you are the one with the radio. What news do you have for me?"

"The radio was smashed in the bombardment," Billy said. "It is only just fixed."

"So you have spoken to Loki today?"

"Late last night."

"And?"

"We are to remain here until further notice."

"Then you will need protection."

Billy smiled apologetically.

"I thank you for your concern, Commander, but as you know, the rules of our NGO and the protocols of Operation Lifeline Sudan, of which we are a part, state that we cannot accept military protection."

"Then you are fools."

"That is a matter of opinion, of course."

"My men are hungry."

The Commander played with the catch of his Kalashnikov as he spoke and I wondered whether it was unconscious habit or implicit threat.

"I'm sorry to hear that," Billy said, slouching his shoulders a little, perhaps with conscious insolence. "But you know we are here to feed children, not soldiers, Commander."

Behind the Commander, a look of painful regret crossed the face of Lieutenant Dit.

"Whether you admit it or not, my soldiers are protecting your bloody civilian operation," the Commander snorted, the almost comic use of the English swearword contrasting with the violent twitching of his hand in his lap. "I hardly think you would be feeding children without them."

Billy pushed his hands into his jeans pockets, and cocked his head to one side as if considering the Commander's demands carefully.

"Extrapolating from the information we gathered yesterday, we are looking at 1,200 households at least requiring supplementary feeding just in Adek," he said, after a while. "So, you see, we do not have food to spare, Commander. And even if we did, you know it is against UN regulations for us to feed the military on either side of this war, regardless of our own feelings on the matter."

The Commander reached for his hip flask with his good hand, and seemed about to make a sudden movement, but Billy raised his hand to indicate he was still talking.

"On the other hand, if your men were to assist in rebuilding the air strip . . ." Billy paused, and scratched at his two-day stubble for a moment. "That would be different. I mean, that would be food for work, Commander. Your men would be employed as construction workers not soldiers."

The Commander got to his feet suddenly, so that Dit had to grab his falling coffee cup and pick up the wooden chair all in one movement.

"You insult me," Commander Wol said.

Dit put the coffee cup carefully on the ground out of harm's way.

"I most certainly do not, Commander," Billy said, remaining seated. "I offer you the proposal with the utmost respect."

The Commander stood there for a long moment.

"You have miscalculated," he said. "You need us more than we need you. Without my men you have no way of clearing the airstrip."

* * *

The Commander turned on his heel in a long stride that became a march. Behind him, his Lieutenant struggled on his shorter legs to keep up, while simultaneously carrying the chair and still maintaining a formal military stride. But he looked back at Billy with an expression that seemed almost a smile.

"He's right of course," Billy said, as the Commander passed out of earshot.

Then, apparently deciding to acknowledge my existence, he turned, and I saw his eyes flick to the lump on my forehead.

"What the hell happened to you?" he said.

"It's nothing," I said.

Billy frowned at the lump again. Then, before I could speak, he picked up the radio transmitter and his guitar from the tarpaulin under the tree, and walked quickly away.

* * *

I was sitting in the sunshine with Adel, wondering what to do if I wasn't allowed out of sight when Sean emerged from his hut, carrying an armful of paperwork.

"Was that the Commander's dulcet tones I heard?" he asked cheerfully. I nodded.

"It's the one thing Billy and I disagree about," Sean said. "Billy thinks he's a revolutionary hero, I think he's a murdering bastard. Either way, we need him."

"What's with the ladies' dressing gown?" I said.

Sean laughed.

"It came in a Christian assignment from some Deep South missionary militias," he said, dryly. "The Commander hasn't figured out it's women's wear and no-one round here has felt compelled to point it out to him."

"I didn't know whether to laugh or cry," I said.

"Both would be appropriate," Sean said.

He held the paperwork tightly against his chest for a moment.

"I'm sorry Billy went off at you last night," he said, rubbing at his beard. "It's just his way."

I nodded.

"Sure."

"He was worried because he thought something had happened to you. He was rightly angry with me too for letting you go in the first place. It was stupid of me. We're not used to accommodating extra people I guess. Billy and I have been working together a long time. It's great that Africaid sent you, but it doesn't mean we've really worked out what to do with you exactly."

I found myself smiling as Sean took the wooden container of goat's milk and poured it over a bowl of cornflakes, thinking how lucky Billy was to have this amiable translator following along after him, clearing up his mess and explaining away his mistakes. Sean seemed to do it as easily as breathing.

"I shouldn't have been there so long," I said. "I just got carried away at the old hospital . . . I was trying to tell Billy last night – I found an amazing thing. A box of medicines. Hundreds of them – six months' supply at least of everything we could possibly need. They were all buried in a series of boxes in a corner under the ground, and most of them are in date . . ."

Sean laughed out loud. I was so surprised that I almost decided to tell him about the man with the white face who had appeared in the hospital, but thought better of it.

"Good old Sudan," Sean said, grinning. "Just when you think you're fucked, the place surprises you. I'll send Michael in the vehicle to fetch them when he's back from the barracks. The way things are going, we might well need them."

I hesitated.

"How long do you think we'll be here?"

I was thinking of so many things then, how I had only half a bottle of sunscreen and a day's underwear left, how hungry I was already, how frightened, how this was the most exciting moment of my life so far, how I wished my mother was alive to hear of it and how relieved I was that she wasn't worrying at home. Most of all I felt curiously exhilarated, as if I had come suddenly to life.

"I think it's going to take about six weeks to get the airstrip fixed," Sean said. "Depending on how much help we get from the army."

"I don't think it will be very much if Commander Wol's got anything to do with it," I said.

Sean laughed.

"Most of that's just shadow boxing," he said. "I'm sure he will help so long as his forces don't come under attack to the north or west where the militias are."

He placed his hand gently on my arm and rested it there.

"I'm sorry. It's hardly the kind of introduction to Africa you were looking for."

I shrugged.

"It's okay," I said. "I mean, as long as we're going to be all right in the end."

"I'm not going to lie to you, Maria," Sean said. "This is a serious situation. But thank God Billy fixed the radio yesterday. We have spoken to Loki and we are advised that, for the moment, things on the ground are relatively secure. The militias are held up west of here close to Aweil where the local rebels are putting up some resistance. That buys us some time. We can probably withstand another aerial bombardment as long as they don't directly hit the shelter. There is a borehole near to here and we have charcoal filters, so we have access to relatively safe water. In any case, there is nowhere we can drive to that we would possibly have enough petrol to reach."

He smiled absently.

"Unless one of us gets really sick, it's just about endurance, and if the Commander's men work fast we could even be out in three weeks – six weeks maximum. Loki can drop food, medicines and essentials without landing. So we wait here. You'll be home by Christmas and ready to start medical school again in January."

The way he spoke both calmed and frightened me, and I saw that he was looking for some kind of response.

"I can manage six weeks," I said. "I might even be useful now we've got the medicines and I won't wander off again." I paused. "I was thinking maybe I could set up some sort of basic clinic at the old hospital. It's perfect. They chose that place for a reason, and it's away from the village if people are contagious. I could train some people here to be nurses and they could take it over when we go . . ."

Sean squeezed my arm where he held it and I looked down at the pattern of freckles on his hand. They seemed clustered into different shapes, clouds and pigs and bubbles.

"We'll see," he said, and I noticed how his Derry accent came through almost as a monotone when he was being serious. "We need to get through a lot of basics in the next few days – survival procedures, what to do in a militia attack, rationing food, making a secure camp."

For the briefest moment, a hummingbird haunted the air like an apparition, its wingbeats invisible and its long bill like a gentleman's pipe, glossy feathers shimmering, camouflaged by thin air.

"We're going to try and get some feeding centres up and running while we're here," Sean continued. "We might manage a health clinic as well. We don't often have the luxury of this much time on the ground. That's another way of looking at it."

I looked at his face. His pale skin was already burned a violent purple-crimson across his forehead and his nose had blistered in the baking sun, but the expression in his eyes was one of pure optimism.

"I'm trying to understand things here," I said. "I thought El Niño had caused the drought which caused the famine. But the other day you said it was man-made."

"El Niño caused the drought, but human beings caused the famine," Sean said. "The Arab Government in the North wants to destroy the base of the Southern rebel forces, the black African armies fighting for independence. For months, even years, militias armed by the Government have been raiding villages in the South, burning, looting, raping, pillaging. Crops and food stores are destroyed, children taken as slaves, as many men killed as they have bullets. The Government supports the militias by bombing supposed 'rebel strongholds' from the air, but more often hits villages and even schools and hospitals. Millions of people in the South have been displaced by this campaign into one of the least hospitable landscapes in the world. The scrubland can barely sustain thorn trees let alone families. So without Western aid, people simply die."

As Sean spoke, he was scratching with his foot in the red dust, drawing a rough map of Sudan and its Southern states.

"We're here in Bahr el Ghazal region," he said, marking a section with his heel. "But it's not just Bahr el Ghazal under attack. With China's help, the Government and its militias are also clearing the oilfields in Western Upper Nile, another Southern state, using a scorched earth policy that is literally burning people from their land. And in the Nuba Mountains, the tribal peoples are being forcibly moved into so-called 'Peace Camps' where only horror and starvation await them."

"But how is this allowed to carry on?" I asked, aware of the naiveté of the question but uncomprehending all the same. "I mean, people know what's happening . . .?"

"After 1992 when 250,000 people were killed, the UN and several large NGOs set up Operation Lifeline Sudan – a dedicated aid operation which was supposed to mean mass starvation could never happen on such a large scale again. But the Government obstructs the aid effort in countless ways – most effectively by refusing flight permissions to bring food, aid and medicine into the country."

Sean looked at me squarely then.

"Make no mistake, the Government wants these people dead," he said. "It is our job to see they fail. Saving even twenty lives is a victory."

In the middle distance Michael the logistician cut across the back of the encampment with his face in shadow, a giant bundle of long wood under one arm, and holding a bucket of some kind of feed for the goats he had bought for us that morning. He was whistling to himself despite his heavy load, an axe with a wooden handle strapped across the broad width of his back. He was wearing Billy's red and blue Tennessee Smokies baseball hat pulled down against the sun.

I thought: "They want to kill Michael because he is a Dinka." But I couldn't comprehend it. Not really. It was only words.

Chapter Six

In the lazy light of late afternoon, the apple tree's black branches are dappled with dying sunshine, and the tiny space of the municipal park is crammed with winter life. Its roof is the sky and three of its wire fences are overhung with unruly tangles of honeysuckle, clematis and ivy. The fourth wall is the side of Nye Bevan House, a short stubby block opposite to mine. It is only 3.30pm, but at this time of year in London the windows are already losing their transparency in the twilight, half-reflecting the black and gold shapes of the dying sun as it cuts through the buildings all around.

My temperature is up again today and the weather is bitter, but I needed to get out of the flat and into the air, and I am sitting on the painted wooden bench next to a planter filled by the local gardening group with coltish, awkward-stemmed geraniums. I can feel the cold coming up from the ground and through my thin coat into the denim of my jeans, but I would still rather be out here.

I realised this morning that I am still angry with Grace. I am angry with her for the photograph that deprived me of the privacy that might have allowed me to move on. Had that picture never been taken, I might have come back from Sudan to an anonymous life. The newspapers and broadcasters and agencies who write to me on various anniversaries of the event itself call it an iconic image, the photograph of me running with my hair on fire reprinted again and again – although strangely it's the one part of it all that I don't ever relive in the shaky cine-film of my own memory. They always ask the same things – in the same handwritten letters on headed notepaper that admire my courage or appreciate how difficult it must be to face the anniversary. Even so, perhaps I would now like to talk about the photograph, or the loss of my 'lover', or even to revisit Sudan? I might even want to tell them how that 'history-changing' moment really felt – a moment that ended up on the cover of *Time* magazine and resulted in a tide of aid moving into Southern Sudan? There

49

has been mention of varying sums – thousands of pounds – for me, for charity, for the village. The photograph itself won dozens of awards and must have made Grace a great deal of money. She was already a well-known war photographer when she came to Adek, but I have seen her name in important magazines since, in *Rolling Stone* and *Vanity Fair*. There was even an exhibition of the pictures she took one night at the cattle camp outside Adek, billed as '*A Sudan retrospective*'. They took me by violent, horrifying surprise one Saturday morning in the *Guardian* 'Weekend' magazine.

Three boys in dark hoods pass my bench, boys I have known since they were five. They are almost men now, long-limbed and loose-walking, their jeans hanging down low enough to reveal two inches below the waistband of their branded pants. They come from families that are poor by Western standards and obscenely rich by African, a kind of mediocre deprivation that is perhaps the hardest kind to bear, where their greatest deficit is love.

The boys look up sheepishly from under their hoods as they pass, pretending to be bad, and I am left alone again in the tiny park with the dogshit and the peace and quiet and the mulchy smell of rotting leaflitter. Below it all I can smell the concrete underneath the soil. The dust from the grey pavements gets up my nose and into my pores until I can feel it turning my skin to grey stone. I have never been able to feel warm again since I came back from Africa. There is always a coldness, deep in the marrow of my bones.

There is so much to look at in this small park, and I recount each part of it to myself as an antidote to the memory I can feel lurking at the fringes of my mind, a shark skirting a shoal of fish at the edge of my vision. I watch the barren branches of the apple tree being possessed by the sharp wind, already robbed of their clothes by the cold and the rain. I notice how the spiders' webs are empty, derelict, patched up, and follow the sluggish networks of snail-trails as they lead everywhere and nowhere, covering the pathways in silvery writings. The snails themselves have packed up their homes and moved on, like travellers moved to a site out of town. The flowers have shut up shop and the weeds lie thick in the borders waging war against once-bright beds of battered orange and fading, forget-me-not blue. A bare trellis climbs the weathered wall of Tutu block without hope of reaching the top – a lack of ambition the Archbishop himself would find incomprehensible. Patches of soil in the cracked brickwork lie dormant. Only the ivy, jungle thick and livid green, still thrives, fighting off other fair-weather tenants and claimants, stretching and spreading itself luxuriously along the fence-posts, basking on the sunny, sheltered side of the park.

I pull out the newspaper clipping from inside my coat pocket and unfold it, careful to protect the ageing newsprint from the harsh wind. Bringing it outside makes it seem safer to me, like a firework or a petrol bomb that can be detonated carefully in a controlled explosion in open space.

I hold the paper there for a moment, unfolded, but I cannot look at it. My head averts itself, aware only of the colours of the page from the corner of my vision – red and yellow and black. The images and smells begin to flood and I close it hurriedly against the noise pouring from the photograph, the stink of it. The horror.

I think: 'Margaret Dyer needs discharging today. I should be at work.'

I think: 'I should have had the flu jab."

I think: 'Mr Shiozaki asked me to water his plants."

I don't let myself think of then.

In the locked shed by the park's entrance, a terracotta army of flowerpots waits for fresh supplies to the front. In the tiny community herb garden, young plants struggle on against neglect and the tug of the winter wind. The rosemary still grows strong and the lavender is thickly scented, but when I bend to check for it I find the oregano is utterly lost.

I pull up the collar of my coat and push my gloved hands deep into my pockets, careful not to touch the piece of folded newspaper, as I pass back through the trellised gate and towards home, knowing my fingers will catch fire if I let the image touch my glove.

I think: What happened ten years ago made Grace famous. That's why she wants to relive it all again.

Chapter Seven

At night, the insect helicopters come – dozens of them, singularly or in pairs. Low buzzing, with drunken captains crashing the arc of the lantern where the lizards lie in wait, green tongues curling their disapproval. Soft-winged moths come to the candle. A stag beetle in full body armour climbs towards the fire, heavy as a locomotive on wheels.

Under the winged copters fly the insect paratroopers: the spitfire mosquitoes and the squaddie gnats freefalling on the tug of the warm wind; snipers darting in and under –biting blood, fattening like cattle.

Where I sit, smoking my one-a-day rationed cigarette, a tiny, shoe-flattened scorpion holds its pincers out in front of itself like a child with sticky hands. As black as pitch and as shiny as night, it is crushed into two dimensions, its poison spent on a rubber sole so that its death is without a sting.

By day, this battlefield is empty – the carcasses of the night before laid out under the creeping fingers of the morning sun. The soldier ants march in formation to the frontlines bearing aloft the copters and the paratroopers, carrying the cavalry of the airborne division back to their mudhill bier. The lizards lie in their beds, the khaki toads retreat like fat tanks, the birds of prey circle the land sorrowfully, the cellophane-winged flies sing of rain, dancing to the wind's skipping beat.

Above the village, the heat lies heavy in the air, pounding the dry earth, stealing the breeze, making sweat pool in the small of a woman's back.

In the morning a voice calls. A soft voice with an African lilt.

"Maria!" the man calls. "Maria!"

The voice is Michael's.

The dawn light leaks weakly through myriad gaps in the thin walls of my tukul, the mosquito net casting shadows on the mud floor. I shake myself fully awake, letting the remnants of the dream-memory fly loosely from my hair and out of the doorway into the pale emptiness of the early morning sky. Michael is standing at a respectful distance from the

52

doorway, holding a tin mug out in front of him. White steam curls from the top of the cup like cottonwool.

"Time for work," Michael says. "The hospital is waiting for you."

He hands me the coffee, which is strong and heavily sugared. He smiles at me, and, god, I actually blush, the way I haven't blushed since the first year of secondary school.

"Thanks," I mumble, my hands burning on the metal mug. It is because he believes in the hospital, I tell myself. He is the only person here who believes in me as a doctor – as someone who actually has something to give. He and I are working on a secret project together in the early hours of the morning before work on the hospital starts – a present for Polio John.

"See you down there," Michael says.

I smile at him sleepily. He is so tall and so clean. I would like to ask him how he does it. When I am covered in sweat and dust within moments of washing, Michael smells always of some old-fashioned soap.

I would like to tell Michael about the dreams I have been having these past three weeks since we've been stuck here in Sudan. They are as vivid and intense as television, stronger than acid: a mass of yearned-for deprivations. I dream of sugar, of chocolate or sugary tea, of thickly salted crisps. I have strange, almost painful, cravings for things I never liked: tinned apricots and pistachio nuts, walnuts and watermelon. I dream of orange juice, sunshine in a glass. Night after night I dream of the sea crashing outside my tukul, thickening the air with salt; of tropical rain falling in a jungle; of the London sleet flying horizontally across the watery Thames. My body seems to know intimately the minerals and nutrients I am lacking – potassium, zinc, oils, water, salt, vitamins – and to dream of them regularly. I don't remember ever learning that at college.

I would like to tell Michael a lot of things, but I am too tongue-tied, too clumsy, and I am hesitant to ask him about his family, his own life in Sudan. He is so private and closed up, even when he smiles his eyes seem to convey a warning. He jumps if you come up close to him, keeping a polite physical distance it is impossible to bridge. Sometimes when I look at him I feel as if he is on television or behind glass or only a figure in a book. But I look forward every morning to the moment when he brings me my coffee, pulling me from whatever strange dreams I am having. And sometimes he is in them at a distance, a person I cannot touch.

Chapter Eight

In the dream I am at the supermarket in London, stopped in one of the aisles near the back, bricked in by cereal packets: blocks of Coco Pops, Cornflakes, Alpen, Quaker Oats, Weetabix, All Bran, Special K. My trolley is over-flowing with food which is spilling out on to the cold, disinfectant-shiny floor. Bright red cherry tomatoes bounce and roll, a giant lettuce is lying cold and shrink-wrapped by my feet, melting blocks of yellow cheese and leaking pats of butter are weeping into the linoleum. I try to catch the torrent of spilling soups and leaking milk, slipping on crumbling loaves of bread, knocked by falling tins of beans and tuna fish and soft fruits. Around me lie boxes of teabags, bags of sugar, pizzas, cut flowers, pastas. At the very top, a dead chicken lies upended, and there is a piece of liver lying bloodied in a polystyrene tray.

As I try to move forward, the trolley jams on its wheels and the food is spilling out and I begin suffocating on my own sharp breath, moving as if under water. The colours are too bright. The green lid of the milk turns my stomach and the Coco Pops monkey seems to swing in a gaudy, cartoon jungle, before freezing again into a still image, grinning with a rictus smile.

An elderly lady stops next to me with a trolley full of empty packets and broken bottles, a binful of shopping mixed up with eggshells and orange peel and wet teabags.

"Are you all right, dear?" she asks, smoothing down her red headscarf with her hand. The cerise of her lipstick is painfully bright, clashing with the unnatural yellowness of her uneven teeth.

Powerless to wake myself up, I stagger against the brick wall of cereal boxes, knocking them to the slick grey vinyl floor, aware that somewhere in the waking world my legs are kicking against the wooden platform of my bed. I try to broaden the shallow breaths in my constricted chest, but this only seems to make my lungs tighter and my head even lighter. The monkey on the Coco Pops box swings again in his unnaturally green jungle and behind him, painted onto the cardboard in childish cartoon drawing, I can make out the scene of a battlefield, red with fresh blood.

I awake with a scream frozen in my throat and my wet sheet imprisoning my limbs like a tightly wound bandage, to the sound of the distant drums beating out a frenetic rhythm somewhere out in the scrubland, calling to another village along the dried out riverbeds of the White Nile.

I sit up, extricating my legs from the sheet, and put on the torch with shaking hands, so that the mosquito net above me is lit up like a shroud and the dark shadows of the inhabited eaves of the tukul begin dancing as moths and insects are drawn by its glow. As the dream's meaning leaks from me like spilt ink, I pick up the packet of anti-malarials I am taking, and trace the contra-indications with a shaking finger, remembering the warning given by a friend recently returned from a Kenyan safari holiday. Feverish dreams, hallucinations, nightmares, all indicated. Without hesitation, I throw the rest of the packet into a cardboard box in the corner of my tukul that served as a bin. Malaria is the least of my worries, and in any case I am running out of tablets.

*   *   *

It was still dark when I went outside to escape the stifling air of my tukul, but the shapes of the straw-thatched buildings were already becoming visible as darker patches of hulking grey against the charcoal black night sky. The stars were fading and the fire in the hearth had died down to its lowest embers and I thought it was probably an hour or so before first light, shivering lightly as the faintest breeze dried the sweat from my face and legs. I could hear Moses, the camp guard, snoring, and smiled to myself, keeping my torch turned off in my pocket, seizing the rare opportunity to just stand and breathe and clear my head of crowding thoughts, watching the dying swirl of the galaxies above.

Standing there in my boots and a T-shirt, it took me a few moments to realise I wasn't alone. Someone else was moving around in the dark without using a torch, scraping or dragging something inside the large foodstores tukul, where all the sacks of grain were kept. As I reached the entrance, wondering whether to wake Moses, a figure cannoned into me so that I fell awkwardly against a heavy object, too shocked to cry out. Pulling my torch from my pocket and flicking it on as I dragged myself upright, I saw the silhouette of a boy still dragging a sack from the tukul. For a brief second, we stared at each other in the torchlight, and I breathed a sigh of relief as I recognised Bol from the night of the bombings. He looked at me and then the floor, and then, twisting out from under the pool of light, Bol ran, leaving me standing with a punctured sack outside the grainstore.

I woke Moses reluctantly, and explained there had been a thief in the camp.

"I sleep only five minutes!" Moses protested. "Maybe less. Maybe two minutes."

He sighed, leaning on the Kalashnikov loaned by Commander Wol.

"Yesterday a sack is also taken." He flashed his ancient torch importantly around the camp perimeter.

"You can't describe the boy?" he asked. "Did you see his face?"

I shook my head.

"When I find this thief," Moses said. "I kill him."

*   *   *

I waited until just after dawn to go to Bol's house, asking directions from a number of people in the village, and getting lost several times crossing through homesteads that looked one very like the other, a series of mud and straw huts clustered together inside perimeter fences made of sticks or occasionally a living hedge of some indiscernible plant. Inside the encampments, people were going through their early morning routines, washing and hanging clothes, building fires, boiling water and great black tureens of sweetened maizemeal, stopping and staring as I passed. Bol lived in a part of the village I had never been to before, and as I walked away from the marketplace, the houses became even poorer, if that were possible, for the people in the houses nearer to our camp were already surviving on nothing. After a while, there were no clothes hanging to dry and no cooking pots boiling. Goats lay listlessly in the dirt, their thin spines exposed. The black-eyed, hollow-faced women who sat at the front of their houses cradling infants no longer looked up as I passed, as if they were oblivious to anything but their own empty pain. I began to tread more and more quietly, showing starvation the respect it was due. It seemed to me that the faces I saw had been rendered by hunger into stark etchings where laughter and pain were the same thin line.

I knew Bol's house because he was standing straight-backed at the fence of his tiny, single tukul compound, waiting, nodding his head when he saw me approach. His thin thirteen year old hands held the fence post in a posture as brittle as glass.

"Can I talk to you, Bol?" I asked, stopping at the entrance to the compound.

The air carried the strong scent of herbs and there was a stronger smell still – of disease or sickness. At the entrance to the family tukul, I could see Bol's sister, Atong, cradling a shrunken child in her lap. The baby's white eyes were wide open and tiny flies crawled across her mouth and up towards the cavity of her cheeks. Bol said nothing.

I tried again.

"Are your parents here?"

Bol looked down at the neatly swept mud floor of the compound.

I tried again.

"Is your mother here?" I asked.

Bol still said nothing, so I walked past him towards the sister who I recognised from the night of the bombing. As I approached, she gathered the child up and pulled her inside the tukul.

Thinking I might find the mother there, I ducked my head down and entered the tukul itself, overwhelmed by bitter smoke coming from a small fire in the centre of the mud and stick hut and by the smell of something rotting. In the corner was a pile of rags jerking slowly up and down in what I slowly realised was the ragged motion of distressed human breathing. Kneeling down, I saw the skeletal face of a woman staring up through unblinking eyes and caught my breath, cursing myself for not having brought my medical kit with me. I looked back at the doorway and saw Bol standing there in the shadows, his eyes bright with tears of pride or shame or both, and I tried to smile at him.

"Everything will be all right, Bol," I said, not sure if he could understand me. "I'll get some medicines, and we'll get food for your family."

The woman seemed to smile at me then, a terrible drawn back clenching of the jaw muscles like a sneer or a snarl that was softened only by the expression of her eyes, two darkly intelligent pools of light that brightened and then faded again. Then she turned back to the tiny reflection of light on the wall she had been studying when I had first disturbed her.

I was examining the smallest child, the baby who was as light in my hands as a doll, when I heard the familiar scrape of Polio John's approach and saw his head appear around the fence of the compound.

He helped himself to a spoonful of the bitter liquid burning at the fireplace, so that Bol growled something at him in the Dinka language.

John said something back, abruptly.

"What are you doing in Bol's house?" John asked me.

I laid the baby carefully back in Atong's arms.

"Can you ask Bol how long she has been like this?" I said.

John spoke to Bol, who did not reply. John shrugged.

"He doesn't know," John said.

"This is very serious, John," I said, raising my voice a little. "The child may not have much longer to live, and his mother is very sick. Bol needs to answer properly. Nothing is going to happen to him. There is no punishment coming for him. I just need him to tell me what's going on."

Again John asked, and again Bol stared at the floor.

In utter desperation, I went over to Bol and shook his shoulder, trying to pull his face round to me, but he only resisted lightly as if he were accepting a punishment.

"You are angry," John said.

"I'm not angry," I said. "I just need an answer, because otherwise I can't help."

Bol began speaking suddenly in halting English.

"Mother is sick," he said in a low voice barely above a whisper. "She is sick malaria, many months. Father dead, militias cut him with machete. This one . . ." he pointed at the baby where his sister cradled her, "hunger sick. All hungry. Mother will die. Waiting to go to father. Father is here."

"Your father is buried here?" I asked, gently.

"He is here," Bol said.

I thought nothing more of his answer then, thinking it was just a different use of language – my incomprehension or Bol's translation to English, not knowing how the Dinka dead are always with their living, buried in the compounds of their houses, sharing in their feast days and decisions, consulted on the smallest thing. I had no way to imagine the richness of a Dinka's relationship with the dead, knowing death only as I had experienced it, and so instead I began with the living.

*　*　*

Later that morning I found Sean back at the fireplace and asked him what we could do for Bol.

"The same as we can do for everyone else," Sean said. "Get some feeding centres up and running, plead with Loki to send food, get him fed with all the others."

"But the family is desperate," I said. "His sister looks like a baby, but she's two years old. The father's dead. His mother is dying."

"And so is half this village," Billy interrupted, entering the conversation abruptly and throwing his daypack down by the fire.

"How did it go with Loki?" Sean asked him, anxiously.

"Same as it always goes with Loki. They want a full fucking assessment."

"We've sent them an assessment."

"They want a bigger one. For the donors. To persuade them to get off their fat, spoiled butts." He laughed humourlessly. "There's going to be a big war in Kosovo. There'll be white refugees. You know what that means."

He lit a cigarette with a flamboyant flick and flare of his Zippo lighter.

"So what's the big deal about this kid?"

I couldn't tell if he was humouring me, taunting me or genuinely interested.

"I just wondered if we could give him some kind of job in the camp. His family is in terrible shape."

"This wouldn't have anything to do with the break-in you foiled last night would it?" Billy said. "Moses has told us all about your detective work. What took you up to this household?"

I felt my face burn.

"I'd promised to look in on his mother . . ." I said. "She's very sick. Malaria, but being starving isn't helping. The boy's ambition is to be a child soldier . . ."

Billy shrugged.

"Oh, and you think he'd make a better architect or a doctor? Or let me see, interior designer . . .?"

The two men exchanged a glance.

"Well, it's a pretty original idea," Billy said, sucking in the smoke from his cigarette. "Give a thief a job so he don't have to steal no more . . ."

"He's not a thief," I said, my voice tight in my throat. "He's hungry." I felt tears prick the corners of my eyes. "And his mother and sisters are half-dead."

"This whole goddamn country is half-dead," Billy said, throwing the butt of his cigarette into the fire so it flared briefly before burning out, "in case you hadn't noticed."

"Of course I have," I said. "Of course I've noticed . . ."

Billy pulled his hat down tightly so that his eyes were hidden by deep shadow and it was hard to gauge his expression.

"Those whores in Loki ought to be on a murder charge," he said, in a violent whisper that was almost a shout. "They won't send food because there's been no 'formal' assessment. I told them on the radio this morning: 'You want a formal fucking assessment, here's mine. People here are fucking starving to fucking death. Now send some goddamn food.'"

"They'll send it, Billy," Sean said, in a calm, reasonable voice. "You know as well as I do, the donors take time to respond."

"They'll send it too late like they always do," Billy said. He stood up in one swift movement, and spat into the flames. "When half the folks round here are already dead."

Sean came across to me then and removed his glasses, massaging the bridge of his nose with his fingers.

"What's the boy's name?"

"Bol."

"You employ Bol if you want to. God knows there's plenty to do around here. You can pay him in food. But if anything goes missing, he's out, okay?"

I kissed Sean on the cheek as I passed him, light-headed with relief, picking up my medical kit from by the fire and checking it for all the things I would need. I would find Michael, I thought. He would know a little about Bol's family and how to help them.

As I walked away, Billy called after me.

"Hey, where's my kiss?"

"Try deserving one," I called back, shouldering my pack and walking out of the encampment in the direction of the village.

Chapter Nine

The day the thundering sound of aircraft came again, I was standing in the shower. It was a new thing, one of Billy's engineering contraptions, recycling the undrinkable water from the borehole. The mud walls smelled of sodden earth and the rough cubicle was inhabited by all kinds of creatures who enjoy the damp, but it is hard to describe the pleasure of standing under a deluge of cold, half-clean water fed through holes in a suspended canvas sack. Over the past few days, when there was rare water to spare, I had taken to getting up early in the mornings before the sack was warmed through by the morning's brutal heat, yanking on the dangling string and holding my face against the freezing torrent, rubbing the grit from my sticky hairline, the stubborn sand that stuck to my skin, scrubbing my face and hair with Sean's dwindling block of aftershave-scented soap before the water abruptly ran out at the end of the jerry can. I had even learned to count under my breath as I washed, timing my shower perfectly so that I was never left with soapy hair.

Standing there in the cool of the palest dawn, with the stars retreating into the sunlight up above, watching their last light through the open roof, was the only space in the day uninhabited by crying children. We had been stranded in Sudan for almost a month by now, with no airstrip and ever-diminishing supplies of maize, cooking oil and beans. Loki promised food would come any day now, and we were building feeding centres, an act of faith that showed we believed that food would come. Our never-ending days began at first light, with those strong enough helping on dwindling rations. Every day there was a feeding, and every day the food was not enough, for the village or for us.

Adek was living on a knife edge of survival and every day that Loki and its donors delayed was a day too long for at least one or two families. Two or three burials were taking place each morning now in the village, mostly elderly people who could not survive another night without food. That morning I was washing and counting and scrubbing into the

61

crevices of my ears and neck with a soap that smelled nostalgically of wet first kisses and fumbling teenage boys, when I heard the roar of a plane up above. I flung myself immediately to the mud floor, crouching in the dark of the cubicle, a vein of fear or adrenalin shooting up from my exposed spine, cursing my own nakedness. We had had a month without attack from the Government bombers and without interference from the militias, long enough to be lulled into some kind of false security, as if we were no longer on the frontlines of a civil war. As the plane roared up above, I felt myself shrinking, dwindling, the way I might appear from the sky to its pilot, dwarfed by a fifty-year conflict in a country the size of Western Europe and a war that was not mine.

I pulled my clothes on quickly over soapy skin and wringing wet hair and pushed open the makeshift screen door of the shower cubicle, crawling out carefully into the semi-darkness. Up in the still pale sky was the outline of a giant white plane, lowering itself heavily like a pregnant animal over the village. I crouched there for a while in the shadow of the wooden cubicle, dripping and dazed and strangely numb, knowing there was no time to get to the bomb shelter and overwhelmed by a profound sense of angry regret.

The airstrip was still weeks off conclusion, but the wooden structures that would become the feeding centres were almost completed, and for the first time I could see the old hospital itself beginning to emerge from its own ashes. At night rather than sit around feeling hungry and helpless, Michael would light fires in violation of the curfew so that our tiny workforce of misfits could see to work: me, him, Bol, Polio John and their friends. Together we were slowly rebuilding the mud walls and cleaning the floors of needles and broken glass. We had come so near to making a difference in Adek that at the sight of the bomber up in the sky I felt more indignantly angry than afraid.

I was standing outside the shower in my soaking clothes, staring upwards, watching the disc of the sun brighten through the grey like a pale communion wafer, thinking it was a beautiful day for the long waking dream of my time in Sudan to end, and lost in the deafening roar of the descending plane, when Billy crashed into me on his way across the compound.

"There you are," he said, grabbing me by my soaking wet shoulder, and propelling me in the direction of the battered white Africaid vehicle.

"We can't leave!" I shouted against the whipping of the wind and the drone of the engines up above. "How can we leave?"

Sand thrown up by the propellers was sticking to my wet skin and forcing me to close my eyes. Billy flung open the rusted passenger door of the vehicle so that it almost came off its hinges, and then climbed into the driver's seat, throwing his filthy flip-flops onto the dashboard. Starting the noisy engine, he actually laughed.

"Jesus, Maria . . . It's food!" he shouted, still laughing. "Up in the plane . . . Food, not bombs . . .! Loki sanctioned it last night . . ."

Billy jammed the Land Rover into reverse and, as I lurched back into the painfully sharp springs and blistered leather of the seat, I stared back at him.

"It's food?" I shouted above the engine, winding down the heavy glass of the window so that my wet hair blew into my eyes and I could barely see where we were headed. "But there's no airstrip . . ."

"We don't need an airstrip," Billy shouted above the wind. "It's going to fall out of the sky."

As he drove, dust flying up around us and in through the open windows, he fiddled with the radio and it buzzed into life.

"THIS IS BRAVO FOXTROT, ARE YOU RECEIVING ME?" he shouted, driving with one hand and squeezing the radio handset with the other so that the black hairs of his arms stood up in the fierce wind.

"GOOD TO HEAR YOU, BRAVO FOXTROT," the radio crackled. "THIS IS LIMA CHARLIE . . ."

"STANDING CLEAR AT THE DROPZONE, LIMA CHARLIE, OVER," Billy said, spinning the wheel so that we came to rest under a row of dead trees.

"I SEE YOU BRAVO FOXTROT," shouted the disembodied voice, and I realised it was the pilot up above.

Billy wound both our windows up, and then removing his seatbelt, sat back and rubbed his hands together the way a weightlifter does before a medal-winning lift.

The plane was directly above now in the lightening sky, its white wings sharp and elegant in the dawn glare, lowering itself as if it were going to land right on top of the village.

"AM I CLEAR TO DROP, BRAVO FOXTROT, AM I CLEAR TO DROP?" the radio crackled.

"DROP THAT MOTHERFUCKER, OVER."

It was beautiful to watch, even as dust and sand spattered the windows in the violent wind of the plane's descent and the roar above reached an ear-splitting scream. The white aircraft seemed to tip and almost fall, and then its long back began to open up gracefully on a vast jaw-like hinge. As it did so, bright white parcels came dropping from the giant mouth, shining in the dawn light, falling like little rectangular pellets of chewing gum that hit the earth with distant cracks and pops and cartoon bangs. As it emptied itself, the plane began rising rapidly, shooting up into the air on its lightened load, and on Billy's radio we could hear the pilot exulting in the zero gravity.

"WHOO-HOO!" the American voice shouted.

"PERFECT HIT, LIMA CHARLIE!" Billy shouted down the radio. "SAFE TRIP HOME."

"GET YOURSELF BACK SAFE NOW BRAVO FOXTROT. LOKI'S MISSING YOUR ASS! OVERNOUT!"

The aircraft circled the village once more in a valedictory lap of honour, and Billy and I climbed out of the vehicle to wave, feeling the rush of warm wind, eyes half-closed against the dust.

As the plane disappeared towards the horizon, there was a deathly quiet, and I felt suddenly lonely, knowing another person had been so near, a pilot heading back even now to the beach-style bar at Lokichokio with its crackling television screen and warm brown bottles of beer.

Billy looked at his watch.

"He'll be back at base in an hour and a half from here," he said wistfully, and I knew he felt it too. "Those Hercs do an incredible speed, and nothing but sky and earth to stop them."

"Do they ever get attacked by the Government?" I asked, and Billy looked away.

"Sure they do," he said.

We stood for a moment in the silence, and I realised that despite knowing that Adek's birds were long gone from the barren, dusty fields, some nostalgic part of my brain was waiting for morning birdsong. Every dawn in Bahr el Ghazal was like a post-nuclear morning, and even today after such drama there was only a dull silence broken intermittently by crickets, and the only birds were carrion seeking out those mammals that had not survived the night. For a moment, standing there in the nothingness, it felt as if Billy and I were the last two people on earth.

"Hope you didn't mind me dragging you down here," Billy said, clearing his throat. "It's kind of powerful, seeing a drop. Lets you know y'ain't on your own out here."

With that, he adjusted his hat, and pulled a makeshift trolley out of the back of the pick-up.

"How did he know where to drop the food?" I said.

"I came out here at first light to lay the markers," Billy said. "Michael had kept them safe from last time we were here. And then I came back for you. Needed someone to help get these damn sacks in the pickup. I sure hope you're feeling strong."

It took an age to load the parcels onto the back of the pick up, and it hurt every muscle in my body to lift them, even with Billy taking most of the weight. Each package was actually a half-tonne bag of maizemeal or beans, strapped to a wooden palette to break its fall. Billy was particularly excited about the palettes, most of which had smashed on impact, and made sure we gathered up all the longest pieces into the truck.

"That's a picnic table right there," he said, eyeing a long bit of splintered wood. "And that's firewood for a month."

He grinned. "And that's a new bedframe for my aching back."

"Was that a friend of yours, flying the plane?" I asked him, as I hoisted up the back end of a palette so he could grip it. It lifted more easily than I expected and I realised I was already stronger than I had been only three weeks ago.

"Lima Charlie?" Billy said. "Sure. I've known Lee a decade or so. He's one of the biggest adrenalin junkies in Loki."

"Why Lima Charlie?" I asked.

"It's a person's initials," Billy said, grunting as he lifted a giant sack onto the pick-up.

"So Bravo Foxtrot is Billy Finn?"

"Exactly."

"So I'd be . . .?"

"Mike Mike. Except you can't be the same name twice."

"I like the name Mike Mike," I said, heaving a giant sack up onto its end, and feeling my stomach muscles tearing with the effort.

"Middle name?" Billy asked.

"No. I've got a confirmation name though," I said, mildly embarrassed.

Sweat was pouring into my eyes and down the back of my damp T-shirt and I was wondering whether there might be water left in the shower later.

"Which is?"

"Agatha."

"Patron saint of nurses."

"Indeed."

I dropped the sack with a thud, and stood there with my hands on my hips, my breath rushing out through my nose and mouth.

"You're Catholic then?" Billy said. "Like Sean?"

"Yes," I said, still out of breath. "My mother is Spanish." I heard the wrong tense, but couldn't bring myself to correct it.

"Marshall's not Spanish."

"No, my father was English."

"He's dead?"

"No. I don't know. He might be."

Billy didn't look up from the palette he was carrying, but he seemed to be waiting for me to say something more.

"He left when I was very young," I said.

I watched the long brown muscles in Billy's back tense and then release as he dropped the palette heavily onto the back of the pick-up.

"Alpha Mike, then," Billy said, wiping his hands on his shorts.

"Alpha Mike," I agreed.

It took us almost two hours to fill the vehicle with sacks and palettes, the pick-up loaded so high that Billy could barely shift the gear stick inside the crowded cab and I had to perch in the open air at the precarious summit of an awkward shaped food mountain on the back, enjoying the open air and space as the truck began moving, eyes squeezed shut against the biting dust and hands gripping at the shifting sacks for support.

It was exhilarating up there as the pick-up gathered speed, and as we slowed up and pulled into the village I opened my eyes to see an excited knot of people had gathered to greet us, a livid tableau of moving colours, green sarongs, blue men's robes and yellow girl's dresses that seemed to tangle and untangle like fairy lights against the backdrop of a buzzing, bustling hum of excitement. In the middle stood the imposing figure of Chief Deng, a head and shoulders above the crowd in his long robe, standing by an even taller Commander Wol, who was leaning on his Kalashnikov and almost smiling, despite his mouth's apparent reluctance to join in with his eyes. Beside him, Lieutenant Dit waved up at me, laughing.

I jumped down from the vehicle to tumultuous shouts and a hundred hands raised in supplication to be engulfed by the crowd, sweating bodies pushing their way through to the vehicle, as some fell to their knees, and others danced to snatches of song and the beat of an invisible drum. It was intoxicating amongst the bodies of the dancing people, and I felt light-headed and exhausted and relieved, and found myself standing still at the eye of a storm of dust and movement, watching Adel and Bol, and some of the other children who were dancing with their necks craned upwards – heads looking up to the sky as if searching for the miracle that had brought food to Adek. Through the thick of the crowd I could see a grinning Billy standing on top of the sacks, passing them down to the men waiting below, and I wondered how he had the strength to keep going when every muscle in my body was crying out for rest and sleep.

* * *

That night there were ecstatic celebrations in the village. A thousand drums echoed in different rhythms from every hearth, and from so far out into the bush that they seemed to come from the empty horizon. It seemed that a message was being passed across the whole of Bahr el Ghazal and into the regions beyond. Food had come to Adek and a village that had been silent suddenly found its voice.

As dusk was falling, Michael called me to the storeroom up at our camp, where the present we had been working on for John for three whole weeks was waiting – a converted tiny-wheeled tricycle that could be worked with the hands. Michael had once seen one in Kakuma, the refugee camp he had grown up in, and had recreated it with love and patience. In truth, the assistance I had given had been very minimal, but I had enjoyed the chance to work with Michael and our shared secret. Preoccupied with the task in hand, Michael had shown a far less guarded side to himself as we worked on the tricycle together, and I realised with a jolt of regret that our time alone together was almost over.

"I think you should roadtest it," I said, pointing at the tricycle.

"Where?" Michael said. "John might see us."

"In here," I said.

The storerooms were half full with grain, creating a ready-made obstacle course. Michael tucked his great, tall frame into something approaching a forward roll position, and climbed aboard the tiny trike.

I pushed him to a starting position, and then he started up pedalling furiously with his hands, far too large for the trike, his long limbs flailing in all directions. Seconds later he crashed hard into a pile of eight great sacks of grain, bursting one and landing winded with two more sacks heavy on his chest.

I ran towards him, hysterical laughter rising in my throat, and helped him pick himself up. Michael was laughing harder than I had ever seen – and covered from head to toe in sorghum flour.

"I always wondered what I would look like as a white man," Michael said, sticky bits of grain stuck all over his head and face, and covering his clothes.

At that moment, Bol ran into the storeroom to see what the commotion was about, followed by Sean and Billy. Three disapproving silhouettes stood framed in the doorway.

"What happened?" Sean said.

I was now half covered in sorghum myself where I had helped Michael up, and stood there embarrassed, wondering how it might look.

"We were testing John's present," I said, after a minute. "Wait there."

Adel was making dinner and I knew John would be there as he always was, watching her shyly and being fed odd scraps of food as she chopped and boiled. I was uncomfortable with the fact that Adel at age fifteen was more or less a child labourer for us at the camp, but reluctant to lose her company. The deal we had struck was that she would remain temporarily, but whenever the school-under-the-tree re-opened she must attend.

Reaching the kitchen hut, I told John and Adel they were needed urgently for a surprise at the foodstores. Reaching the stores, I held my hands over John's eyes and walked him in.

John screamed when he saw the trike, knowing immediately it was meant for him, and everyone applauded when he pulled himself over to it and climbed aboard. When he crashed headlong into the sacks nobody minded. Afterwards, Michael and I took turns at the shower to wash the sorghum from our hair.

*　　*　　*

At around 8.00pm, when I was so tired I could barely stand, Billy, Sean, Michael and I followed the children through the dark to the rickety wooden stalls of the marketplace, where an area had been cleared and drummers and dancers were already celebrating the arrival of food from the sky. In the very middle, next to a blazing fire, a yellow-lit Chief Deng, Lieutenant Dit and the Commander were sitting on a long, knotted length of tree trunk, surrounded by the elders of the village, and they gestured we should sit with them. Michael squeezed up to make space for me between him and Adel on the trunk, and Polio John clambered up from nowhere on to my knee. As the women sang for us, chanting together in a whispering melodic sound that might have come from a seashell, I could feel Michael singing softly next to me. Our bodies were at a polite half inch's distance, not touching despite the cramped treebranch conditions, but he was close enough that I could feel the heat of his breath and the warmth of his body as if it moved in time with the dancing of the men as they dived and jumped in huge whooping dances wearing ceremonial skirts and holding spears. The central drumming rhythm was held by two small twin boys I recognised as cousins of Adel's and I found myself transported backwards as if I were listening to the earth's first stuttering heartbeats, somewhere from under the deep rock itself, as the rhythm of Polio John's rocking in my arms lulled me into a waking sleep.

After an hour or so, Chief Deng stood up and passed a cup along the tree branch. It came to me from Michael's hands, and I drank a draught of a fiery liquid that burned like whiskey and tasted foul: a putrefying vegetable matter that scorched my lips and stomach and then settled into a vicious glow somewhere close to my heart. After each person had drunk and the cup had passed into the eager crowd, the Chief cleared his throat and spoke in English and Dinka by turns.

"In the beginning," Chief Deng said in his low rumble, as the drums beat out the patient percussion to his story, "the world was divided into Divinity and Earth. But the heavens and the down-below were connected by a rope which man could climb up whenever he liked, to visit God."

When he spoke the same words in Dinka, many of the crowd joined in and I realised it was a ceremonial story that each man, woman and child knew by heart.

"God made man and woman from the clay of the riverbed, and called them Garang and Abuk, and they lived perfectly happily, with everything they could want or need."

Next to me I felt Michael shiver lightly, as Polio John stifled an unbecoming yawn.

"God made only one stipulation," the Chief continued, eyeing John. "That the man and woman should live on one grain of millet each per day." He looked into the firelight so that one half of his face was lit yellow and the other was in darkness, shaking the grey-black curls of his head and beard. "But the woman, Abuk, was greedy."

Some of the men in the crowd looked at the women then, as if they the descendants of Abuk should be ashamed, but the women only shook their heads.

The crowd shuddered and strained with expectation, and I found myself thinking of the Northern militias. According to Billy, who heard it from the Commander, their train was already moving southwards towards this village, laden with bombs and weapons, coming to annihilate a people they did not know. In my mind's eye, laughing Arab soldiers played cards inside carriages packed with explosives and the horsemen who followed the train billowed out beyond in their white cloaks.

"When Abuk thought God was not watching," Chief Deng said, raising his voice, "she planted an extra millet seed in the soil and cultivated it. As she did so, her long hoe stirred at the heavens, and God looked down and he was angry."

The crowd sighed mournfully at this, as if hearing the story for the first time. I had read that the Dinka were unusual in worshipping just one God and not many, but I was struck by the similarity to the Christian creation story.

"God called the small blue bird, Atoc, to him at once," the Chief continued. "And he instructed him to fly between Earth and Divinity, severing forever the rope that joined them and creating the blue sky as he flew."

He paused in his speech, and we were all lost in the moment, sitting at the centre of a dustbowl of land where it had not rained in three years, where the soil was bitter, and all that came from the sky was bombs.

"From now on, man no longer had the help of the Gods, and was destined ever more to toil in the hard ground to cultivate his own crops," Chief Deng said, stirring the ceremonial fire with a stick, so that the flames leapt up it towards him. "Ever since, the Dinka have been hungry on this earth."

For a moment it seemed to me that I could see the rope that the blue bird Atoc had torn down, hanging there in the blackness out of the reach of the village. Then the Chief spoke again.

"So, my friends," he said. "A miracle has come to our village today. A miracle we have prayed for these long months.

"The blue bird Atoc flew down today and he gave us food.

"Tonight, we shall eat, and tomorrow; and we shall eat to be strong against our enemies who even now are gathering north of here because they want to see the Dinka wiped from the face of this earth."

There was murmuring at this when it was repeated in Dinka, and some angry shouts, but the Chief signalled there should be silence.

"In honour of what these kawajas – these outsiders – have done for us, there will be a poem."

The people pushed forward at this, clapping their hands. John slipped off my knee, and Adel moved into a space ahead so that she could see.

"Poet Bol," the Chief's voice said.

To my amazement, I saw Bol was being led to the front of the crowd until he stood in the clear space in front of where we were all sitting. His eyes were fixed firmly ahead of him and his back was as straight and tall as if pulled up by a string from the very top of his head. I smiled at him, but he seemed distant, vacant, as if in a trance.

"The poet is possessed briefly by the spirit of Nhialic, the one true God," Michael whispered. "It is a great honour, to speak the words of God."

Bol stood fearlessly at the centre of the circle, and cleared his throat, speaking as if he were reading from his mind's eye. He spoke the poem in the Dinka language first, and then in English, and I wondered if it were Michael who had taught him the words for the translation.

Kawaga
One half of the sacred colours
starlight, in the night sky
the moon over the cattle camp
porridge flour pounded by women
head of the fish-eagle
as it swoops for prey
Strength of leg and arm
and brute force of the elephant
facing its enemy across the plain
colour of gentle rainclouds
Mabior
bull of the women who seek salt
bright scales of the Atoor fish
one half of the Majok and Marial
the markings of the creator
Agher
bright light from which darkness hides

There was a murmur of laughter at first to hear Bol reciting in English, but the crowd quickly fell silent before erupting at the last line into spontaneous applause.

"What does it all mean?" I asked Michael. I was astonished at Bol's prowess and the confident rhythm of his words.

"It is a very clever, very beautiful poem," Michael said in his low, quiet voice, so that I had to strain to hear him. "Bol is a good poet, like his father before him."

"I thought his father was a warrior?" I said.

"Every poet is also a warrior," Michael said. "Every man is also a warrior when he lives surrounded by war."

I shivered to think that little Bol with his soft face and all his cares and worries could one day soon be called to Commander Wol's army.

"What is marial?" I asked him.

I was thinking how the word sounded like my name.

"Marial is the markings of the most sacred bull of all the Dinka cattle," Michael said. "It means black and white as one colour, as one whole marking. Bol is saying that kawaga and Dinka are one."

"So why so sad?" I asked playfully, squeezing his strong forearm and feeling him flinch as I broached the invisible physical wall that had separated us all night despite our physical proximity on the tree branch. "It's a happy poem."

Michael shook his head.

"But it is not true," he said. "Black and white are not one. Arab and black are not one. Dinka and Nuer and Luo – black and black and black – are not one."

Michael stood up suddenly, and said goodnight, and I wondered if I had frightened him away by touching his arm, violating some unspoken taboo.

A few moments later, Sean sat down in the space Michael had vacated next to me on the tree branch. His eyes were bright in the firelight and he was more animated than usual.

"What did you think of the story?" Sean said.

"It was beautiful," I said. "Though I did wonder why it always has to be the woman that causes the end of paradise."

"Greedy Abuk," Sean laughed. "Where did Michael get to?"

I felt myself blush and was glad my face would not be visible in the firelight.

"I don't know," I said. "He just left. Suddenly."

Sean offered me his water bottle, and when I drank from it I tasted whiskey.

"Michael finds these gatherings very hard," Sean said. There was a note of warning in his voice, and I wondered if my schoolgirlish crush on Michael had become obvious or whether Sean doubted the sorghum incident's innocence.

"Michael's wife was killed by the militias two years ago," Sean said, more gently.

"I didn't know," I said.

I suddenly realised how little I had actually ever asked Michael about his life in Adek, beyond his work with us at the camp. Perhaps I had feared a wife or children? Or maybe I had been interested in him only in his context as one of us, an aidworker not a Sudanese tribesman.

"Michael's been through a lot, even by the standards of this village," Sean said. "His family fled Adek when he was a boy after a militia raid in the early 1980s killed his mother and sister. He was educated in Kakuma Refugee Camp in Kenya, which is why he speaks and writes such perfect English. The rest of his family stayed in Kenya, but Michael came back with his father, by now a leading light of the SPLM, the SPLA's political wing. Michael should be one of our top managers by now, not just running the show here – working for us in Loki or in another part of Sudan or in our Nairobi office. I think he could use some distance from this place. But he says he won't leave Adek again. His family were consumed by guilt all the years they were away in Kakuma. And it is hard for the Dinka to leave their ancestors in soil, away from their families."

"Does he have children?"

"Michael's wife was pregnant when she was killed."

Tears came suddenly into my eyes, and I brushed them away carefully.

"It is common in Southern Sudan," Sean said. "To stop the Dinka breeding, that's how the militias think."

I could think of nothing to say that would not sound hollow or empty or clichéd.

"Or they use rape as a weapon of war," Sean continued. "They try to impregnate a Dinka woman with Arab seed. They know a Dinka man will never touch her again. There will be many rape babies in this village, Maria. We can't know the numbers because it would identify the women concerned and expose them to terrible judgement. The levels of HIV here suggest repeated attacks and rapes."

He seemed lost in his thoughts, no longer speaking for my benefit.

"Everyone here has lost someone," Sean said. "Fathers and brothers to the war, daughters to famine and childbirth, mothers to rape and sickness, children to bombs."

I sat there numbly, watching the crowd dancing and swaying and moving to the beat of the twins' drums, raising their hands above their heads in ancient dances that recalled the great cattle stories passed along the Dinka lines for generations.

"But still they dance," I said.

"Dancing is a way of giving thanks to Nhialic."

"Thanks?" I said. "For rape and genocide and war?"

"It is something very difficult for the Western mind to understand," Sean said. "It is part of the Dinka people's extraordinary resilience that they give daily thanks for the simple fact of being alive."

We sat in silence for a while, listening to the drumming, watching the people swaying and jumping, delicate and then heavy-footed, a constantly shifting and undulating firelight tableau as varied and orchestrated as a piece of classical music. Then, shouldering his way through the knot of people, Billy came and asked me to dance with him and, pressed close to him in the swaying crowd, I felt myself carried away with the sudden surprising optimism of it all, the rhythm of Africa rising up through the soles of my feet, the stretched sinews of my calves and hamstrings and spine vibrating with the twins' drumskins. Still I couldn't quite give my heart up to the drumbeat, letting the music wash over me rather than take me over in the way the villagers and the children in their animal skins – and even Billy – seemed to innately understand. I danced still as a Westerner, doubtful, distant and disbelieving, and not yet understanding what it meant to dance.

Chapter Ten

It is bitterly cold in England, more so than any winter I can remember. Everything growing on my tiny balcony is dead, a cramped space cluttered with pots full of knotted brown leaves and decay. The cold gets in deep, seeming to dig down into the concrete pavements and marrow of the bones. The winds along the river are sharp enough to slice a person in two and the elderly tomcat that belongs to the flat downstairs has taken to sleeping on the radiator in my bathroom. I don't think they can afford much heating down there.

It is Sunday today and I am sicker still. Still not at work, hunched on the sofa wrapped in woollens and a thick brown blanket, wondering how much of the chill I feel is outside and how much is inside my body. I take my temperature and it is soaring. I called the hospital and they said there is a nasty bug going round – a winter virus. I hate to be off work and at home. I can't cope with the vacuum of not working, the not doingness. I hate daytime television and the way it illuminates my irrelevance – no white-walled home to trade up, no desire to fit into size zero jeans, no husband to expose on the Jeremy Kyle show. Most of all I hate the thinking. During a headache especially, there is only thinking, when light is too harsh and books are too painful and TV too glaring.

A room away, the kitchen radio plays out a debate, two confident, staccato voices heavy with clever conviction, pondering whether current events in Darfur yet constitute a genocide.

"We'll have to leave it there," the presenter's matching voice concludes.

Sometimes I try to imagine what people in Adek might make of my life here. Of London. Of taps that turn clean fresh water on and off. Of television reality shows, where people watch other people doing things they usually do themselves, and soap operas where people watch people pretending to be ordinary people. Of the traffic lights controlling every street below from some hidden matrix. Of electricity and telephones and

75

gas ovens. Of experts on genocide who have never lost a loved one to the light blow of a rusted machete or the strafing fire of a helicopter gunship.

Adek is always there in my memory, like a scar. Like a stain. Like a piece of unclaimed luggage on a conveyor belt, round and round and round.

As I turn to close the door against the radio the phone rings, and the answer machine projects Grace's distorted voice into the air like a station announcement.

". . . Pick up the phone, Maria . . ."

I almost pick it up and scream down the phone. But I don't.

"Maria, I need to talk to you. And I know you're there . . ."

My attention is held by a photograph next to the phone in a beaten silver frame, an unthinking moment frozen forever under plexi-glass. Billy, Sean, Michael, Grace and I, posing for the camera – Team Adek as Sean described us – taken two thirds of the way through our time in Sudan, when we were all still friends and nobody was harmed. I don't let myself look at that photo very often, although I keep it out on the dresser. Hiding it in a drawer would seem like cowardice. Today I make myself look at it. I look at our sunburned faces and too skinny frames, our hair bleached by the sun, our tired eyes still alive with hope. Sean's worried forehead is at rest for once, his red beard short and his eyes glittering green in the harsh midday sunlight that bleaches out detail and casts deep shadows under the eyes. He is smiling at a camera that must be held by Bol or Adel or perhaps Chief Deng. Billy's leather hat is clamped down hard onto his head and he is laughing, looking younger and thinner and more carefree than I remember him, but then I am ten years older now, as old as he was then. (Really, we were only kids!) Michael's smile is the same white as his stone necklace, his six foot five below-average Dinka frame towering above the rest of us, a green Africaid T-shirt hanging from his wide shoulders. The dark, deep black of his face is cast into shadow by Billy's red and blue Tennessee Smokies baseball hat pulled down on his head against the height of the sun and I cannot read its expression. Grace is a blank canvas, still an outsider. She had only just arrived.

I am the only one not smiling, and my eyes are looking off to the side at something lost to the edges of the picture. The Spear Master perhaps. It seems to me I was always looking for him. Or perhaps I am looking for Bol and Adel and thinking they should be in the picture. I regret it now terribly that they are not.

I look at the photo thinking of the newspaper cutting, now safely back in its envelope, inside a shoe box, at the back of a drawer. As if all those layers and coverings and containers can insulate me from what it contains. In the same envelope is the only other thing I brought back from Sudan with me. A burned, bloodstained piece of paper with a hand-drawn map folded tightly into quarters.

I listen for the river. There is water now in my life. That is how I differentiate when the flashbacks come. Then, there was no water.

I want to rewind to the time of the photograph and change all our endings.

Chapter Eleven

The feeding centres opened in early December, within two weeks of the first food drop and almost five weeks after we had first become stranded in Sudan. The size and frequency of the food drops had accelerated in the previous days, and the Commander's men had worked every hour of available daylight until two large, secure tarpaulin structures were completed: one for supplementary feeding which would support families affected by starvation and one for therapeutic feeding which would help the very worst afflicted of Adek's children and nursing mothers. During the preceding weeks we had gradually come to feel more secure from air attack as there had been no sightings of the Government Antonov plane, and Loki repeatedly assured us UN security were now closely monitoring the Adek area. Sean and Billy had devised an evacuation plan should a Level 4 warning come through, and we were all briefed to have small daypacks kitted out with essentials ready at all times in case we should have to flee into the bush. There was growing interest from foreign media, Sean said, in the plight of three British and American aid workers trapped in the warzone of Southern Sudan, but Loki had imposed a news blackout on the story in case it should attract the attention of Government militias interested in Western hostage taking. Although, logically, the danger we were in was probably increasing, I began to feel less afraid simply because the situation was becoming more and more normalised, and my brain was growing more accustomed to accepting a level of acute watchfulness. Our comforts were increasing as Billy and Michael worked hard to maintain some semblance of order at the camp. As well as the shower, Billy had built an eight-seater picnic table from palette wood with a canopy overhead which he strung with mosquito netting meaning there was a place to eat without being besieged constantly by insects and where our filtered water stayed a few degrees below boiling point. There was a kitchen hut of sorts, an area for goats and chickens, a rough map of the area pinned up in marker pen and all kinds of rotas for cleaning the camp and running the feeding queues. As a final touch, Billy had rigged up a proper gate complete with goat skull at the entrance to the camp bearing the slogan 'Hotel California'.

The morning the feeding centres opened was unbearably hot and dusty even by 7am when Bol, Adel and I set out together across the village on foot. As we walked, we saw how much Adek was changing. The village had been growing since the food drops had begun, with people travelling large distances across the surrounding scrubland hearing of the miracle of food, and as we rounded the edge of the village, we saw that long queues of expectant families were already forming in the heat of the early morning. Hundreds of women were sitting in dusty lines wearing their best clothes, clutching their children and empty pots and pans. The men sat under trees watching the women queue. It had taken a long time to explain to the village elders we were giving food rations to women rather than men because they were more likely to share them with their children and because it would help them increase their status in the village. The women sat mainly in silence, conserving energy for the long wait ahead, but there was an air of excited expectancy amongst the men as they exchanged gossip, also in their smartest, least threadbare clothes for what amounted to the biggest village meeting ever held in Adek. The lines of red and yellow dressed women and the knots of waiting men in their royal blue smocks lent the scene a storybook quality, like the illustrations in a children's Bible.

Bol and I made our way around to the back of the supplementary centre, where Billy and Michael were already organising a dozen or so helpers. Those who needed extra food rations would be fed here, identified on future visits by a blue wristband. Those severely malnourished would be given an orange band and sent to the therapeutic feeding centre next door where they would remain until they put on enough weight to move beyond critical danger. I would run the therapeutic centre with Bol and Adel to help me, and Michael and Billy would run the larger supplementary centre. Sean would oversee admissions.

We watched the first few people pass through the system, desperate and confused. An exhausted-looking woman came in holding a baby to her flapping, empty breast and clutching the tiny hand of another child, whose face was so pinched and distorted his features were barely discernable. Billy supervised the weighing of each of the children, and then measured their height. He slipped an orange bracelet onto the child's narrow wrist, and another onto the baby's arm. The mother looked terrified and Michael spoke to her quietly in the Dinka language, before ushering the family towards where I was standing waiting.

"Your first patients," Billy said, smiling reassuringly, as I led all three to the therapeutic centre next door.

* * *

The day went on as long as the sun hung in the sky, until it became impossible to see a person's face under the shade of the silver tarpaulins. By sundown, our centre next door was filled with hundreds of barely existing women, babies and children lying or sitting in orderly rows, shivering in blankets despite the relentless heat of the evening sun. Those who were strong enough sipped at a weak, sugared porridge from bright orange cups. The weaker children lay silent and still, their breathing raw and too quick, their limbs stiff and their faces taut and lined.

The noise inside the tents rose and fell in counterpoint, in a discordant opera, at times angry and insistent, or melancholic and high-pitched, with occasional bursts of silence that seemed to me to be the most hopeless of all. The rumble of the queue outside barely stopped morning or night as people waited patiently for feeding, or begged for entrance.

A woman died right where she lay, and Michael and Bol had to carry her out to the back and find her husband from the group of waiting men crouching under the shade of the barren mango tree. The man made no sound when he greeted his dead wife, only rocked on his heels and covered his eyes with his hands. Her unknowing child, a barely conscious scrap in a tattered pink cardigan, was passed into the hands of a neighbour to nurse, and I sent Adel to see that he had everything he possibly could to make the child comfortable.

Death was nothing new to Adek, a village ravaged by drought, stalked by disease and contagion, caught up in a war it no longer understood. Death fell from the air in the night when the bombs dropped and whipped through the bare trees with the militia bullets. It waited silently behind the sightless eyes of the sick and hid itself in the long scrub in the shape of anti-personnel mines planted by an invisible enemy. Over recent months the long fingers of starvation had slowly penetrated every family and plucked the weary living from every homestead in turn. The livestock had slowly died away, the wild creatures no longer prowled at night and the trees were empty of birds. Every dusk and every dawn, the cries of the bereaved told of the village's newest losses. The sound of keening women was Adek's birdsong.

Death to Adek was nothing new, but it overwhelmed me like a slow, sagging wave. My heart broke bit by bit, each day in the feeding centres. The sadnesses I had brought away with me from England did not diminish by comparison with the overpowering dose of daily tragedy that surrounded me, but grew bloated on the daily agonies in Adek. Every day brought more and more people, from further and further away, each group in a worse state than the group before. Deluged by a human torrent of arrivals, we worked day and night, night and day, and still we couldn't work fast enough to make room for the new children in the therapeutic feeding centre. Every morning, the bodies of dead children had to be removed to make way for the living, and somehow I became accustomed to lifting the stiff little forms of the dead, the weightless bundles of bones and skin that had become too fragile to bear the force of a human spirit. At night these children came to haunt me, accusing me with their unblinking eyes, the fake, unqualified doctor who could not save them, the despatcher of small souls to the empty sky above.

Waking early one morning a few days or weeks after the feeding centre had opened, I found myself at a point of utter exhaustion, too tired to sleep and too weary to move. As I lay there listening to the drums from the village, thinking of the pink-cardiganed child whose mother had died on the first day and who was now a little better, I looked at my watch to see whether it was time to get up, and the date, the 25th, struck a chord in me. For a moment, my dislocated mind struggled to connect to its meaning. Then, in the din of the Animist drums that worshipped only the Cattle and the Earth and Divinity, my heart picked out a rhythm and my head suddenly cleared and I knew it was 6.30am on Christmas morning.

I got out of bed, suddenly excited as a child, even knowing there could be no snow or presents, thinking of how at home in England there might already be children anxiously awake, studying the shadowy outlines of bulky stockings and imagining their contents in their half-dreams. I thought of the turkeys defrosting overnight in households across Britain, and the peeled potatoes and parsnips in giant saucepans of water waiting for roasting. As I pulled on my filthy boots over blistered, mosquito-bitten feet, I thought of the wrapped packages of school socks and soft slippers our mother would give us each Christmas, and how we would eat and eat until indigestion made us stop. I thought, but not unkindly, of the wasted food and the billion clothes that would be back in the shops by Monday at the returns counter and the toys that would be played with for one day only, and the gargantuan Santas rolling drunk down the high streets and the brawling violence of Christmas Eve that spilled into the hospital where we worked. If I could have eaten a Christmas dinner that day I might have wept with joy or with horror. The thing I would have wished for most would have been a single long blast of cold, fresh, winter morning air.

But then Sudan, after all, has its own miracles. Flapping out of my tukul with unlaced boots and my damp toothbrush sticking out of my mouth, the sight in front of me that morning made me gasp and clap my hands like a child. The barren branches of the mango tree at the centre of the camp had been decorated overnight with silver foodwrapper bells and shiny paper chains, all hanging interspersed with the black, pendular forms of sleeping bats apparently undisturbed by such unexpected frivolity. In the cool light of early morning, despite the amateurish improvisations, the tree was a thing of fairytale beauty: slender, perfectly proportioned branches hung with glittering silver and shiny white, the black bats shimmering in the softest of morning breezes. Standing there, I remembered how Chief Deng had told us during our very first days in Adek that the Dinka believe all ancient trees are the manifestation of Divinity and that it was an act punishable by exile to cut them down. As a symbol of Sudan, there could be no greater emblem than that mango tree. Despite being starved of water and nutrients, and battle-scarred by bullets and machete scratches, it simply and stoically endured.

Celebrating its existence, I stood there thinking of the millions of Christmas trees chopped from European forests to stand slowly browning, dropping their fine green needles into the thick weave of carpets so that the roar of ten million vacuum cleaners rang out on Christmas morning as tables were laid and sleighbells rang on the radio and a million knives sliced through unending fields of vegetables. I thought of my mother setting out her own mother's chipped porcelain nativity set from Santiago de Compostella and unwrapping baby Jesus last of all, and of rushing to the back door in red pyjamas to look for snow. I thought of Billy climbing the branches of the tree quietly in the night, hanging the decorations, knowing it was him, silently thanking him for his effort and thoughtfulness on today, the most homesick day of all.

I stood there a long while watching the tree, its thin beauty defined by a silvery shadow that could almost have been frost. Above me, the sky was the pale azure blue of a cold winter's morning, lit from underneath by the rising sun so that I stood in a cathedral of soft light. And all the while, the drums beat on in the distance: the most uplifting hymns to life I had ever heard. A perfect Christmas morning, without Santas or reindeer or snow, a rare moment in Sudan not tinged by sadness or foreboding. I still had time to make a snowman out of foodsacks before the others awoke, and I set about the task busily, for once living only in the moment, in the morning itself.

Chapter Twelve

Gradually, over the course of those first weeks in Sudan, it came to be one memory in particular that flickered over and over like worn cine film in my mind. I am seven years old and on Brighton pier, tightly wrapped in a beige Paddington duffle coat, red scarf and hand-me-down woolly hat. I am warm and enveloped by my mother's love, and when I clap my red gloves together they make a pleasing muffled sound, and my breath hangs visibly in the air like the white, vanilla smoke of my grandfather's pipe when he visits from Spain. We walk along the boardwalk, where the lurid amusements are already lit up against the pinkish embers of the dying sun, waiting for my five year old brother Matt to finish hurling his ketchup-sodden chips down to the spiralling seagulls. I am watching the grey-blue sea between the cracks in the wooden walkway, pretending to be a pirate walking the plank. Suddenly my mother stops in her tracks, grabbing Matt and I with both hands, holding our duffle-coated bodies before her like two polyester shields. In front of us, a tall, brown-haired man in a long tobacco-coloured overcoat stands with his hands in his pockets, leaning against the gaudy green glass of a fortune-telling machine. His blonde wife holds up a small child with tied yellow bunches, so she can see excitedly inside as her money clinks from the slot and slides down into the bowels of the machine.

Mum begins dragging us away from the stranger, but Matt has dropped something and as he fumbles on the floor, frightened by the gaps between the floorboards that go all the way down to the sea, the man in the overcoat looks up and stares at the three of us, his white hands dropping in slow motion from his pockets to hang awkwardly by his sides.

"Marisa?" he says to our mother, seeming to recover himself.

The girl and the wife are absorbed in the machine. The man picks up the tiny red aeroplane my brother dropped and places it carefully in the

84

hands Matt reaches out towards him, his gloves flapping out of his coat sleeves on the end of their string.

Then, suddenly, mum whirls on the heel of her long black winter boots and spins us away. Mum does not look back, but I do. The man looks back at us, over his wife's shoulder, but he does not follow us.

On the half-empty train back to London, I wait until Matt is asleep on my mother's shoulder before I ask her.

"Who was that man?" I say, resting my head against my mother's thin coat.

My mother pauses only briefly before replying. Her voice is shaking, with the train or with controlled rage.

"No-one," she says.

And then she pushes the sliding train window downwards so that the freezing wind blows into the carriage, and throws out Matt's little balsa wood aeroplane so that it catches the wind and dashes away from the train into the cold night sky.

Chapter Thirteen

In the end, the hospital I had dreamed of opening since Polio John and I had first stood within its walls scrabbling in the mud for buried treasures, opened – like everything we did in Adek – casually, without fanfare, almost by accident. It was nine or so weeks into our stay in Sudan, and the work in the feeding centres had become a blur of exhausted adrenalin. Loki dropped food when the pilots were able to negotiate the complexities of the flight restrictions imposed by the Sudanese Government, or an NGO outside of the official channel, Operation Lifeline Sudan, flew a secret mission under the radar. In the meantime, thousands of hungry, emaciated families continued to arrive at our dusty outpost, far outnumbering the rations we had. Under the methodical leadership of Lieutenant Dit, the Commander's men worked tirelessly at the airstrip in the still, dry heat, their backs bent in the dust, yet there seemed little progress made from day to day. Without the airstrip we could not leave – marooned 1,000 miles from Kenya, and 800 from Chad, with warring armies covering the distance in-between. Christmas had passed, and now the talk was of leaving by the end of February. Africaid had informed my tutors and immediate family of our predicament, asking them to keep the situation from the media – explaining that any coverage would further endanger us, and that, for now, we were as safe as we could be inside a warzone thousands of miles from home.

It was around this time that the weather began further conspiring with the Government against us. For a country that had been three years without rain, a curious thing had begun happening – water levels were rising throughout Southern Sudan. El Niño, the same weather front that had brought drought to Adek had flooded the White Nile's tributaries further up into Uganda. Bahr el Ghazal, a region named after a river, was situated on the White Nile's floodplain and its villages were starting to become sodden with the rising waters. Adek alone was on higher land.

So, we stayed put, and the food drops came down from the sky, a beacon attracting many more thousands of people from across Bahr el Ghazal and up into the neighbouring province of Darfur, drawing like a magnet any family capable of walking. New arrivals told us thousands more people – the sick, the very youngest and the elderly – were being buried daily by their surviving relatives in dusty graves across the plains towards Adek or left marooned in flooded villages facing certain famine and death. Arriving in Adek meant at least a fragile chance of life, however desperately short we were of food. But it also made the village even more vulnerable than before – a sitting duck target for militia attack or Government bombings.

"It's a cat and mouse game now," Billy said.

The Government and the weather had long worked hand-in-hand in Southern Sudan, with starvation a weapon of war wielded with vicious force by the Khartoum Government. Now, the flooding not only increased the levels of starvation, but also corralled people into narrow corridors of land easily attacked. Not only was the village vulnerable to attack from the air by the Government and on the ground by the Government-sponsored militias, but also the warlord Kerubino Kuanyin Bol – one of the former founders of the SPLA – had changed sides yet again, his army rampaging through swathes of Bahr el Ghazal, raiding the population for food, women and child soldiers. The drought also brought neighbouring warrior tribes from all corners of East Africa out of their territories looking for water and food – the Karamajong cattle raiders and the easily riled Toposa were all ready to wage war. Bahr el Ghazal was now host to myriad dangers almost ridiculous in their extremity.

While we, the mice, waited, we fed as many of the people coming to the feeding centres as we possibly could, using crude and terrible measures – literally yardsticks. Age is not measured or celebrated amongst the Dinka, so for the children's feeding centre we used a stick that was one metre long to determine who might come in and out. Taller than the stick, and a child would be deemed too old to be helped. Smaller than the stick, and food and help would follow. It was a cruel process, and children would stand visibly sinking their feet and bodies low into the soil, trying to lose an inch or so from their heights, and I found myself making measurements of such startling inaccuracy that Sean reprimanded me on several occasions. My protestations that a child had experienced a sudden growth spurt upon being fed properly for the first time in weeks, fell on deaf ears.

"We can't feed everyone, Maria," Sean would say, gently.

"Look at her," I would say, holding a child's paper-thin arm up for him to weigh in his own white, sun-freckled hands.

Or: "He's tall for his age . . ."

One day, when Sean tackled me at the line for sending a too-tall child through the wooden gate of the feeding centre, I grabbed the stick and suddenly snapped it in two over my knee, surprising both myself and him.

"What are you doing . . .?"

The waiting crowd took a step back and I realised I must look insane, eyes flashing, dirty hair flying, sweat pouring from my forehead in dusty streaks.

"It's just a stick," I said to Sean.

I turned to the crowd.

"IT'S JUST A FUCKING STICK, OKAY?"

Another stick was found, and it was never mentioned again, but sometimes at night, I sent Bol to desperate families with handfuls of food. Playing favourites, Billy would have called it. I thought of myself only weeks ago standing amongst the debris of the radio hut, saying "I really haven't come here to play God" – yet by now I was so morally afloat as to be utterly at sea.

I understood that feeding a half-dead child did not make logical sense. It was a waste of limited food resources, and would ultimately cause the death of other healthier children who could use the food to get well and strong. Yet, how could a person who starved a half-dead child sleep at night? In a world where our rules were law, a piece of wood decided who would eat, and our exhausted, imperfect minds decided who lived and died, I wished for someone infallible to defer to. But there was only us. The Africaid and UN bosses were distant voices living in another world, and I no longer believed in God.

One particular morning, which could have been any from that time, I was in one of the feeding centres kneeling on the blue tarpaulin floor at the side of a woman whose empty breasts were no longer able to feed the child lying silently next to her, a baby whose tiny pursed lips were ragged with dehydration. I was tired, exhausted perhaps, and I was becoming irritable with the woman's refusal to drink from the plastic orange cup of rehydration salts and sugars I had pressed to her mouth, and my own inability to speak her language. When Bol came up alongside me, distributing blankets, I snapped at him, irritably.

"Tell her to drink, Bol," I said.

Taking the cup from me, he placed his hand on the woman's shoulder – a twisted mass of bone and muscle, knotted like old, dark wood, like walnut – and whispered to her in the Dinka language.

The old woman whispered back in a voice so quiet it might have been only an expiration of dead air.

"What is she saying?" I asked Bol.

As I spoke, the woman knocked the orange cup from Bol's hand, spilling its precious moisture onto the tarpaulin and across my bare knees. She began to weep drily, without moisture, her rattling chest wracked with sobs that shook the fragile machine of her entire body.

The shock of the falling cup made me jump, and I watched the valuable liquid spill itself across the plastic surface into three pale, watery fingers, each of which could have fed a small child.

"What's the matter with her?" I asked Bol, trying pointlessly to catch some of the liquid in my own useless hands, losing it through my fingers and spilling it across my shorts.

"She is crying because she thought she was dead," Bol said, picking up the cup. He pulled a goatskin cloth from his pocket and dried my hands.

"She wishes she were dead," he said, without looking at me. "She no longer has strength for life."

"Rubbish," I said, in a voice I did not recognise. I pulled the cloth from Bol's hands and wiped my damp knees and shorts. My hand shook with anger. "If she has enough strength to cry, she has enough strength to live."

Bol shook his head. He was ashamed of me.

"But the baby . . ." I said, changing tack, trying to find some justification for the fury I felt towards the dying woman. "The child needs her. She can't just give up . . ."

The child did not stir, lying on the tarpaulin next to the woman with his tiny diamond-shaped mouth moving slightly in pain as if he were whispering a song or a prayer. I remembered learning how at a certain point of starvation the body begins to eat itself.

"The child is dying," Bol said. "The woman wishes he were free of pain too."

He lifted the child into the woman's arms and gently manoeuvred her until she was holding the baby against herself. The child stirred a little, and the woman too, and then I could not look any more at the pitiful tableau of mother and baby, but when I tried to look away I only saw the same scene repeated a hundred times over and over throughout the feeding tent. I was lost then in a numb, raging anger that seemed to take over each of my faculties until it had fully submerged my every sense. I suddenly had the overwhelming feeling that I needed to punch someone hard in the face, an unnamed person responsible for this woman's sadness – a crawling militia squatting low in the scrubland, or a Government minister in his gold palace in Khartoum. I imagined the man's look of surprise, hearing the sickening thud of my fist striking his nosebone as he fell backwards into the scrub or fell onto his knees in front of his subordinates. Perhaps I followed this attack with a flurry of punches on this faceless antagonist, maybe I kicked him. I can remember only a pure, unadulterated fantasy of rage. It was a yearning for violent retribution I had never before felt, and it made me dizzy. Leaving the woman for a moment, I stood up and walked to the edge of the giant tent, watching the gentle play of light where a hole in the fabric let a pool of sunshine in. I was breathing heavily, and the plain, dirty white space of the tarpaulin's edge calmed me momentarily.

It was Adel's gentle touch, hesitant on my shoulder, which brought me suddenly back to myself.

"A boy has collapsed outside in the line," she said, her violet eyes full of worry. "Will you come? There are lots of people there. I can't see what is happening."

I was grateful for an excuse to leave the feeding centre. Outside, a crowd had gathered around the fallen boy, and I had to follow in the path Adel made through the people to get close to him. The knot of people were nervously excited, speaking quickly and shouting, and I didn't recognise their mood. Three or four women were chanting in high, feverish voices. Of the faces in the crowd, I recognised only Adel's and she vanished suddenly into the crowd. Still high on anger, I felt mildly invincible, as if were anyone to cross me, they would get what they deserved.

As soon as we got to the boy I realised what was the matter. He was fitting, throwing his arms and legs violently against the soil and banging his head. But as I knelt to protect his head from the hard earth, thinking to use the soft fleece in my rucksack, the crowd hissed and drew back.

I turned to see Bol at my elbow, looking worriedly from the boy to the crowd.

"What is happening?" I asked him, manoeuvring the fleece under the boy's head, and trying to move him into a position from which he was less likely to hurt himself.

His skin was an unusually deep, dark black under the thick dust that covered it, with tribal markings I did not recognise. His right shoulder was badly wounded and leaking blood from a pink island-shaped hole that looked infected. As his legs jerked backwards and forwards I noticed he was wearing a silver anklet with a blue stone in it that rode up his calf with every kick.

"They believe the boy is possessed," Bol said, his hand on my arm like a warning. "They don't want you to touch him. They have gone to fetch the Master of the Fishing Spear."

"Don't be ridiculous," I said. "He's suffering some kind of seizures, and he's got an old gunshot wound to his shoulder."

One of the old women who had been chanting appeared suddenly at the front and began shrieking in a high-pitched voice next to me, where I was kneeling, white spittle flying from her mouth. Her eyes were covered with a bluish film and she banged her head from side to side in time to her own shrieks.

"For God's sake," I said to Bol, my hands shaking as they tried to protect the boy's head from the iron-hard ground. "Tell her the boy has an illness I know how to treat. He is not possessed by evil spirits."

But Bol shook his head anxiously.

"She says you must leave him," he said, pulling at my shoulder. "She says he . . ." he trailed off. "Please Maria. He is a militia from the North."

Having finally manoeuvred most of my rucksack under the boy's crashing head, I looked up at Bol incredulously.

"This boy isn't a militia!" I said. "Look at him. He is nine years old. Eleven at the oldest."

Bol shrugged.

"Maria, that is old enough to fight . . ."

As he spoke, a charged silence fell and I was suddenly aware of the figure of the Spear Master towering over the heads of the crowd. As he stood over us, shaking his spear and murmuring in his low voice, the wounded boy grew immediately quiet, drawing gasps from the crowd. Protectively, without thinking, I gathered his still body up into my arms and stood up slowly, his legs hanging over my right arm and his head lolling over the left as I tried to keep him in a version of the recovery position, worried he might now choke on his tongue. The bright, ragged circle of his shoulder wound was exposed to the light now and I saw there was something – a bullet, or shrapnel – lodged in it. Since the Spear Master's intervention, the boy appeared to be either unconscious or sleeping.

I moved forward, but the crowd did not step out of my way, and for the first time in Southern Sudan I felt frightened not of the enemy, or of the landscape and its inhospitality, but of the villagers themselves. I looked around desperately for Sean or Billy, but I knew both would be inside the feeding centres and oblivious to what was happening outside.

The Spear Master stood still a step away from me and I marvelled at the strength in his body and the benignly authoritative expression on his face. In all these weeks I had only ever seen him as a figure standing on the very edge of things, a shadow under a tree observing us from afar. Up close, he was magnificent, his naked body painted completely white and then marked by great swirls of reds and greens. Against the chalky complexion of his painted face, the whites of his eyes seemed flecked with bright yellows and reds. For a moment, we studied each other coolly, as if the rest of the crowd were not there. Then, unexpectedly, the Master of the Fishing Spear stood back to allow me to pass. Behind him, the people stepped back murmuring, and I walked as fast as I could between them, the unconscious boy in my arms.

As the crowd parted, I saw Sean's worried face advancing towards me through the gap in the crowd, with Adel struggling to keep up at his side.

"Bring him to the hospital," Sean said quietly as he reached me, putting his arm around my shoulder as he spoke and studying the child's sleeping face. "Quick as you can. Billy is there already. I'll try and keep everyone else away for a moment. It's vital the Commander doesn't know the boy is here."

At the hospital, we lifted the boy onto the makeshift operating table Billy had made from scrubbed wood and reinforced palettes as a surprise for me in some distant time weeks before. Billy lifted his legs into a proper recovery position. Then, as the boy lay still on the table, my legs gave way beneath me and I found myself holding onto the wood for support.

Billy looked at me calmly from across the table. He looked at the boy's right shoulder quickly and seemed to size it up with a brief wave of his long fingers.

"Tweezers, a scalpel, needle and thread and local anaesthetic if you have it," he said, and I saw with relief that he was in perfect control. "And heat some water."

In my fantasies of re-opening the old, derelict hospital, now patched together by the Chief's men and long mornings I had spent there with Bol, Adel and Polio John, I had imagined my first operation in the hospital in grandiose terms. A broken leg that I would perfectly splint together, or a machete wound that I would beautifully clean, cut and sew like an experienced surgeon. Opening the hospital had been something to aim towards, something achievable in the midst of so much failure, an unconscious desire, perhaps, for my own, ordered, spotless fiefdom in a place where everything was so utterly out of control. But, oh, how Africa mocks our vanities. In the event, I could only watch Billy, whose quiet dexterity in bullet-removal suggested an unexpected level of experience. I, the Chief Surgeon, Sister and Senior Consultant, was so utterly exhausted I could only watch, dizzied by the hot smell of the boy's blood.

Over the past weeks, and even in England, reading the security briefings Africaid had sent me before I travelled, I had pictured the Northern militia enemy in so many ways: torching the hospital in the early dawn, creeping through the night with a knife in his mouth, smiling safe in a Northern barracks as hate-filled bombs rained down on a defenceless village. I had hated him, and felt afraid of him and hidden myself from him, but I had never thought of him as an eleven year old boy with a beautifully-curved skull, long, dark eyelashes and a silver anklet like a girl's. And so, in the hospital I had built as an act of defiance against the militias of the North, I found myself willing a militia to live. A child militia barely of secondary school age in Western terms, but a militia all the same.

"Did my first bullets in Bosnia," Billy said, in answer to my unspoken question as I stood, having regained control of myself, dabbing iodine around the neatly stitched wound.

"You were a soldier," I said.

My voice sounded childishly thick through my tear-torn throat and nose.

"Special Forces at one time."

A whole array of thoughts clicked into a string of sense, like a matching line on a fruit machine.

"Gonna be terrified when he wakes up," Billy said, laying the boy's arm across his body.

I watched the boy where he lay on the table, and wondered what terrible crimes he had committed against the tribes of Southern Sudan, and what had been done to him to make him capable of those things.

"Why did you stop being a soldier?"

Billy paused, concentrating as he examined the rest of the boy's body for injuries.

"Because of war."

We worked in silence for a while, and then the sound of angry voices broke into the quiet of the empty hospital, and Billy and I stood looking at each other, waiting to see who had come for the boy. Seconds after the voices, Commander Wol squeezed his seven-foot frame through the low doorway, his Kalashnikov slung casually across his back and his good right arm pointing angrily towards the boy. It was the first time I had ever seen him without his dressing gown, in full, badly matching combat fatigues, and it made me realise how the dressing gown somehow downsized the threat of him – as if he were only a comic book Commander and his gun were a mere toy. Today, even in the dim light inside the hospital, the Kalashnikov seemed glitteringly oiled and as hyper-real as the grim expression on the Commander's face. I wished Lieutenant Dit were with him, the only person capable of reasoning with him when he was in this mood.

"I understand you have a prisoner of war here," the Commander said, coldly and without greeting, as Sean came through the doorframe behind him, signalling us to remain where we were.

"Commander . . ." Sean said, continuing a conversation. "Let me be clear on this . . ."

The Commander advanced towards the boy on the table, and I found myself placing my hands protectively across his unconscious body.

The action must have reminded me that I was in charge, because I heard my voice suddenly speak out in tones I did not recognise, all traces of dizziness and weariness gone.

"Commander Wol," I said. "I'm afraid an operation is in progress and you will have to leave my hospital now."

"Your hospital!" the Commander spat. "So, now a patch of dust in Southern Sudan belongs to you, Dr Maria?" He laughed bitterly. "How quickly the helpers become the colonisers."

His eyes flashed and his mouth twitched, but I knew that however much the Commander threatened and blustered, I had not picked the boy up from the path of the Spear Master only to lose him to the SPLA.

"Your presence here is against the Geneva Convention," I said, with greater confidence. "Unless, of course, you are here for me to treat that arm you are always so reluctant for me to look at."

The Commander stood for a moment, glowering at the boy's prone form, and surveying my iodine-stained hands and Billy's blood-stained T-shirt with a tired, empty disgust. Wasting medical resources on a militia was clearly not on his agenda. Then, to our utter amazement, he turned on his heel and exited the hospital, taking some of the straw roof with the top of his head as he passed under the doorframe.

"Go Maria," Billy muttered, following him outside into the bright sun.

The men stood outside talking for more than an hour, and I found myself inside, listening, standing sentinel over my first and only proper patient, who stirred occasionally but did not wake. As well as the anklet, he wore a shell necklace around his slender neck, and his closed eyes were deep set in his small curved head. He seemed completely at peace on the operating table and I wished him the blissful ignorance of unconsciousness for as long as possible. In time soon enough, he would awake to his own memories, and an uncertain future many miles from home.

* * *

That night I asked Michael if he would help me speak with the Spear Master.

"I cannot," Michael said, with unexpected force.

"But why?" I asked.

"He is dangerous to you," Michael said.

"He seems to be helping Chief Deng's wife," I said. "There are so many plants and herbs I don't understand how to use . . . He knows so much about how to treat the things people here suffer with . . . Something incredible happened to the militia boy when he stood over him. I want to learn . . ."

Michael sat down next to where I was sitting on the log by the campfire. He looked closely into my eyes so that his own light brown irises danced in the firelight.

"The Spear Master is not your friend," he said.

"But, we've never even met . . . not really . . . I would like to get to know him . . . He's the spiritual leader of the village . . ."

"Last time the white people came here, very many people were killed by the Government. He believes you will bring the same curse upon Adek village . . . That is what he is telling the people. To stay away from you. To flee back into the bush. To starve rather than take your food or medicines."

"But we are saving lives," I said, stupidly, hearing the uncertainty in my own voice. "Look at all the food that arrived today . . ."

"That is why the elders allow you to remain," Michael said. "The village is divided, Maria. Elders to one side, Spear Master to the other. There is much you are unaware of."

"And the boy?"

"His presence is allowing the Spear Master to win his argument. You are insulting the village by placing him in a Dinka hospital."

"And should I run some kind of apartheid system at the hospital where only Dinka patients should be treated? I cannot believe you of all people would wish that, Michael. He is just a boy, for God's sake."

"In our country there is no such thing as 'just a boy'."

"How can you say such a thing?"

"When just a boy kills the ones you love, talk to me then of children," Michael said, and he gathered up his tall body in one swift movement and left me sitting alone by the fire.

* * *

It took three days for the child militia – who had wide, pitch black, terrified eyes when he awoke, and whose name was Manute – to become strong enough to sit up on the camp bed Billy had set up for him in the hospital. He remained a curiosity among the other new patients brought across from the feeding centres, but two of Michael's most trusted men guarded him morning and night, protecting him from the attentions of the Commander or the actions of any villagers intent on revenge.

After a week, Michael conducted a quiet interrogation on Commander Wol's behalf. His polite questioning could not disguise the obvious dislike and mistrust he had for Manute. The boy answered all the questions in a deep, cracked voice that seemed to come from the pit of his stomach. He had been born to a Dinka slave taken from a Bahr el Ghazal village and raped by her Arab captors. He had been amongst the militias since he was a small boy, living off the scraps of food they provided. He had no family he knew of, and no idea which village his mother had been taken from. As he spoke, I could sense Michael's resentment of the boy diminish slightly. Manute had been fighting for three years, but mainly working as a scout ahead of the advancing armies. His bullet wound came from a militia's gun as he deserted, creeping from a dug-in sand barracks north of Darfur by night. He was looking for his own people, he said. The people of his mother. Someone had told him she was a Twic Dinka from the lowlands close to Adek.

Michael agreed that Manute was a Dinka name, but still doubted his story.

"So are the militias coming?" I asked Michael. "Is that why he's here?"

Michael moved his heavy shoulders almost imperceptibly.

"They are always coming," he said. "It is always the turn of this village eventually. Sometimes an attack every few months. Sometimes three in a week. Sometimes a year between attacks. But the militias are always coming."

"Do you think the boy – Manute – has actually killed people?" I asked, voicing the concern I had felt since our conversation the previous evening. "I mean, is he a soldier or was he a scout as he says?"

Michael looked at his hands.

"It is possible he is only a spy," he said.

I was more troubled by Manute's presence than I liked to admit, and often found myself watching him as he sat up in his camp bed looking at the wall, muttering to himself in his low, sandpapery voice. He was obviously traumatised, yet it was the thought of what he might have done that frightened me most. For long periods of time, he was cold and strange, his black eyes as empty as a heroin addict's. At night, he screamed so much that he kept the other patients awake. Only when he slept did he look like the young boy that he was, his hard man's face with its hollowed circles and baggy skin relaxing into a child's sweet expression, the curls of his eyelashes folded together as if in prayer. Then, no longer afraid of him, I would stroke his head as his dead mother the Dinka slave might have done, hoping to soothe his subconscious as the creases fell from his forehead.

Chapter Fourteen

Waking in pitch darkness one day a week or so after the hospital had opened, I found myself unable to go back to sleep despite a deep exhaustion that cut through to my bones. My stomach transmitted the dull ache that came from a repetitive diet of wet grain and dry beans, and my body was painful and feverish. The cries of the children at the feeding centres carried on the night wind, sometimes insistent, other times barely audible as if my bed were marooned offshore, rising and falling with the breeze. Flicking on my torch, I pulled out a paperback thriller of Sean's I had already read three times, but the sentences jumbled on the page until they became only a series of unconnected words. Putting the book down on the earth floor, I searched the straw of the roof with the torch's beam for Laurel and Hardy the spiders instead, wondering if Michael had finally killed them.

"The fat one is poisonous, Maria," he protested daily.

The more death I was surrounded by, the more sentimental I became about the spiders. They, after all, had existed in the tukul long before me.

"I will never understand kawajas," Michael sighed, when I tried to explain.

Catching sight of Laurel in a deep corner, I lay on my hard bed scratching a mosquito bite, thinking over the events of the previous night. We sat up only rarely together in the evenings now the feeding centres had opened, but yesterday had been an exception. It had been Billy's birthday and Commander Wol had donated a bottle of contraband whiskey and Sean had invited Chief Deng to join us at the fire, and Adel had cooked us a feast where somehow the dark red beans hadn't tasted as bitter and there was rice from somewhere for the first time in weeks, and Billy had played his guitar, and Michael had even sung a little, songs from his father, the fisherman-turned-SPLM politician. As he sang, I saw in him a capacity for joy that was still intact somewhere underneath his grief, and it made my heart lift with possibility. And then I had ruined everything by arguing badly with Chief Deng at the fireplace, talking about the new Sudan, that future Utopia for which the SPLA fought and the villagers died. The independent Southern Sudan would be a socialist democracy, the Chief explained, where people would have basic rights and freedoms, and the country's as yet almost untapped riches of oil and diamonds and minerals would be shared lifting millions from poverty.

"Will there be freedom of religion?" I had asked.

"Of course," the Chief said.

"Even to be a Muslim?"

Since Manute's arrival, I had begun to see the war in far less simplistic terms.

"There will be no Muslims in the New Sudan," the Chief said, laughing kindly. "They will all be in North Sudan."

I had laughed too.

"It's not religious freedom if you don't have any Muslims," I said, smiling.

Michael had tried to intervene, but the Chief was suddenly angry.

"There will be no Muslims, Maria," he said.

I felt angry tears springing to my eyes. It had been a long day in the feeding centres, and at that moment I desperately needed to feel we were on the right side of the war. There was something else too, a light fever in my brain, a slight shiver. I didn't feel right but couldn't put my finger on it exactly.

"How can you say that?" I asked the Chief. "That makes you no better than the North who forbid you your gods . . ."

The Chief glared at me and I tried another tack. "It's not because the militias are Muslims that they are your enemy. I have Muslim friends in England. Pakistanis, Iranians, English Muslims that would not hurt a fly – people you could love . . ."

The Chief had stood up angrily – the first time he had ever shown me anything but kindness.

"I have read about your perfect England," he said, "where you have all kinds of abominations. Homosexuals and drug addicts roaming the streets. Families that do not know each other, pollution from factories thickening the air . . . Children who do not know the shape or the sound of a cow or the names of trees . . ." He laughed bitterly.

"In London, as you yourself have told me Maria, there are people who choose not to finish the food on their plate so that they can be thin like the Dinka. Imagine! That people should be prized on how starving they are! You will forgive me if I am not prepared to be lectured by someone from such a society on the failings of my own . . ."

I looked around for Michael, hoping he would at least understand what I meant, but he stared back at me painfully. Billy was sleeping drunkenly by the fire, propped up against a log.

"And now we find out you are a friend to the Arabs, Maria," the Chief said, angrily, before gathering up his blue robe and leaving the fireplace. "No wonder you are happy to harbour their militias at your hospital!"

"Chief Deng . . ." I called, as he walked off. Michael followed behind him, exiting with the briefest of nods.

I got up to follow them, but Sean placed his hand gently on my arm.

"It doesn't matter," he said, soothingly, in his way. "He'll have forgotten about it in the morning."

"It matters to me."

"It's only drink, and exhaustion and passion," Sean said. "Those are difficult topics. You might feel their views are unjust, but you haven't gone through what these people have."

I saw the Northern Irishman in him then, a man who understood what it meant to take sides.

"But it matters to me that we are on the right side of this war," I said.

My head was spinning although I had drunk only moderate amounts of whiskey that evening. "It matters that these people – our friends – are not monsters."

"If they are our friends, how can they be monsters?" Sean said.

"But people in the North of Sudan must think that about their friends . . ."

"And they would be right too."

"I don't understand," I said.

Sean poured himself another cup of Jim Beam and added a splash of water before offering the bottle to me. I shook my head.

"Both my older brothers joined the paramilitaries when they got to 15," he said. "And you may find this hard to believe, but neither of them is a monster."

I took the whiskey from him after all, splashing it into my metal mug from Millets that seemed to permanently retain the heat of the day.

"Have you ever been to the North?" I asked.

"Yes, once," Sean said. "I was in the capital, Khartoum. Like a lot of Arab cities, it is beautiful in a dusty, busy, noisy way. The heat and the traffic fumes are overwhelming. You can stand right at the confluence of the Blue and White Niles, though they both look brown and muddy. When you go there you realise it is a completely different country to the South. There are cars and roads and palaces and shopping centres and there is air conditioning, and everyone is in Arab clothes. The people look totally different. Even the markets are different, full of dates and mangos and flour for flatbreads. There are top class hotels with marble flooring and gold taps. Things that people in the South couldn't even begin to imagine."

"How did the North and South end up as one country?" I wondered.

"When they carved up Africa with the other European colonialists, the British stuck everyone inside the same borders, into the same country. It was the opposite of divide and rule – combine and rule. It meant that the former colonial power would be called upon again and again, a way of keeping British interests alive."

"Do you think people in the North know what is going on in the South? I mean the teachers and the office workers. Do the ordinary people know about the bombings and the rapes and the militias?"

"I don't suppose they are fully aware of it," Sean said. "It is a vast country and the Government of Sudan controls the media. It is a war hidden in a vast area without electricity or roads or communications. People in the North are violently afraid of the South and its armies and its desire to inflict pain on them. And remember that power is held by the few in the North of Sudan. Only a handful of Arab oligarchs and landowners live in luxury. For the rest, life is a struggle. Joining the army or the militias is a way to survive." He shrugged. "A civil war that has been raging for four decades can only disfigure both sides."

* * *

Sean and I had spoken for a while afterwards but when I awoke in the darkness, it was Chief Deng and Michael I thought of, desperately upset that I had argued with them, but also still feeling they were wrong. Rather than relive the conversation again I decided to get up, sliding my feet into my battered blue flip-flops and, pausing to flick the wood spiders from my damp towel, walking out into the unlit camp. Showering under a sky lightening towards grey velvet with a few stubborn stars still glittering above me, I began to feel a little better, luxuriating in the 90 second torrent of cool well water before pulling on cleanish shorts and a recently washed T-shirt. The headache I had been carrying the past couple of days seemed to shift slightly and I felt light-headed as the warm air dried my wet hair.

Pausing at the embers of the fire, I thought about filling the heavy kettle and making tea but found myself pulled by a strong desire to take a walk through the approaching dawn and watch the village awake from beyond its perimeter. I had precious little time to explore now that the work at the hospital and the feeding centres had become so unforgiving, and I longed to walk out to the fringes of the bush and beyond, away from the dung fires and the scent of boiling butter and wet mealie-meal to an empty landscape where children did not cry and queues of women did not watch my progress with hopeful, desperate eyes.

Too impatient to return to the tukul for my boots, I left in darkness in my flip-flops, my feet joyfully liberated from the heavy, sweltering leather they had been encased in for weeks. In my shorts' pocket, by some small miracle, was a single, slender Lucky Strike cigarette, and I had the idea of smoking it somewhere I could watch the dawn's red sun tip over the straw huts, flooding them with fiery light. After so many weeks of violent, oppressive heat, the air felt deliciously cool on my clean skin after my shower, and I found my spirits lifting as I walked.

The watercolour sky was slowly lightening, a pale eggshell grey tinged with pink brushstrokes where it met the earth, and I longed to be there at the empty horizon, a single black silhouette like the dark mango wood carvings I had seen at the roadside near Loki, a lone shape rising from the curvature of the reddish earth. Passing through the camp entrance, I picked up speed, smiling at the slumbering form of our guard Moses, the sleeping sentinel, his shadow nodding against the butt of his rifle. I walked with the morning heat haze rising around my half-bare feet, slipping through the compounds of sleeping tukuls where white smoke crept on its belly along the earth from the embers of the previous night's fires. I walked with the dawn in front of me, and my damp feet gathering dirt with every step, listening for even the faintest trace of birdsong in this place where so much that had been living was dead. As I walked, I felt the tension that knotted my shoulders and gnawed at my stomach slowly lifting, as if I were unfolding like a piece of paper. There is always hope at dawn, I thought, even in Africa.

As the first yellow rays of sun were within moments of lighting the sky, I realised I was at the turn-off for the path to the SPLA barracks where the soldiers of the rebel army trained and slept. I had been walking unconsciously, thinking only to clear the village, but now I saw that by turning left I would arrive at Commander Wol's lair. Overcome with curiosity about a place so vociferously declared out of bounds, I decided to continue a little way along the path towards the barracks and stop once they were in view.

The path took me gently uphill through scattered trees and sharp scrub and then into a field which appeared like a vision and into which I stepped into eagerly, luxuriating in the feel of actual grass licking up against the sides of my exposed, already filthy feet. The sun was fully over the horizon now, and after weeks living in a hot, empty, grassless dustbowl the setting was as completely perfect as a hot summer's day on the South Downs. When I closed my eyes I could smell rain-dampened grass and rabbit droppings and light cigarette smoke, and the musty wool of my mother's old orange picnic blanket. The lackadaisical drone of a mosquito became the sound of a distant A-road, and my mind filled in birdsong, a stiff bank holiday breeze and thick cut ham sandwiches. No wonder, I thought, the Commander didn't want anyone coming here. Where the rest of Adek was picked over by hunger – every exposed shoot sucked dry, every fallen seed eaten – here was a living field that existed outside of drought or famine. The thin grass was yellowed and ravaged by lack of rain, but in Adek, this might have been Eden.

I walked further into the field, and lighting the cigarette I had reserved long ago for a great moment, and which had appeared in my pocket this morning like a sign, I exhaled a plume of white smoke, which tasted bitter after days without smoking, and made me cough a little. I stood looking down at my bare toes, the dirt and bruises and bites cast into absent shadow by the angle of the low sun, and was contemplating removing my flipflops altogether when something unnaturally white caught my eye. I bent to the long object, and as my hand touched it I realised it was a fragment of bone. The sunlight caught another white object in the long grass and I made out the shape of a long femur, a thighbone too long to be a goat's and too thin to belong to a cow. As I looked around, I saw similar objects almost delicately scattered, whitened like driftwood by the harsh glare of the sun. My brain knew what they were before my heart would accept them, or perhaps it was the other way round – that my mind was unwilling to breach the staccato beat's distance between knowledge and intuition. They were human bones, that much was certain: femurs and fibulas with the periosteum long worn away to compact bone; a humerus; a great jaw bone from some man that must have once stood seven feet tall. By the upturned root of a decapitated tree stood a pile of skulls, and the trainee doctor in me recognised what the human being rejected: that they were each child-sized, of varying ages nought to five years old.

I was standing there, the forgotten cigarette burning quickly between my fingers, thinking of my mother, buried deep and intact under the earth, wondering why these bones still lay here – whether nobody knew who the people were, or whether they had some plague or curse that meant no-one would touch them, or whether it was simply tradition for people here to rejoin the earth exactly where they fell, when my eyes answered their own question. There were mechanical parts to this tableau too: bullet casings, shrapnel, the broken wooden handle of a gun. Next to my feet was a dull, rusted object I recognised belatedly from a brightly coloured canvas chart Sean had shown me on the aircraft on the way in to Sudan, and which now hung in the storeroom. It was a landmine. A small, smooth disc of moulded metal or plastic with a circular pattern at its centre, like a fallen miniature hubcap or an ice hockey puck made with deadly intent. The butt from my cigarette, where I must have unthinkingly dropped it, lay carelessly next to it, a half-inch from detonation.

Minutes or hours could have passed. Time went into freefall, bearing no relation to the prescribed divisions of the clock. I felt lightheaded, sick, floaty. As I contemplated the landmine, three feet away, I realised why the field was untouched by those hungry enough to have explored every inch of territory for hundreds, even thousands of miles. In the long grass, I saw now there were dozens more mines of differing kinds. Fist-shaped mines stuck into the grass like stunted cobs of grey corn. Crudely-made mines with sprung coils hanging out like entrails where they had already ripped open and done their deadly work. My mind was in overdrive, seeking all available information, and my body was flooded with a freezing liquid that might have been my own blood. With effort, I forced my brain to swim against the tide of my confusion, rewinding it to the plane conversation I had had with Sean, and two words came back to me: Stand Still. I swore at myself then. I was in a field off the beaten track where nobody need pass for days. Nobody would even know I was missing. Sean had given up demanding that I check in with him all the time, and would simply assume I was up at the feeding centres. At the feeding centres, Billy would think I was at the hospital with Michael, and vice versa. It might take hours or days for them to find me, and I was standing on a small patch of ground on which I did not dare even to redistribute my own shaking weight.

"Oh, God," I heard my voice say, and wondered at its tone. My baby blue beach holiday flipflops mocked me from below the line of my hips, my bare, dusty toes emphasising the childish vulnerability of my predicament. If I had been wearing a sombrero I would have felt no more foolish, though a hat might have offered some protection against the slowly increasing violence of the rising sun.

Stand still. A standstill. Time stood still. The sun beat down without rhythm.

"Help!" I shouted, after a time, hearing my own thin voice, like a child playing games. What a stupid little word 'Help' seemed when no help was coming. Still I shouted it until it became a meaningless sound, a noise like any other, the sound of a frightened animal.

Time stood still and still I shouted, hoarser now, and exhausted with the effort of shouting and remaining still, every muscle tensed, and still the sun beat down, burning my face and neck and the pink tops of my exposed feet. Hours passed and I began to hear drips of water somewhere, and I longed to turn in the tiny space I stood in and find it, and lick the moisture from the dry earth. In my mind, a waterfall lay just behind the tree with the bodies, and the water was sweet and cold and plentiful.

I shouted thick-tongued at the burning disc of high up sun, until I heard my mother's voice.

"Maria!"

I closed my eyes, drawing comfort from her presence in the minefield. It was so hot, I told her, quietly, and I was so terribly thirsty, and the effort of keeping completely still, balancing on one leg slightly more than the other to take turns on each, was beginning to take its toll. There was no respite from the heat. Sweat slid from my hair and forehead to join the deep pooling in the cleft at my collarbone, and I began to imagine that a bead of moisture might spring from my leg or foot and trigger the landmines with the tiny blow as it fell. It seemed that it had been dark and then light, but perhaps it was only the passage of the clouds up above the South Downs where I was standing with my mother and a half-eaten picnic, where brightly coloured kites even now were troubling a cloudless sky. I was angry with my mother because she wouldn't let me sit down.

"DOCTOR MARIA!"

It was the tone more than the voice I recognised, its tremulous snarl scattering the air like white waters disturbed by a ship. I opened my eyes to see Commander Wol standing ahead of me where the long grass started: a long tall figure in a ladies' dressing gown belted unfashionably tightly over long desert combat trousers. It was the first time I had seen him since the confrontation in the hospital that seemed part of a distant past my brain could not fully recollect.

After standing still so long, I almost ran towards him, but his voice cut across the thirty or so feet between us like a gunshot.

"Stand still. Stand exactly where you are."

My body froze again. I barely nodded.

"Are you hurt?"

I tried to reply but my parched tongue was thick in my mouth.

"Thirsty."

"Keep completely still or you will kill us both."

I nodded, but keeping still suddenly felt utterly impossible. Every muscle seemed poised for flight. My left leg twitched, and seemed as if it would walk by itself. I held onto my own violently shaking arms and legs rigidly, as someone might cling to a fleeing dog.

Without warning, the Commander carefully removed his dressing gown to reveal a pair of oversized camouflage trousers and a long, winding, upper torso cut across by great snaking scars. Then he detached a long thin machete from his heavy belt. Laying his AK-47 on top of the dressing gown, he sprung down onto his haunches, reaching ahead and around himself in one-inch strips with the point of the machete, holding the knife carefully at a 30 degree angle so that he was prodding slowly and ahead of himself. Each time he finished a tiny patch of soil or grass, he marked the area with a knife or with sticks, and then he walked his crouching legs an inch or so forward.

Standing on my fixed spot, I could only watch dry-mouthed in a state close to dreaming, breathing out only with each step he took. Only the surreal edge that had taken over my reality kept me from shouting. The very core of my brain, I realised, was refusing to accept this was really happening. That my casual stupidity had led to this man risking his life.

It took well over an hour for the Commander to reach me, during which time neither of us spoke, although once he looked up and grinned through his good two front teeth. At no point did his machete appear to come into contact with any buried mines, although he three times changed direction and marked one of the corners with a cross of two sticks. As he reached me, he stood up, and I found myself acutely self-conscious. The moment seemed almost impossibly intimate – a connection between two people which was powerfully unique. Half a step away from each other and we might both be dead. Of all the points leading up to this moment, this was the most utterly powerless I had ever felt.

I don't really remember the next part. My legs swayed a little in the heat and the Commander lifted me as if I was a little child, and with my eyes closed we passed slowly back through the minefield along the route marked so painstakingly by the Commander. As we reached the path, the Commander set me down and I threw up a few times into the bushes. I had nothing to wipe my mouth and for a while that bothered me more than everything else put together.

When I turned back to the Commander he was wearing his dressing gown again and his usual aloof scowl had returned to the gap between his moustache and his goatee beard. His face slid with sweat.

"I need to go back to camp," I said, shivering, and my voice sounded small enough to slip between the stones beneath my feet.

"We will go to the barracks," the Commander said.

I had no strength to argue.

* * *

Ten minutes or so later, I was sitting in a high-roofed tukul on the only chair in the district, inside the perimeter of the SPLA barracks. In front of me was a field table spread with meticulously hand-copied maps, detailed with coloured pencils and sprawling handwriting. The Commander was preoccupied with a crate at the back of the room from which the barrels of several Kalashnikovs protruded. His own gun, an ornate piece that would not have looked out of place in some colonial museum, leaned heavily against the mud wall of the tukul and I saw the scratches across the wooden handle that Bol said each corresponded to a life lost by the enemy. The heat seemed to fall in sheets around me, and the air was heavy with the threat of a far off storm. As the adrenalin left my body, I felt my eyes droop and my neck fall forward. I felt hot and cold at the same time, as if I were an ice cube melting on a hot plate.

I sat up a fragment of a second later to find a bottle of Jack Daniels under my nose, its black and white label like a cameo from another life, the distinctive curve of its glass belonging to a long shelf at the back of a bar, or stuck with a red candle in the bathroom of a student flat.

I accepted the bottle gratefully, and drank down a draft that burned my lips and made my throat hurt, but did not seem to warm me beyond where the liquid touched.

"Thank you," I said.

The Commander nodded that I should swig again.

"For rescuing me, I mean," I said.

The Commander shrugged.

"Your friends are coming for you," he said. "I have sent for them."

"Where did you get that?" I asked, returning the bottle for him to drink.

"Christian supporters," the Commander said, standing awkwardly at his desk so that he seemed to regret having given up his wooden chair. "Missionaries. Comrades." He spat a long squirt of liquid between his teeth onto the dusty floor.

"Americans," I said.

"Of course. Jack Daniels, I believe, is an actual American man."

I smiled despite myself, but pressed on.

"Is that where the guns come from?"

The Commander smiled, and the scar on his cheek leapt like a fish, but did not reply. A silence stretched between us, broken only by the low buzz of a hornet drifting somewhere outside the tukul. A rivulet of sweat trickled down my right cheek and dripped onto my collarbone. My jaw was trembling, and it made my teeth rattle almost imperceptibly in my mouth. I found myself desperate for a cup of plain English tea with milk and sugar.

"What happened there?" I asked eventually, wiping my forehead with the sleeve of my T-shirt. "Out in the field where the bones are."

The hornet entered the relative cool of the tukul via the open doorway and spun lazily around the upper air like a boater on a lake. My mind, afloat with alcohol and relief, seemed to follow it.

"Militia attack," the Commander said. He leaned his long frame against the field table opposite me.

"The last time the Muhraleen came, they razed large sections of the village. We cleared mines from the marketplace and the areas where people live, but there are still many areas mined around the village itself." He refolded his arms, so that his withered arm was supported by its healthier twin. "Villagers know the signs: the long grass, the fruit in the

108

trees, the skeletons. More than thirty villagers lie there unburied in that patch alone."

I wanted to speak but I could not, and the Commander seemed lost in his own reverie. I was in shock, I thought.

"That was our punishment," the Commander said, "the last time white people came to Adek. The people who left the hospital you are rebuilding."

We shouldn't be here, I thought, watching the hornet. We are dangerous.

"Adek has always been this way," the Commander continued. "What you would call a sitting duck. Our position to the North of Bahr el Ghazal makes us particularly vulnerable to the Muhraleen. We are high up on the flood plain. Now we have drawn fresh attention to ourselves."

"Why not move?" I wondered. But I wasn't sure if I had spoken.

"We cannot leave our land," the Commander said. "Our ancestors are here. They live in the trees, they till the earth when we are sleeping. Those whose bodies lie in that place – in that field – their spirits are trapped there by the mines, and they cannot roam the lands in peace."

The Commander, I remembered came from Eastern Equatoria, from Nimule or one of the other villages close to the Ugandan border. He was a Madi, a Nilotic tribe like the Dinka.

"But your family is buried far from here . . .?" I said.

I heard my voice make its polite enquiry at a distance, as if it were a recording. My vision was beginning to slip and stagger, and through a narrow tunnel of light I watched the Commander drink from the bottle and study the amber liquid as it settled.

Turning from the bottle, he said:

"I have family here too. Chief Deng is my brother."

I was puzzled. The men's animosity was well documented by village gossip. The surprise shook my brain, briefly righting my vision. I thought: They look nothing alike.

"I thought the warrior clans and ruling clans were separate," I murmured.

"They are," the Commander said. "Deng's father adopted me after my own father gave his life to protect him. He was his bodyguard."

"But you are not friends?"

The Commander was facing the wall of the tukul when he spoke, so I could not see his expression. There was a long pause.

"No," he said.

I continued, recklessly. After the minefield, I realised I no longer feared the Commander.

"Were you ever married?" I asked.

The dizziness was returning now, thicker and blacker. The tunnel of my vision was surrounded by dark, scratchy shapes, as if someone had taken a blunt pencil to the surface of my retina.

The Commander snorted through his nose.

"I think I hear your comrades," he said, although I still heard nothing but the hornet and the pounding that had started up moments earlier inside my chest.

I don't remember anything after that – or nothing that I can swear to as being real. I don't remember Sean and Michael coming into the tukul. I don't remember swaying on the chair and falling sideways to the ground, toppled like a sack of mealie–meal falling from a plane, a dead weight that hit the ground solidly, without splitting. I don't remember Michael carrying me to the Spear Master or anything else that followed. I remember my dreams though. And they were real enough.

*   *   *

When I awake the first time, I am lying in a narrow tukul lined with black and white animal skins. I feel strangely calm and reassured as if this is the place I have been waiting to wake up all my life. I am wearing a faded yellow oversized T-shirt I don't recognise and my body is heavy under a thin blanket that is pleasantly rough against my skin. The air is thick with the sharp scent of bitter herbs and my body is colder than ice, my blood turning solid in my veins. Within touching distance, a solitary ox stands squarely on the solid muscle of its four legs, covered in deep black and white markings like a glossy magpie of hallucinogenic proportions. It turns its huge, horned head towards where I am lying, and for a moment, he and I look at each other, the bull's eyes like deep wells of black water. His hooves are polished almost to the lustre of glass and painted with dotted lines of bright colour like an aboriginal painting. His horns are decorated with dyes and decked with heavy wooden bells that chime low as the giant ox gracefully swings his head. His coat gleams like a rich woman's fur, groomed over and over until no imperfection diverts even a single hair from its velvet course. He swings his head away again, and I feel strangely bereft.

Something is Going to Fall Like Rain

*   *   *

Next time I awake, I see the Spear Master kneeling at the fire in the middle of the tukul, stirring a great metal pot with intense concentration. In the firelight, he seems even younger than he had looked the day Manute collapsed at the feeding centre. I am so cold that I cannot move: a deep, thick chill that starts at my heart and makes my bones ache violently. I know it is pointless to resist this cold – that some part of me inside is frozen solid. I watch the doctor dip a small wooden cup into the boiling pot, drawing out a draught the size of a shot glass. The steam curls around his ash-painted face, highlighting the tribal scars around his eyes. He brings the cup to where I am lying, and I sip the bitter liquid up, with the sense that this has happened several times before. The pulp is familiarly thick and green, bitter and boiling, and swallowing it is an effort. I retch a little as it goes down, and then the burning fluid begins its work, tracing a livid course down through my neck and chest, scorching my stomach so that the flames of the fire seem to lick at my solar plexus, a pulse of acrid heat spreading towards the frozen wasteland of my heart.

Then, without warning, I am sitting in my mother's garden on a rickety wooden chair by a big white tub over-run by geraniums, feeling the cold coming up from the ground and through my thin black overcoat into the worn denim of my jeans. The turquoise paint on the chair is blistered, and comes off in flakes where the wood takes my weight. No-one has sat on this chair I think, for a long time. I cross my legs, and hold my hands in my lap. I look at the struggling geraniums, which have lost most of their thin, red, clockhand petals to the cold and the battering wind.

I think: "It's too cold for the geraniums. They should be inside."

Then I notice something amongst the barren twigs of the wintering azalea bushes that seems wrong, and I get up to look more closely, my cold jeans clinging hard to my legs. A loosely coiled spring of violent metal lies open in the soil, already sprung, its vicious heart wide open. My mother must have stepped on it as she tended the flowerbed, and I run into the house calling her name, stepping over the white bones of my ancestors lined up in pairs on the linoleum of the hallway like so many muddy boots.

*   *   *

Later, with growing anxiety, I realise the village is on fire, that Adek is burning. I struggle in my blanket, but my legs are a dead weight, and I have to drag them slowly, inch by inch towards the doorway of the tukul. The bull is gone, leaving only pigeon-toed prints in the dust that I blur as I pull myself across the harsh grit of the earth. Acrid smoke chokes my throat and my eyes are streaming with soot and tears, and at the doorway, I see everything I have come to love drowned in flames. The blazing silhouette of a girl comes towards me and it is Adel, and I am screaming now, crying out with every last gasp of smoke in my lungs, and then suddenly I am screaming clean air, deliciously sweet and fresh like spring water, and I am aware that someone unseen is holding my shoulders and whispering to me, singing songs I don't recognise softly in my ear.

* * *

In my dream I am on the shores of my grandparents' town of Tarifa, lashed by a standstorm that is catching my breath and dashing it out to sea. Beyond the green-blue of the waves I can see Africa lurking like a caged animal – a huge presence like a streak across the sky. To a continent achingly adrift, my own tiny sadness is the most minuscule of fractional echoes, the smallest bleep miles offshore. And suddenly, like a lost trombonist reunited with the world's largest symphony orchestra, Africa and I are hitting the same sad note over and over, in a jarring blast of klaxon noise that brings me to my knees in the hard sand.

* * *

The next time I awake I feel strangely absent. Neither hot nor cold, neither sick nor well, neither happy nor sad, as purely and impersonally existing as the steam floating up from the cooking pot towards the hole in the tukul's thatched roof. The snaking flames of the fire move together in an ancient pattern of red and yellow and white light, and I am aware I am on fire but without pain, feeling the flames licking over me like a gentle breeze. My mother kneels next to me, gently wiping the sweat from my forehead. I try to whisper to her, but she places her forefinger to her lips. She looks exactly as she does in the photographs I have kept of her, the pain gone from her eyes and the grey pallor of her skin and lips replaced by the pinkish flush of an afternoon spent outside in the hot

African sun. She smiles at me and strokes the skin of my cheek and I float on the breath of the wind outside perfectly supported by love. For all the words I have to say, there is no need.

*   *   *

Five days later, I found myself lying on a blanket on a bed-platform in a tukul I didn't recognise, with Adel pressing wet rags to my face and humming softly. I fought to sit up, my head clouded with cotton wool languor, and limbs heavy as lead. Billy was leaning over me in the twilight, his cowboy hat tilted to one side, his shirt tied like a jumper around the brown muscles of his narrow shoulders.

"There you are," he said.

Next to him, Adel smiled shyly, showing two rows of tiny white teeth strung like freshwater pearls.

My tongue was hard and swollen in my mouth, as unwieldy as a sea cucumber.

"Sorry," I said, thickly.

Billy lifted a metal canteen to my lips, and I drank the juice inside. It was warm but deliciously sharp, like passionfruit or grapefruit juice.

"How long have I been here?" I whispered to Billy, now that my dry lips could move.

"Three days with the witch doctor, three days here."

"Shock, or sunstroke?"

Billy laughed.

"It's malaria, doctor," he said. "You must have felt sick for days."

I lay back down on the soft bed, wondering where I was.

"Is this Chief Deng's tukul?" I asked, closing my eyes against the brightness of the room.

Then, through sleep, I heard my own voice again.

"I was in a minefield," I said, to no-one in particular.

*   *   *

When I awoke again it was night. I shifted in the bed, assaulted by a wave of savage hunger – a sure sign I was getting better. I was starting to assemble my dreams one by one on a long thread of consciousness, pulling them together like a string of beads, when I realised with a start there was another person breathing in the room. I sat up in a movement that astonished my stomach muscles, and made out the long shape of a man lying on the floor sleeping. In the grey light leaking through the roof of the tukul I could make out the startling slope of Michael's left cheekbone and the narrow curve of his shoulders. He seemed peacefully asleep, and for that I felt grateful. Perhaps it was because the minefield had suddenly made Sudan's war come luridly alive, but in that moment, I felt incredibly relieved not to have made a fool of myself with a man whose experiences I now realised were deeply, terribly untouchable. Lying there, in his dark room where once he lived with his wife, I wondered how I could have presumed to sully her memory with the cheap thoughts I had of his long, spare limbs and the curve of his strong back and the promise in those tawny oval-shaped eyes. The minefield had shown me, if I had needed showing, that being in Adek wasn't a game or an experience or an escape, but something far more profoundly real. And in that moment I was desperately glad we were sleeping together like this, chastely, like friends or siblings: me on his bed – where on long hot nights I could now admit I had too frequently imagined myself – and he on the floor, even as his chivalrous kindness embarrassed me.

Lying there completely without tiredness for the first time in months, I felt the same sense of safety I had felt in Michael's presence on that first night in Southern Sudan, when he had dragged me from my tukul during the bombing. The shivering noise of his breathing soothed me, easing the loneliness I felt knowing that my mother was gone again, vanished with my fever. The thought kept playing over and over in my clear head: I could have stepped into the minefield, but I didn't. I might have died – of malaria, from a mineblast – but I did not. Perhaps it wasn't so remarkable. The act of not dying, as every doctor knows, is a deep and unconscious reflex in us all. In Sudan's terms, I had not come any closer to death than a child who runs across a busy London road. All notions of probability ran away from me then. What difference is a one in ten chance, if you are the one and not the nine? Yet still I felt that something had changed: that I was now living in extra time, in a space I did not understand.

My mind floated away, liquid again, pondering the thin tightrope of life and death, the watery thread we mistake for a great river. I thought of the Commander, whom I now owed my life, crouching in the dust, feeling forward every step with the pinpoint tip of his machete. If we truly understood how fragile life was, I thought, wouldn't we proceed like that with every step through every day of our lives?

Something is Going to Fall Like Rain

Lying there on the hard platform of Michael's bed wrapped in his often-darned yet still impossibly white sleeping sheet, I was suddenly aware of the vast dark arc of the African sky above, its black heart pulsing with the flickering of the awakening stars that the Dinka believe are distant cattle camp fires of people who live in the sky. I thought of Bol's poem and how it described the night sky, like the black and white bull, as being everything at once, dark and light, night and starlight, absence and presence. That night, I dreamed in black and white, the colours of nothing and everything chasing each other into a spiral like cream stirred into coffee. And then at last, I slept, pulling Michael from his fitful sleep on the dusty floor into my lucid, fevered dreams.

Chapter Fifteen

I was three weeks sick with malaria before returning to work in the hospital, newly empathetic towards the patients who came in sweating and shivering and shouting for their mothers and those who simply lay prone under trees shaking in silence, lost entirely to life in the grip of a repeated attack. In Adek, we lost people to malaria all the time, and I began to wonder whether the quinine I was doling out from the buried medicine chest was really more effective than the treatment of herbs and barks I had been given by the Spear Master. Soon, I would have no choice but to learn his medicine, as the hospital's supplies were dwindling even as the food drops attracted thousands more people to Adek. Despite what Michael had told me about the Spear Master's anger with the white visitors, he had saved my life, and I desperately hoped this could be the beginning of some kind of relationship between us.

For my own part, I had gained a curious celebrity by surviving the minefield, meaning visitors to the hospital came not just to see Manute, the injured child soldier from the North, but also to stare at me, his doctor. It gave Manute and I strange kinship, which I sensed we both needed, even if we were barely able to communicate in one another's languages.

I was on my way to the hospital one early morning after the malaria, when Billy came back excitedly from the day's food drop, stopping me at the gate to our encampment to show me the four parcels he was carrying under his arm. Three were from his friends the pilots – little gifts we had come to rely on to make life more bearable in Adek. The first contained cigarettes, coffee and dried mangos; the second, water-purifying tablets, carbolic soap, pens, paper and painkillers. The third contained a packet of marijuana which Billy used both to bribe the soldiers and for personal use. The fourth, astonishingly, was addressed to me.

"Maria Marshall, c/o Lokichokio," Billy read out, studying the

116

battered manilla envelope. "Hope there's nothing in there that couldn't survive a 2,000 feet drop . . ."

He read the back of the envelope as he handed it over.

"M. Mendez . . . The Latino doctor boyfriend?"

"My brother," I said, taking the envelope from Billy. "Matthew."

"Different surname?"

"My mother's."

"Must be worried sick."

"I don't know how much he will know. Africaid are keeping it hushed up, aren't they? In case someone thinks of kidnapping us?"

"That was the plan. But we're on the news and all sorts now, according to my pilot buddies," Billy laughed. "Been on CNN for weeks. Why do you think they ain't bombing the fuck out of us any more? Cuz the whole goddamn world is watching. Bet your old BBC's even woke up to the action."

It hadn't occurred to me that the longer our isolation went on, the greater the outside world's concern would be. I tore open the envelope anxiously, but it was a birthday package, obviously sent long ago. At that point, Matt could not have known anything was wrong – and he still might not realise the full gravity of the situation, I thought. He lived in his own twilight restaurant world, working long hours in a Soho basement kitchen. He rarely saw daylight, let alone the news. A part of me was thankful that my mother was not alive to hear of her missing daughter. A worrier by nature, she would have been sick with distress. Our family had always been the tiny unit of the three of us – mum, Matt and me. At least there were no other relatives to see us on the news and panic.

"When's your birthday?" Billy asked, leaning over me to read the card, which pictured two fluffy kittens tied with red string and the words 'To Someone Special'. Matt specialised in bad cards, bought in the newsagent on Old Compton Street, around the corner from where he worked on Greek Street.

"December 3rd."

"That was months ago! It's February. Why in the hell didn't you tell us?"

"I didn't realise it was my birthday on the day itself, and then, well, there seemed no point celebrating it afterwards."

"Shit. Happy birthday."

I was laughing, but something in Matt's looping handwriting made me stop. I caught Billy looking at me oddly as I turned the package over in my hand, suddenly not wanting to open it.

"I'll leave you to open it in private," he said, with one of his rare shy grins. "Need to take this ganja over to the Commander."

"Save some for a birthday smoke?" I said.

Billy grinned.

"Sure," he said.

I sat down on the bed platform in my tukul to open the package properly, slitting through the thick brown masking tape with my penknife. Apart from the card, inside the parcel were two small packages wrapped in sparkling paper, and at the very bottom were five squashed chocolates that had melted deep into their wrappers so that they were soft to the touch and without shape. I knew them all from the colour of the papers: Hard toffee. Praline. Chocolate Brazil nut. Strawberry Cream. Caramel Cup. I thought of Matt choosing them carefully to go inside the package with a grin. Praline was mum's favourite. Matt's was the Brazil nut, mine the strawberry cream. Caramel Cup was a wild card. Toffee was the only sweet that hadn't melted on the long journey, more than 3,000 miles and an airdrop from England.

Sitting there I thought of all the things I could have had from London – all the things I wanted and missed. Selfish things, not real things like antibiotics and morphine and iodine. I had long ago run out of shampoo, and I had only a tiny dab or so of moisturiser left. These were things that in the absence of a hot bath or nice shoes or a sit down toilet, could make you feel suddenly human, even glamorous, again. I thought of a hot bath and a clean towel. A good book. A single squirt of perfume. A bunch of daffodils tied with elastic bands. A handful of purple, juice-thick blackberries hand-picked from a hedgerow. A glass of sweet, clear tap-water. A haircut. Clean sheets. A book of poems. A dog's bark. A takeaway curry. A bottle of blood-red wine, or cold, cloudy beer. A municipal swimming pool full of freezing, deep blue water and children splashing about ignoring the NO BOMBING signs. Freshly washed, still-warm clothes from the tumble drier. A walk in a wet pine forest, crushed needles under foot. A packet of crisps so salty and vinegary they could make your mouth sing. The Top 40 countdown on Radio 1 on Sunday nights. A new pair of box fresh trainers. A hot date. A busy road. Birdsong. A bridge over a river. Strong fresh coffee. A pint of deliciously cold milk swallowed down without breathing. A folded newspaper and a slice of hot buttered toast. For a moment the list seemed endless. But as I turned the bright sweets over in my hand glittering gold and purple and green, the vibrantly wrapped jewels of chocolate seemed the antidote to every deprivation my brain could dream of. These, after all, were things from another world – in their way as miraculous to Southern Sudan as any deep space asteroid fallen to earth. I thanked Matt silently as I piled them up on the bed like a handful of lost sea treasure.

It took me a while to find Adel and Bol, who were in the storeroom together, and sprang away from each other guiltily when I approached. I sought out Polio John too, finding him pedalling alongside Michael's long-legged walk, the pair of them heading out to the feeding centres. I led all four to the shade of the barren mango tree, where I pulled out the chocolates from a sticky pocket, having tried to remould them into their various distinct geometric shapes.

The three children looked on puzzled, but Michael laughed as he bent to let John climb down onto the fallen tree branch we used as a bench.

"Sweets," Michael said.

"Chocolates," I said. "From my brother, Matthew."

"I have never eaten a chocolate," Michael said. "But I have read about it. The raw material, I think, comes from Africa?"

I nodded.

"One of the slave crops: coffee, sugar, cocoa," Michael continued.

I was embarrassed, and unsure whether he wanted to try one. The children hung back too, as if startled by the colours.

"I have always wondered," Michael said, "what chocolate tastes like."

"Which colour would you like?"

He smiled.

"I think green, for Africaid."

Polio John chose the gold toffee. Bol waited for Adel to take the caramel cup and then took the purple Brazil nut, leaving me with my old Christmas favourite, the Strawberry Cream.

Inside each tiny, glittering package was a squashed, wet sweet, too sticky to unwrap. I licked mine straight from the wrapper. Eyes closed, I held the chocolate in my mouth for a moment, sucking at the strawberry sugar, playing with its sensuously thick texture with my tongue, letting the chocolate fill my mouth and flood my brain with endorphins, my mouth flickering with remembered pleasure and a thousand memories of trips to my grandparents and Christmases and birthdays and passed exams, the link between taste and memory as strong as an internal slideshow after so long without anything as harsh or chemical as processed sugar.

When I opened my eyes, I saw that Adel was standing with her mouth half open, her eyes wide with wonder, and that Bol was sucking his Brazil nut thoughtfully, but below us, Polio John's face was contorting as if he were choking. He stood twisting his jaw left and right, eyes bulging, poking a filthy finger into his mouth and making a low sound in the back of his throat. Realising he had the toffee, I tried to tell him to chew gently, but it was too late. John pulled a sticky wedge of sweet from his mouth with three fingers and held it up. Embedded in the toffee was a single perfectly-formed incisor, bright white against the chocolatey mass. He spat blood onto the floor by the fire and looked up accusingly at me, where I stood trying not to laugh.

"Yuk!" John shouted, spitting red again as Adel watched in alarm.

Bol stood staring at his friend, while folding his purple wrapper carefully and placing it in the pocket of the shorts Billy had given him. Michael laughed out loud, the happiest I had ever heard him.

"Sorry, John," I said, but John was sulky-faced and frowning. He dragged himself backwards away from the fire in disgust before climbing aboard his tricycle, and Bol and Adel went after him.

Still laughing, I looked over at Michael and he was looking disconsolately at the empty wrapper of his praline.

"You didn't like it?"

"It's . . ." He smiled shyly. "It's wonderful."

He screwed up the wrapper into a perfect metallic green ball. "If you could make the taste of pleasure into a thing, it would be that taste."

He had a slight smudge of chocolate on his lip, and whatever I had promised myself only nights ago in his tukul it was all I could do to resist the physical urge to kiss him where the melted smear blended into the blackness of his skin. But when he spoke I found myself stopped once more by the distance between us.

"The problem is, I should not have eaten it," Michael said.

He looked at his feet.

"We Sudanese grow cocoa in a place called Equatoria in the South of the country. It is a beautiful place where coffee and chocolate and wonderful things grow, but people there grow crops they never eat or even taste. The cocoa growers never taste their chocolate – at least not until Nestlé or some other big corporation processes it on another continent and sells it back to Africa at 100 times the price. People in

Equatoria have never eaten a piece of chocolate or tasted a cup of cocoa. Where Africans grow coffee there are international laws that make sure we cannot process it ourselves. Our sugar must be raw and unrefined until it comes back to us in bags with English writing or in a can of Coca Cola. And people wonder why Africa is so poor? Because we still grow the slave crops at slave prices. Trade keeps us poor."

I was stunned into silence, never having heard Michael speak more than a few sentences in a row, and never as passionately as this.

"But you drink coffee and I have seen you have sugar ..." I said, weakly, casting about for something that could restore the Quality Street miracle. "Why not chocolate?"

"This is impolite of me," Michael said. "This is not the way I should show gratitude for you sharing your gifts with us. I apologise." He hesitated. "I should explain that my wife came from cocoa-growers in Equatoria. She came to Bahr el Ghazal for me. Her father was a very educated man – one of the leaders of the revolution. He wanted her to be a doctor ... It was he who taught me that Africans should not eat chocolate."

This was as much in terms of personal detail as Michael had ever told me.

"I am so sorry about your wife," I said. "It has never seemed the right moment to say that to you."

I could still taste the last of the strawberry cream in my mouth, but it seemed a sad taste now, a taste of things gone that could not be resumed, the taste of the gulf between Michael and me.

"Thank you, Maria," Michael said. He got up, pocketing the little green ball of guilt. "And thank you for the sweet. I didn't mean to spoil your gift. Sometimes I think too hard about things, that's what Billy says."

I went back to my tukul to unwrap my presents, the momentary intoxication of the chocolate dissolving into the thin taste of empty saliva. Inside the first thin package of purple sparkling paper was the new Radiohead album, OK Computer, that there was no hope of playing as we had no CD player or electricity for that matter. In the second was a slim volume of poems by W.H.Auden and I flicked through it greedily, enjoying the unfamiliar sight of words typed onto a printed page. From inside the cover fell a bright, slightly blurred photograph of Matt and his blonde, curly-haired boyfriend Charlie on a winter sun beach somewhere. They looked tanned, happy and healthy. Behind it was a second photograph – a tiny baby with curled fingers and a squashed, red, wrinkled up face. A baby who looked like babies should, the sort of baby I had not seen in five months in Sudan. Its fat rude health and the clean white blanket it was wrapped in seemed almost obscene, and I flipped it over, unable to look any more at its pudgy, squashed-up face. "Richard Milligan 03/11/97 9lb 4oz," it said in blue biro. A friend from work, Sarah – a hearty physiotherapist with a stockbroker husband – had had a baby son, their second. Without knowing exactly why, I wept.

A thin piece of airmail paper told me not much and a great deal, all at the same time. Matt and Charlie had gone to put flowers on Mum's grave on November 8th, which would have been her 45th birthday. It had been constantly raining in London since I had left, and a sombre mood prevailed in Britain. Matt had been appointed sous-chef at the restaurant he worked for. The hours were long and the clientele finicky, but he was working with the finest imported ingredients and he had seen Posh Spice through the window of the kitchen when she had attended a special charity opening night.

"So we're both feeding the starving, Maria," Matt wrote in his deadpan way. "It's just most of the people I'm feeding deserve to be dead."

I sat for a moment with my head in my hands, knowing I was late for the hospital, but lost momentarily in the dull, insistent sound of distant city traffic and the pink neon lights of Soho, and the smell of rain hitting wet streets and the view from the window of Matt's south-of-the-river bedsit, where three too tall towerblocks stuck out at striking intervals, scraping the London sky. I thought of baby Richard, born by blessed accident of geography to suburban parents with two big dogs, a semi-detached home and a shiny estate car, wrapped up in organic terry towelling and rubbed in delicate oils and watched over by a Lithuanian au pair. For a cruel moment, I almost hated this child who had yet to do any living person a scrap of harm, but perhaps after all it was myself I was picturing, fat in a crib and already measuring my deprivations with differing howls of self-pity. I thought of Michael and his own lost child, and tried to imagine him standing on my friend's ostentatiously crunchy gravel drive among the manicured pots of privet, loading up the 4X4 with the vast amount of baby equipment apparently necessary for an afternoon trip to Brent Cross shopping centre.

What was I doing here, I wondered? How had it come to be February? I was two months late back to medical school. I shouldn't even be here.

I had left my own trajectory and was orbiting some other, lost path, thousands of miles from home.

Then, tying on my boots, I pushed all these thoughts away with a shake of my head. I was late for morning feeding and I had promised to look in on Chief Deng on the way. Everything outside the act of tying my shoelaces and smoothing down my shorts and running in the morning heat to the feeding centres would have to wait.

Chapter Sixteen

I am up on the roof of the building, the place where the Ghanaians showed me you could get to all those years ago when I was escaping the long lenses of the press pack below. Since I last came up here, it has been colonised by young people, dotted about with cigarette butts and the ends of joints stuffed with tiny torn-off pieces of coloured cardboard. There are empty, dented blue and silver lager cans up here and the cardboard and bone carcasses of Chicken Cottage dinners, and the occasional flaccid debris of a used condom. Someone has left a sodden old salad cream coloured blanket out in the wet and there are a couple of rickety red plastic chairs I recognise from the pub on the corner. The kids come at night in their hoods and their tracksuits, and the rise and fall of their street patois is inter-cut with bursts of angry music. But the rooftop is empty now, during the day.

I have made a mess of my life I think, standing with London spread out below me like a dirty tablecloth into which you could jump and disappear. Up above, two helicopters buzz like angry insects, chasing each other in irritable spirals. It is a Saturday, and down below I can see the snaking column of people coming along Victoria Embankment on the northern bank of the Thames headed for Westminster, protesting against the unfolding genocide in Darfur. I have been on these marches before, buoyed up by the optimism of the hoarse and footsore throng, walking with the cold of the pavements coming up through the soles of my trainers, thinking about the feeling of hard, red, stony earth between my toes and the relentless heat of the drylands burning the skin of my neck. I have stood in Trafalgar Square and huddled anonymously into the lee of a family, listening to speeches both outraged and pleading, a high-pitched sound and fury apparently inaudible to the people whose offices lie hundreds of yards away inside the Palace of Westminster. I had planned to be there today with one of the neighbour's lads, a tall bookish boy with old-fashioned glasses who intends to study politics at university against the wishes of his parents and likes to protest about things. I should be there but this morning I reached a sudden clarity about my fever – or have I known it all along? — that it is not flu or a virus, but the return of the malaria, ten years on. Like clockwork, like Grace, like all my chickens coming home to roost.

Standing here watching the trickle of protesting ants down below bunching and spreading, unaware of the legions of armoured police vans already lining Horse Guards and the small streets off Whitehall, I admit to myself for perhaps the first time, that the malaria is not the only recurring damage from Southern Sudan. That a decade ago a part of me died in Adek's marketplace. That my label of 'survivor' is not the whole story because not all of me survived. After Sudan, something closed off hard inside me, suddenly and painfully, as if a part of my inner self had been cauterised without anaesthetic, irreparably and violently damaged. Something burned and blackened began lurking in the corners of my imagination, a wounded minotaur stalking the bloodied chambers of my heart and mind.

There were people, of course, who wanted to help me. God knows my brother tried, and there were friends and colleagues whose kindness was overwhelming. But how could I accept help when the people who were killed that day had none? Why did I deserve the relief of a psychologist's couch, lying in some suburban office with the sounds of traffic passing below salving the sores and lesions of my conscience, when those who had truly lost everything and everyone they loved had only bitter herbs dried in the harsh sun to rub into their open wounds?

Yet today the crowd below rebukes me. I was the one that got away, and I have not helped those who saved me. It is still going on, the slow planned annihilation of black African Sudan. What happened that day in Adek village was only the rehearsal. A million people have already died, but that is nothing to what the Government and militias have planned for Darfur. There were so many things we didn't understand then. How the Chinese were already working the remote oilfields, supplying themselves with oil and the Sudanese Government with weapons to keep the oilfields clear and the dictatorship in power. The people who lived up on the surface above that black gold dreamed only of water, but their presence was an inconvenience and they were cleared like fields of weeds, burned and butchered and piled up high. Now Darfur resounds to the same widows' cries – its air is thick with the same murderous smoke and its fields run with blood. Meanwhile, the ceasefire in place in Bahr el Ghazal is heavily endangered, even now. Should it fail, Adek will be on the frontline once more when the Muhraleen horsemen come with their torches, guns and machetes.

My limbs frozen with malaria and my hands shaking with a terrible violence, I dare myself to look at the piece of stale decade-old newspaper in my pocket, but instead my fingers go automatically to the back of my neck, to the skin graft that came from my thigh. The skin is bunched up and textureless.

Standing on the roof, I haven't even the courage to jump.

Chapter Seventeen

I had been back at the feeding centres for a couple of weeks when Bol came running into the larger of the two high-roofed tents, his face covered in dust and sweat and worry.

"Maria! You must come quick!"

The baby I was struggling to persuade to feed burst into violent tears in my arms, and I gestured for Bol to keep his voice down.

"Is it Manute?"

My first thought was always for Manute. I worried that someone might harm him at the hospital or cause him to flee before his wounds were fully healed.

"It's Mrs Deng – the Chief's wife . . ." Bol said, in an urgent whisper. "She's having the baby . . ."

I shifted the child's weight in my arms so that he stopped crying suddenly. I was getting stronger now after the illness, and seemed better able to cope with life in Adek since the events of the minefield.

"The women don't like us to interfere in childbirth," I said. "She'll have the village midwife with her, and Adel will be there. She is almost a nurse herself now you know . . ."

"Adel is asking for you," Bol said. For a moment, he looked as if he might cry. "The Chief is asking for you . . . There is something wrong . . ."

There was no time to fetch the vehicle, so we ran most of the ten minutes to Chief Deng's compound despite the furnace of the afternoon heat, arriving sweating and breathless. A group of women were standing outside the main family tukul in bright sarongs, and they hushed their voices when they saw us approach.

"Mrs Ajuong," I called, recognising an old patient who I knew could speak a little English.

Mrs Ajuong grabbed my hand and pulled me through the waiting women to the door of the tukul, through which a muffled screaming came

127

in indistinct bursts like gunfire. Inside the door, Chief Deng was waiting agitatedly, pacing up and down.

"She won't see me, Maria."

"Men are forbidden to see women in childbirth, aren't they?" I said, in what I hoped was a soothing voice. "Even Chiefs?"

I was trying to avoid interfering, as I knew well the wrath of the midwives. There were certain aspects to Dinka medicine that were not for Westerners or even witchdoctors.

"It is not going well," Deng said. "It has been twenty-four hours already. You must help her."

In the background, the screaming stopped, and I saw that the absence of sound made the Chief more afraid than the noise itself. This was his second wife, I thought. This must be her first child.

"Please Maria."

"It will make problems."

The Chief walked to the door of the tukul and stopped at its entrance. He spoke without turning back to me.

"Adel's mother died in childbirth," he said. "I could not bear . . ."

When he turned back to me, I nodded.

"You'll need to send someone to the hospital to fetch the medical equipment I need," I said.

"It is already done," he said.

*   *   *

Time slipped away after that in the way it does during moments of intense concentration, flowing into the oddly cool air of the makeshift birthing room – a mud-walled bedroom with a patched-up mosquito net where the Chief and his wife normally slept. As part of medical school training we were required to assist in several births and I struggled to remember the procedure, as Adel ran in and out fetching towels and hot water and keeping admirably calm for a fourteen year old girl whose father's young wife was in agonising labour. I wondered then whether she had witnessed the death of her own mother in childbirth. There are so few secrets in Dinka life.

My biggest fear was that the baby might be breeched or that Mrs Deng would need a caesarean – an operation I had never even observed – but it seemed to me she was only exhausted after months without a proper diet, and I concentrated on bringing her fluids and sugars up, watching the colour come back into her grey face. In truth, I had done very little when the baby's shocked head appeared suddenly through the blood and watery mess on the towels I had laid across the dirt floor on top of the animal skins and sarongs. When the child itself slid out after it, a beautiful baby boy with a tangle of wet hair and a squashed, triangular-shaped mouth and Adel's almond-shaped eyes, I was stunned more than anything that such a thing was possible, staring at the cord I should have been cutting with a wonder I had felt only a few times before in medicine. After so many months of prising the hard little bodies of dead babies from their parents' reluctant arms, the act of laying a living, breathing newborn child into a mother's trembling hands seemed nothing short of miraculous. The Chief named his fifth child and first son Akak, after his own father, and refused to believe I had played no real part in keeping his baby boy and wife alive.

At the campfire that night I was euphoric with adrenalin, filled with a nervous energy despite the exhaustion I felt from the five hours or so I had spent with Mrs Deng. Billy was also in celebratory mood, having just finished a new palette wood and tarpaulin extension to the feeding centres in which we could treat the malnourished elderly – a group he and I both felt we were failing in our efforts to feed Adek's most vulnerable. We sat by the campfire smoking a large roll-up built from pure African grass, and drinking whiskey donated by the Commander. Adel and Bol were still at Chief Deng's compound, and there was no sign of Michael or Sean. No longer used to alcohol, I felt as giddy as a teenager and curiously untouchable, as if the bush itself were a benevolent force intent only on protecting me. For the first time since I had stood in the minefield, Africa seemed suddenly once more both benign and hopeful and I felt myself smiling at the darkness out beyond the fire where the village lay.

"Have you ever noticed how all babies smell like hope?" I said, pouring another generous inch of Jack Daniels into my tin mug.

Billy laughed, leaning back against the fallen log, his hat in his lap, offering a rare sighting of the thick, dark brown suede of his hairline.

"I noticed you smell like iodine," he said, looking up to where I was looking down on him. He sniffed the air. "And soap." He sniffed again. "And something else unmentionable, like blood."

He handed me the joint.

"Chief Deng's wife is only twenty-three years old," I said. "She's the same age as me."

"And?"

"I thought she was about forty."

"African women work hard. They have a lot of kids."

"They lose a lot of kids."

I was thinking of the children we had lost that morning at the feeding centre. Four tiny children who left behind flesh and bones so insubstantial it hardly seemed necessary to bury them. A light breeze would have blown them to Lual Aghony, the Dinka's promised land.

"Today, it was four to one," I said. "Four to famine and disease. One to us."

"One to you," Billy said.

He was worrying at a hole in his red Willie Nelson and the Outlaws T-shirt, and I wondered if I should offer to sew it for him with some medical thread.

"One to Mrs Deng," I said.

For a moment, I thought Billy was putting his arm around me, but then his hand came away jumping, and I saw he had trapped a large flying insect that must have been crawling along my shoulder.

"Don't kill it, Billy."

"Why not?"

"Because it's not poisonous."

"How do you know?"

"Because if it was poisonous you would already have stamped on it."

Billy flicked the insect away into the darkness and it started up an angry whirring somewhere by the kitchen hut. A log cracked under the flames, and I poked it with a stick, pushing it up closer to its neighbours. Billy had lit the fire for food, but the thought of eating made me feel tired. I hadn't had much appetite since the malaria.

"Do you know what Bol asked me today?" Billy said.

"Was it about girls?"

"How did you know?"

"He's in love with Adel," I said.

Billy sat upright and lifted his hat back on to his head in one movement.

"Seriously?"

I laughed.

"What are you, blind?"

Billy tapped his foot with the stick he was holding.

"I'm happy for them," I said. "Adel likes him too. I can tell."

"But, shit, she's way out of his league . . ."

I laughed at Billy acting the outraged parent.

"I don't think he's planning on asking her to the prom. Anyway, he's good-looking, and he's a poet – every girl's dream. Everyone likes him . . ."

"This ain't no soap opera, Maria," Billy said. "Adel is a Chief's daughter. She can't just . . ."

He stopped abruptly, placing his hand on my arm. A second later, Bol's face appeared in the firelight.

"Hi Bol," I said, too brightly. "How's Mrs Deng?"

"She is very well," Bol said.

"And how's Adel?" Billy asked, casually.

I nudged him painfully with my elbow.

"She's fine," Bol said, head down, looking at the fire. "She's with Michael and her father attending the birth."

"Have a drink with us, Bol," I said. "We're celebrating."

"Celebrating?"

"The birth of Akak Deng."

Bol sat down next to us, a bit warily I thought. Perhaps we were more drunk than we realised, or maybe he was just nervous of Billy's teasing.

"Have you seen Sean?" I asked him.

"Sean is in his tukul," Bol said. "He is feeling sick of the stomach." He lowered his voice. "The Chief is very pleased with you, Maria."

"Well, you can tell the Chief that it was his wife who did all the work," I said. "I had nothing to bloody do with it."

Billy poured a splash of whiskey into his own cup, and handed it across to Bol.

"Stop it, Billy," I said, trying to take the cup from him.

"It won't hurt him," Billy said. "It's only a splash. Go on Bol."

Bol sipped from the cup, coughed and made a face.

"What d'you reckon?"

"Nice."

"You liar!" I said.

"The boy needs to learn how to drink whiskey," Billy said, pouring Bol another slug.

"He's thirteen years old," I said.

"It's your initiation soon, right Bol?"

"Yes, very soon," Bol said, accepting the cup and screwing up his face as he drank.

"So he's nearly an adult," Billy said. "It's like turning twenty-one in America. Except they cut your face and send you off to the wilderness for a few weeks to see if you can handle it."

I had become used to the weals and welts and blistered patterns of scarification, but the thought of Bol's handsome face being cut still made me wince. The Dinka cut their faces in long lines following the slant of the eyebrows, and I had occasionally been called on to clean a wound that had become infected. If the lines were cut too close it was hard for the skin to heal.

"In Tennessee, you just get one of these," Billy said, pulling down his pants an inch at the back to show a small tattooed cross at the base of his spine. The middle section of the cross was perfectly aligned with the tan-line where his walnut-brown back met the pale white skin below his shorts. I wondered that I had never noticed the top section before.

"What does it mean?" Bol asked, apparently as fascinated by the startlingly bright white flesh below the tan-line as by the tattoo itself.

"It's a symbol of Christianity," I said. "Christians believe God sent down his son to earth, and people killed him by nailing him to a cross."

"Why did they do that?" Bol asked.

"Because, they didn't understand him," I said. "I don't know. It's just a story."

"A long story," Billy said, slurring his words a little.

He laughed.

"Funny how this war's supposed to be Muslims versus Christians, yet there ain't a damn Christian in Bahr el Ghazal province 'cept those who changed their names Biblical for food . . ."

We talked for a while about Gods, until the whiskey was half empty and Bol had dozed off in front of the fire with the effect of the drink and the effort of understanding the language.

"He's a good 'ol boy," Billy said, raising his mug to Bol. "One of the finest."

"Would you like a son?" I asked. "I mean – do you want kids? Are they in your plans?"

"Sometimes, I think so," Billy said. "But sometimes I think I'm better at being on my own." He shrugged. "My own parents didn't do so great, you know?"

He lowered his mug.

"Why, you offering?"

Bol stirred a little in his sleep and I got up and lifted him by the shoulders.

"Bed!" I said, firmly directing his sleep-heavy body in the direction of his tukul. "Drinking whiskey with the grown-ups. Off you go and get some sleep. There's a big drop tomorrow. You and Billy need to be up early."

Billy and I sat in silence for a while, watching the yellow flames flickering and jumping. The fire was low now, and I went to the woodpile and lifted a split log, checking for wood spiders before carrying it across to the fire and placing it exactly as Billy had shown me a few weeks and a lifetime ago.

"What are you thinking about?" I asked him.

"I was thinking about Bol. How he feels about Adel. That first thing you feel for someone."

His answer took me by surprise.

"Who was your first love?" I asked, taking the joint from his hand and closing one eye against the pungent smoke.

"My wife," Billy said.

I exhaled slowly.

"You're married?"

"Not exactly," Billy said. "Just never got divorced."

"That makes you married."

"I was sixteen years of age, and it was nineteen years ago."

"That still makes you married." I calculated. "And thirty-five years old."

We sat for a while, looking at the fire and its shapes. The patterns in the flames, the swirls and dragons and snakes and grasses, told me I was more stoned than I had realised. Billy's brown eyes were half-closed against the smoke from the fire.

"Her parents had the neighbouring farm," Billy said after a while, as if that explained it all. He laughed. "It was a good blending of cattle stocks."

"How was the blending of human stock?"

"Terrible," Billy said.

I heard myself giggle inappropriately – the effect of the grass.

"It only lasted two years and by then we couldn't stand the sight of each other," Billy said after a while. "Problem is divorce ain't looked upon too highly in Tennessee, even if Dolly Parton did sing about it. So, I did a runner. Walked out one sunset and never went back." He whistled a bar of a country song I half recognised.

"So you ran away and became an aidworker?" I said, helping myself to more whiskey, having made the calculation I was going to have a bad headache in the morning whether I had another drink or not. "It's a romantic story."

"Aidworker by way of McWorker, soldier, sailor, thief . . . All the things a man does on the run. Anyway, we're all doing it . . ."

"Doing what?"

"Running."

"Who's we?"

"Aidworkers. UN people. NGO staff."

"What about Sean?"

"Youngest son of missionaries," Billy said, shrugging. "Lived in Africa most of his childhood. Congo, Eritrea, Angola, then back to Belfast by eleven for his teenage years. He's still doing the same, but without the God stuff. His parents were running, and now he's running the only way he knows how. He's got two IRA brothers, one's in prison and one's on the run. You could say running runs in the family."

"Aid work and terrorism are pretty diverse ways of earning a living."

"Is that so?" Billy said. "I s'pose you noticed our hosts in Adek village – the Sudan People's Liberation Army? There's a hundred different ways to try and change the world, not just those that are lawful."

"They say Commander Wol has killed 1,000 men. Aidworkers don't kill."

Billy laughed.

"Oh, you'd better believe it."

Billy took the bottle from me and drank a long swallow from it.

"Were you really a thief?" I said, changing the subject.

"Only once. In Mexico. Stole two fishes from a market stall."

"And now you're feeding the five thousand," I said.

There was a long pause then, filled by the distant crying of the children at the feeding centres, a sad lullaby borne on the wind. It seemed to ebb and flow like the songs that carried from the cattle camp to the empty scrubland beyond. It was a desperately sad sound, the inverse melody of the sound a mother makes when she sings her child to sleep. Without warning, a lone tear tripped down my cheek. I was drunk, I thought, and homesick and suddenly at terrible odds again with this strange world in which I was trapped.

"Do you miss your folks?"

I wiped the tear on my hand, and it made a mark in the dust.

"I miss my mum and my brother and my friends," I said. "How about you?"

"I miss my folks of course," Billy said. "But I'd rather miss them at a distance than hate 'em close up."

"My mother died just before I came here," I said, surprising myself. "She had bowel cancer."

Out loud it didn't sound as bad as I had feared. I wondered why I hadn't said it in all those weeks.

"At last it makes sense," Billy said. He let out a long low whistle from between his front two teeth.

"What makes sense?"

"You'd just finished your medicine degree, but you couldn't save your own mother. And that's why you're in Africa."

Whiskey flooded my brain like white rage.

"Jesus," I said. I was shaking. "Who died and made you Jerry fucking Springer?"

"Who's Jerry Springer?"

I laughed despite myself.

"Sometimes I wonder what planet you're from," I said.

"I've been on Planet Africa a long time. Who's Jerry Springer?"

"A US TV talkshow host. He gets desperate messed up people up on stage and then offers them single sentence, trite self-help-by-numbers solutions to their woes."

"Ah, I see. I knew I was missing some great television back home."

"That's only the half of it."

"But I'm right?" Billy asked.

"About what?"

"With the trite pop psychology?"

"Does it matter?"

"Yes."

"No, you are not right."

"In no way at all?"

"My mother didn't want saving. She wanted to die. She wanted an end to the pain she was suffering."

"As I said. You wanted to save her but you couldn't."

"Just don't take up psychology professionally, okay?"

I felt Billy stiffen next to me.

"What?"

"It just gets me, is all."

135

"What?"

"Women are always the same. It's always, hmm, let's see what makes Billy Finn tick. Let's bring out all his dirty washing and air it and have a good ol' look ... I bet you've reached a million ground-breaking conclusions about how fucked up I am and why ... Did he have a bad childhood, tick – a messed up marriage, tick – a screw loose somewhere in his stupid head, tick. I can feel you prying into the tiny corners of my mind, and let me tell you, you ain't gonna find anything noteworthy there at all."

Billy had raised his voice to a growl I didn't recognise.

"You're the one with the theories," I said. "You're the one obsessed with working out everyone's motivation for everything ..."

"And you don't think about it all? About what the fuck we are all doing in this goddamn shithole? Jeez, you are even more stupid than I thought ..."

"Why are you being like this?"

"Because your bullshit is tiring me."

I surprised myself then by bursting into tears.

"Aw, shit ..." Billy said, reaching his arm around me.

I shrugged him off.

"It's fine," I said. "It's nothing to do with you. I just keep crying at the moment. I can't stand any more at the feeding centres. I can't bear the hospital and I can't cope with being stuck here. It's too much ..."

I was properly crying now in great wrenching sobs, whiskey-liberated tears for the children at the centres and the birth of Akak Deng and for my mother and myself. My hair had fallen out of its tie and into my face, and I pushed it angrily out of my eyes, trying to breathe and stop the torrents of water falling from my eyes.

"Damn," Billy said. "I don't know what gets into me sometimes."

"I do," I said. "You're a complete arsehole."

He put his arm back around me and I let him keep it there, but only for a moment. It was disconcertingly comforting, the warmth and strength and heaviness of it. But I was still angry with him and I pushed Billy off and sat up, away from him.

"If you must know, Doctor fucking Freud, my mum was pretty depressed most of our childhood," I said. "Our dad was around when I was born, and then when mum was pregnant with my brother, Matt, he left. He went, and he didn't come back, and we waited all this time, and my mum used to say 'He's gone away, but he'll be back soon,' and after a while we realised that wasn't true. So mum was pretty depressed and in denial about everything, and she was kind of hard to live with. And the only time she used to smile was when she talked about Africa. Even when she was dying her face would light up talking about the Sahara or the Kalahari tribesmen or the flamingos that make the Great Lakes turn pink, or the souks in Morocco. Matt and I grew up knowing we would come to Africa one day. We both loved it like no other space or place. Our own garden was a little domesticated piece of the Masai Mara. Until I was seven or eight, I thought that jungle had the texture of ivy, that lions were giant tomcats and that the whole continent looked like brown concrete. So that's why I'm here. Only it's hard to explain to someone that you hardly know, especially when they ask you rudely on your first day in the field without even looking at you, you know?"

I pulled a cigarette from Billy's packet, and stood up to light it from the fire.

"You know, you're right," Billy said. "I am an asshole."

"I should go to bed," I said.

Chapter Eighteen

I have asked myself the same questions a thousand times about the night Chief Deng's son was born. Why hadn't I just gone alone to my hard bed under the mosquito net as I had done all those nights before? Why had I drunk so much whiskey when such a long morning lay ahead and the work in the feeding centres had grown so hard? Why hadn't I listened to the small, tired voice inside my head that kept telling me to stop?

Maybe it was because we had buried those four children that morning, three little daughters and a son belonging to families newly arrived from the bush: children who seemed so small and delicate, their skin papery enough to blow away had they not been wrapped in white muslin and weighted down by stones from the dry riverbed. Maybe it was because the loneliness of four unpredictable, harrowing months under the vast emptiness of the African sky had just reached breaking point. Maybe it was the miracle of Adel's brother's birth, the surprise of something so startlingly hopeful in an arena of death and despair. Maybe it was just plain, unadorned physical need. In the end, of course, wondering why doesn't change anything. What happened happened, and although we couldn't have known the consequences we might have known no good would come of it.

It was my fault. I want to be clear about that. That night, the night everything changed, I could have just gone to bed and nothing would have happened. But feeling the unfamiliar comfort of a loose connection with another person, I was suddenly afraid of being once more alone. So, instead of going to bed, I sat down again with Billy by the fire. And as the whiskey levelled off lower and lower in the bottle and the unbroken heat grew more bearable as the night reached its dark heart, I stood up, took Billy's hand and led him after me to the hard bed I had slept in those last twelve long weeks. For a while, we lay fully clothed in the hot darkness, not touching, listening to the scratching of the creatures that lived in the roof, while above us the mosquito net seemed suspended in the air like a ghost, caught by the moonlight that leaked into the tukul. For a moment the simple act of not being alone seemed to be enough. Then, as I was falling into sleep, Billy pulled my face towards him on the pillow stuffed with my clothes and kissed me hard, his sour tongue tasting of whiskey and cigarettes and his hair smelling of sweet African grass. I remember forcing his sharp stubble against my face, needing the friction, wanting to scratch my own face raw, climbing onto him so that I could feel the hardness of his body against mine, wanting to feel something, anything other than the despair that had flooded my heart since that morning in the minefield. We had both been months without any form of physical closeness, even a hug, and I found myself pulling off Billy's T-shirt and tracing every long muscle with my fingers and following the long scar under his ribs, struck by the miracle of this sudden physical closeness with another human self, the sudden connection as our bodies slid together in the wet heat. He smelled of sweat and dirt and wood smoke and I drank in the scent thirstily, sick of the antiseptic smell of the hospital and the porridge steam of the feeding centres and the hard familiarity of my own body. For one long moment of silence interrupted only by the whisper of falling clothes and the screams of distant cicadas, I felt as if I had never been this close to another person in my whole life, as if the thin glass between our two selves had fractured and fallen away. I remember that I paused for a moment with Billy underneath me, his eyes wide open looking up at the roof so that I could see close up the speckled stars and planets of his brown irises, twin universes in sepia, struck by the thought that I had pictured this moment the very first time we met. Only I had imagined it simple and unemotional, like sex in a film, driven by uncomplicated need, by the hot nights and the death all around and two people's need for proof that they were painfully, screamingly alive. I had imagined an age-old formula of physical combinations unlocking a stark relief: the forgetfulness of living precisely inside one moment. I had imagined us in Billy's bed, with him quickly asleep and me creeping back to my own tukul to lie awake listening to the wind and the scratching spiders and the sound of my own heartbeat subsiding. But as it turned out, it wasn't like that at all. For the briefest moment, a single beat of time that was without history or future, Billy looked at me and I looked at him and we understood each other without words, in a silence that was heavy and complete and utterly present – full of remembering not forgetfulness. I found myself crying with my whole body, every wet, living cell awash with tears. Then, as the pulse at my throat restarted, thudding and thumping once more along the tickertape of my lifeline, I was the one who fell fast and soundly asleep.

Chapter Nineteen

The next morning, I awoke alone under my mosquito net in the knowledge that something was badly wrong. A plane was whirring heavily overhead, and in my confusion I thought it must be the Government Antonov with its cargo of bombs. Billy's red Outlaws T-shirt lay on the bed next to me, and I pulled it on as I went quickly to the door of the tukul, my legs wrapped in my sleeping sheet, my whiskey-damaged head banging and throbbing with the drone of the engines. Outside, people were running from all directions across the camp, waving up at the plane. Billy was running ahead of them, naked from the waist up, with the laces of his boots flapping and the belt of his jeans hanging down. Squinting at the sky I saw it was the low-flying Hercules from Lokichokio that was buzzing angrily overhead, lapping the barren fields as if it were unsure where to drop its load.

I looked at my watch. 7.06am. We had overslept by more than an hour. And Billy had not laid the markers for the food drop.

I grabbed a pair of long shorts from the floor of my tukul, pulling on my boots as I ran, laces trailing after me. As I reached the perimeter gate, Billy was already throwing markers into the back of one of the vehicles.

"What are you doing?" I shouted, above the noise of the plane.

"Going to the drop zone."

"You're not going to make it. The plane's about to drop."

"Get out of my way."

"I'm coming with you."

"It's dangerous, Maria . . ."

Billy leapt into the front seat of the jeep, wrenching at the gear stick with a heavy crunch, and I climbed in next to him as he tried in vain to lock the passenger door. Even as he turned the vehicle around, I could see the plane was already dropping.

"Get out of the truck, Maria," Billy said.

Sean appeared at the open window on the passenger side, shouting across me to Billy.

"What the fuck's going on?"

"Get out the goddamn way," Billy shouted back, revving the engine.

"What the hell happened?"

Billy crunched the gears again, slamming the car forward, then braking heavily as Michael's face appeared on the driver's side. I saw the goodness in him then, already half-smiling, thinking to calm the situation, knowing there would be a perfectly good explanation. He looked at me with equal confusion, and for a split second I saw him glance down at the red Outlaws T-shirt and his face seemed both to physically fall and rearrange itself in a single fluid movement.

"They need to get to the drop zone," he said, quietly, pulling the angry blur of Sean aside to let us pass.

Billy forced the vehicle forward in short bursts, piloting it through the tall trees that lined the side of the perimeter and across the edge of the village, throwing up huge chunks of dirt and clouds of dust that made the villagers scatter. He drove with one hand, fastening his belt with the other, and I could not look at his face, concentrating on holding onto door and dashboard, protecting myself with my arms against the rise and fall of the bumping, suspension-damaged vehicle. But before we reached the start of the empty land designated as the drop zone, we could already hear the rat-a-tat sound of the second load of heavy wooden palettes hitting the ground from a great height, like machine-gun fire only louder and heavier. Through the tree cover, I saw the heavy palettes flying from the opening at the back of the plane like tiny specks of black, like birds or bombs.

"DO NOT DROP!" Billy was screaming into the radio as we drove into the dustcloud. "LOKI DO YOU READ ME?" And then: "Shiiiiiit . . .".

For a moment we drove into nothingness, into the eye of a red storm. Then Billy stopped the car suddenly and switched the engine off. We sat for a moment in silence, watching the air dance in thick red and yellow dust, waiting to see if a palette would land on our vehicle – a moment of long drawn-out suspense that felt like a yellow-red ending to the world. The air slowly cleared in time for us to see the suddenly empty plane shooting rapidly up into the air and turning to head back towards Loki. As it rose, Billy wrenched open the driver's door and jumped out, running in the direction of the dropped palettes. Not knowing what else to do, I followed him into the dust.

Billy was running hard and it was a few moments before I caught up with him where he had stopped dead, his breath ragged, his hands on his hips. Dust clung to both our faces where it had settled onto the shiny surface of sweat. As the air cleared, I saw the barren ground adjacent to the drop zone was littered with dozens of palettes drowned in red dust. Ahead of them, a single tukul on the edge of the village stood shattered, splintered into firewood with a great hole at its middle. It was Polio John's tukul, I realised, with a lurching feeling in the pit of my stomach. It was Polio John's home and all I could see was the flattened roof.

Billy got to the crushed tukul before I did, tearing at the mud and earth with his bare hands, ripping wood from wood and levering into the mud with a huge pole that had once supported the doorframe. He had half-disappeared up to his waist before I had even climbed across the broken roof, and I had to scramble past him to gain a foothold in the dry mud and splintered branches. After the roar of the plane, there was complete silence, broken only by our digging.

"John!" I shouted, my voice hoarse with dust and fear. "John!" I used my hands to dig at the straw roof, cursing their fragility, ripping through the woven reeds with broken nails. After a moment, I thought I heard a muffled voice underneath us.

Billy seemed dazed by his efforts and carried on digging, his body shaking violently with the effort or shock or both.

"Billy!" I called. "Under here." I was convinced now that I could hear John's voice, coming from under the roofing.

Billy put his ear to the straw, then pulled his knife out of his pocket and began cutting quickly and carefully through the roof, using the blade to slit out a strip and then tearing away huge pieces with his hands. Then, together, we heaved a huge sack of grain away from its position buried in the ground. The palette around it had splintered and caught on Billy's arm so that it began to bleed heavily. Billy seemed not to notice. He was working methodically now, almost calmly, and I worked next to him, dragging at the straw of the shattered roof, cursing myself because I had no bandage for Billy's arm, nor means of treating John if he came out alive.

Minutes passed that seemed like hours, and then I saw the shape of a shoulder or a knee below the straw and caught Billy's arm as it swung down.

"There," I said.

Billy ripped back the remaining section of roof and mud to reveal John's head and shoulders. The boy's eyes were closed with pain and blood trickled stickily from a gash on his head. He was trapped horizontally to the ground, as if lying in a grave.

"John," I whispered. "We're going to get you out."

"Hullo Maria," John said.

I suddenly remembered his mother was in the feeding centre with his sister, and I almost wept with relief. But John was whispering between clenched teeth.

"Say again," Billy said.

"Baba. My father," John whispered in mixed Dinka and English.

His eyes opened briefly and then closed again.

"We'll find him," I said.

I noticed my own hands were bleeding, and tried to wipe the mud and blood onto my shorts to clean them.

"Okay John," Billy said. "Can you move your neck? Don't try and twist it, just gently see if it moves."

"I can," John said, his lips moving this time to reveal muddied teeth and tongue. His face creased again with pain. "It's my legs."

Billy and I looked at each other. Then, Billy knelt next to him and spoke gently.

"Don't move, John," he said. "We're going to get you out of there, but you need to lie as still as possible while we dig." He turned towards me but did not look at me directly. "Start digging carefully, moving your hands away from his body. Start by his head, like this." He pulled mud away towards himself.

As I dug, almost relishing the punishing pain in my bloodied hands, Billy began slicing and digging again a few metres away from John, calling out for the boy's father, cutting into the roofing with his knife, lifting huge lumps of mud and wood out with his bare hands so that the muscles in his neck stood out at his scarlet throat.

"Where are the others?" Billy muttered from time to time, scanning the empty horizon for our other vehicle. "Come on Sean, where the fuck are you?"

When John was almost clear of the mud, Billy asked me to see if there was a first aid kit or some water in the car. There was only water. Billy trickled some across John's mouth and nose, washing it clear of mud. John spat weakly. Lying free of the mud in a deep trench made by our digging, I could see his legs were badly shattered, his left knee twisted painfully under him and his right thigh bloodied and exposed almost to the bone. His right shoulder also hung badly, as if it might be dislocated.

"We need to get him to the hospital," I said. "I've nothing here."

"Find me two long straight sticks," Billy said, indicating the remains of the doorframe with his head. He was slashing at a bag of grain with his knife so that the grains spilled out on the dry earth. Together, we fashioned a kind of stretcher from the wood and fabric as John opened and closed his eyes, seeming to slip in and out of consciousness.

"What about his father?" I whispered.

"We'll get him out," Billy said, but he didn't look at me when he spoke.

As we finished the stretcher, I recognised the low growl of the other Land Rover.

"I'm so sorry," I whispered.

Billy shook his head.

"Don't be," he said. "It's my fault, not yours."

But it was both our faults, and both of us knew it.

The Land Rover screamed to a halt a few yards from the broken remains of the tukul and Sean leapt out of the passenger seat carrying my medical kit, with Michael and Bol jumping out behind. They took in the scene in front of them with a look of horror and I found myself looking at my surroundings as if for the first time: John lying in agony with his shattered legs, a muddied Billy bleeding profusely from his arm, tying the stretcher with his good hand. Bol jumped into the trench next to John, whispering to his friend.

"Both his legs are broken," I told Sean, quietly. "His shoulder may be dislocated."

Billy stood there, shattered. His body was scratched and battered, his face broken.

"His father's under here, somewhere," he told Sean. "We have to keep looking."

Sean nodded. Michael had stood there, a single, solid tall tree amongst a scene of devastation, doing and saying nothing, but hearing John's father was missing, he began walking around the exposed dirt, studying it carefully and calling softly for John Snr.

Before the stretcher moved off, I felt along the length of John's body, checking at his neck, his spine, his hips and then his legs. I pulled a syringe and a needle from the white medical kit and injected John with one of the hospital's last phials of morphine – drugs we had found together weeks ago, digging for treasure in the burned out ruins of the old clinic. He made no sound when the needle went in, only closed his eyes more tightly. I bandaged the bleeding leg, but left the other leg alone at its strange angle. Then I stroked his face.

"Am I going to the hospital, Maria?" John said, in a strange voice.

"Yes."

"Good."

Sean and Michael lifted the stretcher quickly onto the back of the white Land Rover, and I climbed in with John, thinking to steady the stretcher as the vehicle moved.

Sean pulled a bandage from the first aid kit and threw it at Billy.

"Put that on your arm," he said. "Before you bleed to death."

Then, he threw the vehicle's keys to Michael to drive us to the hospital, but Michael shook his head and threw them back.

"I will stay here," he said. He looked at me when he spoke and his expression was completely empty as if we had never met. "I must look for my friend, John Adior Mapel."

I climbed out of the vehicle, shame burning my face and neck.

"I'll drive us to the hospital," I said. "Bol can go in the back with John and keep his legs and shoulder still."

"Okay," Sean said. "Send back more men from the village to help."

Behind him, Michael was already digging calmly into the dirt, alongside Billy to whom he had yet to speak a word.

I leaned across the battered tailgate at the back of the vehicle to whisper to John where he lay on the stretcher with Bol supporting his head and legs.

"You are so brave, John," I told him. "You are so brave and your mother will be so proud when she sees you. And your sister. They are both safe at the feeding centre. Now try to stay awake for me. Try to stay awake and squeeze Bol's arm when it really hurts."

John nodded, and struggled to speak. Bol put his head next to his friend's ear and listened carefully.

"He is talking about the tricycle," Bol said. "He says it is safe at the hopsital."

I drove slowly between the shattered palettes and back up towards the village, but I could still hear John cry out with every bump of the rough ground, every shout a deserved blow to my guilty heart. Every now and then, Bol would bang on the metal at the back for me to stop the vehicle, pausing to rearrange John's body more comfortably on the stretcher and wetting his mouth and lips with drops of water. He held his friend's body carefully with his own legs and held onto the sides of the vehicle with his arms, trying to stop the bumps from hurting John. Above us the sky was already hot and yellow, the sun now a fully formed ball of fire. I pictured John's father, a gentle giant with kind brown eyes. The sky was so blue it hurt. The day was only just beginning and already we had killed a man.

Chapter Twenty

Everything changed after that day. In one single moment, on one hot night, under the straw roof of a small mud hut in a tiny compound in Africa's largest country which spans a million square miles. A heartbeat of time in the grand scheme of history, but a lifetime in one small village on the frontlines of a forgotten war. On the long nights that followed there was no more sitting up at the campfire, no more whiskey camaraderie, no more putting the world to rights, perhaps because it seemed the world was no longer capable of being righted. None of us – not even Sean – attended John's father's funeral, as it was clear we were not welcome there. There was a sense of mutiny towards our presence from some of the more volatile pockets of the village as rumours spread that the UN had killed a man and injured a poor, crippled boy. Still Adek could not banish us, its villagers as dependent on our presence as we were on them. No plane could come for us, and we could not have survived more than a few hours exile in the hostile territory of the interior. The village would have lasted only days without the food drops.

On the day of the mis-drop another thing happened that gave us all cause for further misgiving. Manute vanished into the bush, and despite all the Commander's protestations, I refused to believe the SPLA had nothing to do with it. The boy had been well for some time – the bullet wound in his shoulder nicely healed and his epilepsy calmer – and I had been keeping him in the hospital more for his own protection than medical necessity. But I was worried that he was now being kept at the barracks by SPLA soldiers and might be ill-treated, tortured or worse. I doubted he was strong enough to make the journey back to the North, and in any case, as a deserter he would have been returning to an uncertain fate. But the Commander became angry when I questioned him, and I knew I had no chance of reaching the barracks without someone seeing me and returning me to the village. Polio John took over Manute's bed in the hospital and slowly I began to accept that the boy

148

soldier from the North was not coming back. Even so, I missed him, the boy with the nightmares and the strange, heavy-lidded eyes.

After the day we dug John's broken body from the earth and rubble, Billy and I avoided each other by unspoken mutual consent. With Adek now increasingly hostile to our presence, Michael left the village two days later in one of the camp's vehicles for Mapel, 100 km away where new feeding centres and an airstrip were being built in advance of food drops, to take some of the growing pressure from Adek. He would see if it were possible to evacuate by that route, or whether it might be a safer location to await rescue. Michael did not say goodbye when he left, or not to me anyway. I was glad when he had gone because every time I saw him I remembered the moment he looked down at Billy's T-shirt where it hung almost to the length of my shorts, his eyebrows puzzled and his beautiful mouth suddenly opened in a sad-shaped O. That moment seemed the start of everything bad that happened that day and afterwards.

Avoiding the camp, I worked long hours at the hospital and ate with Bol and Adel at the clinic, spending the evenings sitting at John's bedside, holding his hands and praying for his legs to mend. They were clean breaks left and right, but with his muscles already wasted by polio they were agonisingly slow to heal. Through his delirium, John was as affectionate towards me as he had ever been and seemed oblivious to any bad feeling in the village as a result of his father's death and his own injuries. But in the night he sometimes cried out for his father as I sat up washing dressings and sterilising needles and bottles, trying to recycle every remaining asset at the hospital. Looking at his unused tricycle gathering dust by his bedside I wished that the stain of what we had done could be as easily removed as a deep red blood spot on a crepe bandage. But these days our shortages were spiritual as well as medical. Hope, of all things, was in the shortest supply.

The truth now impossible to ignore was that Adek had grown desperately weak, stretched along a tightrope beyond what it could bear – bloated like a mosquito engorged with infected blood. Its expansion had been exponential until quite suddenly one day it was no longer recognisable as the place in which we had first arrived – no longer a modest scrubland village but a vast refugee camp, home to tens of thousands of internally displaced people fleeing the militia movements to the North and the famine of the East. The most recent air drops had flown in hundreds of mosquito nets and people had pitched them over tree branches to create thousands of makeshift homes that stretched to the horizon. In the day there were so many thousands of fires feeding so many families that sometimes it seemed as if the entire dustbowl of Southern Sudan must be filled with smoke and noise – the sounds of babies crying, women calling to their husbands, what few animals there were tethered next to where families slept. Every night at dusk, as the white smoke rose into the fireball of the setting sun, it looked as if Adek were ablaze, a muslin-tented, mist-shrouded citadel of smoulder and netting. No wonder Bol told me the young children were getting lost on the way to the well, and the old women complained that the ghosts of the village could no longer find the paths to their old homes.

Returning late one night, I lost my own way, disorientated by the jumbled, ever-changing patchwork of new tents and tukuls. Trying to get my bearings, I stood still for a moment, struck not just by the silence but also by the air of surrender that seemed to spread like smoke through the homesteads. I realised then that between feedings, no-one in Adek any longer walked for berries and roots, that the village had been plucked dry. Apart from the ever-circling vultures, even Adek's birds were long dead, its skies as empty of life as the barren scrub in which no wild animals survived the drought. Only the insects flourished, feeding on the disease and the tiniest crumbs of spilled food and the dried blood of the dead. Watching a trail of ants pass along the ground, undeterred by the solid, pale leather obstruction of my dusty boots, I understood how insects would one day inherit the earth.

Some time past midnight I found the path and followed it back to our encampment, where I was surprised to hear voices coming so late from inside the radio hut. Sean was speaking urgently in turns with the distant, crackling voice at Loki, and I pushed aside the door and looked in. Billy was slumped next to Sean on the wooden bench and I was shocked by the change in him. Heavily bearded, he was wearing filthy shorts that looked baggy on his suddenly thin frame, his battered hat streaked with dust. He was clearly drunk: his body drooping forward to reveal a half-empty bottle grasped loosely at the neck in the fingers of his left hand. The radio room was aggressively hot and claustrophobically dark, except where the tiny, forceful beam of Sean's thin torch danced with tiny insects. The smell of sour alcohol was overpowering.

"SIERRA CHARLIE TO JULIET LIMA. REPEAT: NEED URGENT FOOD DROP, OVER."

Sean was hunched over the transmitter as if he could intimidate the receiver into forcing Loki to respond. I recognised the voice of Billy's

American WFP friend Jorges – a six-foot ex-marine and unlikely Juliet – at the other end of the line.

"COPY THAT SIERRA CHARLIE. NO FLIGHT PERMISSIONS. GoS TRAIN MOVING FURTHER SOUTH. SECURITY LEVEL 4. NOT SAFE TO DROP. ADVISE EVACUATE TO MAPEL. OVER."

"NO DROP IN EIGHT DAYS. THOUSANDS OF NEW FAMILIES IN FROM BUSH. FAMINE LATE WARNING: EMERGENCY. OVER."

"DONOR PROBLEMS STILL HOLD. SPLA OUT OF TALKS. REPEAT GoS TRAIN MOVING. MIKE DELTA AT MAPEL, SECURITY GOOD. OVER."

"HIGH RISK THOUSANDS DIE IF NO DROP NEXT FORTY-EIGHT HRS. TWO ZERO THOUSAND HOUSEHOLDS THIS LOCATION. OVER."

"ROGER THAT, SIERRA CHARLIE. ROGER THAT. WE ARE AWARE OF SITUATION. ADVISE EVACUATE TO MAPEL. OVER."

As Sean stared at the radio, Billy grabbed the receiver with a swipe of his long fingers. Sweat dripped from his face. I was immeasurably relieved to hear that Michael – Mike Delta – was still safe in Mapel, or at least in a secure location.

"BRAVO DELTA TO JULIET LIMA. NO EVACUATE. 100 TONNE DROP, NON NEGOTIABLE. OVER."

Billy slurred when he spoke and only the crackle of the radio could have hidden his obvious drunkenness from the Loki radio receiver.

"NO DROP, BRAVO DELTA. ADVISE EVACUATE MAPEL. OVER."

"DROP FOOD TOMORROW. OVER."

"NO CAN DO, BUDDY. REPEAT NO FLIGHT PERMISSIONS TO BAHR EL GHAZAL. OVER."

"GoS WANT THESE PEOPLE DEAD. OF COURSE THERE WON'T BE FLIGHT PERMISSIONS. SEND THE FUCKING FOOD. OVER."

"ROGER THAT BRAVO DELTA. NO DROP. REPEAT: ADVISE EVACUATE. OVER."

Billy held the receiver hard in his hands.

"FUCK YOU. OVER."

Then, he smashed the receiver into the bottle he was holding and it broke in two.

* * *

Outside, Adel was sitting at the fire. She had been sleeping at the hospital for the past few weeks and I was surprised to see her. Inside the radio hut Billy and Sean were still shouting at each other.

"It's late, Adel," I said, but my mind was reeling. We were completely cut off now, without even radio contact with Loki, our only protector. "You should be in bed."

"What is evacuate?" Adel asked, and I realised she must have overheard the conversation in the radio hut.

I looked at her trusting face and I felt suddenly exhausted.

"It means to leave. To empty. To leave a vacuum."

"Are you leaving us?"

I looked at her, and I wanted to say no.

"I don't know."

I tried to smile at her.

"Maybe we aren't helping, any more," I said. "Since John's accident we've lost the support of the Spear Master, the community leaders, Commander Wol and the village. The hospital has run out of supplies. We are barely feeding a quarter of the people in Adek." I felt sad when I said all this. "Even your father no longer comes to see us."

Adel shook her head, and began mixing the water and porridge with one of the plastic spoons from the feeding centre.

She said something so quiet that I had to ask her to repeat it.

"I said, if you had never come, we would all be dead anyway."

I hugged her then, an arm around her thin shoulder, noticing how fragile Adel felt despite her tall frame and growing woman's body. Even in a country where childhood did not exist, she was still only a child.

"Bol gave me a poem," Adel said, unexpectedly.

"A wedding poem?"

"I think. I think he is asking me to marry him," Adel said. "But I don't know." She shook her head slightly. "It is written down. In English. Bol says he doesn't know how to write our language. I can read some of it, but . . ."

Girls were rarely able to read in Southern Sudan. Not even Chief's daughters. I cursed myself for having been there so long and not having taught Adel to read more than a few basic sentences.

"Would you like me to help you read it?"

Adel nodded her head, but as she handed me the paper, Sean and Billy emerged abruptly from the radio hut, and she pushed it into my pocket instead, with a warning look that told me the poem was our secret.

"What the hell are we going to do now you've endangered the whole camp?" Sean was shouting. "Now we don't even have the option of evacuating."

"I told you the radio in the car needed fixing, you sanctimonious piece of shit . . ."

"And you're in charge of radio ops, you drunken . . ."

The two men stopped when they saw Adel. As we all stood there awkwardly, I noticed how Sean's face had aged since the start of the mission. His hair had grown longer and curlier and the orange was bleached to yellow in some places by the sun and salted by grey. Only his beard remained red. His grey eyes were buried in deep shadow and hung about by bags. Next to him, Billy's grown-out hair and thick, straggly beard lent him the air of a man marooned on a desert island, his eyes curtained by heavy lids that told how long it was since he had last slept properly. Presented by this new crisis my mind somersaulted away, idly wondering what the two men in front of me saw looking at me. My mother's tiny hand mirror had broken in the second week and I could only imagine my appearance. Billy had cut my hair for me one evening weeks or months ago, but it had grown rapidly beyond my shoulders again. My skin felt tight to the touch with constant sun. I guessed I had lost around two stone in weight since coming to Southern Sudan and that my skin would be dull with the lack of nutrients in our diet.

"Why don't you tell Adel what's happening?" Billy said sarcastically to Sean.

Sean gave him a hard look.

"We've got two days rations left at the feeding centres, Adel," Billy said, pulling the cap from his whiskey bottle and draining its last dregs into a metal cup. "After that we're fucked."

"That's enough, Billy," Sean said.

Adel's eyes filled with tears and I went over to her, placing my arm around her shoulders.

"The food will come," I whispered to her, because how could I whisper anything else? "You'll see."

"We've been in worse shit," Sean said, trying to reason with Billy.

"Like when?" Billy snapped.

153

"In Angola, when you and I were taken hostage. In Congo, when the UN wouldn't come. In Rwanda . . ." He stopped as he always did when he spoke about Rwanda. He and Billy had both been there through the 1994 genocide. "In Rwanda."

Billy swayed lightly on the balls of his feet and spat the last of his whiskey at the fire. A blue flame flickered where the spit landed, and then fizzled out.

"Great. We're in better shape than Rwanda. How fucking reassuring. Only a million people died there after all."

He swung himself up into the old army hammock under the mango tree where he had taken to sleeping since the mis-drop.

"I think everyone could use some sleep," Sean said. "In the morning, Billy can fix the radio and I'll speak to Loki again. They'll have to listen in the end."

Billy grunted from the hammock.

"Perhaps you can speak to him, Maria?" Sean said, and I felt my face flush red. Sean turned to Adel as if things were perfectly normal.

"Good night, Adel," he said. "See you in the morning. It will all look better in daylight."

Adel said goodnight and they both went off to their beds, the poem forgotten in my pocket. In the yellow circle lit by the fire, there was suddenly only me, the shadow of the still swinging hammock and the sour smell of stale alcohol. Tiredness overwhelmed me. The hammock slowed, moving like a pendulum towards stop. Billy's old leather boots were faintly visible in the moonlight at one end and I moved to the other side, where his sunken face was lost in beard and shadow.

"Don't sleep here Billy. You're exhausted."

Billy moved his head jerkily towards my voice.

"Where should I sleep, with you?"

His voice was abrupt, and his reply took me by surprise.

"I meant, you should go to bed," I said, evenly.

"I'm staying up in case there's a drop," Billy said. He voice was so slurred it was hard to distinguish the syllables. He was mortally drunk.

"There's no drop tomorrow. You heard what Loki said."

"I'm staying up," Billy said.

His voice was a petulant child's.

"I know how you feel," I heard myself say, speaking above the noise of my own screaming guilt. "We did something terrible. But we didn't mean it to happen. We made a mistake . . ."

"A mistake?" Billy cut in. "Someone got killed and a kid got crushed – all for a drunken fuck . . . And you call that a 'mistake'?"

It occurred to me then that despite the forced intimacy of the past three months, I didn't really know Billy at all.

"We should never have gone to bed too drunk to wake up," I said. "That was a mistake. But I don't think I made a mistake sleeping with you, and I'm sorry you think of it as a drunken fuck."

"Oh, well, here's some news for you, Maria, just because we're in the middle of a goddamn warzone doesn't make it meaningful, darlin'. This ain't *Out of Africa*, so you'd better just get over it . . ."

"I am over it," I said. "You're the one sleeping up a tree out of your mind with self-pity. I'm getting on with it, trying to make amends, seeing what I can salvage from this whole mess. You're the one who's given up. I thought you were supposed to be some kind of hero."

Billy had rolled over in the hammock so that he was facing the tree, causing it to swing again. I waited for it to stop, listening to the creak of the ropes in a silence filled with the sound of the fire, and the crickets calling out to one another and the whirr of bats' beating their wings. Then, as the ropes stilled, feeling suddenly empty, I walked away.

Back inside my tukul, I undressed slowly in the warm darkness, pulling my hair out of its elastic band and dipping a corner of my towel into my water bottle to wipe my face. As I dragged off my ragged denim shorts, my torch beam glanced on something small and white on the floor. Adel's poem, folded into a careful square, had fallen from my pocket. Bol's poem to Adel, written on paper neatly torn from the notebook I kept at the hospital. Climbing into my sleeping sheet and tucking the mosquito net around me like a shroud I unwrapped the paper parcel carefully, shining my torch onto Bol's tiny handwriting, the letters carefully aligned across a neat, lightly sloping trajectory in beautifully copied letters, framed by the dirty brown of my hands.

> Her red brown skin alight
> like mud sand where a fire has been.
> Malual, colour of antelope
> hiding in elephant grass.
> Daughter of Adek,
> reddish water of the White Nile
> flowing upstream to the green sea
> to the white-toothed mouth of the river
> far to the north of the lands we know.
> Daughter of Adek

the burning acacia branches
of your long arms,
your red-brown neck.
I am the flatlands, the seroot fly,
you are the sky above Jabal Marrah,
and there are not oxen enough
at any man's cattle camp.
The warrior clan will never be chief
and the antelope will not come
to the watering hole of the lion.

Switching off my torch, I repeated the last line to myself in the semi-darkness. It wasn't a wedding poem at all. It was a poem telling Adel why Bol could not marry her: why the warrior and royal clans could never be one. Sitting on the edge of my bed I wept then, into my hands, thin tears that fell to the thirsty mud floor. Then they were gone, swallowed by the hard Sudanese soil that feeds on tears and blood.

Chapter Twenty-One

I was up at the hospital the following morning looking for Adel when I felt the breeze shift, almost imperceptibly at first. There was a low, heavy buzz like a mosquito cloud forming and then the dust began choking itself, whirling in tiny winds that caught in my throat. I looked up at the sky, but saw only the wisps of straggling clouds. The cold azure blue hurt my eyes where I had wept the night before. As the noise of the wind grew louder, one of the women waiting for treatment dragged herself up on her sticks, her blurry eyes darting across the heavens, startling her little grand-daughter by pulling her suddenly upright. We all looked up together at a sky that had been empty of planes for many weeks. It seemed to me the clouds were moving too fast.

I called Bol outside.

"Is it the Government bomber?" I asked.

He shook his head.

"Then it's Loki," I said. "They must be sending food after all."

I had yet to give Adel his poem, and I felt awkward standing there with him, knowing his business. I wanted to speak to him about it, but it wasn't the time or place.

"It's not the food plane," Bol said, his eyes shadowed by his hand, straining up at the sky. "It's too small."

The tiny speck in the sky was moving quickly towards the northern edge of the village, and I wondered suddenly if the plane was planning to land.

"The airstrip's not finished," I heard myself say.

"It must be Loki," Bol said.

"Maybe it's Michael?" I was powerless to stop the eagerness in my voice.

We began running towards the airstrip, joined by a fast-flowing river of people jostling and elbowing and craning their necks towards the sky, shielding their eyes from the midday sun. Even the sick and the half-

157

dead were scrambling from tree to tree, dragging themselves from their hearths, joining the throng.

The parched earth seemed to vibrate with the rumbling of their shouts. "Food is coming, food is coming."

As we reached the airstrip the air was already dancing with the force of the descending plane. Tiny beads of whirling grit stung my eyes and scattered the waiting silhouettes like maize-meal, leaving only the strongest standing there, the dust rising around them with the wind, as if the fierceness of their hunger had become visible at last.

My own hunger raged suddenly through my body, now that food and perhaps even deliverance, was a possibility. The aircraft descended on the village in an angry blur, screeching down dragging its feet, scattering elders and villagers into the scrubland. The village seemed to scream with one breath. In the final seconds of its landing I had to close my eyes and mouth and cover my nose with my hand. Particles of grit, carried by the air, whipped and bit into my face and legs. The plane roared and then stopped suddenly, spluttering like an old man, spitting red dust. The villagers stepped out silently from the long shadows of the afternoon. There was a silence as loud as the noise before. The air had stopped dancing. No-one spoke, not even the elders or the crazy women, who were staring mad-eyed at the aircraft resting in the clearing. For the first time I realised what it must have been like when we arrived that first day from Loki from the perspective of the villages on the ground. I was sure it was Michael, even thought it could make no sense for him to have returned in a plane. I was longing to speak to him, to explain everything, to ask his forgiveness for what had happened to Polio John's home and for what I had done to earn his disapproval.

It was a Buffalo aircraft, much bigger than the single-engined Caravan that had flown us in to Southern Sudan, but much smaller than the Antonovs that dropped food when they came from Kenya and bombs when they flew in from the North. It was a plane capable of holding many tonnes of grain and medicines and people too. I saw Billy reach the airstrip out of breath, and I waved to him, exultantly, but then I saw his face reddening with anger and I knew something was badly wrong. Seconds later, the back of the plane began opening slowly like a yawning mouth.

As the plane opened, a curly-haired white man stepped down wearing a khaki military-style uniform, a red and white bandana and mirrored aviator sunglasses. The American flag was sewn on the back of his jacket, and next to it the letters US-O-S. He strode towards me without extending his hand. I felt hope crumble into flat disappointment.

"Delivery for Commander Wol," the man said, in a strong Southern American accent.

I was disappointed but also puzzled. Surely Loki wouldn't send food to Commander Wol?

"Commander Wol?" the man repeated slowly, as if I might not speak English. "Leader of the SPLA round here . . . Big tall guy, beard, usually attired in pink?"

Billy reached the plane before I could reply.

"I hope you got some food in there, buddy," Billy said.

He spoke quietly but emphatically, and the vein at his temple stood out from his forehead. Still, he seemed sober this morning, and calmer somehow, though he still hadn't shaved his shaggy beard.

"Sorry, but I got a delivery for Commander Wol," the man said. "The contents ain't for discussion with no other person."

"Then get the hell off our airstrip," Billy said.

I was lost in utter disbelief, staring at Billy open-mouthed, wondering if he were drunk after all.

"Are you out of your mind?" I said. "We are desperate for food and medicines . . . And we need to evacuate. This plane could take us home . . ."

But Billy spat on the ground.

"What food and medicines you carrying, bud?" he said.

The man removed his mirrored shades and looked at Billy squarely.

"One last time," he said. "This cargo is for Commander Wol. It is a MI-LI-TARY cargo."

I tried to talk to the man then, thinking there must be some kind of miscommunication – that if only he knew the desperation of our situation he would give us the food.

"Look at these people . . ." I said, pointing out the people who stood expectantly at the airstrip, their stomachs distended and their long legs too thin to support their tall frames. "They are starving. You are the only plane to fly in days, and the only aircraft to land in six months . . . The Khartoum Government has been blocking permission for aid flights. We have food rations for only a few hundred and there are thousands here. We have no clean water and no medicines. I beg you, if you can help us . . ."

"Guns and Bibles," Billy shouted, and I saw that he was up in the body of the plane throwing down boxes as a second man wrestled with him. He was holding a Kalashnikov in one hand and with the other he emptied a box of Bibles down onto us, the pages flapping white against the hard, red earth. In front of me, a book lay open at Leviticus. I closed it and picked it up, fearful that Billy seemed to be aiming the gun down at the SOS man.

The villagers stood staring, watching the white people fighting, not understanding why there were no white sacks of grain inside the plane. A low, loud murmur spread through the crowd, an unfamiliarly angry, aggressive sound.

The man produced a pistol then from a holster inside his fishing jacket and shot it twice in the air. The crowd pulled back.

He spoke without looking directly at Billy.

"I'm counting to three and I want that gun down."

Billy reluctantly laid the Kalashnikov down across one of the boxes, but the man still stood there with his pistol, a pious sneer across his face.

"One last time," he said, turning to me. "Where might I find Commander Wol?"

I was shaking, but suddenly unafraid of him.

"You can shoot that gun all you like," I said. "In fact you might as well shoot all these people now and leave them all for dead. Look at them. They are barely alive. You could have brought them food and you have brought them books and guns. That's tantamount to murder."

The man adjusted his aviator sunglasses and looked at me strangely then, as if I were a particularly stupid child.

"What good," he began, patiently, still holding the cocked pistol, although pointing it casually now at the ground, "is bread, when the people do not have eternal life?"

"Tomorrow morning, like every morning, we will be pulling the bodies of the dead out of the feeding centres and gathering them from under the trees and stacking them in shallow graves . . ." I said, still thinking if only he really understood what we were facing he would turn the plane around for food.

"What use feeding these good people to send them to the holy fires of eternal damnation?"

"These people are not Christians," I said. "They believe in one God, but it's not your God. It's Nhialic, the Divinity."

The man smiled then with a curious noise in his throat that was halfway between a laugh and sneer.

"They are pagans," he said. "But God has a plan for them, to rise up against the infidel."

The dying, proud people of Adek understood not a word of what this man was saying, and for that I was grateful. They were people on the frontlines of a war so far from their own making that they were almost an irrelevance, like the random spot where a landmine took hold in the soil or a bomb fell. A pen scratched in Khartoum and a village fell. A Hallelujah uttered in Utah and villagers in Adek fell to their knees. I was lost in these thoughts when I saw a dark-haired woman in her late-thirties step out of the front of the plane, dressed elegantly in a white linen trouser suit and immaculate navy blue flak jacket, which she wore casually like a fashionable gilet, as if it were a particularly windy day on the deck of a St Tropez yacht. She jumped down easily from the cockpit without extending the ladder. She looked bored as much as anything, her eyes hidden behind expensive black sunglasses, Gucci perhaps, or Chanel. Even her straw hat was tied on by an Audrey Hepburn white scarf.

"Put that goddamn gun away," the woman said, and the man reluctantly relocked the safety and returned the gun to its holster.

She approached in a cloud of almost forgotten scent – of soap and perfume and hairspray and myriad other things, washing powder and fresh laundry and moisturiser and insect repellent. Unable to speak with the surprise of this brilliant-white vision of almost God-like freshness, I found myself staring open-mouthed, as if the woman had suddenly materialised from the pages of Vogue.

"Grace Mulholland," the woman said in a low-voiced French Canadian drawl, approaching Sean and I, extending a lightly-tanned hand with French-polished fingernails and an expensive Swiss wristwatch. "*Time* magazine."

She smiled a red lipsticked smile and her white teeth glittered in the sun.

"Sorry about these dumbfucks."

As she stood there, I caught the scent of myself for the first time in weeks or months, a low smell of woodsmoke that hung about my clothes and hair, blended with stale sweat and the antiseptic overtones of iodine. I pushed my hair back from my face with my hand and realised my forehead was coated in thick red dust where the swirls of grit thrown up by the plane's landing had stuck to the thin film of sweat that covered my face. I wiped my dusty hand on my filthy shorts, tied at the button with string, before shaking the outstretched hand. To her credit she did not wince when she took it.

"You must be Maria," she said.

I nodded, puzzled.

"And this must be Sean?"

I turned to see Sean approaching at a jog.

"Quite the celebrities," the woman said, with a dry smile.

"The airstrip isn't ready . . ." Sean said, by way of introduction, taking in Billy's angry face, the SOS man and Grace Mulholland, all in one shocked movement.

"Well, it obviously is," the woman replied. "A little bumpy is all . . ."

She jabbed a ringed finger at the plane where Billy was standing watching the proceedings with mutinous eyes. "These guys are after the local SPLA Commander. I just needed a lift. Been trying to get in here for three weeks, and I'm pig sick of Loki." She smiled at me and her eyes, teeth and skin shone luminously like a backlit advertisement for some kind of miracle face cream. "So many married men."

"Have you brought anything useful with you?" Sean asked. "Food or medicines? I mean, we're very short . . ."

"I've brought myself," the woman said, cutting him off abruptly. "That's usually a way to kick the donors into spending their millions." That implausibly white smile again. "And I've brought a way to get you out." She jabbed her finger at the plane. "Word is, you're trapped here."

The woman brought a blue, square-shaped bottle of Kenyan spring water to her lips, beaded with moisture from the fierce cold of the plane at altitude, and I thought about its unboiled taste, the clear deliciousness of a pure liquid that lacked tin kettle taint or traces of charcoal that leaked from the camp filter. My lips felt dry enough to crack.

"It's up to you," the woman said. "You can come with us this afternoon. Or Loki said that if we land successfully they will send a plane for you in forty-eight hours. Midday on Friday. "

She smiled.

"Of course, I'd rather bring you back with me. Better for the story."

My mind was turning somersaults, literally spinning so that I felt an almost fairground-ride sickness. Go home? Could it be that simple? After all these months of watching and waiting, were we just simply to get a lift back like a taxi ride and never ever come back again?

"Do you by any chance have a cigarette?" I asked the woman with strained politeness, and she pulled a neat hardpack of Lucky Strikes from her bag.

"Take the packet," she said. "I've got tonnes in the plane. I usually use them for bribing soldiers." She laughed and lit one herself, leaving a neat pale red lipstick mark on the brown filter, before proffering the packet to Sean.

"I don't smoke."

I lit a cigarette from the packet and inhaled.

"Thank you," I said.

"So you wanna show me around?" the woman said.

"That won't be possible, Ms Mulholland," Sean said, coldly. "We can't show press around without permission from Loki."

"Don't be a bore," Ms Mulholland said. "I've come all this way . . ."

"Well nobody asked you to," Sean said. "And there are procedures . . ."

"Are procedures feeding these people?" Grace asked, looking around at the pitifully thin people gathered at the airstrip. "Because they look hungry to me."

She pulled a giant lens from the smart black camera-bag she was carrying and fitted it to the body of an old style film camera.

"It's up to you," she said. "But I usually find there's nothing like a set of photographs to get those donors' minds focused on helping."

"You could come to the hospital," I said.

Sean nodded reluctantly. He was torn, I could see, between dealing with the journalist and dealing with the fundamentalist mercenaries who were still cluttering the airstrip with crates of guns and boxes of Bibles. For my part, I felt strangely starstruck, as if we had just been visited by a glamorous deity whose surreal presence might yet have the power to save us all.

"We've only an hour or so before this plane goes back," the woman said. "So, we'd better get going." She waved up at Billy, familiarly, and he glared down at her.

"I see Billy Finn's let himself go," she said. "Used to be cute."

She lit another Lucky Strike from the butt of her dying cigarette.

"Let's go and get some shots of these malnourished kids anyway."

*   *   *

163

On the way to the hospital Grace Mulholland told me all about herself and the story she was writing about the American donors who wouldn't help Sudan. She explained how the Sudanese Government was perpetuating genocide against the people of the South and how the whole thing was really about oil that they'd found in the Western Upper Nile region, which the Government wanted and was the reason it was burning all the villagers off the land.

There was a rumour that the US intended to bomb the North, but it was nothing to do with the war. The US was after a Saudi Arabian terrorist called Osama Bin Laden accused of making chemical weapons in a factory in Khartoum.

"There's another way of looking at it of course," Grace said. "The US President has been caught with his pants down, a sex scandal involving a White House intern. The case for impeachment against him is growing. Fighting terrorism is a mighty wholesome distraction for the Clinton Government right now and Bin Laden's in the frame. His friends are Sudan and Afghanistan."

She laughed. My head was beginning to spin.

"Most stories come down in the end to oil or sex. In this case it's both. Everybody wants it to be a religious war, of course. Islam versus Christianity and guess who're the bad guys?"

She stopped a moment to take a photograph of a little girl carrying her sister tied up in a sarong bundle on her back.

"Anyway, these gunrunners are the only psychos who'll fly in," she said. "I paid 1,000 bucks for the lift. They're on their way to buy back Dinka slaves from the slave market at El Obeid. It inflates the prices of slaves enormously. Used to cost two heads of cattle per person, and then thanks to the evangelicals it's more like 200 bucks a go." She laughed easily. "So my passage buys back five people. Hard to know if that's good or bad, but then that's the wonderful thing about Africa – everything is so marvellously morally ambivalent."

It was a mile or so to the hospital and somehow I seemed to be carrying most of Grace's cameras as well as my medical kit. Grace was walking along writing as furiously fast as she spoke, pausing every now and again to use the smaller Leica camera she carried on her shoulder and keeping up a rapid commentary on everything she encountered.

"Oh nice," she said, framing a shot. "Kind of picturesque here, isn't it? Sort of how you imagine Galilee or Nazareth, like those illustrations in the Children's Bible. I've been to Sudan before, but only to the North.

Northern Kenya's a bit like this though."

"How do you know Billy?" I asked.

Grace laughed, a tinkling, shivery sound like broken glass shaken in a cup.

"Oh, you know how it is in our game," she said. "Have you . . .?" She studied my face for a moment, which flushed bright red under her gaze. "I see you have . . . Ha." She laughed. "I was stuck for months with him in Rwanda in '94, before they cleared us all out so they could start the genocide. He stayed of course. That's why he's so fucked up. Never forgave the UN, or himself. Although God knows what else he could have done. I remember there was a story about a school. He was a marine, of course, before. Special Forces. Hated being unarmed, I suppose."

She paused with the length of her cigarette hanging delicately out of her lipsticked mouth to take another photograph.

"A waste really. He always seemed a bit broken after that."

We reached the feeding centres before the hospital, and Grace started down the path before I could stop her.

"I'm not sure if we should be going to the feeding centres," I said, hesitating where the path turned off from the main village thoroughfare.

"Maria, darling," Grace said, soothingly. "We need to go wherever the children look the most starving. I'm sorry, but that's how it is."

Half an hour later and Grace was lying with surprising agility across the blue tarpaulin of the feeding centres despite the weight of her flak jacket, leaning upwards, the long lens of her largest camera inches from a feverish mother nursing a pitifully thin child. The child's eyes rolled in her head and the mother seemed to ignore the camera's presence, only moving to flap at the seroot flies with her skeletal hand.

"This is Mrs Maduot," I said to Grace. "She has HIV after being raped by the militias. She has no husband and has lost one child already. This child may not make it either."

Grace pointed to the notebook on the floor behind her.

"Write it all in there for me," she said.

I wrote the names of all the patients and their rough ages in careful capitals, giving a brief description of each. The other scribblings in the notebook seemed to refer to troop movements and militia attacks and I realised that Grace was far better informed than we were.

The photographer worked quickly through the acute admissions section, and I bit my lip as she leaned into the faces of the children, her cameras clicking and whirring as she snapped the shutter down. I understood why it was necessary for her to take the photographs, but it still seemed somehow wrong. Without food, these white tents were little more than dying rooms. As Grace knelt and crouched and lay, occasionally moving a mother's hand or adjusting the lens on her camera, it seemed a cruel, undignified last intrusion, filled with a promise neither of us could actually fulfil.

I was concentrating so hard on Grace and the needs of my patients that I didn't hear Billy walk in behind us, but I heard him clear his throat with his distinctive cough and knew it was him.

"These kids marasmic enough for you?" Billy asked quietly. "Or do you want us to find some who are dying a bit harder?"

Grace stood up slowly, dusting specks of dirt from her white linen suit before she replied.

"Ah, Billy," Grace said. "Glad to see the cowboy machismo remains under that ghastly Grizzly Adams beard." She picked up her camera and took a picture of him standing there, hands on hips, a glowering silhouette with the light from the tent opening pouring in behind him.

"What are you doing here?" Billy said.

"On holiday, darling, what's it look like?"

"Your plane's leaving in fifteen minutes."

"How kind of you to let me know. That's just enough time to get to the hospital and back out to the airstrip."

"That bug-assed, Bible preaching pilot says he ain't waiting for you neither."

"I take it you won't all be coming with me? It's a gamble . . . The next plane might never come . . ."

Billy turned on his heel then, as if nothing further could be gained from the conversation.

"Have a shave, won't you darling?" Grace called after him, and smiled at me conspiratorially.

"Well, he hasn't mellowed with age," she said. "Shall we get going?"

If it were possible, Grace Mulholland looked even more out of place inside the hospital. Too clean, too fit and healthy. Too Western. A woman from outer space with gym-toned calves and triceps and impossibly white teeth. The beds around her looked ramshackle by comparison, which I suppose they were. The bedlinen looked filthy, the dressings badly applied, the thirty or so patients desperately poor and ill.

"Shit," Grace said, whistling between her perfect white teeth. "This is as bad as I've seen."

She walked straight over to where Polio John was lying, staring at her open-mouthed, as if a miracle had walked in through the door.

"What happened to him?" she asked.

I felt my face fall.

"John speaks English," I said, evenly. "Why don't you ask him yourself?"

Leaving the two of them talking, I walked away and fetched a cup of water for one of my elderly patients who was struggling to sit up from the floor. Grace sat on John's wooden platform bed and the two spoke earnestly for a while before she took some photographs, concentrating on the injuries on his legs.

I introduced Grace to the most acute patients on the ward one by one: the TB patients with their wracking coughs and paper-thin chests, those with undiagnosed HIV whose skin was yellowish and whose bones seemed as if they might shatter with only the tiniest of blows. Those with acute diarrhoeas whom we could no longer keep hydrated in the unrelenting heat. Two men bitten by mambas, a girl with an unexplained gunshot wound and a child with a scorpion scratch completed the list of the sick. I told each of their names to Grace and she wrote them down.

"Come and sit here for me," Grace said, calling me over to the bedside of Aneta-Maria, a child with acute malnutrition whose mother had died and who still wore the tattered clothes she had worn when she was admitted. For months we had not wanted to name a child who seemed as if she were simply too fragile for this world. But the girl had won through, and despite my protestations Adel had named her Aneta-Maria, the child with Western and Dinka names. Not that I was about to tell any of this to Grace.

"Oh no," I said, realising she meant me to be in the picture. "I'll get Adel for you or one of the other nurses."

"This is about Western aid," Grace said. "We need to show it's getting there. Anyway, as I said, you're quite the celebrity."

"What do you mean?"

"Oh you know how the world loves a missing white woman. The American media's over-excited by ex-Special Forces hero Billy Finn, the Irish papers are all over missing Sean Donnelly. But the Brits are wetting themselves over Maria Marshall, the 'Angel of Sudan', missing for six months among the natives!"

Grace laughed.

"It helps that some friend of yours has released a gorgeous picture of you at some graduation or other," she said. "Meanwhile, your fellow medical students have been organising vigils down by the Thames. It's textbook tabloid stuff."

"But people must be worried . . ." I said. "Have you heard anything about my family? My brother Matt must be worried sick . . . Africaid said they would inform relatives not to panic, but if we're on the news . . .?"

"Your brother looked fine last time I saw him on CNN. Handsome, isn't he?"

"Matt has been on CNN?"

"I told you – you're quite the celebrities . . ."

I was suddenly overwhelmed by the thought of our faces, mine and Matt's, on television. Perhaps our father had even watched us, not realising who we were.

"Look, you're nearly home now," Grace said. "And you're going to have quite a story to tell."

Stunned by this news, I found myself complying with the forcefulness of Grace's wishes, doing as I was told, cradling the child's body in my arms. Aneta snuggled in instinctively. An orphan, she responded to any kind of human touch with a trustingly unconscious affection I found myself returning despite the artificiality of the situation. She was one of my favourite patients, repeatedly returning with malnutrition simply because there was no close or extended family to feed her. I had frequently entertained fantasies of adopting her and taking her back to England, except I knew in my heart it was better for her to stay with her own people and not be transplanted into another world far from the cattle camps and Adek's vast skies.

"That's great," Grace said. "Just hold it like that."

But as the camera clicked I felt false and uncomfortable, violating Aneta-Maria's instinctive responsiveness for a cause she could not understand. She spoke no English and my own grasp of Dinka was even by now only polite and low-grade functional. I laid her back down on the pillow I had made from sacking from the food bags, sewn into a long, filled rectangle to support her nodding head.

"I'm sorry," I said. "She needs to sleep."

The photographer began protesting, her red mouth in a pleading pout, but as I adjusted Aneta-Maria's blanket we both heard the same noise at the same moment: the roar of a departing aeroplane making its run at the landing strip.

Grace looked up as if she could see through the straw roof of the hospital.

"Jesus H Christ!" she said, quietly. "Those goddamn, good for nothing, shit-for-brains evangelicals . . ."

We ran outside together and watched the plane climb into the cloudless sky – the sudden loss of possible escape registering with both of us simultaneously. I had felt terribly unready to leave only that morning, and yet now, when the chance had gone again, I desperately wanted to be airborne and away from this place, on the way home to security and comfort. The feeling of being trapped spread through me like a paralysis. Up in the sky, the plane became smaller and smaller until it was only a speck and my eyes hurt with straining to pick it out from the background of the brilliant blue. When it was gone, and only the empty heavens lay above us, I saw that there was genuine fear spreading across Grace's shockingly beautiful but suddenly not-so-confident or self-assured face.

"I fucking hate Africa," she said.

* * *

Grace kept up a volley of abuse against the Christian pilots all the way back to the airstrip, and it took the appearance of Commander Wol, a vision in pink striding across the plain in his half-open dressing gown to bring her to a standstill.

"What the hell is that?" she asked, open-mouthed, as he appeared, using his gun as a walking stick, an ammunition belt slung diagonally across his shoulder like a curious, rusty sash.

"That's Commander Wol," I said.

"Well, I've seen some things in my time, but never a ladies' dressing gown worn with a Kalashnikov."

"You'd like him," I said. "He's not all that bad when you get to know him."

"He's got the look of a mass murderer to me."

"Well," I shrugged. "There is that."

Commander Wol came straight for us, as if we were a target in his sights, moving across the plain with his customary agility and flanked by the sensible and affable Lieutenant Dit.

"Dr Maria," the Commander said, with a little bow of his head.

He looked at Grace for a moment.

"And this must be the famous photographer?"

"Grace Mulholland," Grace said, shaking his hand.

"I'm afraid I can't allow you to take any pictures of my men for intelligence reasons," the Commander said, showing his two good teeth, and I realised he was instinctively flirting with a beautiful woman. "But I myself will be available for interview."

"Excellent," Grace said, recovered now from the fact of her sudden exile in the badlands of Southern Sudan. "It seems I'll be here another few hours – at least until I can get on the radio to tell those goddamn gunrunners to come right back here."

I must have flushed because Grace looked at me hard.

"What?"

"Billy smashed the radio, last night," I said.

"That redneck motherfucker," Grace said, and I saw the Commander wince to hear swearing emitting from a lady so superficially fragrant.

"Thank God for plan B," Grace said. "Friday, 12.00 hrs. Less than forty-eight hours time. We can all go together, which will be better for the story."

"You are leaving us?" the Commander said, looking at me this time. Grace after all was only a visitor. Our abandonment amounted to a full-scale betrayal.

"I don't know," I said for the second time in only a few hours.

The thought of leaving filled me with hope and dread, guilt and elation, fear and yearning. I could no longer imagine being without these friends, without Adek's open spaces, its vast horizon, its night-time canopy of stars. I did not understand how I would return to normal life while this parallel universe existed out here in the bush, in the middle of one million roadless, pollution-free, internet-virgin square miles. A universe where these people would face constant attack from the Sudanese Government and their sponsored militias over and over until they were eliminated, while more than 3,000 miles away I went about a normal, Western life of blissful worrying about traffic congestion and house prices and what shoes to buy and whether I was a little overweight.

"One thing I have learned about white people," the Commander said, addressing himself to Grace and pulling his dressing gown tightly around himself so that it hugged the contours of his bare chest. "Is that 'I don't know' usually means whichever truth is most unpalatable."

Something is Going to Fall Like Rain

*   *   *

We sat up at the fire that night for the first time in weeks and even Billy sat with us, strumming his guitar and sharing his whiskey. We all had the sense, I suppose, that our time was coming to an end. Rescue was coming on Friday, in less than forty-eight hours, and we all wanted to make the most of the short time we had left in Southern Sudan. I felt giddy with the thought of escape but terrified by the idea of release, a prisoner with Stockholm syndrome or a freed animal that dares not leave its cage even with the door open. I was puzzled by these feelings, but then I realised how much I had come to value the simplicity and immediacy of Southern Sudan these last months. Food and water. Night and day. Life and death. No bullshit in between.

As we sat looking into the flames, sharing stories and jokes with Grace who told us with brilliant detail of everything that had happened in the past eight months, brightened and cheered by the presence of a new person with the power to lift our stale five-month old dynamic from the mess it had become, I missed Michael even more keenly than usual. It seemed such a long time since he had been gone, as if he had been part of a previous era, a different Adek, the right one – where men were not killed and boys not crushed by falling aid, and child soldiers didn't go missing from the hospital, and Billy and I were able to bicker and laugh at the fireplace, and the work we did actually seemed to make a difference. In that world, we were moving forward. Since Michael had left, ours had become a looking glass world, where however much we ran towards our goals we were really moving backwards, away towards the horizon. In the last few weeks we had not been even running to stand still, and a part of me felt Michael was the only person alive who could have changed that.

Bol was at the fire, talking quietly with Billy, and I wanted to speak to him about his poem, knowing I could not avoid Adel forever, and that sooner or later I would have to reveal its contents to her. I suppose I wanted to make sure that Bol understood how Adel really felt, although I guessed it couldn't make any difference if the village truly opposed a match between the warrior and ruling clans. I wanted them to challenge the village at least, not just to accept their fate. I wanted them to run away together. But it wasn't for me to interfere and there was nowhere for them to run away to. In any case, Bol was keeping his distance from me – perhaps suspecting Adel would have taken me into her confidence.

171

Adel arrived with her father late in the evening, when the fire glowed with low coals and the younger, thinner mango wood had burned to ash. We were laughing at something when they arrived suddenly from the shadows and I realised self-consciously how long laughter had been gone from the camp. Grace was sitting up on the wooden tree branch shining her torch on every giant insect that loomed into view by land or air, and she shone its beam directly onto their faces as they arrived as if expecting something far more malevolent than a man and his daughter enjoying an evening stroll.

"Ah, so you are all awake," Chief Deng said, sweeping his robe up around him as we all stood up to greet him. "It is almost like old times."

He sat on the low camping stool Sean had passed down to him and we sat down again at the fire. Kneeling next to him, I saw Adel try to catch Bol's gaze, but his eyes were firmly down, only the crown of his head visible where he sat cross-legged next to Billy.

"I would like to say a few words to you," the Chief said.

I felt Sean shift awkwardly behind me, wondering what new problem we had caused in the village.

"In recent weeks, there have been many problems in Adek village," the Chief said. "A man was killed and the villagers were angry, as is their right. A boy lies injured in hospital."

I felt myself redden still further, but the Chief smiled beneficently in the sudden flash of Grace's camera, showing his straight, white teeth. Next to him, Adel was still looking at Bol's downturned face.

"The period of mourning for the man, John Mabior, is now ended," Chief Deng said, "which allows me to return to your hearth."

"And I have more to say to you. Before you came, Adek village was facing a death sentence. Our cattle were dead in the fields. Every household was in mourning. We were tested beyond what even we as Dinka could bear. Led by some influences, the village has not always remembered that."

He sipped politely from the glass of whiskey Billy had poured for him.

"In the past months, you have given us something perhaps more important than food and water or protection from the militias, although you have also given us these things. You – Sean, Billy and Dr Maria – have given us a fragment of hope. You have showed us, that even as obscure and as small as we are, our international brothers are watching over us, that the world feels our pain. Before you came, we only knew isolation in this terrible genocide. We were forgotten, lost. You have not chosen to be our guests for these many months – your long visit was decreed by fate. But you have been guests in a way we as Dinka understand. You have worked hard for your stay and given us much, even friendship."

A small tear crept from Adel's eye and splashed down onto the hands she held clasped in front of her.

"Now it is time for you to leave, and you do so with our blessing. We only ask that when you are gone you remember your brothers and sisters in Southern Sudan and the ways in which we are the same as you. We ask you that when you return to your homes, to more comfortable places without war or hunger, or to other countries with new problems, that you will not forget us. We, for our part, will remember you."

The Chief clapped his hands together after that as if to signal that the formal part of his business was now over.

"To thank you, we would be honoured if you would all attend the harvest celebration which takes place tomorrow. It is up at the cattle camp, which under Dinka law is not open to outsiders. However, at the village meeting today, the villagers voted that this should be waived as an act of gratitude to you all. It is to your own credit that Adek no longer sees you as outsiders but as friends."

Everyone jumped up at that, and I found myself hugging the Chief. All these long months I had dreamed of visiting the cattle camp, the Dinka's most sacrosanct space: a place where the cattle were kept in safety and imbued with spiritual significance because of the sacred nature of the cows themselves. Michael had told me long ago of the place itself, its quiet, almost eerie quality at dusk and dawn when the white smoke of hundreds of burning dung fires shrouded the animals to keep the flies from their beautiful hides, and of the cows themselves, painted with reds and ochres and soft blues from clay, and decorated with bells and religious objects. I had been there in my imagination and even in my feverish dreams, but never imagined I would actually see it for myself, accepting my exclusion as a Westerner. Like Sean and Billy I was completely lost for words and could only accept the offer with a feeling of excitement and honour. And of course, I hoped that Michael might come back for the harvest dance, the most important date in the village's calendar.

* * *

173

That night, Grace slept in my tukul because there was no other place for her to stay in safety within the compound except Billy's bed and she said she had been there, done that, in Rwanda, in another warzone, in another place where no-one would listen to the warnings of the local people or of the aid agencies. We lay companionably enough in the thin darkness, although I seemed to be the one taking up the least amount of space in my own bed, pushed to the outer edge while Grace sprawled diagonally, her long, tanned arm slung behind her head. It was hot in the tukul, and the night was heavy around us as if the rocks beneath us were sweating beads of molten earth. The air was completely still and strangely pressurised as if a storm were coming. With amusement, I watched her remove her make-up with a packet of industrial strength facial wipes: a toning and moisturising ritual that seemed to belong to another era and another world.

"I'm amazed we've been invited to the harvest dance," I said, borrowing a wipe to remove some of the thick dust from my own face and neck. "It's an anthropologist's dream. Outsiders just don't get to see in to these events."

"What gets me is that there's no goddamn harvest," Grace said.

"Of course not," I said, smiling into the semi-darkness and remembering a conversation I'd had long ago with Sean when we had watched the villagers dancing together despite the death all around them. "The Dinka thank their Gods for what they receive, not for what they need. Even if the Gods give them next to nothing, harvest or not, they dance."

"I don't think I'd be dancing if I lived in this shit-heap," Grace said.

I sat up slightly then and looked at her, noticing how vulnerable she looked without her make-up. I had thought she must be nearly forty, but now I realised she was probably not much over thirty years old. The Dinka would understand the use of warpaint, I thought.

"The point is we should all be dancing," I heard myself saying. "All the time. For everything we have, which is unimaginable riches compared with what little this village has to dance for."

"God, why are aidworkers always so goddamn earnest?" Grace said. "You're doing a great job, your conscience is clear, you're going to heaven – where's the need to go on about it?"

I smiled despite myself.

"I'm not really an aidworker," I said.

"Well, all the more reason to cheer the fuck up."

I struggled to think of Grace and Billy together, the coupling of an inflated bicycle tyre and a sharp pin, or a dog and a tiger. In twelve hours this woman had swept through the camp like a rainstorm. I suddenly wished she had been here all along.

"Are there really lions in this village?" Grace said.

"I don't think so. I don't think there's anything much left alive out there in the bush except militias. Who told you there were lions?"

"That Polio boy. The one at the hospital. He said he had been attacked by lions."

I was astonished that John would try to protect us. He knew the falling palattes had been our mistake, even if he didn't know why the mistake had been made. The fact of his having tried to conceal our murderous error moved me almost to tears.

"Is that what you were looking out for at the fire?" I said. "Lions?"

"I just felt the boy's story didn't add up," Grace said, indignantly. "That's all."

I was suddenly conscious that the sheet we were sleeping in was covered in grime, but then Grace was no longer immaculately clean, her white suit smeared with red Adek dust, and the French polish of her fingernails already turning reddish brown. It made me both wince and smile to think the pillowcase below her head was stuffed with my filthy clothes. In all these months there had been so few visitors to the private world of my tukul. Michael had charged in and grabbed me on that very first night when the bombs were falling. Billy had been here just that one time. Laurel and Hardy were only spiders. Adek was an outdoor place where no-one spent time inside a hot tukul except when they were sick or sleeping.

Grace reached over to my side of the bed and fished in her bag for something. Her hand came back holding a neat, silver compact mirror that she flipped open at its hinge. The starlight pouring in through the thin roof caught the metal briefly as it passed my face.

"God, keep that away," I said.

"Why?"

"I haven't seen myself in the mirror for almost five months."

"Aren't you curious?"

"Not really."

"Sure?"

"Maybe a bit," I said.

I held the torch and Grace held the compact so that the small oval of space was lit yellow, shining from the shadow like a Tudor miniature: an intimate portrait blurred by poor light. In the middle, framed perfectly by the silver edge of the mirror, was a woman with dark hair streaked brown and tan by the sun, and blue irises muddled by the glare of the torch beam: eyes and cheekbones defined by tiny, crisscrossed lines of sun damage. The skin tones and blemishes were bleached out by the light, yet I was still startled by the dark brown colour of this woman's skin and her hollow, sunken cheeks and eyes. An unexplained bruise shadowed one temple, and her lips were split into a thousand tiny, hairline cracks. Dirt hovered in an eye corner and along her hairline was a noticeable streak of deep red dust. I didn't recognise the woman at all. And most of all I didn't recognise her expression. Hard-looking, old. Those pale blue eyes blank as duck eggs. Then, the portrait seemed to settle and it was my mother looking at me – a too thin, dark-skinned version of myself with hard eyes and worry lines.

"And?" Grace's voice broke into my thoughts.

I snapped off the torch.

"I wish I hadn't done that," I said.

"Don't think about it," Grace said.

Her arm was still across me where she had placed the mirror back into her bag and she moved it now with a small shrug, wriggling lightly so that her head was in the crook of my shoulder and her hand across my hip. I lay there, slightly uncomfortably, wondering if she had fallen asleep.

After a few moments Grace sighed.

"So, you want to have sex?"

The scratching of the tukul roof seemed very loud then, as if all the insects above us were held in noisy suspension, and the rats and rodents were preparing to turn their backs and look away.

"I don't think so," I said.

"You don't sleep with women?"

"Sex just seems to make such a mess of things."

"Well it will if you sleep with goddamn Billy Finn . . ."

I laughed.

"I liked goddamn Billy Finn," I said. "I thought it would help somehow. That it would be a night off from it all. A few moments respite from death and despair. I was desperate."

Grace laughed.

"For something that would make me feel alive."

"And did it work?"

I found myself telling Grace everything – how we had overslept the food drop, and tonnes of palettes had fallen on the houses at the edge of the village and crushed John and killed his father. How we were murderers now and had lost the faith of the village until that very evening when Chief Deng had come to the fireplace. I had been so long with no-one to listen to me that I spoke in an urgent, unthinking stream of thought, barely pausing for breath. I told her about Michael and how I had an inappropriate and clumsy crush on him, but that he had lost his wife and unborn child and how the knowledge of these unfathomable losses made me feel petty and insubstantial and small. That I might even have loved him, but now I would never know because Billy and I had slept together and Michael had realised when he saw I was wearing Billy's T-shirt and now he hated me and had gone to Mapel. How I had only slept with Billy anyway because of boredom and fear and the need to just feel another person's skin and exit from the visceral horror of my own brain for a few brief moments' lull from a time that had become so unrelentingly, soul-destroyingly, bitterly hard. I told her that Billy had called it a drunken fuck but that it hadn't been, not exactly, more that it was a there-and-then moment that would have made no sense outside of that time and place. I told her about Adel and the poem I was carrying in my pocket that carried the news that Bol would never marry her. I told her about standing in the minefield hardly breathing, surrounded by landmines and sunbleached bones and the consequences of what had happened last time white people had come to Adek. I told her that I was an imposter, not even a qualified doctor. That I had come to Africa on a borrowed fantasy, my mother's. I was here living her life and not my own because I had no idea what I wanted or who I was. I told her, hesitatingly, slower now, how my mother had asked me, her doctor daughter, to help her take her own life, sparing her the last agonising weeks of bowel cancer.

"And did you?" Grace asked, as my rushing narrative trickled suddenly to silence.

"The hospital let me care for her at home. And I promised her that the next time she came close to death I wouldn't intervene."

I was completely dry eyed when I spoke, and very calm.

"Only I couldn't bear to watch," I said. "I didn't think that if I watched her I could bear not to help her. So, instead I sat in the garden on an old wooden chair amongst her geraniums in the freezing cold for a part of an afternoon, and I left her to die completely alone. And I have spent a part of every day since trying to find a way to live with that."

Grace said nothing.

I said nothing.

"We only get one chance at the big things," Grace said, after a long while. "That's the cruelty of it."

I wept then, and Grace held me, and for a moment it seemed that everything would be all right.

"You're a good listener," I said, after a while.

"It's my job to be."

"Is this how you conduct all your investigative interviews?" I asked. "In bed?"

"To tell you the truth, I don't sleep well in the bush," Grace said. "Not alone anyway." She laughed. "If I were in your shoes I'd have been in Billy's bed from day one, even with his nightmares and his snoring. That was kind of what happened in Rwanda. It was his tent or the thought of being asleep alone when the Interahamwe came. I loved him of course in my own way, and perhaps he even loved me in his."

She looked at me carefully.

"You don't love him though?"

"No." I said. "Definitely not."

"And Michael?"

"It's too clichéd."

"I'll take that as a yes."

I thought of the first nights I had spent in the tukul, and the loneliness and fear I had felt.

Grace shook her head against my shoulder.

"I knew that Polio boy wasn't attacked by a lion."

"I was so frightened when we first came here," I said. "I was afraid of the dark and the spiders and the snakes and the armies and the militias and the bombings. But most of all I was afraid of making a mess of things."

Grace held me tight against her so that my face was in her shoulder.

"Get some sleep, sweetheart," she said.

Chapter Twenty-Two

I have to look at the calendar on the back of the kitchen door to remind myself where we are in time. Sudan was ten years and a millennium ago, 1998 – two years before the fireworks lit up the snaking line of the river, showering the banks with greens and reds and paving the narrow riverside streets with golds. Three years before the Twin Towers, those lofty symbols of Western might, were pierced by terrorist planes and people stopped wanting to live here by the river because of its proximity to the concrete and glass bunker of MI6. In the before times, when there was still a bright new peace in Northern Ireland, I remember hoping that people would get a bug for it, start spreading it through the Balkans and the Middle East, even as far as Southern Sudan and the dark heart of Africa's largest and longest-running war.

The truth is that the turn of the millennium made stupid optimists of us all. On the night of the failed fireworks, when I stood on the roof with my neighbours as we drank cheap cava from plastic glasses and watched the sky light up white and green and red, I thought of going back to Sudan in search of some kind of closure, to find my own ending to it all. Then, as the years passed and I did not go back – too afraid of opening old wounds, too scared of what I might find, too fearful even to look at photographs or newspaper cuttings – I came to realise that not everyone gets a Hollywood ending with all the threads of their life story neatly tied off. I had survived the fires and explosions and guns. My only physical scar was across my neck and ear and hidden by my hair when it eventually grew back. Who was to say my ending wasn't only this? A quiet existence in an empty flat by a dirty river. Compared with the loud, hot violence of life and death in Sudan, did I have any right to complain?

The kitchen is pleasingly cold and I lay my head on the fake-marbled worktop, enjoying the hard, cool formica against the thudding pulse in my temples. My temperature is higher again today, 40°C, and I struggle to pour a glass of water for myself from the fridge, adding hard globules of ice from an ancient tray that smells of old plastic and frozen peas. I swallow two huge paracetamol, which seem too powdery and dry and weighty for my throat, and squeeze an orange with an old metal juicer that used to belong to my mother, drinking it down for vitamin C. My vision is blurry but stable, and I have become accustomed to the pounding in my head now, a kind of painful heartbeat that seems to tighten with my in-breaths and loosen as I breathe out. I should try to call Matt or one of the neighbours. I should go to the hospital before I get too weak. I am sure it is malaria now. I need choloroquine or mefloquine, drugs I haven't prescribed in a long time. There is no Spear Master to save me this time, only myself. But for what? That's what I'm thinking. For what?

Just now I had the curious sensation that Commander Wol was lying on my sofa in his dressing gown, his long legs hanging over the side. Of course, when I looked again it was only the old blanket I slept in last night given curious human form by the afternoon shadows, but I feel superstitious about going into the room to phone the hospital. As if there is a presence there. And I have this sudden desire to turn on the news – as if something is about to happen.

There is a strange sound, which I realise is the rattling of the ice in my glass of orange juice where my hand is shaking, or maybe the chattering of my teeth.

And then the doorbell rings suddenly and insistently in a series of tinny exclamations.

"Maria!" A lipsticked mouth at the letterbox.

On the sofa the blanket seems to stir and move.

I close the kitchen door quietly and sit down on a stool, steadying my hands on the worktop.

I want them all to go away.

Chapter Twenty-Three

When I awoke in my tukul the next morning at some time barely past dawn, there was no sign of Grace except for a boomerang-shaped hollow in the bedclothes and the perfumed smell of her hair on my threadbare pillowcase. I got up slowly in the pale light, shuffling my bare feet into flip-flops and picking up my towel from the bent nail on the back of the door. Grace's compact was still on the floor and I snapped it open, smiling grimly at the sleep-swollen face in front of me. In the shower, I used the mirror to make sure my hairline was fully rinsed of grit and that my face and neck were properly clean, and to scrub my teeth hard with the frayed fronds of my ragged toothbrush. I was getting used to myself again, but I still looked at the face in the mirror as someone detached from the person who held it, a sibling or a lookalike or a parallel self. The length of my arm seemed to represent an unbridgeable gulf of experience.

By the time I had showered and dressed carefully in my cleanest clothes in honour of the harvest dance, it was almost fully light, and I sat for a while at the fire, building the embers to a blaze and brewing coffee from the neat brown and cream packet Grace had brought in with her from Kenya, enjoying the comfortingly familiar smell of the steam whistling through the metal spout of Billy's espresso maker. The single cup I poured black into a blue-flecked tin mug was scalding hot and deliciously bitter. Its burning taste on my lips and mouth seemed another tentative step back towards the world I had come from, and another step away from the place I was leaving behind.

After I had drunk the coffee, I smoked one of Grace's cigarettes sitting in a shaft of soft, almost opaque sunlight that fell through two branches of the mango tree, and it felt the perfect morning with the sun on my face and so many cravings satisfied at once. Then, I walked to Billy's tukul and knocked on the door.

Muffled noises came from inside.

181

"Wait a minute," Billy called, but I was already opening the door.

In the gloom of the hut, Grace was clutching the dark bedsheet around herself, leaving Billy's naked torso exposed to the light spilling in through the door. I stood there for a moment, enjoying their discomfort. Then I threw Grace's compact lightly across the room to the bed so that it landed without accusation on Billy's thigh.

"You forgot this," I said.

It was a moment of perfect symmetry: Billy's alarmed expression half-hidden by his beard, Grace actually blushing in the bed. I was relieved to find I felt neither jealousy nor irritation. I merely had the sense of a necessary balance restored.

Billy was propelling himself out of the bed and I threw him his khaki shorts from the floor.

"I've just made coffee," I said. "Will you have some?"

"Look Maria . . ." Billy said, zippering himself up to comic effect.

Grace pushed past him, wrapping herself neatly in Billy's navy blue cotton sleeping sheet and adjusting it around her breasts as if it were an impossibly glamorous, shoulderless ball gown. Her hair fell immaculately down to her shoulders in loose curls, and her eyebrows arched by degrees like the architectural sketch of a particularly graceful building.

"Coffee's great," Grace said, and smiled her irresistible smile. It seemed we were somehow co-conspirators. "Black, no sugar . . ." She turned to Billy who was standing in awkward dishevelment, groping in the half-light for a cigarette. "How d'you want your coffee, hon?"

I looked at Billy and he seemed to have physically shrunk, as if his skinny body was trying to hide itself behind that enormous bushy beard.

"I think I know by now how Billy takes his coffee," I said, walking out of the tukul and back into the morning light. "And anyway, we don't have milk or sugar."

*　*　*

Up at the hospital that last day I was acutely conscious that we had only a single day left in Adek – a final twenty-four hours with which to make impossible peaces, attempt inadequate thank yous and say inexpressible goodbyes. Lost for how to spend my last morning with so many endless things that needed doing, I spent it cleaning up the way my mum would do before we went on holiday, scrubbing and sweeping, preparing for departure in the only way I could think of, trying literally to tidy up after myself. After a couple of hours, Adel joined me, and we worked for a while in a companionable silence before she brought us both cups of water and we went to sit outside in the shade and drink them together.

"I can't believe we are leaving," I said to Adel. "There's so much we have left to do . . . I haven't even had time to talk to you about the poem . . ."

"You don't need to read me the poem," Adel said. "I know Bol doesn't want to marry me. It doesn't matter."

"He does want to marry you," I said, looking at my hands where they cradled the earthenware cup – a red handleless vessel made from Adek soil. "He's just trying to do the right thing. He doesn't want your family to disown you. He wants what's best for you."

"If he loved me," Adel said, "he wouldn't have gone to join the SPLA."

I sat fully upright then, suddenly, spilling some of my water on to the floor. It disappeared immediately, swallowed by thick dust.

"Bol hasn't joined the SPLA . . ." I said, hollow-voiced. "He wouldn't. He's a poet. And he's needed at the hospital. He can work for Africaid after we've gone. He doesn't need to be a soldier."

"He is the son of a great warrior," Adel said.

"He's a bloody idiot," I said, frightened and angry and upset. "I'll go and speak to the Commander and get him dismissed at once."

"If you do that you will humiliate him," Adel said, and I could tell she still loved him from the expression in her violet eyes.

"Well, better humiliated than dead."

"Bol will not agree with you."

"He's a thirteen year old boy."

"He's fourteen years old," Adel corrected me. "And he is a man."

We sat quietly for a while listening to a solitary bird sing mournfully up in the leafless branches of the breadfruit tree behind the hospital. Then, it stopped and the silence seemed too much, broken only by the shivering of the bare trees in a sudden rare light breeze. I pulled the poem from my pocket.

"I'd like to read this to you anyway," I said.

Adel took the paper from me.

"Please don't," she said.

"It's a beautiful poem," I said.

"Bol only writes beautiful poems," Adel said, pushing the square of paper into the waist fold of her sarong.

* * *

The rest of the day passed in a blur of activity. I packed up my rucksack with a few necessary things for my journey home and shared the rest between Adel and John. I found the WH Auden anthology my brother had sent me and took it across the village to Bol's mother to keep for a time when he could become a poet again, in case I did not see him to say goodbye. She wept when she saw me and I had no way in Dinka to tell her how sorry I was, and could only hold her against the torrent of her anger and tears. Almost without point I left her what medicine I had left for her malaria and TB. They were drugs that I knew were unlikely to be replenished once we were gone.

In the afternoon, I gathered all the nurses together at the hospital and told them how important their work was and how help would be coming and that other NGOs would soon send some more Westerners and Sudanese doctors to help with their training. I went to take a last look at the feeding centres and promised myself I would be back, that I wasn't abandoning these people, not now, not yet. I sat on John's platform bed and held his hand and said I would be back to see him the next day to say goodbye properly, and I promised him that one day I would get him to the big ICRC hospital at Loki where they could fit callipers to his legs and he would walk again. My promises were as heartfelt as they were hollow. I had no way of knowing whether I would ever be back in Southern Sudan.

As I left, I felt my pockets and went back again to John's bed where he lay feigning sleep.

"Cigarettes, John," I said, in our familiar routine from the old days when John would sleep up at the camp and we still had a seemingly endless supply of duty frees. John must have noticed the packet of Lucky Strikes that Grace had given me.

A small, dark hand bearing a white packet appeared from under the blanket.

"Smoking's bad for small boys," I said. "Especially small boys in hospital."

"Give me something else, then," John said, and it gladdened me to see he was growing closer again to his old self.

My mother's engagement ring was in my pocket where it always was, carried everywhere, but too small for my long, large fingers. John whooped with delight when he saw it, straining his face to squint at the tiny diamonds inlaid on cheap silver. His dirty hand seized it greedily and placed it on his fourth finger, where it fitted perfectly, the first time anyone had ever worn it since my father had left my mother twenty-two years before.

"I'm so sorry, John," I said, kissing his forehead. "I'm so sorry about your father and about what happened to your legs . . . Of all the people in the village to hurt . . ."

John held the ring out in front of him, apparently ignoring what I was saying.

"It's nice," he said. "It sparkles."

"It's a ring for a wedding."

"Can I give it to a girl one day?"

"I would love it if you did. Do you know which one?"

"Yes, of course," John said. "But it's a secret for now."

* * *

By around 3.00pm I was back at the camp, leaving some final instructions with one of the needs assessment nurses from the feeding centres, in time to see Commander Wol striding in, wearing freshly laundered dressing gown, combats and high boots. Commander Dit walked up behind him, and by the gate I could see a group of his men waiting and wondered if Bol was among them. The Commander looked enquiringly at his gun, which was forbidden inside the Africaid compound, and I nodded not to worry. What did it matter, I wondered, when by tomorrow this camp would once more be an ordinary part of the village, swallowed up by the frontlines of the civil war.

Sean, however, took a different view.

"I'll have to ask you to leave your gun at the gate, Commander," he said, emerging from the radio hut with a red plastic mug in one hand and a sheaf of paperwork in the other.

"And tomorrow and the day after when you are no longer here?" the Commander said.

"We are still here today, Commander," Sean said. "And so I must ask you stick to our rules as laid down by Operation Lifeline Sudan."

"But there are already guns in this encampment," the Commander smirked. "Perhaps you should ask your own staff why they feel it is necessary to carry them?"

As if on cue, Billy arrived from the feeding centres with Grace, carrying a sack of grain up on his back. I noticed he had shaved since the morning, and seemed restored – physically at least – to a look of his former self, his chin bare, his hair cropped back to its usual short length and his stance more straighbacked than I had seen in weeks or months.

The Commander's eyes followed him.

"But then perhaps old soldiering habits die hard?"

Sean looked at him coldly but did not take up the Commander's bait.

"I am leaving now in any case," Commander Wol said, irritably. "I only came as a courtesy to inform you that myself and a group of my men are leaving now for the cattle camps. Lieutenant Dit here will remain at the barracks to take command should anything untoward happen. Reports are that the area north of here is lying quiet today, but the militia train is still moving south and we cannot leave the area undefended. "

"I'll be here, Commander," Billy said.

He was washed and clean and sober. Grace had made him handsome again.

"And miss the harvest dance?" Sean said.

"Someone should stay," Billy said. "Anyhow I need to fix the radio."

I thought of him fixing the small black box all those months ago after the bombing on my first night in Southern Sudan, of how strong his fingers had looked and how impenetrably hard and cold he had seemed.

I asked the Commander how long it would take to walk to the cattle camp, and he looked at me curiously.

"Are you planning to march with us, Dr Maria?"

"I'm feeling sentimental I suppose," I said. "I haven't seen anything of Bahr el Ghazal except this village. And we're leaving tomorrow . . ."

"Then you shall march," the Commander said.

"I'm not sure it's such a good idea," Sean said.

"I'll be with the Commander," I said. "And a dozen armed men."

Sean's eyes said that it was this that worried him, but I was determined to go all the same. I wanted to talk to the Commander about Bol. And since the day he had pulled me from the minefield I had felt no fear of him.

"All right," Sean said after a while. "I'll drive a group up to the cattle camp and meet you there. Perhaps, Commander, you can spare one of your men to show our vehicle the way?"

* * *

At first we walked the paths that I knew well, the Commander and I up in front with the men in pairs behind, and it took an hour or so to reach parts of the scrubland I did not recognise. We passed through dense jungle and thick trees hung with vines and into clearings overhung by thin acacia bushes on all sides, passing along avenues lined by the skeletons of tall trees that had perished in the drought. After a while, the walking grew more difficult. Towards the flatlands where the frontlines shifted and stuck, the White Nile had recently flooded its banks, swelling all the tributaries to the south including the Jur River close to Adek. Although it had not rained now for two years in Bahr el Ghazal, much of the low-lying land was heavily flooded with stagnant water, from which rose clouds of biting insects.

The Commander removed his dressing gown and handed it to a young colonel, who folded it carefully and held it out in front of himself so it should not go near the water. Following behind the Commander's seven-foot frame, I disappeared several times up to my waist in the viscous, sharp-smelling, green-yellow liquid, regretting my decision to walk.

"So now you see how the Sudanese travel," the Commander said. "This is how your patients have been reaching help, Dr Maria."

A leech had attached itself to my upper arm and I had to find a dry lighter in my upper pocket so the Commander's man could burn it off, blood flowing freely and mixing with the river water until I felt dizzy in the heat.

"In a few days you will be home," the Commander said. "No more leeches. No more famine. No more disease. What will you do?"

"I don't know," I said. "Go back to work at the hospital in London, I suppose. Or stay with Africaid. I was thinking this morning that perhaps I could get a job in Loki or even back in Southern Sudan?"

"Fantasy, Dr Maria," the Commander said. "You will not come back to Southern Sudan."

"How can you be so sure?" I said.

The Commander studied me for a moment while we walked.

"Perhaps I am wrong," he said. "Maybe it's just that you will stay away a long while."

A river snake slid past us and under the water, a shadow under the murky surface. I felt something brush past my legs. I was desperate to get out of the water now, my neck covered in fresh welts where the mosquitoes and midges were biting. We were walking through a malarial swamp, I realised, feeling suddenly foolish and lost, despite the fact that the soldiers clearly knew the route well.

"There are crocodiles in this part of the floodplain," the Commander said, slipping the safety catch off his weapon and holding it above him, out of the water. "So, please take care."

When we reached dry land again, the Commander re-fixed the safety catch and lit a cigarette, guarding the flame from the hot, light breeze, and passing it to me before lighting one for himself.

"You said that someone in the camp had a gun."

"Yes."

"Billy?"

"Danger is very near us," the Commander said. "And Billy wants to die a soldier not an aidworker. That is what he said."

"And what did he mean?"

"The aidworker wrings his hands and survives. The soldier takes his enemy with him when he goes to Lual Aghony, the Promised Land. One dies helpless or flees. The other will stay to do his duty to the end."

"And can a white man go to Lual Aghony?" I asked.

"Perhaps," the Commander said. "All things are possible."

We walked on through a long avenue of tall trees, our waterlogged boots squelching in rhythm with the men behind us. My toes felt hot and raw where they were rubbing on my wet, muddy socks and a brown-green film covered my legs all the way up to my waist. I was determined not to complain, but increasingly wished I was in the rickety comfort of Sean's Land Rover, my shorts soaking wet and chafing as I walked.

"I have noticed you have built no church in the village," the Commander said, continuing our conversation. "And that when the American man came with the Bibles you refused them."

"I don't believe in God, Commander," I said.

"You don't believe in God, or you don't believe in the Christian Gods?"

"I don't believe in any God. But your Gods seem more real to me than any Christian God, at least," I said, hesitatingly. "Your God-spirits live in the trees and the wind and the skies. It makes sense to me to worship real things that affect every day life. The Christian God, well, he doesn't seem worth believing in to me. He is supposed to be a God of love, yet he leaves people starving to death and bleeding on battlefields and takes children from their mothers. That is not love."

"I suppose not," said the Commander, dryly. "But you surely do not believe we can control our own fates?"

"I have to believe we can," I said. "Otherwise, why try to change anything? Why would I treat people in the hospital? Why would you take up arms against the powerful Government of the North?"

"Perhaps because that is what fate has decreed," Commander Wol said. "Have you thought of that?"

We walked on for a while on dry ground, enjoying the freedom from the stinking water and the biting insects.

"Dr Maria," the Commander said, his hand on my arm. "You can surely see that you have changed nothing in your time in Sudan? Nothing of real substance, I mean. You have affected a few lives for the better, of course, but this is a war measured in millions. Already more than a million people have died. Our village is only a tiny place."

Perhaps it was exhaustion, but my eyes stung with tears.

"I don't mean you in particular," the Commander said, more kindly. "I mean white people in general. Africa is a juggernaut that takes years to change direction. The colonialists managed it in some areas, but this part of the continent is still living the way it has done for thousands of years. How would three white people stranded in a village change that?"

I had no tissue to wipe my eyes and used the damp seam of my stinking T-shirt instead. The liquid stung my eyes.

"Oh dear," the Commander said, ruefully. "Now that is why I always feel that white women are not right for Africa. You should be at home in a cold climate with a nice husband bringing home food, sharing a life together. A woman of your age should have children, not be adventuring out here in the bush with soldiers. Women take things too personally. This is a war, Dr Maria, and you are only a tiny part of it. We are all just tiny cogs in a machine controlled by destiny. You mustn't take that to heart."

"But even if we have only helped a few, doesn't that still matter?" I said. "Maybe we have helped someone stay alive who might otherwise be dead? What about the people we have fed in the feeding centres and trained to work as medics and the women who have given birth safely at the hospital and the men whose gunshot wounds we have patched up and malaria we have healed? Would it have been better if we had left them for dead?"

"No, Maria," the Commander said. "But you must understand that their lives are as vulnerable now as the day you arrived."

He stopped the party so that he could drink from his hip flask and offer me a swig which I declined. I drank heavily instead from my water bottle, feeling the tepid moisture momentarily refresh me.

"You saved my life," I said. "You could have left me."

"It was my fate to save you," the Commander said. "Perhaps it still is. The big question of free will is this. Will the West truly come to the aid of Southern Sudan in its hour of need? This is only smoke and shadows compared with the fire that is coming. The North means to wipe all the African peoples off the map of Sudan."

"I don't know what the West will do," I said. "There is so much other noise that drowns out what is happening here. It's like a roar. Before I came here, I didn't even know where Southern Sudan was, let alone that it was in the middle of a civil war. That's why we need Grace's pictures. To wake the world up. Then people might listen."

"But perhaps they will listen too late," the Commander said.

"And then?"

"And then there will be a genocide," the Commander said, quietly. "And your Western governments will have Southern Sudan's blood all over its hands."

I looked at him squarely as we walked, and he looked back at me. I knew the Commander was speaking the truth and yet there was something bothering me.

"Where is Manute, Commander?" I said.

"Manute?"

"The boy from the North. The one the villagers believe is possessed by evil spirits and you tried to arrest in my hospital."

"I have no idea, Dr Maria."

"Bullshit."

"I can assure you, I have no idea." The Commander snorted. "Perhaps your little friend has gone back to join the murdering militias."

"He was a scout," I said. "A lookout."

"I repeat your own word to you. Bullshit."

"How can you possibly know?"

"Because I have seen that look in a boy's eyes a thousand times before," the Commander said. "Don't tell me you haven't seen it? It's the look that says he has killed. That he is so ruined now inside that he can never again be made whole. It is not his fault. It is the way of the militias. But it makes him a deadly enemy – one that must not be mistaken for a mere boy."

"And where is Bol?"

The Commander looked at me squarely.

"He is with us," he said. He smiled, almost regretfully. "He was always with us."

"And do you hope that he will soon have that look too?" I said. "The look of a killer?"

"If it pleases Nhialic, yes. We need fighters in this war."

"Then what about the blood on your own hands?"

The Commander sighed then, as if dealing with a difficult child.

"Bol is bright, brave and robust. And his father was a famous warrior in Adek. We don't receive many recruits of his calibre. He has the potential to be an officer, even a Commander."

"And he is thirteen years old," I said.

"Ah well," replied the Commander, laughing easily, "you know the Dinka do not measure age as you do in the West. How do you know he is thirteen years old? He may be small for his age. Anyway, far younger boys than he are fighting this war in Southern Sudan on both sides."

"Then I will have to report you to the UN for breaching the Geneva Convention," I said.

The Commander laughed uproariously. "And do you think they will come to find me here in the middle of the bush, hundreds of miles from roads and good food and air-conditioning, to punish me?" he asked.

"The boy is a poet," I said, almost in a whisper. "He is not a fighter."

"And will poetry deliver the Dinka people from slavery?"

"Bol's family need him."

The Commander snorted contemptuously.

"It's funny how you didn't think of that when you took him to set up your feeding centres," he said.

"He was paid in food, and it kept his family alive."

"And when you are gone? How will you keep him alive then?"

An uncomfortable silence grew between us and we walked on through the scrubland in silence, listening to the excited chatter of the Commander's men. The harvest dance was one of the highlights of the year and the low position of the sun in the sky meant it would almost be beginning.

After a while, the Commander spoke again.

"I know you came here to help us," he said, more kindly. "I know you came with good intentions. I have seen you working in the feeding centres from dawn long into the night. All I am saying is that it may not be enough, Dr Maria."

Exhaustion flooded my heart and radiated through my body to my limbs, as if my extremities were filling slowly with sand. There was a long silence as we walked through a deep dry riverbed.

"One day perhaps we will live in a time for poets," the Commander said.

The dry land grew harder yet, more solid underfoot, and still we walked on, with the crack of dead wood under our feet and the noises of evening, the crickets and the fruit bats starting up in the trees. We had been walking in near silence for almost an hour when I asked the Commander to tell me what had happened to his hand.

"An accident," he said tersely.

I was tired and impatient to arrive. I no longer cared if I angered the Commander.

"What kind of accident?"

The Commander said nothing.

"For God's sake," I said, impatiently. "What can it matter? I'm leaving tomorrow. What harm can telling me possibly do?"

The Commander grunted.

"When I was a boy, in the time before the animals died, a lion came to Adek village," he said. "I was on the outskirts of the village one day, visiting . . ." here he paused with an uncharacteristic air of uncertainty, ". . . someone I was fond of." He looked down at his hand. "Then I saw a brown flash disappear into the scrubland, and shortly afterwards I heard a woman scream. When I reached the clearing where she was standing I saw that the lion had the woman by the throat. In those days, before I was a soldier, I was armed only with a knife, and I threw myself onto the body of the beast and plunged into its flesh many times, up to the hilt, until it lay dead."

"What was her name, the woman?"

"What does it matter?"

"It matters for the story," I said. "I am trying to picture her."

"Nyibol," the Commander said.

"Did she survive?" I asked. "Did you save her life as you saved mine?"

The Commander snorted.

"I did."

There was a trace of bitterness in his voice I could not quite pinpoint.

"And did she marry you as your reward?" I asked, teasingly.

"No, she did not," the Commander snapped.

He turned angrily to his men, some of whom were lagging behind, and shouted at them to keep up, and I realised I had touched on dangerous territory.

"I only ask about your hand in case I might find some way to treat it," I said.

The Commander eyed me warily.

"The injury is almost three decades old. I doubt even your Western medicine can fix wounds so ancient."

"Let me see," I said, reaching for his hand, but he dropped it awkwardly and held his arm away from me as if embarrassed in front of his men.

"Some other time, perhaps."

The Commander seemed to struggle with himself for a moment, as if he both wanted and didn't want to divulge some secret.

"You may not know that I myself was once a poet," the Commander said. He coughed into his hand, a polite little noise. "A wedding poet like Bol."

I was astounded at this, and looked at the Commander for a moment, trying to imagine him as a young man, before his scars and injuries, before his heart had hardened to stone and was still a porous, malleable thing. Somewhere inside the Commander that soft kernel of a person still existed, I thought. I had seen it that day in the minefield.

"And Nyibol was your lover?" I asked.

"Nyibol was Deng's sister," the Commander said.

"Chief Deng's sister?"

"Yes. And mine too, but not by family blood . . ."

"From when Old Deng adopted you. Because of your father's service."

"You were listening."

"I'd like to hear more."

The Commander began to tell me the story then despite himself, much in the way that I had told my own story the previous night to Grace. How many stories we are hiding, I thought, as he haltingly explained what had happened thirty years ago in the same village we were now walking away from. How many stories make up a man.

When they were both fourteen years old, young Wol and Nyibol had experienced a fleeting moment of happiness, but a year into their love affair, a lion had come upon Nyibol in the clearing where they met each day. The Commander had fought the lion to the death, but when his lover had dragged his unconscious body back to the village their lovemaking had been discovered. Nyibol had been sent away from Deng's family to become another man's wife in distant Equatoria. Three years later she had died of malaria. The part of Wol's hand where the nerve had been destroyed by the lion's bite served to remind him every day of what he had lost. Wol the poet had been sent to Uganda where he had studied politics and philosophy at Makere University in Kampala, before volunteering to join the Ugandan army, where he served alongside such luminaries as a young Idi Amin. When he returned to Adek years later, it was as the ultimate soldier: a well-trained, battle-fit man who did not much care whether he lived or died.

"It is the fate of the warrior clans and the royal clans to remain separate," the Commander said.

"The antelope will not come to the watering hole of the lion."

The Commander looked at me quizzically.

"Spoken as a Dinka," he said.

"It is from a poem of Bol's," I said. "It seems he is to suffer the same fate."

"Why do you say so?"

"Because he is in love with Deng's daughter, Adel."

The Commander paused.

"Then, yes, you are right."

"But perhaps it could be different. Things could change."

The Commander snorted into his beard.

"Well again that depends very much, Dr Maria, on whether or not you believe in fate."

* * *

As the smoke of the cattle camp drew into sight, the colonel handed Commander Wol back his dressing gown with a ceremonial bow, and he put it on carefully.

"You know, there's something I've been meaning to tell you about your robe," I said, watching him smooth the material against his skin.

"What is that?" the Commander said, tying its rope around his waist, and replacing his ammunition belt on top.

I hesitated. As the words formed in my mouth they felt suddenly cruel.

"It is a very fine garment, Commander," I told him.

"Thank you, Dr Maria."

"I'm not really a doctor," I said. "Not yet anyway."

"Don't be so sure," the Commander said.

* * *

We reached the cattle camp by late dusk, in time to see the white smoke from the dung fires filtering the brilliant red sunset to a pale pink smudge. Beneath the noise of a thousand insects kept at bay by the fires, a distant drumbeat pounded out an ancient message to the Gods.

"The most important sight in any Dinka's life," the Commander said quietly, as I stood in awed silence, astonished by the glowing dots of the tiny fires that shone like stars through the gloom of late dusk and the vast numbers of cattle drifting through the haze, wandering unherded in a gentle, seemingly ordered traffic. The cattle camp had the feeling of a ghostly church populated not by humans but by an animal congregation, the pink cloak of sunset lending the sacred space a haunting beauty and the icing sugar smoke floating like incense up through the rows of beasts and towards the great cathedral of the late evening sky. We were hidden in a frying-pan-shaped dip in the landscape which seemed to contain the mists and fires, making them invisible from the plains above. The cries of unseen men and haze-hidden cattle echoed around us as if we were walking back through time to a place of safety, where ancient peoples still lived as they always had.

"All of Adek's cattle are kept here, away from the village, away from the Arab marauders," the Commander explained. "I must ask you not to touch, or even to approach any of the animals. It is forbidden for any woman to do so by Dinka law."

We walked carefully between the cattle, stopping now and then to study from a discreet distance the decorations that covered the animals' heads and bodies, making each animal appear distinct.

"They have diminished in number due to the drought, but we still have 100 or so heads of cattle belonging to the village," the Commander said. "Our cows are sacred to us, and they live out their mysterious lives here, each individually named and adorned by a man in the village."

He took my arm sadly, leading me between two great-horned animals that seemed to nod at our presence and demand some kind of bow.

"Only in the last resort will we kill these animals," the Commander said. "When they die, the village dies too."

We followed the drum beat through the dim light to a clearing, where young men daubed in white ash were dancing in a circle, making the distinct shapes of cattle horns with their outstretched arms, and the women stood round the edges clapping and wailing. The Commander led me to a large fire at the perimeter, where a woman was spooning a thick whitish paraffin-scented liquid into small gourds.

"Whether the harvest is one single grain or a multitude of crops, the village must still dance," the Commander said, flicking the flies from his exposed neck. "We dance every night for the gifts of the day, even when those gifts are hunger and sorrow and anguish. But the harvest dance is the biggest dance of all."

"Then we are very ungrateful in the West," I said. "For we only thank our Gods when they deliver."

The Commander emptied a gourd straight down into his stomach without swallowing. Then he offered me the gourd shell and I held it as the woman filled it with the liquid.

I drank from it as he had done, but found it impossible to keep down, coughing and retching into the dry dirt, the lining of my throat and stomach burning with acid.

"It's not Jack Daniels," the Commander laughed, throwing another gourd-full straight down his throat. "It's made from sorghum. It can make you blind."

Sean and Grace walked over to us then, and I saw Chief Deng and Adel were with them. Deng and the Commander greeted one another coldly and it made me suddenly sad to think of the rift between the two brothers.

"What the hell happened to you?" Grace said, looking aghast at my filthy wet shorts and T-shirt and the smears of greenish-brown that adorned my legs. "We've been here hours."

Deng and Adel burst out laughing.

"We went the scenic route," I said.

Grace took my arm and made me stand with her while she took some photographs.

"This is fucking amazing," she said, adjusting a lens as I held a flashbulb for her. "National Geographic, here I come."

The women were dancing inside the circle now, the dust from their feet throwing up clouds and shadows against the fire, and the men were around the edge, still moving to the same heavy drum beat, still making the shapes of bullhorns with their arms and bodies, as if they were now one with their cattle. The air was heavy with wood smoke and it was entirely dark now in the clearing, even with the full moon hanging above. The flames of the fire seemed to devour the light and soon I could barely make out the shapes of the figures as they swayed and crouched and stretched and spun in showers of dust.

"All this time, we haven't seen the dancing," I shouted into Grace's ear above the beat of the drums, feeling my hot breath bounce off her cheek. "We've heard the drums every night but we've never seen it."

Grace looked at me, her brown eyes shining in the firelight, softened by the warm glow of the embers of the fire and whatever she was drinking from a small brown gourd.

"You were right about the dancing after all," she said.

After a while, Chief Deng led Grace and I to the outer circle, where we joined the women in the clapping as the young male dancers whirled past whooping and stamping and whirling their arms. At the very centre, two small boys were beating out the rhythms of the ceremonial drums and I found myself transfixed by the rapid rise and fall of their tiny hands. Inside the inner circle, I was amazed to see the normally reserved Sean dancing with the men, apparently abandoned entirely to the drumbeat, lost in a world unseen.

I turned to Chief Deng, who was standing still watching his daughter dance.

"I thought Michael might have been here," I said.

"I thought so myself," Chief Deng said. "He promised to be back by today from Mapel, for the dance. Perhaps security prevented it."

"In any case, it might have been too painful for him," I said. "There would be too many memories of his wife."

The Chief studied my face carefully before he replied.

"I myself lost a wife," he said. He nodded his head kindly as he spoke. "I thought I could never recover from a loss so deep. Aling and I had been friends since our childhood. Yet now I am happy with another wife. It is not uncommon in Southern Sudan."

He smiled at me again.

"Michael will not always be mourning," he said.

But I will never see him again, I thought.

The Chief shook my hand warmly in the African handshake.

"I am going back now," he said. "I will walk and be back long before dawn. I am going home to my wife and our baby. I am too old for dancing."

Standing on the edge of the circle, I saw Adel's young silhouette rising and falling with the other dancers, her young body moving fluidly to the beat of the drum with an innocent sexuality touched by a more knowing sadness. She danced beautifully but her face had lost its lustre, that astonishing flush of first love, the sparkle in the eyes, the feeling of having captured something that no-one else could ever experience, and her posture was flat and defeated. There was nothing to say to her that could make it any better and I left her alone with her sorrow. Instead, Grace and I drank small sips of the firewater and the broths of bitter leaves that the cattlemen used to keep themselves from sleep, and smoked the pipes that were passed along the line of villagers, and soon we were whirling with the women, white ash adorning our faces, lost in the drum beat, eyes closed, in a trance that seemed to link back millions of years to when men and earth and cattle were one nothingness.

*   *   *

When it was just less than a full hour from dawn, Sean rounded us up and directed us towards the vehicle, where Commander Wol was waiting with Adel.

"All aboard," Sean said.

We said our goodbyes to the cattle camp elders, tired but elated, and climbed into the vehicle. Grace went in the enclosed front with Sean, waving me to squeeze in next to her, but I had the sudden desire to travel in the back of the pick-up and feel the cool wind on my face and to open my eyes and see as much as possible of my very last dawn in Southern Sudan. I was a little high from the pipes we had smoked and the liquids we had drunk and as the colours of early dawn faded upwards it seemed to me that there must be someone operating a giant switch somewhere out of view just below the horizon. The Commander climbed in next to me and laid his rusted old AK-47 across his knees, and for once Sean made no comment about him carrying a weapon on board one of the Africaid vehicles despite the No Guns sticker on the window.

Resting my tired limbs against the cool of the metal, I arranged myself carefully in the back, bracing myself for the bumps ahead, and studying my filthy legs and shorts still coated with dried mud from the arduous journey down. Sitting next to me, Adel passed me a small white shell she had found somewhere in the sunken basin of the cattle camp.

"It means Southern Sudan must have been under the sea once," I said, putting my arms round her like a seatbelt.

"What is the sea?" Adel asked.

I laughed then, lost for a way to explain, realising that of course no-one in this landlocked country had any more concept of sea or waves or the power of the tides than they had of peace.

Sean drove hard through the scrubland, the vehicle throwing up clouds of red dust that covered each of us in the back with a thick blanket of soil that stuck to our sweat and filled our streaming eyes. Adel hid her face in her dress which steadily stained a deep orange and, from my luxurious perspective behind battered sunglasses, I saw even the Commander had closed his eyes against the flying dust and grit. Conversation in the back was impossible against the wind and the bone-crunching tips and drops of the Land Rover as it lumbered with elephantine grace across the potholed landscape. The first rays of the rising sun faintly warmed the metal back of the pick-up and the dust covered me like a blanket as the landscape whipped by, and I was filled with a sense of privilege to be there, despite everything, riding through Africa in the open air, seeing a land made unreachable to other visitors by war and famine. I slept for a while despite the bumping and grinding, lost in a kind of trance brought on by the dancing and the spirits and the singing, exhilarated by a sense of freedom I had not felt in months. I dreamed of the mists of the cattle camp with the dung fires burning, only the smoke came thicker and blacker from the fires and the cows seemed smaller and further away.

I awoke choking, acrid smoke constricting my chest, my eyes on fire underneath their lids. All of my instincts seemed to fight against each other as my suddenly alert brain sought to make sense of the evidence brought to me by each of my overloaded senses. An area that only hours ago had been teeming with thousands of displaced people – the sick and the dying from outlying villages – was barren of all but the signs of hastily stamped-out fires. The trees appeared to have been slashed by some giant monster, great cuts bruising the trunks and branches torn out everywhere. There was no sign of life, just an uncanny emptiness and a burning smell too acrid for woodsmoke.

Then, as the Land Rover rounded the final bend before the village and we emerged through a thicket of tall trees, the explanation lay before us. Adek was on fire.

Chapter Twenty-Four

The doorbell is ringing in long bursts now, over and over, making me worry about my neighbour Mr Shiozaki, an elderly Japanese painter with a nervous disposition and a fear of loud noises that dates from the Second World War. I've tried turning up the television and putting on my iPod headphones but still the insistent drill of the bell is making it impossible to think. My headache is banging and throbbing as if someone has taken to banging directly on the temporal nerve, and every metallic ring goes through my brain like a sharp wire through a hard-boiled egg. I pull my mother's blanket around myself, as freezing as I was hot before, my teeth chattering and my body rigid with muscle contractions. It is possible this ringing is not outside at all, but in my head. Perhaps I am further along than I realise, already moving towards cerebral malaria or liver failure.

The Commander has woken up from his nap on the sofa and is standing in the kitchen doorway, filling its narrow frame with his giant height, his large hands covering his ears and his dressing gown rumpled into tiny creases. His eyes look tired and haunted and he scratches irritably at his beard. Then he turns on his heel.

"I am going to answer it," he says, over his huge shoulder.

I pull myself off the chair I am sitting on with great effort, the black and white kitchen tiles shifting in front of my eyes like a chessboard seen under moving water. My feet seem a long way down, and my body is convulsed by shivering. Sweat streams from my forehead and into my eyes, and I smell my mother's fear in her old blanket as I pull it around myself, trying not to trip on its neatly stitched edges where they trail on the linoleum floor.

I reach the hallway as the Commander reaches the front door, his big hand on the loose mechanism of the latch I have been meaning to fix for months. The letterbox lifts and falls against the single coat of thin white paint on the back of the door.

"Stop!" I shout, and the Commander looks around at me, wide-eyed. "Don't open it!"

He is about to open it, I know he is, when a woman's voice comes through the pushed-open letterbox and startles him away from the door.

"Open this door immediately, Maria. I know you're in there."

The voice throws me completely as I don't know whether the person is real or imagined. The doorbell, thankfully, has stopped ringing, and my shivering is returning to a more normal level, allowing me to relax my jaw muscles and bring my hands around myself, holding the blanket against me.

"Don't make me kick the goddamn door in . . ."

The voice sounds so familiar I want to hug it.

"Who are you?"

"Who am I?" There is a familiar laugh. "Maria, this is Grace. Grace Mulholland."

I can't handle this. I seriously can't handle it. First the Commander and now Grace. My flat isn't big enough for every one of the cast of thousands who were there in Sudan to come and take up residence.

"Go away!" I shout.

"Go away?"

A pair of grey kohl-rimmed eyes and then a lipsticked mouth appear back at the letterbox.

"Jesus, Maria, it's taken me ten fucking years to find you. I'm not going to go away."

"Please," I say. "I'm sick."

I am pleading now, begging her. My eyes are hurting in their sockets like balls jangling in a pool table's pockets and I need to sleep.

The Commander has vanished back into the living room or run upstairs and I have slid down the white wall to the brown floor of the tiny hall, my back burning against the radiator piping and my vision blurring.

"Go away. Go away. Go away."

I know only this mantra will keep Grace from me and the past from finally intruding so far into the present that a schism will occur and I will be trapped forever in the living hell of what happened ten years ago and has kept on happening every day and night that I have closed my eyes ever since.

"Please go away!"

As I whisper the words, I can hear the door coming in. I can see the useless latch bending against the cheap Yale and the square mechanism of the lock itself twisting sideways. I can see the white door swinging inwards towards me and a woman falling in on top of it, her shoulder against its red front, and her hair in her face. She rights herself quickly and pushes the hair out of her eyes and it is darker than I remember and her face is older, but she is still surreally beautiful like a film star from another era.

"Sorry about that," Grace says, without the remotest air of apology.

I look around for the Commander, but he has vanished with the shock of her. The same grey eyes, surrounded now by narrow lines. The same look of outraged honesty.

"Commander Wol was here," I mumble, and I see the puzzled look in her eyes. "You've frightened him. He was here and now he is gone."

"Maria . . .?" Grace is coming towards me, open-mouthed with alarm. "What the hell is wrong with you?"

I tell my mind to block her out, to prove that she is not here, only a figment of my imagination, another ghost from then that has hunted me down to my flat by the river.

"Maria!"

I try to close my eyes and force myself to concentrate, but she is holding my face and looking at my eyes and I can feel my wet head boiling between her two cool hands.

"Call 999," I hear her say to some invisible person. "Ask for an ambulance."

Chapter Twenty-Five

In the marketplace, plumes of black smoke rose from the fiery roofs of every tukul and fireballs fed by the straw buildings blew across the sky. My eyes tried to close against the thick, treacly air as it danced with swirls of black burning ashes that made the wind appear on fire. A burning piece of paper flew on the breeze into the centre of the marketplace and landed bumpily, jumping before settling on a blackened mound I slowly realised was the body of a woman, lying among a hundred others, stained black with ash and red with blood. When I bent carefully to the woman, I saw with numb calmness it was the Chief's young and beautiful wife, Mrs Deng, lifeless with the remains of their dead baby somehow still cradled in her hands, as bloody as the day I had delivered it. Around her the bare earth was strewn with slaughtered, half-burned bodies weeping red-black that pooled lightly against the duller red of the earth. The brutally cloying, repulsively sweet smell of burning flesh was in my throat and nose and I coughed bile into my hand trying to rid myself of its acrid, staining scent.

Everything fell into calm slow motion then, the stillness of the scene strangely beautiful. The marketplace had the neatly methodical air of a tableau, or some ancient battle scene artwork in which every lifeless body had been ordered to suit the painting's composition. Walking amongst the bodies, I found myself marvelling at the tiny details of death. The way a woman's beautiful necklace was cut neatly in two. The way an elderly man's broken jaw was fixed into a rictus smile. The delicate arch of a child's foot. As I picked my way through the jumble of bodies, I found myself staring at the corpse of a pregnant woman, the baby expertly cut out of her with a single knife wound. The child was nearly full-term and I found myself wanting to pick it up and hold it, but none of my limbs were responding to my commands, as if they too had been rendered from my body with a machete's blade. Floating above my body looking down, I saw myself bend and pick up a battered bullet casing that seemed too small and empty to be capable of harm. Then, as the weak morning light flickered on the burnt brass of the casing, my lost self caught sight of something familiar that wrenched me back into my body once more.

Commander Wol was standing over the body of a man, his hands across his mouth, and tears falling from his eyes, and I saw it was Chief Deng who lay there, yards from his wife, in the tangle of bodies. Wol dragged him up and over his shoulder and pulled him from the burning pyre, howling now with grief and rage, and I could not watch him. I looked around for Adel, wishing to spare her the sight of her parents, but I couldn't see her anywhere near.

Again and again I stooped to lift an arm or to take a pulse, but the cries I heard were only the whisperings of the wind in the burning trees, or the distress call of a bird or a falling tukul collapsing in on itself. I found my friends one by one. Moses the camp guard who we had teased so much about sleeping on duty, finally at rest. The long, tightly-muscled body of the Spear Master, painted white for the harvest celebrations and now streaked with red. Mrs Ajuong, my favourite of all the nurses. I looked at her and then I thought of Polio John, lying defenceless with two broken legs at the hospital we had built together, and I started running, not caring that the path under my feet was lined by the bodies of the dead. I thought of everyone I loved as I ran. I thought of Michael who had not come to the cattle camp, and of Billy. Of Bol and Manute. Of Aneta-Maria. And then names began falling like tears around me.

*   *   *

The hospital looked as I had first found it all those months ago with John: burned out, ruined, uninhabitable. Ashes turned once again to ashes, and dust to dust. All the long hours and days of work we had put in to rebuilding it, gone in minutes of wilful destruction. The stronger part of the mud walls still stood and some of the roof remained, but mostly it was derelict, small fires still burning away at its corners. I could tell from the detritus in the entrance that the drugs and provisions had been looted and the beds wrecked and torn apart. In the doorway lay two Muhraleen fighters, their white head-dresses bloodied and their clothes and beards red with dust. They were the first casualties I had seen of the Arab forces – the first Muhraleen fighters I had ever seen – and I was startled both by how small they looked and the way they looked so familiar, like young men who in other circumstances you might have gone to school with.

I hesitated at the doorway, prolonging the last moment of ignorance, not wanting to see inside, but knowing I had to find John in case he were still alive. Then, in the dim, smoky light I saw a sight that I did not expect and that made me cry out aloud. In a pile of bodies close to the entrance, I saw Bol's oval-shaped face, expressionless in death, his eyes closed tight against the atrocity that surrounded him. His curls looked soft and wet in the gentle light of the dawn, and when I pulled him from the jumble of the dead his body was intact and still warm. He had died from a bullet wound, and I begged God or some other deity I did not believe in that it had been quick. If the boy soldier had held a gun it had been taken from him by looters, but inside his pocket was his usual piece of paper and the stub of a pencil, and I knew he had died a poet too.

I was still holding Bol tight to me as if in a dream, when I heard a noise behind me – a cry like a wounded animal's – and I spun round, making my way quickly into the shadowy darkness at the back of the building where the matting roof still held stubbornly intact. For someone, anyone, to be alive, seemed a miracle of such proportions that I almost wept, my heart beating against its own rhythm in recognition of another living soul. As I made my way around a fallen branch that had once held up the central section of the roof, my heart leapt to see there was a boy crouched low in the corner, resting himself on Polio John's tricycle.

"Manute!" I called out, recognising the shape of his head and the long, elegant, slope of his neck into his narrow shoulders. "Thank God!"

But the light glinted suddenly off something in his hand, and I saw he was holding a kalashnikov in front of him, the way a man would hold a spear.

"Manute?"

Manute rocked back on his heels and as my eyes grew accustomed to the thin light, I saw something strange had happened to his expression, as if he were completely absent from his own body, or merely inhabiting his own corpse from some remote place.

As I moved towards him, he cocked the gun and trained it towards me in a single jerky movement, as if controlled by strings from up above in the dark roof. He looked both more sturdy and more hollow than when I had last seen him, as though the muscles in his arms were made of some light but immensely strong substance.

"Manute," I said, softly. "It's me, Maria. You have nothing to fear."

A birdlike cry came from Manute's throat, the same sound I had heard from the entrance. His eyelids fluttered as if he were in great pain. He was barely taller than the length of his Kalashnikov.

"It's okay, Manute," I said. "I know you had nothing to do with this. We all love you very much."

But as I spoke, a fear was growing inside me, that Manute had killed the people in the hospital, and that he had shot Bol, and that he had led the Arab militias straight to Adek village along the back routes, knowing the harvest dance would have been this weekend.

Then, I saw he was wearing something on the finger that held the Kalashnikov trigger. My mother's engagement ring glittered in the light creeping through the smoky holes of the tukul.

"Where is John, Manute?" I asked, more coldly now, but Manute only shivered. "Where is the crippled boy who had that ring? Why do you have his tricycle?"

I continued to advance, not knowing what else to do, just believing that if I could get to Manute and hold him as I had held him in the hospital he would go back to being that sleeping boy, the beautiful child with the striking dark eyes and the man's deep voice.

I was still six feet away when he spun the Kalashnikov round with that sound again in his throat, the one all animals in terror share, even humans. I was five feet away when he shot himself, and four when his head dropped forward and exposed the space where his brain had been.

I started back to the camp by the back route from the hospital, moving carefully now, studying every single thing that moved, stopping now and then to suppress the screams inside my own throat. My body was trembling from the cold flood of adrenalin and my teeth chattered lightly against each other. My eyes seemed as accurate as a rifle sight, and my hearing was clear and precise. In my hand was the ring that Manute had been wearing, but I had no idea how it had got there. As I walked I could smell the snuffed out bodies around me, the bitter-sweet smell of death catching at the back of my throat and slashing at the sharp breath that came from my lungs until the stink of it became unbearable. I tried to focus on reaching the radio room at the camp, but something in me kept stopping. Every few steps or so I would catch a sign of life in a dead villager, a movement in a stiffened finger, a clench of a jaw muscle, a glimmer of spirit in a whitened, staring eye, the flicker of a foot or a finger amongst the bodies of the dead. Yet every time I bent to them, I found I was mistaken, that it had been a trick of the light or the light breeze, or merely imagination.

On the path around the back of the marketplace, I stopped at the body of one of the Commander's young soldiers and the oddly misplaced familiarity of his clothes made me want to stop and weep. A boy who should be playing football, he lay on his front on a pile of bodies, the word Beckham written in white across the back of his red Manchester United shirt.

I had no way of knowing where the others were, and it seemed for a moment to my numbed mind that I might be the only person left alive in an entire village of dead people, like the Creation story in reverse, the last woman in a paradise that had fallen as far as hell itself. But as I walked past the burned out remains of the Spear Master's hut I saw I was not alone after all. The Witch Doctor's Marial bull was standing in the middle of the battlefield, a lone living presence of breathing flesh and moving muscle in a scene of carnage, looking about him with tosses of his massive head. His coat shone black and white, and his brightly-painted horns seemed to belong there in the garish field of bloodied clothing and disturbed red earth. Only the heavy weight of his gleaming body seemed out of place against the wasted life around him. He was too full of life, a bull standing over the spectacle of human butchery, a scene from a Western abattoir in reverse. He stood for a while, and then moved off, leaving me once more completely alone with the dead. Inside my distracted mind, I found I was keeping a running toll of the murdered against a list of those who might still be alive. There were many hundreds dead and yet that might still mean many thousands had escaped. To where? Back out to the inhospitable bush where other cruel deaths from thirst and hunger and sickness awaited them? My mind flitted from thought to thought without settling and, all the while, I kept on walking towards the encampment we had built so many months ago under the barren mango tree, not thinking of what I might find there.

* * *

I reached the camp to find it ransacked, encircled by a perimeter fence now burned and charred like a giant oval scorch mark, many of the buildings inside still ablaze. The 'Hotel California' sign Billy had painted in another lifetime was trampled into the dirt, cracked in half, the word California hacked in two. The inner fencing was torn down, and the fire where we had sat so many long evenings was stamped out, the bare earth around it strewn with possessions. The camp had been thoroughly pulled apart, water containers overturned, food looted, Billy's picnic table macheted to pieces. A deflated football sat forlornly in the hearth, its vinyl outer coating melting into the fire's ashes like a leaking marshmallow. Billy's coffeepot lay in a black pool of grinds, its handle dripping molten plastic into the mud. Michael's knife was there too, left inexplicably in a pile of clothing from one of the tukuls. I stooped to pick up a piece of purple glittering plastic and almost wept realising it was a sweet wrapper, one of the Quality Street my brother had sent for my birthday, stuck to a shattered CD case where a bootprint had muddied the words 'OK Computer'. Turning, I saw my own tukul was burning, its coconut matting roof still on fire. My disordered brain thought of Laurel and Hardy the spiders, saved from Michael's murderous attentions all these long months. The fate of bulls and spiders was easier to consider than the human cost. That was already beyond comprehension.

I was barely able to orientate myself in the chaos of the ransacked camp, and it took me a moment or so to realise the radio hut was the dismembered tukul to my right. Perhaps I already knew what I would find as I walked towards the mess of matting and roofing, a wooden post sticking out sideways like a broken spine, because I registered the crumpled body lying in the fallen doorway without surprise. I knew it was him even before the familiar shape of his body registered itself through the sluggish confusion that threatened to overwhelm me.

Billy's dirty white T-shirt showed a single entry wound between his shoulder blades. If he had had a gun, the militias had taken it when they had fled, but as I pulled his body towards me I found hidden under him the radio and receiver from which I could hear anxious voices shouting his call sign and his name. The stars and stripes shorts I had thrown at him across the tukul twenty-four hours earlier were streaked with dust, and his legs were twisted under him, and I heard a scream echo that I might have made with my mouth or only my mind. I moved towards his body on limbs I could no longer feel, knowing it was him, knowing and yet not wanting to reach him because then all doubt would be driven away. I looked up at the dawn instead, where the unknowing sun did not hide itself, and the clouds continued to drift across the sky without the decency to stop and pause at the sight below them. My eyes were dry and tired, as if they knew tears were of as little consequence as a few drops of rain on an earth parched by months of drought. I could hear shouts and voices around me, but I was lost in the shape of Billy's head, the way his brown hair had a texture like suede, pointing in different directions, following the shape of his hat. I had seen him fully hatless only once before, on the night when we had poured our separate longings into one another, with the insects up above scraping out a rhythm in the roof, pulling and scratching at one another as if we were each dying of a separate loneliness that only physical pain could awaken, each trying to save the other from the desperate feeling that whatever we were doing couldn't ever be enough. Unable to look any more at that face and all the conflicting things it meant to me, I picked up Billy's hat and placed it gently over his eyes as if he were merely sunbathing in his hammock in the gentle morning light.

*　*　*

I don't know how long I stood like that but suddenly I saw that Commander Wol was running towards me, his arms extended, holding an AK-47 in each hand. The Commander was screaming, but the wind was twisting the words from his mouth and the rushing in my ears smothered his voice. His expression was terrifying, and I wondered what harm he could mean and what he was screaming as he threw himself on top of me, knocking me into the dust, his dressing gown blackened to the colour of his own skin. Then, hearing a volley of shots ring out I flung my face down into the bare earth, tasting the soil with my open mouth.

After what felt like hours, although it may have been only seconds, an agonisingly sharp and anxious pain in my arm distracting me from fear, I pulled myself from underneath the Commander, heaving him over so that the wounds on his strong chest lay exposed where his gown had fallen open. In the middle of the camp, two militias lay murmuring in the throes of death, their bodies twisting as if controlled by invisible ropes. The burning tukul had fallen, but there was no sign of Adel. My arm was badly broken and bleeding, but the Commander's body had taken the bullets meant for me.

Fresh gunshots sounded in the distance. Flames were licking and spreading where the burning tukul had fallen.

"We need to move into those trees," I told the Commander. "I'm going to try and drag you."

But even as I spoke I knew I could not drag a seven foot man with gunshot wounds, even without a broken arm. Instead, with my good arm, I found the Commander's hip flask in his pocket and dribbled a little whiskey onto his lips so that he opened his mouth a little. Water fell onto his face and I realised I was crying.

The Commander tried to speak, but blood dribbled from the corners of his mouth. I knew he was trying to tell me to go.

"How can I leave you?" I whispered to him. "When you have twice saved my life?"

His tongue seemed to flicker against the tide of blood in his throat but no words came. With great effort, he moved his fluttering hand to pluck at the top pocket of his camouflage jacket and I slipped open the pocket, careful not to apply any pressure to his shattered chest. Inside was a beautifully delicate hand-drawn paper map of the area around Adek and I knew he meant me to use it to escape, but it was badly stained with blood and tore as I unfolded it.

"Thank you, Commander," I told him. "You rest now."

The Commander seemed to smile and I knew he was already moving through the blackness towards a tiny white dot on the horizon, the distant cattle fires that the Dinka believe mark out the beginnings of Lual Aghony, the Promised Land. He smiled even as the spreading stain of blood darkened the material of his dressing gown and the dry, bare earth where he lay with his AK-47 in his hand, and I wondered if Nyibol was waiting for him there. Against the sound of the pain in my arm I heard the whispering of the wind in the trees, and the sound of soil slipping gently against soil, and the clouds soft movement through the air, and the falling of starlight to earth and I knew then the Commander was already becoming each of them.

I went then to the bodies of the militias, feeling curiously close to them after hearing something so intimate as their dying whimpers. I was floating above the searing pain in my arm, where I could see the ulna bone protruding obscenely through the broken skin of my swollen forearm, and it made me strangely sad to think of these two young men so far from home, with no-one to hold them when they died and perhaps no clue as to why they were fighting in this remote, godforsaken, arid part of a country where they had no desire to live or raise families. They looked to me like brothers and I wondered if they were and whether this was of some comfort to them in dying, knowing they were not alone. I stood there pondering their deaths because I didn't know them, when all around me were the bodies of my friends.

Something is Going to Fall Like Rain

* * *

I was aware of how bad the fire was only suddenly, and then the noise of it came roaring into my consciousness, the tukuls crashing and burning ahead of me, the heat of the blaze suddenly acutely uncomfortable. I began to move away from the fire's terrible force into colder air, but then, through the circle of flames, I saw Adel kneeling down amongst the debris, holding herself tightly as if in prayer, and I knew she had seen her parents, her baby brother, maybe even Bol, and I turned back and began running towards her through the fire. As I reached her the tukul behind us – Billy's tukul – began to fall around us with a terrible splintering sound. Finding Adel's body with my hands, my eyes closed against the thick smoke, I lifted her somehow under my good arm, the searing pain in my broken limb stopping me perversely from passing out in shock and smoke and blood loss, and sheltering her with my body, I began to carry her frozen form out from the flames and I was aware that my hair was on fire as I walked.

* * *

I don't know what happened next but suddenly Lieutenant Dit was holding me, speaking in a soothing voice, my head wrapped strangely but neatly in his shirt. Somehow I was telling him that the radio was working – that Billy had fixed it, and that even now voices from another world were shouting at the other end.

The pain in my arm was making me dizzy, and I leaned on the Lieutenant, feeling the strong beat of his thudding heart through his combat vest, suddenly aware of Billy's stopped heart and the Commander's silent chest, of all the stopped hearts in Adek village, dozens of them that had been beating as normal only this morning.

Adel knelt on the ground in front of us, seemingly unharmed but frozen with horror, locked into a state of shock.

"Where is Michael?" I asked Dit, and I did not recognise the husky, cracked sound of my voice, burned by firesmoke. "Where is Sean? Where is John?"

Somehow, around us, the clouds continued their silent passage, the earth still turned on its axis, the sun still burned and the stars waited to become pin-pricks once more in the black night sky. The soft wind still blew tumbleweed through the wrecked encampment. And then, as the stabbing, aching agony in my arm intensified, hearing the sound of aircraft up above us and hearing the shouts of Dit's men that help was coming, I blacked out, no longer able to bear the pain in my own heart.

Chapter Twenty-Six

"Been in the wars?"

The cab-driver was barely awake. Dawn was breaking softly in a dirty yellow haze along the motorway slip-road. Two miles east of Heathrow at 7.25am and the traffic had already slowed to a steady, stuttering stream. I looked up at the grey-blue eyes in the rear-view mirror, stalling with a vague smile, seeing myself as he could see me – hair shorn, thick dressings at my neck and ear, left arm in plaster. No longer equipped for small talk, I momentarily had no idea how to reply.

"Yes," I said and somehow my voice held firm, my throat taut as the sling that held my broken left arm close to my body, as if I were permanently guarding my ribs.

With my right arm, I sipped from the Evian bottle I had bought at the airport, its clear plastic containing the miracle of clean, chilled water bottled for my convenience, swallowing the painkillers the nurse had given me in Loki. Next to the fridge at the WH Smith at Terminal 4 arrivals, the front pages of the day's newspapers dripped with the blood of the 'Adek Atrocity'. Grace's pictures had gone all around the world and I could see my hospital, even now, folded over on the front page of the Daily Mail where it rested on the cab-driver's front passenger seat. I wanted to scream at the cabbie to unfold my friends, to stop dripping his coffee on their faces.

"Do you mind the radio?" the cabbie asked.

I said 'no', but he wasn't really listening, fiddling with the radio for the traffic news, swinging the black cab from lane to lane, watching for gaps in the choked up motorway. A badly tuned news programme reported that the American Unabomber had been sentenced to four life sentences for a bombing campaign that had taken three lives. It was raining steadily on the concrete outskirts of London, where rain had no consequence, meaning only that commuters flicked on their side-lights

213

and turned the radio up against the sound of water hitting glass. No-one fell to their knees. Nobody stopped their car and danced for joy.

At the airport, Africaid was holding a press conference. It would be hearing even now how the UN security planes had come in within hours of the raid, summoned by aidworker and former US Special Forces hero Billy Finn in a last act before he died. His buddy, Jorges, had heard Billy's last moments through the crackle and static of the radio transmission from Loki and immediately scrambled two aircraft to our location. As one of the injured I had been carried unconscious onto the first plane, waking smothered in a blanket as the plane took off to find myself separated from Adel, Grace and Sean and everyone left alive that I loved. As the plane lifted clumsily from the airstrip I had seen Michael down below, running towards us with Polio John in his arms, waving up desperately at the aeroplane, but the screams I had made to the pilot went unheard over the plane's engines and when I tried to undo my seatbelt to run to the front a security man had held me down and buckled me back in.

My arm was operated on the same night in the Red Cross hospital at Loki, and then after forty-eight hours being splinted and plastered and treated for shock in the cheerful brick building, I was medevaced, or evacuated on medical grounds, to Nairobi and then London. I repeatedly asked for information on Michael and John, on Grace and Adel, on Sean, but none was forthcoming. My burned hair cut short and the scorched skin of my ear and neck carefully dressed with advice to seek further, cosmetic medical help in England, I was simply given an unfamiliar set of clothes borrowed from other Westerners at the UN base, dosed up on painkillers and told to rest.

Two days ago, on May 15th, as I had passed through the traffic-choked streets of Nairobi in a taxi, one of Grace's pictures had appeared on the front page of every British, Kenyan and American newspaper and probably many more besides. I was frozen in a single moment of horror, my hair on fire, running through thick smoke and a knot of yellow flames, carrying Adel's limp body as blood streamed from a cut on my temple into my eye. I couldn't recognise myself any more than I could recognise the picture of Billy on the inside pages where it wouldn't scare children from the news stands, his bullet-ridden body twisted in the dust. Logic not memory told me who these strange, agonised people in the photographs must be.

This morning, the 16th, after landing at Heathrow, I was supposed to be facing the reporters from Sky News and CNN who were now furiously organising trips into the field regardless of flight permissions from Khartoum. Adek, the UN assured us, would now be fed and the injured treated, and the Government warned by the international community over the actions of the militias. Instead, when I got to the airport, I had found myself slipping away from my Foreign Office minders and straight past the media scrum who were looking for someone with blackened hair and bloodied clothes, not an ordinary-looking, freshly-washed tourist in oversized American hand-me-downs and a floppy hat pulled down over my head and ears. Only the arm in a cast might have been a clue to the waiting reporters, but no-one looked up as I slipped through the barriers.

As I walked straight into a waiting taxi, I worried my brother had said he would be there to meet me, but I could explain later.

"What you done to yourself then?"

The news had finished and the cab-driver was smiling in the rear-view mirror, flashing straight white teeth surrounded by greying stubble, pushing back the sliding window to communicate better. He had been handsome up until recently, I thought, tall and solid with a silver-grey crewcut and the beginnings of a cabbie's sedentary stomach poking up at the steering wheel. His eyes in the rear-view window were kind, his mobile mouth pouring out a stream of chatter into the vacuum of passing traffic. Half his words were lost to the wind sucking hungrily at his half-opened window.

"Accident," I called back. "My own fault really."

"I should get that looked at by a British doctor," the cabbie winked.

British doctors were on the way to Adek now. Doctors and sanitation experts and feeding centre coordinators from Rome and London and New York. Millions of dollars in aid had been released. It was too late for Adek, but there were a thousand other villages in Southern Sudan. If those 300 dead saved the life of 2.4 million souls perched on the knife-edge of famine, did it not make heroes of every one of the dead? And yet, what use was a dead hero to Adel, a teenage girl who wanted only her beloved Bol and his beautiful poems.

Outside the bubble of the taxi, a sleek, dark Mercedes A-class slipped by in the fast lane. Through the left-hand window I watched a youngish man in a navy blue saloon car stuffing an Egg McMuffin into his mouth. The yolk was dripping from his lip as if in slow motion and onto his suit jacket so that I could almost smell the glistening sliver of spat sausage that had slipped out onto his lapel. He was wiping his mouth on the back of his left hand, holding the wheel in his right, spraying his breakfast into the mobile phone clamped between his ear and his shoulder. With a shock, I realised the radio was playing one of Billy's campfire guitar songs from a world away, an old Willie Nelson melody, 'Mammas don't let your babies grow up to be cowboys . . .'

The cab was stop-starting along the Chiswick flyover now, airborne in an avenue of bright billboards. Eight months ago I had made the same journey in reverse under a similarly slate-grey bucketing sky and noticed none of the same things. The posters seemed terrifying to me now: the giant lipsticks promising slick kisses, magazines screaming promises of better sex, adverts for supermarkets with glistening plates of food thirty feet across. The big boy's buildings, the corporates, the conglomerates, the capitalist chapels of consumerism lined up on both sides of the road like opposing armies intent on violence. The tall, glass-fronted GlaxoSmithKline building reflecting the clouds as if it were creating them and pumping them up into the air. The empty glass Ark stood grounded on dry land, sitting astride its own Godless in-land Ararat. Above the noise of the traffic, it seemed to me I could actually hear the sky-scrapers scraping the grey sky.

I watched a black, hearse-like Land Rover overtake us, thinking how the funerals in Bahr el Ghazal would be over now, the dead buried before I had even left the hospital in Loki. I had repeated the names of those killed quietly to myself over and over these past three days looking for a pattern, but I could see only randomness, as if the names had blown across the marketplace like leaves carried by the wind and some had landed in the fire and others had floated safely into the scrub.

On the flyover, the cab stopped suddenly as if in mid-air, leaving me at eye level with a Gap Kids poster in which a line of children wearing bright smiles and khaki cotton leapt out of a white background, and the shock of them almost made me scream. They were so tall, so well-fed, so normal, that they seemed obscene in their camouflage trousers: doe-eyed, made-up children in combats that would never see battle, never load a weapon, never retch at the scent of blood and gunsmoke.

I thought of the sad little figure of Adel who had visited me in hospital, and the way her face had aged with pain overnight, and how she was a woman now, her adolescence stolen, her shy smile disfigured by grief. I had begged her to come to England with me, to come and live in a place where there was no war or famine and where children went

216

to school and to swimming lessons and played with toys. But she had smiled at me, sadly.

"Adek is my home," she said. "If I leave it, then isn't that what the militias want?"

Her violet eyes were fierce and proud and perhaps for the first time I saw what it meant to be a Chief's daughter, and it made me ashamed that I was running away to safety even though Sudan was not my home.

Adel told me that John was safe and that he had saved little Aneta-Maria from the hospital, dragging her into the tiny space of the medicine chest we had unearthed all those months ago. When Michael had found them, they were almost dead from suffocation.

John had told them how Manute had come into the hospital with the other soldiers, and wrenched my mother's wedding ring from his finger. Manute had whispered something to John as he had done so, telling him to get out of the hospital. But there had been an exchange of gunfire in which Manute had killed an elderly patient and that then seemed to trigger something in him so that he was suddenly firing indiscriminately across the hospital, round after round, killing the militia soldiers as well as villagers as they tried to flee. Bol had been killed, unarmed, carrying one of the elderly women patients, a friend of his mother, to safety. In the commotion, John had dragged himself and little Aneta-Maria to the medicine chest and climbed inside.

So these were the five children I had loved most in Sudan. Adel, Bol, John, Aneta-Maria and Manute. Two of them dead, and none of them children any more.

"Stupid bastard."

The cab driver swerved, narrowly avoiding a people carrier switching lanes, wrenching me back into the present. I wound down the window breathing in deeply, sucking in the street sounds of approaching suburbia, watching the empty-faced commuters line up nose to tail, forming the slow human and metal chain of the early rush-hour. As the A4 bled seamlessly into the jumbled road network of Central London, I saw the giant flagship Tesco pass to my left, stocked with unimaginable riches, a plastic palace of produce, a cathedral-sized monument to the Western way of life. The skyline was closing down now, as the cab inched slowly through Earls Court. The motorway vista had given way to cramped streets, houses stacked on top of each other, cafés spilling onto the pavement, shopfronts hidden by hordes of people of every colour and language and religion moving in ant-like columns, making their way to shops and offices, a network of boxes in which people lived and ate and worked.

As we crawled along at eye level with the flaking paint of neglected bedsits, glimpsing leafy squares through the traffic, I heard Chief Deng's voice in my mind, repeating the questions he had asked so often up at the camp.

"Why?" I heard him say, quite distinctly in his deep baritone. "Why would anybody want to live in such a place?"

Seen through his eyes, the city I was born in seemed obscenely self-important for a place so choked up and cramped, so poorly organised a way of life. I looked for the flat horizon out of habit and found it obscured by the maze of narrow streets and the hubbub of the morning rush-hour, the curvature of the earth hidden by terraces, by the brown oxygen-starved trees, by the glowing traffic lights, by the people pouring across pedestrian crossings and pushed off the pavement to walk in the gutter. It was unimaginable to live like this, without the horizon, without the smell of mud and straw and the stillness of thousands of miles of open space. Adel could never live here, nor Michael. Nor Bol or Billy either. Desperately, I forced myself to tune back into the cabbie's narrative. He was into a long story about giving up smoking, prompted perhaps by the cigarette I didn't remember buying or lighting, but which was burning between the fingers of my shaking left hand.

"Then, one day I found I didn't want one any more," the cabbie said and it seemed to me that giving up was always the same, like having your heart-broken or losing hope.

I thought of Michael. He had been wounded in the leg reaching Adek from Mapel, Adel said, but was refusing to go to Loki to be treated in the hospital.

"He is treating himself," she said. "He is staying with Sean in the village to bury the dead and show the new aidworkers how to help."

Michael hated me for what I had done and I hadn't even had the chance to tell him goodbye. Now there were even new aidworkers who might actually be able to make a lasting difference.

"Michael asked if you were gone safely home to England," Adel said.

"Tell him, yes, I am," I said. "And tell him I am sorry."

"Sorry for what, Maria? There is nothing to be sorry for . . ."

I hugged her close to me.

"There is everything to be sorry for," I whispered into her hair.

Something is Going to Fall Like Rain

The cab swung sideways towards the river and the dirty Thames opened up to our right, a vast grey space lined with matchstick bridges above which the sky hung like a painting, clearly visible once more.

"Where do you want, love?"

When I had exited the press conference so suddenly, I had thought of going to my brother's flat in Camberwell to sit it out, wait for the furore to die down. But Matt, of course, would be at the airport looking for me. It had been stupid to run away, I thought, but I couldn't bear the idea of going back to Heathrow.

"Do you know where Camberwell Cemetery is?"

"Old one or new one?"

"New one."

"Honor Oak?"

"If you don't mind."

"It's your money," the cab-driver said, settling back in his chair and tapping the metre box where it ticked away like a heart.

Stubbing out my cigarette carefully in the plastic ashtray, I saw how my sunburned brown fingers were dark with callouses, my fingernails jagged and torn. I had scrubbed them in the hospital and in Nairobi Kenyatta airport while I waited for the flight home, but I could see that dirt still clung to them, tiny particles of the life I had come from tracing my heartline along the length of my palm.

The cast on my left arm was dirty with dust from Loki, the same dust that blew across from Sudan in the hot winds that breathed across the scrubland. Closing my hand tightly, I could feel the pulse of the village trapped there like in one of Bol's poems, in the creases and folds of my skin, and in the deep lines etched across the landscape of my fingers, flowing gently along my bloodstream to my heart. In the pocket of my unfamiliar American jeans was a flower-shaped leaf I had picked up at the harvest dance and secreted in my shoe, thinking to give it to Adel the next day. My mother would like it, I thought, pulling it from my pocket where it was wrapped around the bloodstained, hand-drawn map folded into quarters that Commander Wol had passed to me as he died. She had always preferred trees to flowers, and it was from Africa, the place she had dreamed of since she was a girl walking the south beach at Tarifa staring at the brown-green land mass of Morocco that was almost near enough to touch.

Chapter Twenty-Seven

I awoke in my own hospital, two floors below the geriatric ward in acute admissions, with a network of drips and taps and wires protruding from my skin, held together by white sticking tape.

"Dr Marshall," the woman standing over me said, smiling, and I recognised one of two nurses recently arrived from Trinidad and Tobago. They lived near me, close to Lambeth Bridge, in a flat cramped with health professionals from the developing world, a whirl of colour and cooking pots, chilli and chicken, Urdu and Spanish and Swahili.

"Have I been here long?" I said.

"A day or two."

I looked at my hands for any trace of jaundice.

"How is my liver?"

"Your liver's fine me darlin'," the nurse said. Her neat white badge said 'Nurse Sally Benedictine'. "But we nearly lost you. Temperature like that an' all! And you a doctor!"

I remembered something strange then.

"Who brought me in?"

"Nice American lady and a young boy. They were mighty concerned about you."

"And now they've gone?"

"Only to fetch you some clean clothes my dear."

My head throbbed suddenly on the pillows as my brain fought with the painkillers and whatever dosage of chloroquine they were giving me to fight the malaria.

"I need to speak to them," I said.

I started to drag myself up, but the wires pulled and I couldn't see a way of disentangling myself from them.

"No sense rushin'," Nurse Sally said, pushing me back firmly onto the white pillows. "They'll be back soon."

I noticed cards laid out neatly on the windowsill and I wondered who else had been in to see me.

"Only most of the geriatric ward, half the consultants in the building and that handsome brother of yours."

"How is he?"

"Worried sick. But he had to go back to work. He says he'll be back after his shift."

"He's a chef."

"I know," Sally said, handing me a big Tupperware container packed with food. "He brought you this. It's been all I can do not to eat it myself."

Sally fussed around me and I let myself drift with the painkillers for a while, thinking how a hospital looked so different from the bed, the lights so bright, everything so linear and sharp, a white world of bleach and fluorescence and peeling pea green paint. I missed suddenly with all my heart all the people I had been dreaming of and thinking of in my fever, as if I had just lost them all over again, freshly killed in the marketplace.

I was watching the hands of the clock move slowly forward, imagining the healing of my body like a short film playing under a microscope and thinking absently of the food Matt had left for me, when a woman tore aside the curtain Sally had pulled thoughtfully around my bed.

"Thank fuck for that," the woman said and kissed my forehead with force.

Seeing Grace made me smile despite myself.

"What are you doing here?" I asked.

"Well, Maria, thanks for the welcome . . ."

"It's great to see you . . ."

"Yet you've been avoiding my calls for three months?"

"I didn't feel able to speak to you," I said. "I've been angry with you. With myself. There's been something wrong with me since then."

"Like recurring malaria?"

"Well, yes, and some kind of post-trauma thing. I should have got help. I've been in a terrible mess and I didn't realise. I mean, it's been ten years."

I paused, letting my head rest on the pillow.

"Is that why you're back now? Because of the anniversary?"

Grace pulled a face.

"Yes and no."

She called behind the curtain.

"William, could you come here a moment."

A boy stuck his head through the curtains, holding them closed around his neck so that for a moment he appeared disembodied. I knew who he was instantly, without having to calculate ages or facts or circumstances. It was written in the shape of his head, where the hair was cut short and patterned like suede. It was in the cat-like ovals of his brown eyes and their lashes, and in the curl of his mouth.

"Hi William," I said, sticking out a hand full of drip-lines and attachments from on top of my blanket.

William stuck his own hand through the curtain as someone might stick out a tongue and we shook hands carefully. He was tall for ten years old.

When he had vanished again from behind the curtain, I turned to his mother.

"So what are you thinking?" Grace said.

"Honestly?"

"Honestly."

"I'm thinking, how the hell did you end up with everything?" I said.

Grace put her head on one side – a funny little mannerism I remembered from a decade ago, like an echo.

"Ah, you did mind about Billy," she said. "I wondered about that at the time."

"I didn't," I said. "Or at least I only minded a bit. I meant that somehow since Sudan I have spent the last ten years un-existing, while you have William and a brilliant career."

"It was different for you," Grace said. "You had lived there. You knew those people. You knew which body belonged to which other body. You knew who the hands and feet belonged to. You had spent months in terror, living with the threat of it all. I just parachuted in and out. And I had seen it all before. After Rwanda, I just shut up shop emotionally. It's taken me years to hack back through the ice."

"I have been angry with you," I admitted. "Because of the photographs. But now you are here I only feel happy to see you again."

"Those damned photographs," Grace said. "I hate to look at them. Never had more commissions of course. Won an award or two. But my heart wasn't in it any more. And I was pregnant . . . you realise who this is, of course . . ."

"You called him William," I said. "That's nice."

"We've been home in Canada pretty much since he's been born," Grace said. "I ditched the dangerous stuff for portraiture. Actors and musicians and politicians mainly. Celebrity horseshit. Brad and Angelina's new baby, that kind of crap. Would you believe Hollywood stars actually get a kick out of using a Canadian ex-war photographer?"

"It sounds glamorous."

"It isn't."

"So, you still didn't answer my question, not really."

"Why now? Well, last summer we went to see Billy's family in Tennessee. Then we saw Sean. And now we're here to see you – the final person in the jigsaw."

"I'm glad you came," I said. "You might have saved my life."

"Hey, you're the famous life-saver," Grace said. "The 'Angel of Adek', remember? They used that photo on the cover of *Time* . . . That image must have been in a hundred magazines and newspapers in the US, Canada, UK, all over Europe . . ."

"I don't remember it," I said. "Or not when I am awake anyway. I don't remember carrying Adel. I don't remember being on fire or running or anything. A part of me doesn't believe that it happened. Even looking at the photograph, it seems to be someone else. I felt such a fraud. The Commander had saved my life twice while I was in Sudan. Whatever I did for Adel must have been instinctive, which means anyone would have done the same. And what that photograph shows is a sham. I was only a passenger, a passerby. They used my photo because I was white . . ."

"You were a hero, black or white, like it or not . . ." Grace interrupted.

"Because that was what suited you, and suited the people you were selling the photo to . . ."

I was shouting now, sitting up in the bed. I hadn't shouted in a decade, and it felt good, all that surging anger, that sudden sense of actually being alive, of being something more than a faint whisper in life's auditorium.

"It was a lie, Grace – a journalistic lie that made a great photo, a good story and a shocking front page . . . But it had nothing to do with reality. NOTHING . . . Being on fire does not make someone a hero. It makes them a victim. There is a difference you know, whatever our screwed up celebrity culture says. And, by the way, there was nothing heroic about what I did. What was I going to do, watch a little girl burn to death? If you want heroes, look at Bol, look at Commander Wol, look at Adel. But they aren't worthy of the front page of a newspaper because they're black Africans. They're supposed to die horrible fucking painful deaths.

Worst of all, it was all our fault. All of it. All those people would be alive if we had never flown in on that mission. The militias only attacked that village because we were there."

"Bullshit. The militias are attacking villages every day. They burned a whole town yesterday in Darfur. It hasn't stopped just because you're in hiding after someone dared call you hero."

I glared at Grace then, suddenly hating her immaculate make-up and her chichi silk top and her beautiful son and her clever career and her award-winning ability to ignore the truth.

"Don't think I don't know why you've come here . . ."

Nurse Sally appeared then, dragging the curtains apart.

"I think that's enough . . ." she said. "Dr Marshall needs to rest."

But Grace stood her ground.

"Why have I come here, Maria?"

"For more photos. For the exclusive. For some fucking anniversary bullshit, like every other hack in town."

Nurse Sally, a woman of solid forearms, had Grace by her slender arm, but she turned her head and held onto the bedframe.

"We came here because we wanted to ask you something," Grace said. "A favour. I want to take William to Southern Sudan in September – to Adek, for the tenth anniversary of his father's death. I would like it if you came."

The nurse dropped Grace's arm.

"I'm fetching Sister," she said.

"It's okay, Sally," I said.

*　*　*

Grace stayed an hour or so longer and we talked about Southern Sudan. We talked about Billy's burial, out in the bush in his hat and boots because Sean had promised him he would be buried in Africa and not sent back to American soil. He had been buried in a Dinka warrior's military ceremony, next to Bol and Commander Wol in a neat row and close to where Chief Deng and his wife and baby were buried. Someone from the US embassy in Nairobi had come out to witness Billy's interment on behalf of the family. Sean had read one of Bol's poems at the ceremony.

"Sean was in Montreal for a conference recently," Grace said. He's doing good. He's living in Kigali and has a Swiss girlfriend who works for the UN. She's cute but kind of earnest. He said he'd tried to get in touch . . ."

"He did. I couldn't cope with it. With anyone from that time," I said. "And now?"

"I don't know."

"You'll think about Southern Sudan?"

"You're going to take a ten year old boy to a warzone?"

"There's a peace accord at the moment. You wouldn't recognise the place. You can even fly in and out of Juba these days. Loki is tiny in comparison with the city it once was. The Government has finished with Bahr el Ghazal for the moment and moved one state north to Darfur. It's a mainly Muslim area, but the people there are Muslim Africans, not Muslim Arabs. It's still Arab against African but without the religious divide. Up there they call the Muhraleen militias the Janjaweed but my God their tactics are familiar – villages burned and looted, cattle stolen, crops destroyed, mass murder, women raped and children taken as slaves. I was there in December, overwhelmed by sickness and déjà vu . . . Meanwhile, the rebels are not what they were. There are factions within factions. A decade of blood lust and babies born of rape, of burning and killing, has affected everybody on every side. If possible, it's even darker now. Something even more evil is hanging over the middle of the country. The peace talks stall one more time in the South and there will be full scale civil war again, maybe worse than we've seen."

Grace's voice had risen, and she checked herself, unconsciously smoothing the frown from her forehead with her hand.

"I don't understand," I said. "After everything that happened ten years ago, there were so many promises, but people have gone on dying in different villages in their millions and still only the aid agencies are helping them . . ."

"Africa is about small miracles," Grace said. "And for now Adek at least is peaceful and flourishing. That's why I thought of going back there now. There might not be another chance to visit before they start trying to ethnically cleanse the area again. No-one knows how long the rebels in Darfur will be able to hold out or how long before the Government decides to re-open the war in Bahr el Ghazal or the other Southern states. The peace process is on the verge of collapse, but there is this window of opportunity . . . I am terrified that if we don't take it, William might never be able to see the place his father died."

"You don't need me to come."

"No, but I'd like you to."

"No cameras?"

Grace's face twisted against the promise.

"I just ask you to consider it," she said. "Darfur needs every bit of publicity it can get ... And the South too. You know what the consequences are if the peace talks fail."

"We're not going to Darfur."

"Well, we could. Afterwards."

"Grace ..."

"Think of it, Maria," she said. "A photograph of you back in Sudan. It could be another *Time* cover – it could raise all those questions, the tenth anniversary and still people dying in the same way ... You said it yourself ..."

I closed my eyes against the force of her persuasion.

"It's not just that," she said.

"Oh?"

"I just think if you could see it now, as it is, it might help."

"Help with what?"

"Un-existing."

"Meaning what exactly?"

"You said you were un-existing. A way to start existing again is to go back, see that things have moved on, changed. To stop the moment repeating itself over and over in your mind. I know you think I am a monster, Maria. Maybe I am ... Maybe we all are, or the way the world is, we'd never get out of bed again."

"You coped, I didn't. I don't think I understand why."

"I'm an old pro, Maria," Grace said.

"At what? Surviving massacres? You're only ten years older than I am ..."

Grace was silent for a moment.

"It was a long time ago – but do you remember a famous photograph of a vulture standing over a tiny emaciated baby, a dying child crawling to a feeding centre. It's a horrific image. The bird of prey is waiting for the child to die."

"I remember it."

"It was taken in Sudan in 1993. Five years before we were there."

"Don't tell me you took that picture. Wasn't there a furore about it? Why not throw rocks at the bird, why not pick up the child? Why hadn't the photographer intervened?"

"The picture was taken by a guy called Kevin Carter. A South African who had grown up photographing the brutality of apartheid. The picture won the Pulitzer."

"So what's your point?"

"Kevin Carter's dead. He killed himself a year after the Pulitzer. A year after Sudan."

"Did you know him?"

"No," Grace said. "But I knew of him. I knew his face. I'd worked in Soweto and in the townships when I started out. And, when he died, it scared the shit out of me. I thought, if I care about this stuff it's going to kill me. So, I began shutting everything down. Coming home and wiping it from my memory. But I couldn't do that this time . . ."

"Because of William."

"Yes."

This confessional moment ended abruptly as Grace shrugged her shoulders and fixed me with one of her mischievous smiles.

"You haven't asked me about Michael," she said.

"No."

"Do you want to know what he's doing?"

"I don't think so, no."

A pause.

"He's living in Nairobi. One of the big cheeses in Operation Lifeline Sudan. Looks after refugees from the conflict as part of UNHCR. I expect he even comes to London every now and then for conferences . . ."

I heard myself reply despite myself.

"Is he happy?"

"Is he married, is that what you mean?"

I twisted in the bed, and my stomach muscles punished me for the sudden movement.

"Don't be ridiculous."

"A blind person could tell how you felt about him," Grace said. "You never stopped staring at him when he was around, and your voice used to go funny when you spoke to him. Even Adel used to laugh at you."

Just then Sister O'Reilly appeared at the curtain alongside the anxious face of Nurse Benedictine.

Grace sighed, finally defeated.

"William, say goodbye to your Godmother . . ."

"Hey . . ." I started to say, but Grace put her finger to her lips.

Billy's son stood obligingly on tiptoe to offer a reluctant cheek to the wired-up sick woman in the hospital bed and I air-kissed it, conscious of the smell of him, all soap and washing powder and young skin. He had his father's eyes, even more so close up, and the simple fact of his being alive made me want to weep and smile all at the same time.

"I'm really glad about William," I said, as Grace kissed me goodbye and William ducked out of the curtain.

"Me too," Grace whispered. "Even if he is the son of fucking Billy Finn."

"You loved fucking Billy Finn."

"I did love fucking Billy Finn."

"You know what I meant," I said.

"Yes," Grace said. "So you see, I don't have everything after all."

* * *

That night I called my brother Matt for the first time in months, to thank him for the food.

"You scared me, Maria," he said, taking the call on his mobile out in the tiny three feet square back yard behind the basement where he worked, amongst the piled crates and dog-ends. In the background I could hear the clatter of the kitchen.

"I'm so sorry," I said into the mouthpiece of the hospital phone. "And not just about the malaria. I'm supposed to be your big sister. I've been so absent since Sudan. Since mum died. Could we be friends again? I mean properly?"

"Come and eat at the restaurant as soon as you're better," Matt said, generous as ever. "I'll get you the best table for people-spotting. You can spy on the rich and famous and I'll sneak one of your favourites onto the menu."

"I'd love to," I said. "But I'd also love it if you and Charlie came to me for dinner. I'll do one of mum's Andalucian specials."

"Sopa de gato?"

"Or a lamb stew."

"I'd love to. I can't remember the last time someone cooked for me."

"I'll be out of here in a couple of days. I'm going to try to get some help. For the panic attacks. I can't stay in hiding forever."

"I'm so sorry, Maria," Matt said. "I haven't known how to help you. I saw you all over the papers but I didn't know how to help."

"You have helped, Matt," I said. "You've always helped."

"You know, Maria, I've been meaning to tell you something . . ."

Matt trailed off and the clamour of the kitchen grew louder in the background.

"Whatever it is it can wait," I said, but kindly. "I've already had quite a few surprises today."

"I don't want it to wait any more."

Another long, clattering pause.

"When you came back and your picture was everywhere, our father – our dad got in touch. He'd seen you on the news, and watched me on CNN. He said he wanted to see us."

"And what did you say?"

"I said . . . I'm sorry, Maria, I told him to get lost. I figured he'd had twenty years to track us down if he'd wanted. I told him we didn't want to see him. I thought, well, you had enough going on. So I didn't tell you, and then time passed and I couldn't tell you, and God, I haven't known what to do about it . . ."

"You did the right thing."

"Really?"

"Really."

"I mean, I wondered what he looked like . . ."

"He's quite handsome," I said, without thinking.

"How do you know? From mum?"

"I saw him once on Brighton Pier. At least I think it was him. Mum freaked out."

There was a muffled voice speaking at Matt's end of the phone.

"I have to go, Maria," Matt said. "Can we talk about it all though, soon? Mum and dad, and all that stuff?"

"I've got things to tell you too," I said. "Hard things. I'll call you as soon as I'm out of hospital. You only get one chance at the difficult stuff. Someone told me that a long time ago."

Chapter Twenty-Eight

I am sitting in the verandah bar, on the terrace of the Norfolk Hotel in Nairobi, listening to the familiar sounds of the tropical night, calling crickets and cicadas and the whirr of midges and mosquitoes mingling with other noises completely unfamiliar during my previous time in Africa – silvery spoons tinkling against china dessert bowls, wine glasses clinking on a tray, the sound of the large white grand piano from the bar indoors.

The waiter, dressed in neat cream shorts, white knee socks and a crisp white shirt, asks me if I would like another gin and tonic.

I shake my head.

"No, thank you," I say.

"Still waiting for your friend?"

"Yes."

Nairobi is not what I was expecting. My only other experience of Africa is so different that I have the strange sensation that I have stepped off the plane into a different era, a colonial time long past, a place of tall white shuttered windows, mahogany planters' chairs, dark wood floors and cream walls. The dress code and the gin cocktails are little changed since the days when Hemingway stayed here, in the distant times when the hotel was still miles outside the capital, a hunting lodge in the Kenyan bush. But the Norfolk has long since been swallowed by the city of Nairobi itself, cheek by jowl with the unofficial bus station and the craft market, sucked into a blur of traffic and street-sellers, gaudy hoardings and exhaust fumes.

I look up from my drink into the blackness beyond the yellow lamplight and there is a beautiful couple walking towards me, a perfect symbol of the new modern Africa. The woman is in a stunning floral print dress and sling-back canvas shoes, short-haired and bare-skinned except for a touch of lipstick. The man is tall and dignified in a well-cut dark linen suit, greying at the temples where his neat hair curls into the

230

blackness of his skin. They are speaking urgently to one another and it takes me a moment to recognise Michael, his hair clipped short and his cheekbones sharper, the pale brown of those startling eyes defined by a patchwork of tiny sun-lines. He walks easily in his suit, as if he has worn one all his life. He sees me and it is too late to run – he is coming towards me all smiles and twinkling eyes and I feel suddenly drab and overtired from the night-flight from London and deathly pale next to the black lustre of his healthy, exercise-fit skin. I feel sick and dizzy and high.

I stand up and we embrace awkwardly. I am conscious of the woman's eyes on my back.

"Maria, this is Gabriela," Michael says.

We shake hands, eyeing each other carefully.

"I have heard a lot about you," Gabriela says.

He lifts a chair backwards for Gabriela to sit down and seats himself, ordering a black coffee and a gin and tonic from the waiter. His calm confidence reminds me of the way he would feed the goats, letting them know he was their friend, but also very much in charge of the physical space around him.

"I'll have a beer," I say. "A Tusker."

The black man in the white tuxedo on the grand piano is playing Richard Clayderman competently but regretfully, as if he wishes he were playing another rhythm, anything but the strangely sanitised form of music flowing from his fingers.

"I'm sorry we can't stay long," Michael says. "We're under a three-line whip to attend an event across the road at the National Theatre." He gestures across the wide street from the terrace to a wooden and glass building I hadn't noticed. "It's a play about landmines."

He grins suddenly. "It's probably dreadful, but it comes with the territory. Gabi is the UNHCR landmine lady."

Our drinks come and Gabriela excuses herself briefly, the heels of her canvas shoes clicking softly on the terracotta tiles as she makes her way along the terrace to where the rest rooms lie out of sight from our table.

"It's good to see you," I say. "You look so different."

Michael says nothing, fishing into his inside jacket pocket for something.

"Gabriela seems nice," I say.

Michael's hand leaves his pocket and comes out with a filthy but neatly-folded piece of paper. He has a new watch, no longer the scratched Seiko with the battered strap. He is not wearing a wedding ring.

"I've kept this for ten years," he says. "I didn't know how to send it to you, and I didn't want it to just come through the post and shock you. Now seems the right moment . . ."

He pushes the grubby parcel of paper towards me, and despite his outward confidence his hand is shaking.

"Bol left it for you, before he left to join the SPLA," Michael says. "It was with his sister Atong, who miraculously survived the attack. I was to give it to you but I thought I might never see you again. We never even said goodbye, Maria . . . You were up in the plane . . . I could see your face in the window . . ."

"I was screaming for you . . ." I say, closing my hand over the tremor in his palm where it holds the torn letter. "I was crying and begging them to turn the plane around . . . I could see you, with Polio John . . . I was so frightened . . ."

"I found him in the medicine chest with Aneta-Maria, he was barely breathing . . . I found him in the hospital near to where Manute . . . Manute and Bol . . ."

I held tightly onto his hand.

"I'm sorry about Billy," Michael said. "When I heard he had a son, I thought . . ."

"You thought he was mine?"

"You were in love with him."

"No. You're wrong. I was in love . . ."

Gabriela slips soundlessly back into her seat.

Michael and I drop hands and I place the letter carefully into the pocket of my jeans, like a secret. It nestles there next to Commander Wol's parcel of map that for an entire decade I have not been able to touch. Both pieces of paper are folded the same way.

I take a long drink of cold, flavourless beer. Michael sips his gin and tonic, heavy ice cubes crashing against his glass. Gabriela stirs her coffee slowly and lifts the small, neatly wrapped piece of chocolate from under the silver spoon on her saucer, handing it to Michael. He unwraps it, seemingly without thinking, and drops it into his mouth. He has changed so much, and yet his mannerisms are acutely, almost painfully familiar, hanging in the air between us like echoes of tracer fire.

Gabriela looks at her watch, her tight black curls dancing in the candlelight.

"It's almost eight o'clock," she says. "I could go alone . . ."

Michael shakes his head.

"They are expecting us both."

He waves the waiter over and asks him for the bill.

"I'll get it," I say.

"You are a doctor now?" Michael asks. "A consultant?"

"Yes," I say. "I look after old people."

Gabriela stands up in a burst of floral repositioning, collecting her canvas bag onto her shoulder and adjusting her dress in one fluid movement.

"I'll see you tomorrow," Michael says. "Wilson airport, 9.00am. For the flight up to Loki."

"You're coming with us?"

My heart jumped then in a tiny internal tapdance.

"Of course. It's not often I get to go back home. You will find Adek very changed."

* * *

I watch Michael and Gabriela pass out of my sight, disappearing into the car park of the National Theatre, joining a stream of other well-dressed couples, his hand lightly steering the small of her back through the crowd. I am almost tempted to follow them, just to watch the curious new Michael – a suited, new watch-wearing, chocolate-eating, Visa-card owning city-dweller. To watch them together. To imagine his hand in the small of my back.

Instead, I let the barman bring me another Tusker, and with pale hands I slowly unfold the fragile piece of paper Michael gave me from its awkward origami. It is smeared with muddy fingerprints and still bears smudges of Adek's red dust. I read the careful handwriting slowly, my mind awash with a memory so strong it is physical, every needling word making me want to laugh and cry. I want to hold Bol's narrow little face in my hands. I want to see the quiet way he moves his head when he speaks. I want to hug his thin body. I want to listen to his stories. Instead I have only his poem, and that must be treasure enough.

> Maria, woman of kawajas,
> daughter of far off lands,
> you have no cattle name
> you have no village in Bahr el Ghazal
> but still the cattle-fires in the sky
> above Adek,

will burn for you each night.
I name you now, Ma Kuei Acoot,
the short-horned bull
a warrior amongst the herd.
Kuei for the fish-eagle
whose head of black and white
is as precious as the Marial markings
on the most sacred of cattle.
And our tribes will be allied
where the wetlands meet the dry earth.
You are a Dinka now
Ma Kuei Acoot
and so I will see you
once more in Lual Aghony

Tomorrow, Grace and William will arrive from Canada and we will all fly to Adek together.

Chapter Twenty-Nine

I barely notice it at first. A slight shift in the wind, the sensation of something impending, a heaviness in the air. Around us, in the bustling thoroughfare that has returned to Adek's marketplace, I can hear the bare trees whispering. I stop stock still and drop the gourd I am carrying so that it hits the parched ground with a sharp pistol crack. Above me, the sky is darkening thunderously and I wonder for a moment whether this is it, the end of the world. Ahead of me I can make out the bright silhouette of Adel, a fiercely tall woman in her mid-twenties, standing outside her tukul, her arms around Aneta-Maria, pointing up at the clouds. From this distance I cannot see it, but I know that glittering on her finger is my mother's engagement ring, given to Polio John by me and by John to her. A decade or so on and the three orphans – Adel, John and Aneta-Maria – have made their own family.

Feeling afraid of the thickening darkness, I begin running towards Adel through the strangely oppressive, almost familiar heaviness of the air, my feet slipping on the bare red earth, the smell of damp soil suddenly deep in my nostrils. But long before I reach her, I feel something wet and gentle, almost imperceptibly touch the top of my shoulder where the muscle meets the bone, and suddenly I understand. I stop, putting my hand to the spot, touching it with my finger. Bringing my hand up to my face, I see what touch tells me but my soul does not believe. At the tip of my index finger, glistening like a tiny, empty world, is a single droplet of moisture. Even as I examine it, I feel another one hit my collarbone, sliding down my bare arm leaving a streak like a scar in the dust. Then another hits my nose and my mouth and then my face is wet, my eyes thick with water as I try to look up at the rumbling sky. I am running now, running looking upwards, running wet and exultant and brimming with the lunatic promise of it all. The shouts of the village are in my ears and people running from every direction, chasing the water pouring from the heavens.

It has rained only twice in fifteen years, and now it is raining, raining, raining, in a pattering rhythm between Divinity and Earth, lashing drops of clear water connecting two separate worlds separated for so long by drought. Holding my eyes open against the torrent of water, I can see that Grace has stopped the Land Rover in the middle of the old marketplace and climbed out with William, and if I narrow my eyes I can see Billy there beside them too, his face turned upwards into the rain, and for the first time I glimpse the way the Dinka's dead are not lost but always in the place they are buried.

Behind them, Polio John is hopping from metal leg to metal leg in his Kenyan trainers, as agile and upright on his callipers as any young man in the village, dancing in the rain with Adel and Aneta-Maria. And it seems to me that just as Billy is here, Bol is there beside them, smiling and dancing as he sometimes had by the fire, as if nobody could see him, and that Chief Deng and his wife, and the Spear Master and even Manute, and all the other faces gone all these years from Adek have come out into the marketplace to witness this miracle of the rain.

The son of the Spear Master is the ghost of his father, lost in the jerks and rhythms of an ancient war dance, the white ash that covers him washing slowly from his skin so that the blackness of his face and torso reveal him to be only a man after all. I watch him fade to black under the force of the pouring torrent, under a sky filled with the thundering screams of the Dinka spirit-gods as they witness the watery connection between heaven and earth.

All the while I am scanning the horizon for Michael, looking for his tall frame amongst the villagers, wanting to share with him the miracle of the rain. It is our fifth day in Adek with Grace and William and tomorrow we are due to fly back to Loki. From there, Michael has invited me to visit his home in Nairobi. He has a small house with a tiny, fragrant garden, in the suburbs of the city.

"On the evening I saw you, after the show," he told me, after making his hesitant invitation, "I told Gabriela that things were over between us. She is a wonderful woman, and it is not fair to her when my own mind is elsewhere. I hope we will be friends."

He didn't look at me when he said this, but we were sitting in our old positions by the roaring light of a flickering campfire, on the edge of a large NGO compound far more ambitious than anything we ever built in Adek village. Around us the bugs jumped and cicadas sang, and the stars were brighter even than I had remembered them during all the long years in London gazing at a dark grey sky. Our three tents – mine, Michael's and Grace's – were pitched in a neat row behind us, and we had just finished a familiar supper of rice, goat's meat and fire-smoked beans. We were sitting on a log with a foot between us. The air was thick and still with humidity.

"There are jobs at the Kenyatta Hospital in Nairobi in geriatrics," Michael said, after a while.

I said nothing, but took his fingers in mine.

This morning, a day after Michael and I sat up half a night watching the fire and the stars, it is hard not to believe the rain has come just for us – for our visit and for all those who were lost.

In the marketplace, among the rain-blurred figures of the whirling witchdoctor, the metal-legged John and his young family, Grace and William and all the ghosts of Lual Aghony, people are dragging pots and pans and gourds from their tukuls and out into the open, gathering the water, standing with their mouths open to catch the cool cloud-liquid, dragging their animals out under from the cover of trees so that they too can drink and wash the years of dust from their thin coats. I can hear them all clattering and whooping and screaming and singing, the village brought to life by rain like an ailing plant, Adek alive once more.

At last I see Michael, smiling and waving as he rounds the bend by the marketplace. Then with my eyes tightly shut, the way the Dinka listen, I can hear distant gunfire and I know that Commander Wol is firing his rusted AK-47 into the air. I open my eyes and see them all there, everyone lost in Adek known and unknown to me, but then the dead fade into other shapes, the wet and shining faces of the living, and I do not begrudge them their passing. The miracle of the rain, an everyday miracle made extraordinary, is wonder enough. Standing there on water-drenched soil by the barren but still enduring mango tree, I feel as if my heart might split with hope. And Southern Sudan is wet with promise, a shocked land of sodden villages and rain-happy dancers, lit up by the brightening sky.

Acknowledgements

This book has been a long time in the writing and there are many people to thank. Firstly, my agent Lizzy Kremer and her assistant Laura West at David Higham Associates who have believed unfalteringly in this story. Also Reportage Press, particularly Rosie Whitehouse, Laura Keeling and Charlotte Eagar, for their faith in Bol, the Commander and their friends.

I must also thank my former editors Rosie Boycott and Chris Blackhurst for sending me to Southern Sudan in the first place. During those early trips, photographer Michael Dunlea was a tower of strength. Of all the tireless and dedicated staff of Operation Lifeline Sudan, Unicef and War Child working in Sudan in the late 1990s, Musa Bundugu, Sally Burnheim, Gillian Wilcox, Norman Sheehan and Bill Leeson deserve special mention.

None of my experiences of Sudan would have been the same without the vast presence of aidworker Johnie McGlade, or friends of War Child and No Strings, James Topham, Neil Morrissey, Hugo Speer and Adrian Dunbar. Although written about Southern Sudan, some of this story also bears testimony to the aftermath of a massacre I witnessed in East Timor in 1999, an experience also shared with Johnie and Bill, and with photographer Nigel Wright, and which the Centre for Anxiety Disorders and Trauma at King's College Hospital helped me to survive.

I would also like to thank the Daily Mirror, and editor Richard Wallace in particular, for continuing to send me to Africa. My more recent work there with Oxfam has been hugely supported by the charity's Sam Barratt, Katie Abbotts, Claire Lewis, Rebecca Wynn and Alun McDonald, and illustrated with instinctive flair by Daily Mirror photographer John Ferguson. Sam, John and I recently travelled to Eastern Chad together to meet those displaced by the Darfur conflict into the perilous refugee camps along the Sudanese border, and the similarity of their stories to those I heard in Southern Sudan a decade ago is chilling.

Something is Going to Fall Like Rain

In terms of expertise, I must thank Dinka academic Kuyok Abol Kuyok for his patient checking of the text; the journalist, Jacob Akol, for his experienced eye; Godfrey Lienhardt's wonderful book, *'Divinity and Experience: The Religion of the Dinka'*; and British paediatrician Dr Kerry Robinson. All mistakes and inaccuracies, however, are entirely my own.

Most of all I owe an immense debt to the people of Southern Sudan, and those in Bahr el Ghazal in particular. It is impossible not to be moved by the generosity of those who have absolutely nothing, and not to be awed by the pride and resilience with which the tribal peoples of the South keep on existing despite every continuing effort by governments, armies, flood, famine and pestilence to wipe them from the continent. The Dinka are an extraordinary people, and it has been a great privilege to observe their culture, humour and strength.

To early readers Libby Brooks (without that pen and notebook, who knows?), Mary Powell and Glenys Kinnock, your thoughts and support have been invaluable. Neil Michael helped me start to think of Sudan as a fictional story. The Renegade Writers, especially Dreda Say Mitchell and Mary Long helped me keep writing. I must also thank Claire Dauncey See at UWCSEA, and Professor Robert Young at Wadham College, Oxford University (now at NYU) for introducing me to Africa through literature. Not forgetting that so many friends have helped me keep the faith along the way, particularly Lucy Powell, Nicki Casali, Victoria Gallant, Rachel Reid, Cara Lavan and too many more to mention.

I would also like to remember my cousin Stephen Jones who died too young as I was finishing this book, and add that enormous thanks are due to my family. To my parents, Patricia and David Wynne-Jones, for teaching me to love words. To the Tiplers and our beloved late grandparents for being the uncomplaining cast (and props) of earlier stories. Finally, I would like to thank Claire Wynne-Jones and Dan Bardino just for being themselves, and Cheryl Clarke for everything.

Oxfam in Southern Sudan

Oxfam GB has been working to save and rebuild lives in Sudan for 25 years. When war erupted in Sudan in 1983, we began by providing emergency water to people who fled the terrible violence. Over the following two decades, we have helped some of the most marginalised and devastated communities by providing vital water, healthcare and basic shelter, and responding to disasters such as the food crises in Bahr el Ghazal in 1988 and 1998.

During the long and devastating civil war fought between Northern and Southern Sudan, up to two million people have been killed and four million made homeless. The 2005 peace agreement brought decades of fighting to an end, but for many of the millions forced to flee there is little to return to. So many years of bombs, suffering, and marginalisation have left Southern Sudan one of the most under-developed and impoverished regions in the world.

Oxfam GB is working in some of the most remote and neglected areas with communities and local partners to help put peoples'shattered lives back together. We are drilling boreholes to provide a steady supply of clean water, constructing new latrines for schoolchildren, supporting villages to start farms, grow food and care for their livestock, and responding to humanitarian emergencies caused by ongoing violence and natural disasters such as flooding.

Although seemingly simple, the provision of clean water can have a transformative effect on communities. Around a quarter of villages rely on river water as their main source, which can make them vulnerable to water-borne diseases, such as diarrhoea and cholera. Lack of water sources can have surprising knock-on effects on issues like school attendance, with children taken out of the school in the dry season to collect water for their families.

In the dry and dusty Southern Sudanese village of Mirindanyi in Western Equatoria state, an Oxfam water pump is benefiting the community there.

"Before, it took two hours to the river to collect the water, then two hours back," says local resident Floris Fazir, pausing to heave a 20-litre container on her head. "In the dry season, we got the water from a scraped well on the river bed, and that was dirty. We would get sick often. But water from the borehole is sweet to drink."

The peace in Southern Sudan is precarious. But for places like Mirindanyi, once on the frontline of the civil war, it is bringing new hope and opportunity. Where once villages were abandoned as rebel and Government forces battled back and forth through the remote bush, with Oxfam's help, people are slowly getting back to living normal lives.

Oxfam GB has also been providing clean water, sanitation and other aid to over 400,000 people affected by the conflict in the Darfur region, in the west of the country. However in March 2009 the Government of Sudan revoked our registration to work in Northern Sudan, along with 15 other agencies. We are extremely concerned about the impact this will have on millions of poor and vulnerable people in Darfur and the rest of Northern Sudan. Meanwhile our work in Southern Sudan continues. Oxfam GB is also still working in Eastern Chad close to the Sudanese border, where we are assisting hundreds of thousands of refugees from Darfur, as well as those affected by Chad's own internal conflict.

With your support we can continue to help the people of Sudan. Five per cent of the proceeds from the sale of this book will be used to help this work.

If you would like to do more visit www.oxfam.org.uk/sudan where you can keep updated with the situation in the region, make a donation, read stories of hope and pledge your campaigning support.

REPORTAGE PRESS

'Switched-on, ethical, grown-up publishing' – Daunt Books

Reportage Press is a new publishing house specialising in books on foreign affairs; non-fiction, fiction, and reprints of classic pieces of journalism from the past.

Each of our books has a charity chosen by the author and part of the proceeds from the sales of the book is donated to that charity.

For further details of current and upcoming titles visit our website at www.reportagepress.com.

REPORTAGE PRESS

ALSO FROM REPORTAGE PRESS

The Budapest Protocol
By Adam LeBor

'A first class political thriller' – Alan Furst, *The Spies of Warsaw*

As the European Union launches the election campaign for the first President of Europe, Miklos Farkas is brutally murdered in the Hungarian capital. His journalist grandson Alex investigates his death. He soon discovers a chilling conspiracy rooted in the dying days of the Third Reich, one that will ensure economic domination of Europe - and plans for a new Gypsy Holocaust.

The hunt is on for *The Budapest Protocol*. Alex is soon drawn into a deadly web of intrigue and power play, a game played for the highest stakes. But Alex too is haunted. He must battle his own demons as he uncovers a shadowy alliance that the world thought had been defeated for good.

Powerful, controversial and thought-provoking, *The Budapest Protocol* is a journey into Europe's hidden heart of darkness.

Part of the proceeds from *The Budapest Protocol* go to the Medical Foundation for Victims of Torture.

Available at www.reportagepress.com.